SHANGHAIED!

Clint turned up the alley. Worms gnawed at his vitals, and his eyes, cold and gone gray as the night fog, darted at every hiding place. His callused thumb found the iron hammer of his rifle. The gravel alley crunched underfoot.

He caught movement out of the corner of his eye and a swinging piece of lumber flashed out of the shadows, crashing into the barrel of his rifle. Then powerful arms enveloped him and a blow racked the side of his head. Clint dropped to his knees and rolled out of the man's grasp. Instinctively, he scrambled to get his back to the wall. At the same time he pawed for his Colt's revolver—and found the holster empty.

Clint tensed. The four men had him cornered, and they were moving in to take him. . . .

Also by Larry Jay Martin

EL LAZO
AGAINST THE 7TH FLAG

THE DEVIL'S BOUNTY

By
LARRY JAY MARTIN

BANTAM BOOKS
NEW YORK • TORONTO • LONDON • SYDNEY • AUCKLAND

THE DEVIL'S BOUNTY
A Bantam Domain Book / August 1991

ISBN 0-553-29154-8

Published simultaneously in the United States and Canada

PRINTED IN THE UNITED STATES OF AMERICA

RAD   0 9 8 7 6 5 4 3 2 1

For my brother,
REX L. MARTIN
who had to be much more
than that

CHAPTER ONE

FROM THE DEEP SHADOWS OF A RAVINE BRACK-
eted by river willows, four robed men—strangers to
this quiet riverside—watched in sullen silence. At the
sound of approaching hoofbeats they hunkered down,
hidden by the cleft's edge, and waited.

Beneath a towering gnarled cottonwood, Apolonia Vega drew rein on her sorrel stallion, tossed her
long coal-black tresses out of her eyes, and watched
the hundred-fifty-foot steamer *Senator* churning up
the wide Sacramento on its way to the newly platted
city of the same name. Voices floated across the water
singing to the tune of the popular "Oh, Susanna" that
she had heard so much in the last year. The singers
were accompanied by two amateur instrumentalists
perched in the midst of piles of cargo on a large bail
of hemp rope, fiddle and flute in hand.

> I came from Salem City,
>   With my washboard on my knee,
> I'm going to California,
>   The gold dust for to see.
> It rained all night the day I left,
>   The weather it was dry,
> The sun so hot I froze to death,
>   Oh brothers don't you cry.

The voices began to fade as the steamer drew near
and the men realized that a beautiful señorita sat
astride a handsome tall stallion watching their progress.

Men crossed the boat from the far side and a group of men five deep in slouch hats, brown canvas pants, red and blue woolen shirts, and knee-high hobnail boots, with picks and shovels and packs, crowded the portside rail. In almost reverent silence, as even the flute and fiddle players had stopped to stare, they waved to her. She stole a glance over her shoulder up to the road forty paces behind and above her and saw that her *dueña*, her chaperon, Tomasa Madariaga, was engaged in lively conversation with the old vaquero, José Romero, who drove the buggy.

Apolonia carefully returned the wave, her hand concealed from those who watched over her. A foot-stomping cheer arose from the festive mass of gold hunters.

Across the fifty yards of water separating the shore from the double-decked steamship, barn swallows dipped and dove. They, too, seemed to revel in the simple exchange of people so close in distance, yet so far apart in culture. A regal blue heron winged overhead with the aplomb the Californio señorita was expected to observe in this situation.

Apolonia smiled for the first time that afternoon. With even more exuberance the song resumed.

> Oh! California,
>> That's the land for me,
> I'm going to Sacramento,
>> With my washboard on my knee.

She had seen many such men pass over her father's rancho on foot and on horseback, and many more filled large boats to the rails and small boats to the point of swamping, heading for the gold fields.

She had seen almost as many return, half starved, dejected.

But there were a few who had hit it big, and Sacramento City and the recently renamed city of San Francisco grew by leaps and bounds as a result of stories told and retold, growing in splendor with each telling—streets paved with gold, nuggets for the taking. She remembered eight years ago, as a young girl of ten, visiting Yerba Buena—now booming San Francisco, but then little more than the squat Mission Dolores and a few huts among sand hills, reached by slopping across the wide mud flats at low tide, or small boats at high. It was said the city was now twenty-five thousand strong, a mass of men and tents and clapboard buildings that filled every square foot. On one patch of public land south of the city, facetiously known as Happy Valley, over a thousand tents of cotton duck and rubber, known to the miners as Mr. Goodyear's finest, swelled out of the earth like a mass of pointed blisters.

The *Senator* blew its mournful whistle, rounding the bend in the distance. The exuberant voices and the thumping of the steam pistons disappeared, and Apolonia nudged the stallion on down the riverside trail, enjoying the afternoon sunshine, though she knew she should not.

Her father had forbidden her to take her usual afternoon ride, and for the first time she could remember she had willfully disobeyed him. Had her chaperons, Tomasa and José, known of his edict they would never have allowed her to ride away from the hacienda. She had been careful not to let them see her anger or hear of his.

Glancing up at the afternoon sun, she wondered if it was four o'clock yet. If so, Gaspar Cota, the reason she had disobeyed her father, would be arriving at the hacienda of Rancho del Rio Ancho. Her father would even now be sending one of the Indian serving women to find her, and when her absence was discovered, he would fume in anger.

Apolonia bent low in the saddle to make her way under a dense thatch of overhanging river willows, her tight black riding jacket biting into her stomach. Clearing the branches, she straightened and smoothed the long velvet-trimmed skirt that demurely hid her ankles and most of the leather *tapaderos* protecting the saddle's carved wooden stirrups.

She sighed deeply, wondering if she had the

slightest chance of dissuading her father from his plans. Then she set her jaw with determination. She would not marry the pompous ass Gaspar Cota, a man almost twice her age. A man whom she detested. She would not!

She raised her arm to fend off the river growth, encouraging the stallion into a shadowed cleft where the willows were the thickest. She gasped as strong hands encircled her waist and she was suddenly jerked from the saddle. She tried to scream, but the ground rushed up and her breath was expelled by the slamming blow to the trail.

Her eyes swam; she fought for air. Masked faces! Powerful hands pinned her to the sandy trail, then hauled her to her feet.

She gagged and fought the callused hand covering her mouth. Her eyes flared, her view filled with brown teeth behind a soup-strainer mustache, and the laughing face of a man looming in front of her—dressed in Chinese robes. He held a cloth bag, reaching to put it over her head while unseen hands pinned her arms to her sides.

With a rush of strength, she kicked out and buried her pointed high-top shoe in the burly man's crotch.

"Aiee, ye bitch!" he screamed.

Apolonia clamped her teeth into the rough palm covering her mouth and got the salty taste of blood before the hand jerked free. She realized the man with the cloth bag had cold blue eyes the instant before he snarled and dropped the sack into place over her head.

She struggled against her bindings and the fear of darkness, managing a muffled scream. Then the cloth was bound tightly around her mouth.

She felt herself being hauled up and winced when her stomach slammed across the saddle. She struggled against the tight, suffocating ropes and gag, and bile choked her. She was afraid she would vomit, which would have been life-threatening with her mouth bound. Trying to calm herself, she began silently to pray.

"Apolonia!" a nearby gruff voice rang out. José—it was old José! He would make them stop.

She jerked away as a pistol roared near her ear. Then the horse bucked with a bone-jarring dance and she was almost thrown from the saddle. To her relief, the animal quieted—but she could feel its shivers through the saddle and wished she could comfort the horse with a stroke on the neck or a quiet word. Strong hands shoved her roughly back upright.

Apolonia, her ears still ringing from the blast, heard a low moan, and despair flooded her for herself, and more so for old José. Even through the cloth, the acrid odor of gun smoke seared her nostrils.

With its rider bound tightly to the saddle, the horse was led away. Apolonia began to sob, but quickly quieted, steeling her resolve not to show these barbarians any weakness. *Pray, Apolonia, do not cry.* In the distance she heard the shouts of her *dueña,* but they faded, as did the moans of her old friend, her father's trusted vaquero.

The horse's hooves sucked at mud, then finally quieted, and she heard the men dismount. Her knowledge of English was good enough that she understood the gruff voice instructing her as she was jerked from the horse, placed on her feet, and made to walk.

"Don't ye be fightin', now, me pretty Polly. Ye best get used to it. It's a long, long trip for ye." The voice didn't waver as strong hands hoisted her easily, then deposited her against the hard wooden ribs of what she knew must be a small boat. Waves lapped at the sides and she heard the boat scrape against the bottom, then felt it levitate away from a muddy shore. It rocked violently to the side as others clamored in and jostled her roughly with knees and backsides when they took their places on the thwarts.

The oars clattered into place and began to dip in a steady rhythm. One of the oarsmen whistled a lively tune, grating her shattered nerves. She struggled against her bonds, and faith waned. With each stroke she was farther and farther from Rancho del Rio Ancho. The bilge water in the bottom of the boat soaked through her clothes and she shuddered, but not from the cold.

She wished she had obeyed her father.

CHAPTER
TWO

JOHN CLINTON RYAN SAT ASTRIDE HIS PALOMINO
stallion, Diablo, one long leg hooked over the pommel, his wide-brimmed hat pushed back on his head,
exposing a shock of sandy hair.

Behind him on Front Street men hustled in every
direction—afoot, horseback, and in every possible
horse-drawn contraption, including a fire wagon that
careened by with bells clanging and buckets banging
and men hanging on desperately to its wooden sides.
He admired the four matched grays that pulled it, as
well as the kelly green brass-trimmed wagon with the
yellow words MONUMENTAL FIRE COMPANY painted
boldly along the length. San Francisco had already
burned twice this year.

But it was the sight that stretched before him
that caused his real wonder. More than eight hundred ships—a winter forest of barren masts—covered
the bay beyond the tide-out mud flats. Even more
wondrous was the sight of two corpses, heads grotesquely canted, tongues distended, swaying with the
quiet roll of the ship from the yardarm of a sixty-cannon U.S. frigate moored not more than a cable's
length from shore. Examples, he had been told. Left
hanging to discourage the rest of the crew from deserting and following the thousands of others who
had left their ships to the watery graveyard the bay
had become.

Clint Ryan had had his years at sea, and her cruelties were usually no surprise to him. But for the U.S.
Navy to leave two of her own to be picked at by the

seabirds and stared at by throngs of Chileans, Chinese, Australians, Sandwich Islanders, and thousands of others from every nook and cranny and filthy crevice of the earth's ends? His mouth dried and his brow furrowed at the sight of it.

Reining the big stallion away, Clint urged the powerful animal into the milling throng on Front Street. Little puffs of dust led the way as they plodded through the hock-deep powder, passing tents and clapboard shops, weaving through horsebackers and wagons laden with freight. It was not the California Clint was used to. No lethargy here, no *poco tiempo*, no *mañana*. These men were going somewhere, each with a determined stride, each with a set to his jaw and a gleam of hope in his eye.

Clint drew rein and glanced at the long, permanent wooden building in front of him. It stretched along the street for well over a hundred feet. Glass, in several huge three-by-six-foot panes, covered the length and advertised to those on the street the longest bar in San Francisco. A year ago a two-by-two panel of glass was a rarity in California. Clint looked above the amazing wall of glass and read the garish sign, THE EL DORADO SALOON, in bold two-foot gilded letters.

He had been most of a month on the trail, El Camino Real, traveling from the sleepy pueblo of Los Angeles up the coast to Santa Barbara, where he spent some time with friends. Then he had gone on to see for himself what he had heard was happening in San Francisco.

Clint had originally come to California because it was his job. A sailor went wherever the ship he was currently signed on went. But she ran aground and broached, and he found himself a resident. At first his mind was set on getting back at sea, but being blamed for the wreck of the *Savannah* had changed all that.

Three years in California had given him a new hope, a life on the land, a life as a landowner. The upheaval and political change in California during those three years made any planning speculative at best. But during a trip deep into the Ton Tache Valley, as the large central valley of California was known to the Mexicans and Indians, he had solidified his hopes. On the banks of the river called Kaweah lay a beautiful live-oak-covered, river- and stream-fed rancho. A fertile land, home to elk and deer and wildfowl of all kinds. With grass belly deep and rich. Land suited for the raising of cattle and horses. Land claimed only by the Yocuts Indians, and he had already made his peace with them. Now the problem was garnering title, making the land—the dream—his.

It had been a long trip up El Camino Real and Clint ran his tongue over gritty teeth. He was dry as dirt.

Reining the stallion to a rail that he recognized as the purloined boom of a ship, he shouldered the palomino between a bay and a dappled gray. He dismounted, loosened the palomino's cinch, untied his saddlebags and draped them over his shoulder, pulled the revolving breech Colt rifle from its scabbard, and started for the batwing doors that welcomed all comers to the noisy saloon.

Assailed by the odor of tobacco smoke, sweat, and dirt, he crowded between men of all sizes, colors, and descriptions. There were Peruvians in wide flat-brimmed hats with tassels bobbing from the rim, Chinese in robes with long queues hanging to their waists, Chileans in hats like upside down bean pots half hiding dark-skinned faces, which rose out of slitted wide-striped ponchos. Californios, dressed as Clint was in embroidered jackets and *calzonevas* with flat or slouch hats, carried reatas even into the saloon. In addition to foreigners, the room teemed with men from every corner of the United States and her territories—most of them sporting hobnailed boots with their canvas pants tucked in and flannel shirts covering long johns. Each had at least a knife at his waist and many had hatchets on their belts to boot. Most had one pistol, and some a pair, shoved into their belts. A few, like Clint, carried rifles or shotguns as well. All looked as if they were more than proficient with the weapons they toted. And the weapons appeared to be needed: More gold covered the fifty round wooden tables, where men drank or gambled with dice and cards, than Clint had expected to see in a lifetime.

Shouldering his way between two miners clad in red shirts, canvas pants, and brogans, Clint bellied up to the bar and leaned his Colt's rifle against it. Six bartenders, big enough to handle beer kegs with ease, were stationed along the bar at twenty-foot intervals. They hoisted whiskey bottles and drew foaming mugs of beer. Mirrors as tall as the glass panels out front lined the intricately carved backbar, spaced between mahogany columns topped with sculptured gargoyles who glared down with evil relish through clouds of tobacco smoke at the crowded mass of sweaty men.

More bottles of liquor graced the backbar than Clint had seen in all the saloons from Mystic around the Horn to California. Maybe more than he had seen in all the ports he had called on in his twelve years at sea.

Champagne, Holland gin, sauterne, peach brandy, and whiskey in bottles of every size and description perched on multilayered shelves up to the ceiling and stood six deep on the backbar. Ale kegs in twenty different varieties hunkered under the brass-trimmed forebar. Labels in languages Clint couldn't read invited him to become lost in their elixir.

Suddenly the saloon quieted, as if a blanket of silence had been laid across it. Clint turned to see what the attraction was. Half a head taller than most of the men in the room, he could easily see why the deference was paid to the beautiful golden-haired woman who had entered through the batwing doors. Her Jenny Lind parasol, which perfectly matched her emerald green gown, twirled as the crowd parted to allow her to pass. In a wave from those by the door down the hundred-foot length of the bar, hats were snatched from heads. In the sudden silence, her laughter tinkled like silver bells as she crossed the room and disappeared up a short stairway near a small curtain-covered stage.

Dogging her steps, hat in hand, revealing his shining bald head, a man followed her closely. His eyes worked the room, taking note of any threat. As the curtains closed behind them, the room resumed its raucous roar. Clint overheard the word *sultry* and wondered if it was a description or a name.

Clint realized she was the first woman he had seen since he entered the city earlier in the day, and the first sunlight blond he had seen since he'd arrived in California years before.

Yes, San Francisco had changed in the three years since he had visited the quiet town of Yerba Buena while serving on board the brig *Savannah*.

That had been before the revolution, before the Treaty of Guadalupe Hidalgo, when the hide, horn, and tallow brig had struck a reef off Pt. Concepción, broached, and sunk with the loss of fourteen hands—men Clint had sailed around the Horn with. Quade Sharpentier, her captain, had made a formal accusation of Clint's malfeasance. But Clint was not at fault. He'd been below, asleep after twenty-four hours on duty, so he had been made the scapegoat by her captain. A U.S. warrant still existed for his arrest, he was sure, but he was unconcerned, as the thousands of men in San Francisco had something else on their minds. Gold.

And its glitter paled all other concerns.

The bartender stood across the bar, a knotty-faced man without eyebrows who looked as if he were first cousin to a bulldog and who wore the same disdainful expression as his brother gargoyles above.

"Well, mister, you drinkin' or leanin'?"

Clint's eyes narrowed, but he decided a drink was more important than trading insults or blows with an overworked bulldog bartender.

"Drinkin'. Give me a whiskey."

"I got fifty-four kinds of whiskey, emigrant, and twenty-five varieties of ale, and I ain't got no time to educate you. What'll it be?"

Clint leaned a little closer to the man, and his eyes hardened. "The closest kind."

The man's lip curled in a half smile. He reached for a bottle of Noble's Finest and upended it until the shot glass filled exactly to the ounce line. Holding the glass out of Clint's reach, he snarled, "Half a dollar."

"Half a dollar?" Clint grumbled in surprise.

"Same price as every saloon in San Fran, emigrant."

Clint dug into his pocket and tossed a handful of silver pesos clattering onto the bar.

"You best get to the diggin's, emigrant, and get you a satchel fulla gold. Boss don't like me takin' this greaser money." He paused as he eyed the money and Clint. "How come a Boston-talkin' man's a-wearin' those fancy Mexican duds?"

Clint didn't give the question the respect of an answer, just reached over and took the shot glass out of the man's hand, held it to his lips with relish, and upended it.

"Another?" the bartender asked. His mouth curled with the smirk-grin. "Or would you rather try the local swill?"

"How much for *aguardiente*?"

"Two bits."

"That'll do."

The bulldog bartender bent and pulled a clay bottle from under the bar, removed its carved pine plug with his teeth, and poured Clint another shot in the same glass. Clint dropped the coins on the bar and the man swiped them into his palm, then moved to another customer.

A few feet from Clint, a voice rang a mite louder than the others in the bar. "An' that's so much horse dung."

Clint turned to his left and immediately spotted the two men, who were arguing nose to nose. A man leaning on the bar between Clint and the two picked up his glass and discreetly moved away. The one with his back to Clint stood straight and stiff, dressed in a smartly tailored black swallowtail coat and matching pants with a narrow-brimmed city high hat—the only one in the room. His boots shone with a bootblack's gleam, and he leaned on a gold-handled walking stick. The other man, of an equal height with the dude but with an ample girth, sported homespun clothes and a slouch hat, and his red shirt was splattered with tobacco juice—but he gave no quarter to the better-dressed man. He glared, his red face whiskey blotched from too much time holding up the bar.

The man spat a stream of tobacco juice, missed the cuspidor, and backhanded the dribble from his chin. "Louisiana's Senator Soule is a no-account, and all he's doin' is gummin' up the works." Homespun glowered at High-hat and backed up a step as others moved away and gave the two more room.

"No-account?" High-hat repeated in a distinctly French accent. "M'sieur Soule has served Louisiana with honor, and it is M'sieur Daniel Webster and M'sieur Seward who continue to keep California out of the Union."

"No, my frog friend"—Homespun's voice rose, and the crowded saloon began to quiet—"you and your kind not wantin' another free state is what's keepin' us out." Others in the crowd jeered at the Frenchman in agreement.

"Slavery is not the issue here," the Frenchman countered, his walking stick pounding in anger on the board floor. "We, too, want California in the Union. She is the gateway to the Pacific, to China, the Japans, and Hindustan, the fulfillment of our destiny as a great nation—"

"As long as you slavers keep men in chains and the planters have all the money," Homespun interrupted, "this country will never be worth a fiddler's length of gut."

Some of the crowd stirred in anger with this slight on the Union. Homespun rested his hand on the butt of the small cap-and-ball Root Patent Model pistol shoved into his belt next to a foot-long, leather-sheathed Arkansas toothpick.

But the Louisiana Frenchman was not deterred. "We abide by the law, M'sieur, as educated men should. Money follows those who toil with honor and use their God-given wits. And the law allows the ownership of slaves to help with that toil."

"Evil is evil, frog. Keepin' men like dogs and hog-gin' all the money in the country is evil."

A man as large as Homespun stepped out of the crowd in-between the two. He turned to face High-hat, his face nearly as black as the Frenchman's city suit. "We bes' be gettin' on, now, Massa LaMont."

"Stand aside, Gideon."

"But Massa—"

"Aside, Gideon."

"Yessa," the black man said, but his eyes pleaded.

The Frenchman lifted his walking stick and shook it in Homespun's whiskey-blotched face. "Ignorant men such as yourself do not understand the economics of this great country and should not sully her name."

"Ignorant?" Homespun started to step forward, but the bulldog bartender swung the stubby double barrels of a scattergun across the bar.

"Outside, Vester Grumbles. You, too, Frenchy, or I'll blow you there."

Both men cut their eyes at the bartender and saw dogged determination.

"Sure as I'm Luther Baggs," the bartender said, lifting one hairless eyebrow, "I'll cut you in half." He motioned to the batwing doors with the scattergun. The saloon crowd faded back as if he were shaking the tail of a venom-spitting eight-foot timber rattler.

The Frenchman was the first to move, brushing past the man the bartender had called Grumbles, and the crowd parted. "I will be pleased to take my satisfaction outside, with pistols or fists," he said loud enough so all could hear. But if he carried a pistol, it was well concealed.

He was ten feet away when the glowering Grumbles came to life, jerking his Root and leveling it on the Frenchman's back as the hammer ratcheted.

Clint brought the heavy stock of his revolving breech rifle up in a sweeping motion, cracking Grumbles's forearm and knocking it upward. The Root's spat flame and smoke with a resounding blast that rocked the saloon but harmlessly holed the sculptured lead ceiling. Before Clint could close with the man, the black was on him. Two massive blows smashed Vester Grumbles, snapping his neck back and crumpling him to the foot of the bar. His head cracked soundly on the brass footrail, his arms splayed, sending a spittoon spinning and its contents of cigar butts, tobacco juice, and spittle flowing. Then he lay unmoving among soaked sawdust and peanut shells.

The Frenchman's look went from shock to revulsion. "I should have known he was a coward."

Fear reflecting in the large brown eyes in his otherwise stoic face, the black glanced from man to man in the crowd, trying to weigh their thoughts. His gaze centered pleadingly on the man he had called master.

"I surely sorry, Massa," he mumbled, mostly for the benefit of the crowd, fearing he was about to be set upon and hanged from the nearest rafter, or whipped until dead—as he would have been for striking a white man in Louisiana.

With a booted foot, Clint toed the Root pistol aside and out of Grumbles's reach, just in case he awoke soon, but his face was already darkening with a massive blue lump the size of Gideon's fist, and he looked like he was out for some time.

The Frenchman moved closer to Gideon, his walking stick in one hand, the fancy gold handle shaking in the slave's face. "You know better than to raise your hands to a white man." The Frenchman's voice rang cold and aloof.

"I know, Massa LaMont, but—"

"Never again, Gideon. Never again, or I'll take the cane to you." He raised the walking stick threateningly.

Clint's jaw knotted with this change in events.

"Yessa," Gideon mumbled, and his gaze sank to the floor.

"That's the damnedest thing I ever heard," Clint managed, and some of the men in the crowd echoed his sentiment.

"Sir?" the Frenchman fixed his eyes on the newcomer.

"He knocked the gun aside, Massa," Gideon said quietly.

The Frenchman hesitated a moment. "I guess I owe you an imbibement, M'sieur, but we'll not discuss the discipline of my man, which is my business alone."

"Let me see, here," Clint said, studying the well-dressed man. "You owe me a drink, but you berate this man who saved your life sure as the sun rises in the east? That Root carries four more shots."

The Louisiana Frenchman puffed up and threw his shoulders back. "Do you desire the drink, M'sieur?"

"Soon as you thank this man and offer him something other than that fancy crutch across his back." He motioned to the big black man, who shook his head as if trying his best to silence Clint.

"This man is my property. It is his responsibility to protect my life—"

"Not in California, not to my way of thinking. Here a man steps up or stays out . . . his choice." Those nearby clamored in both agreement and disagreement.

"I told you to take it outside," Baggs snapped. He motioned toward the batwing doors with his scattergun. "You, too, emigrant." He locked gazes with Clint.

Clint shrugged his shoulders, reached over and upended his *aguardiente*, then headed to the door. The crowd parted, making way.

Deciding he had had enough of the El Dorado and saloons for one day, Clint moved straight to his horse. He shoved the rifle into its saddle scabbard, cinched the big palomino tightly, and mounted just as the doors swung away and the Frenchman, followed closely by his slave, stepped through. From behind, where the Frenchman couldn't see, Gideon nodded and flashed Clint a quick smile.

Clint backed his horse out from between the other horses and reined away. He'd ridden only a few paces when, at the roar of a gunshot, he instinctively dropped low to the saddle. He spun the palomino to face the threat.

The Frenchman lay sprawled on his face in the dust, his arms and legs unmoving and splayed abnormally, a red splotch growing on his back. Vester Grumbles stood on the boardwalk, the smoking cap-and-ball in his hand. Gideon stared at his fallen master. Then Grumbles swung the muzzle to the slave.

Clint jerked the leather thong binding his sixty-foot woven rawhide reata to the saddle. Almost as quickly as he could form a loop, it cut the air. The reata dropped over a surprised Grumbles and snapped tight, throwing off his pistol's aim, then sending the Root's spinning away. Clint dallied the reata on the high pommel, spurred the palomino, and reined him away in the same motion.

With three of the big horse's powerful strides, Grumbles flew off the boardwalk and landed with a rolling dust-raising crash on the street near LaMont. When Clint was sure the Root's was left behind in the dirt, he reined the palomino and spun the animal to face the spitting man whose face had plowed a furrow in the dust.

"Don't even think about picking that Root's up," Clint warned, resting his hand on the butt of the Colts pistol at his waist. Grumbles fought to get to his knees, then slowly climbed to his feet. He eyed the Root's, a few feet away.

"Don't," Clint repeated coldly.

Grumbles slowly worked the loop off his torso and discarded it, then cut his eyes back to the black man. His free hand came up to rub the side of his swollen face. "I don't care if you're white, green, or purple, free or slave, don't you ever raise your hands to me again or you're a dead man."

Gideon, showing no emotion except for the tightly balled fists at his sides, nodded at Grumbles, who walked to his bay horse and mounted. He spun his horse away from where Clint sat, but paused long enough to look back over his shoulder. "We'll meet again," he called out.

"If we do, it could be the last time for you," Clint said, recoiling the reata, his tone in deadly earnest.

Grumbles gave his heels to the bay and galloped off, threading through the busy street. The saloon began to empty as men crowded out to view the fallen Frenchman.

Gideon stopped near the Root's, gave Clint a quizzical look, then, when Clint nodded, bent down and picked up the little pistol. He hurried to where Clint sat the palomino.

Barrel in hand, he offered the pistol to Clint, who shook his head. Gideon shoved the Root's in his belt and watched Clint in silence for a moment. He cleared his throat. "Sir, after I bury M'sieur LaMont, are you in need of a manservant?"

Clint was taken aback by the change in the man's speech, which even had the hint of a French accent. "You . . . you talk different now."

"I've lived and worked all my life among the educated and studied their ways, but they preferred I speak in a manner they would not consider 'uppity.' " He glanced back at his fallen owner. "But there's no need for that now." He found Clint's eyes. "Might you be in need of a manservant?"

Clint chuckled at the thought. "You're a free

man now. You don't need anyone. This is California, and she'll be coming into the Union free. You'll get along here fine. You got a punch like a mule." Clint watched the man's worried expression change to a blank one. Then Gideon's face lit. "Looks to me," Clint continued, offering encouragement, "like when you bury that Frenchman, you bury his chains along with him."

"A free man?" Gideon said, looking doubtful, then grinning. "A freedman!" But his grin faded. "I'll bury him, surely, for his mother and grandmother were kind to me and mine, and he and his brothers were kind enough in their arrogant way, but I need the manumission papers to be free."

"Not here. Like I said, California is gonna come in as a free state or she'll revolt and become an independent sovereign nation. Folks here, at least most of them, don't abide with owning slaves, nor with the kind of thinking your mas—your former owner had. Take care of yourself. I'm Clint Ryan," Clint said, and extended his hand. Gideon looked at him for a second, then grinned and shook.

"Gideon."

"No last name?" Clint asked, knowing from his experience with black sailors that many carried only one handle. "Hell, take his. He won't be needin' it."

Gideon muttered the name to himself a couple of times.

Clint tipped his wide-brimmed hat. "Nice to make your acquaintance, Gideon LaMont. It has a nice ring to it."

He spun the palomino and urged him away. "Good day, Mr. Lamont."

But the black didn't answer. He grinned, and repeated, shaking his head in wonderment, "Gideon LaMont, a freedman."

"Hold up there," a voice commanded from behind. Clint wheeled the horse, his hand finding the butt of the Colt's. A tall redheaded man stood with fire in his eyes, one chiseled granite hand clasping

Gideon's shoulder roughly. In his other knotted hand he held a shortened 1841 Hall's rifle with a big .54-caliber bore—aimed at Clint's midsection.

"Keep your hands where I can see them and dismount. This Hall's carries a double charge and half a barrel fulla chopped-up square nails."

"And you'll cut down half the people on this street if you let loose," Clint cautioned, his voice steady.

The man freed Gideon's shoulder and tapped the star on his chest. "If I do, it'll be legal."

Clint nudged the stallion back next to LaMont's body and dismounted, careful to keep his hands in plain sight of the man. Diablo snorted and pranced, nervous with the nearby dead man and smell of blood.

"I'm City Marshal's Deputy Thad McPherson. What the hell happened here?"

"Wasn't them," one of the miners called out from the crowded boardwalk. The others chimed in agreement.

McPherson glanced at them, then quickly returned his eyes to Clint. "Then who did the shootin'?"

Luther Baggs shouldered his way through the crowd. "A fella named Vester Grumbles."

"Shot him down in a fair fight?" McPherson asked, still watching Clint.

"Maybe . . . maybe not," Luther said with a shrug of his shoulders.

"Cold blood, from behind," Gideon offered.

"You keep your mouth shut." McPherson raised his voice derisively and glared at Gideon. "Your testimony's no better than that mule's." He motioned to a big Roman-nosed animal tied nearby.

Gideon folded his hands behind his back and shut up.

"He's right," Clint said. "The man was shot from behind. He never had a chance."

"I know Vester Grumbles," McPherson snapped. "He's no backshooter."

"Maybe not before today." Clint's voice remained steady. "Now he is."

"What's your name?" McPherson stepped forward, the muzzle of the Hall's held ready, his green eyes studying Clint carefully.

Clint glanced over the crowd before he answered. The last thing he wanted was for the law to discover the outstanding warrant for his arrest, and a name could put McPherson on that track. "I'm known as Lazo."

"That some kind of greaser name?" McPherson asked, his mouth pulling back in a lazy smirk.

"It's a Mexican name," Clint stated coldly.

"What's your other name?" McPherson's thumb never moved from the big hammer of the Hall's.

"Lazo. That's all there is."

"Well, Lazo, you be on your way." The deputy motioned with his stubby gun.

Clint wasted no time and mounted. He hesitated before he spurred Diablo, then looked back at the deputy. "Mr. LaMont there is a free man and he had nothing to do with this. Ask any man who was in the saloon."

Half the crowd on the boardwalk chimed in their agreement. The rest sullenly held their tongues. Surprised, Gideon shook his head, fully expecting a lynch mob to emerge from the crowd like the head of Cleopatra's deadly asp from a basket of figs.

"You got a name?" McPherson asked Gideon.

"Gideon . . . Gideon LaMont."

"What's this man's handle?" McPherson poked the still body at Gideon's feet.

"He's Henri . . . Masters," Gideon said, his voice gaining confidence, but he glanced at Clint to judge his reaction.

Clint smiled, but only with his eyes. The former slave was learning fast.

"Did you know him?" McPherson was beginning to doubt the whole exchange.

"He was my associate. A fine man," Gideon said, smiling a little too broadly. "Bought a lot of enslaved folks and set them free. I owe him a lot and I'll see to his buryin'."

"Good," McPherson said, but his expression still reflected doubt. "That'll save the city a little money."

"I got a row to plow," Clint said, and spun the stallion away.

"Don't plow it too far," McPherson snapped. "I may want to talk with you again."

"I'll be around," Clint's voice rang out, but he didn't turn, and Diablo plodded unhurriedly down the road.

"Get this man off the street," McPherson instructed, and Clint heard Gideon's voice, strong and clear.

"Yes, sir."

Then the big horse wound its way into the crowded street out of earshot. Clint reined away, out of sight of the trouble, at the first intersection.

As the stallion clomped along, kicking dust in front of him, Clint decided he had had enough of the city. He yearned for the clean fresh-smelling countryside. He spurred the palomino into a canter and headed for the sand hills that ringed three sides of the growing town.

Just as he neared the last of the tents, two vaqueros flanked him, riding at the same pace.

The man on his right, astride a big red roan, doffed his sombrero. "You are the man they call El Lazo?"

"I've been called that, by friends in the south."

"You must come with us."

Clint rested his hand on the butt of the Colt's pistol shoved in his belt. "And who the hell are you?"

"I am Sancho Guiterrez, the head vaquero and *segundo* of Rancho del Rio Ancho." The man snatched a leather pouch from his belt and handed it across to Clint. It weighed heavy with gold—and gold was something Clint would need if he was to stock the Kaweah ranch.

"And where do we ride?" Clint asked in a considerably more agreeable tone.

"We don't ride. We take the boat. To Rancho del Rio Ancho, on the river Sacramento, the home of Don Carlos Vega."

Again Clint hefted the weighty pouch. "Lead the way, amigo." He smiled, tucked the pouch into his belt, and followed the vaqueros, who reined around and galloped for the bay.

CHAPTER THREE

THE ANCHOR LANTERN CAST A PALE CIRCLE ON the quarterdeck and reflected off the encroaching fog, a single glowing eye glowering from the mizzenmast of the full-rigged packet ship *Amnity*.

At one hundred seventy-five feet, the *Amnity* reigned among the largest of the more than eight hundred hulls anchored in the San Francisco Bay. The dark and fog precluded admiration of her black-painted hull, green-painted deckhouses, and bright varnished bends, as the four hull planks below the deckline were called. Her decks were naked pine, continually holystoned with sand to keep them free of stain. Her mainmast rose one hundred sixty feet from the water to her main truck; her foremast was only slightly shorter; and her mizzenmast, near where her captain stood on the quarterdeck watching with interest, was only slightly shorter yet.

Fully loaded, the packet's main deck lay nine feet above the water. Now, her holds empty, she rode at fourteen. The quarterdeck rose another six.

With no idea what was happening, the fourteen feet seemed a thousand to Apolonia Vega as she spun upward, suspended from a light block and tackle, still bound in her sackcloth and trussed like a keg of molasses. She expelled the breath she had been holding only when she felt the reassuring support of the solid deck. The sounds of the quiet creaking of the rigging and yardarms were unfamiliar to her, but the slight roll told her she was aboard ship.

On the quarterdeck in the darkness, Isaac Banyon

stood with his large sun-reddened hands clasped behind his back, his booted feet spread wide in a stance acquired from twenty-five years riding the pitching decks of a dozen ships. He wore no mustache, but his steel gray side beard joined chin whiskers in the New England manner, and the whiskers fell in waves to the middle of his wide chest. He was often misjudged as fat, for he was as deep as he was broad, and his girth at the waist far exceeded even his barrel chest. But he carried little extra weight; rather, he was built much like the hogshead barrels the *Amnity* normally carried in her hold. Many men would have allowed themselves to go to fat as master and owner of the *Amnity*. But not Cap'n Moses, as his men referred to him in private, for his piercing gray eyes and wavy beard portrayed that biblical image. Among other attributes he carried from his Quaker upbringing was a reverence for hard work. And he neither drank the demon rum nor smoked tobacco.

He served the Lord through his own liberal interpretation of the Bible, and he served himself— mostly himself—with hard work, and expected no less from his men. His was one of the few ships that had not lost a man to the diggin's, for he ruled her with an iron hand—and it rested on the butt of an Aston cap-and-ball pistol that always protruded from his belt while in port.

Bringing one of his rawboned, bony-knuckled hands up to his chin, he rubbed his whiskers, watching the men hoist their fragile burden aboard. They got her to her feet and guided her, still bound, gagged, and blindfolded, aft to the communal passenger quarters, disappearing into the hatchway below the quarterdeck.

Banyon clasped his hands behind his back and paced the windward side of the quarterdeck, satisfied that this would be a profitable voyage. Profitable indeed, as his cargo continued to grow in quantity and, with the addition of Apolonia Vega, certainly in quality.

" 'Tis the devil's work ye do, Isaac Banyon." His wife, Lucretia, startled him from behind.

"Damn ye, woman," he snapped, "ye move around this ship like Satan's own apparition. It is the Lord's work I do, as I have always done."

"Don't blaspheme in my presence." She drew the dark cloak she wore tighter around her face while Isaac glared at her. After more than a year on board, she still had the sallow withered look of a winter-trapped, parlor-bound New Englander. "Trading in flesh is not the Lord's—"

"Quiet yourself!" He took a step forward and she gave a step, her watery eyes wide. "The Good Book supports my every act. 'Smite the Philistines,' it says. The heathen China Marys and the papist whores of California who follow the edicts of a Roman master have no place in God's perfect world. They are the Philistines of our time."

Turning with a whirl of her cape, Lucretia faded back out of sight. Banyon heard her footfalls on the ladder to the main deck. Then her voice rang out clearly: "Do ye unto others, Isaac Banyon."

"Get back to your tatting, woman, or ye'll find yourself on the next ship back to Pennsylvania."

"Ye'd like that, left alone with the devil's cargo." Her voice disappeared with her footfalls.

He should never have allowed her to come along. *A fool's errand*, he cursed himself. Had he any idea he would be involved in trading the goods he now carried, he would have left her home. But how was he to guess? Opportunity came in strange ways, and a man had to be ready.

Banyon clasped his hands behind his back and paced the rail with angry strides. The deck rang with his heavy footfalls; then his anger wore off and his steps quieted. After a few moments he stopped, dug into the pocket of his heavy woolen coat, and pulled out a pipe. He knocked out the dottle and repacked it, content with his place in the scheme of things. He lit up with a sulfurhead that flared for a moment in the darkness.

Before Banyon had half finished the pipe, Harlan Stoddard, his first mate, scrambled up the quarter-deck ladder.

"No problems with this one." Stoddard smiled, revealing yellowed teeth beneath the soup-strainer. He rubbed the back of his thick neck with a ham-sized hand. " 'Twas clean as a newly honed knife blade."

"And is she the beauty it was said she is?"

"Even better, I would say, Cap'n. The best of the lot."

"Good. Set an extra deck watch tonight, just in case ye were followed."

"No chance of that, but as ye wish." Harlan Stoddard flashed a grin that reflected his yellowed teeth in the lantern light, then turned to head for the fo'c'sle and to call the watch. His massive shoulders gathered and he put both hands on the rails. With the skill of a man long at sea, he slid to the lower deck without putting a foot on a rung.

"Did ye have ol' Abner take her a smock?" Banyon called after him.

"Aye, Cap'n, like always."

Banyon waited until his first mate disappeared into the forward fo'c'sle hatchway, then started aft. His pace quickened and he took the half ladder two rungs at a time. He entered his wide cabin and was disappointed to see Lucretia not in bed but sitting in her rocker. Even in the cabin and already in her heavy nightgown, she wore a flowered coal-scuttle bonnet. She read the Bible.

Lucretia looked up, her eyes still reflecting condemnation, but her voice had softened. "Are you ready to retire?" she asked.

"Not quite yet. You go ahead. I want to check the rudder gear . . . been binding up a bit." He moved to the supply closet, picking a swinging coal-oil lantern off its hook as he passed. Entering, he pulled the door shut behind him and carefully turned the lantern down until it barely glowed. Then he knelt and pulled away the deck boards where the control cables passed below through the closet to the rudder block and

tackle ten feet below. Carefully, quietly, he climbed
down into the dank musty passageway with barely
enough room for his massive bulk, until he reached
the lower deck level. Moving forward a few feet into
a cleft, he searched the splintery bulkhead in the
darkness and found the tin can top that he had carefully placed over a quarter-inch borehole. He swung
it aside and peered through.

"I shall *not* remove my gown," the girl's voice
nervously rang through the plank walls.

By all that's holy, she is a beauty, Banyon thought
as he pressed closer to the peephole to watch the slender girl, whose gleaming black tresses hung to her two-
hand-span waist. Dark eyes flashed, contrasting with
a perfect complexion as light and clear as alabaster.

"Either you'll do it, or the cap'n will have the
men do it for you," cackled old Abner, the ship's supercargo, his voice whistling through the spaces of
missing teeth. Then, gaining a touch of compassion,
his look softened and he ran a bony hand through his
wispy hair. He scratched his liver-spotted pate.
"Please, lass, take off your clothes and put the smock
on. 'Tis a decent if simple gown and 'tis an order from
the cap'n. Put your'n in the sack and I'll store it for
ya."

"But why? Why am I here?"

"There are others like ya in the passenger's cabin.
You'll be able to join your own kind as soon as you're
settled in a bit. I'll give ya ten minutes, lass. Then, if
you've not complied, I'll have to tell the cap'n, and
he'll send the men."

She glared in anger and weighed the alternatives.
"Then leave me."

As old Abner pulled the door to the little cabin
shut, Banyon pressed so close that he could feel the
wood grain in his cheek. The girl turned her back to
the door and faced the peephole, then began to un-
button the tightly fitted jacket and blouse. Banyon's
breath quickened when she slipped out of the jacket
and her full breasts were outlined under the white
chemise she wore beneath, dark-peaked circles testi-

fying to the chill of the cabin. She untied her long skirt and it fell away to the deck. Her legs were slender and long, and smooth below the white pantalettes that covered them to just above the knee, exposing the skin between them and her calf-length stockings.

"Damn," he mumbled when she picked up the smock and slipped it on over her head without removing her undergarments. She stopped and stared at the wall, and Isaac held his breath. After a second she bent and recovered the skirt, stuffing it and the jacket into the sack she had been provided.

A sharp knock on the door snapped her head around. "Enter," she said, her voice as cold as the bay that lapped the hull just outside the cabin.

"Are ya done?" Abner asked, standing in the hatchway.

Without speaking, she handed him the sack. He ruffled through it, then looked up.

"Sorry, lass," he said, "but you'll have to shed the boots an' . . ." his eyes found the floor, "an' whatever else ye have on under."

"What?"

"All but the smock."

"*Chingaso*," she spat.

"Don't understand that Mexican." He smiled wanly, showing gaps where teeth should be. "An' it's probably jus' as well."

"Out," she said, and shoved the door in his face.

Banyon felt the grain of the wood as his eye bulged, but she merely raised the hem of the gown and worked the ties at the back of her chemise.

"Isaac, are you all right down there?" Lucretia's voice rang out, and Isaac jerked back, cracking his head on a crossbeam.

He hurried out of the cleft and glowered up into her pale face, lit by the lantern she held.

"I'll be along. Get ye to bed, woman."

"Is the steering gear all right?" she asked, but her voice rang with sarcasm. " 'Tis the fifth time you've checked it since we've been in San Francisco Bay."

"To bed, woman. I'm coming up."

She was in bed, asleep, or pretending to be, with her bony flannel-gowned back to him, by the time he had stripped to his faded red long johns and joined her.

Though neither of them could hear the quiet sobs from the cabin below, Isaac Banyon forgot his prayers, his thoughts centered on more earthly matters, and it was a long time before his breathing evened out to match Lucretia's.

CHAPTER
FOUR

IT WAS AS DARK AS A BLIND MAN'S HOLIDAY BY
the time Clint and the vaqueros neared the shore
where Rancho del Rio Ancho stretched for over four
miles. By that time Clint, Sancho, and Enrico Alverez
were fast friends.

The two vaqueros were men not unlike those
Clint had spent the last three years with during his
meanderings through southern California. Like most
vaqueros, at first Sancho and Enrico had been skep-
tical of a tall, sandy-haired, blue-eyed Anglo who
wore the embroidered jacket and *calzonevas* of the
vaquero, but after several hours aboard the little
donkey-engine steam-powered scow and conversations about mutual acquaintances they had all ridden
with, he was accepted.

As gruff as he had seemed at first, Sancho turned
out to be a comical man quick to smile and full of
stories. Even more importantly, he was a second
cousin to Inocente Ruiz, the *segundo*, or foreman, of
Rancho del Robles Viejos in Santa Barbara, where
Clint had worked for a while. It was Inocente who
Clint had saved from a sure death with his quick and
proficient reata work—and who had given Clint his
Californio nickname, El Lazo, the lasso.

The scow rounded a bend and Sancho rose from
his seat on a pile of cast iron bound for the diggin's.
Stretching, he kicked Enrico, who was dozing on the
deck.

"It is time, Lazo," Sancho said as Enrico climbed
to his feet. They picked their way through barrels and

crates to where their three stallions were tethered. The men saddled and bridled the horses, then waved to the captain of the little work boat, who steered as close to the shore as he could in the darkness. They mounted and Clint leaned forward in the saddle, squinting into the black void, searching for the wharf or landing he was sure would mark their departure spot.

Instead, Sancho's exuberant yell startled him as the vaquero gave spurs to his stallion. The big bay lunged forward, gathered its powerful haunches under it, and cleared the scow's low rail. Enrico followed, and Clint gave his spurs to Diablo. The big horse hesitated a half second, then followed. They hit the water with a tremendous splash and disappeared into the murky depths. Clint kicked free of the stirrups and slipped out of the saddle, clinging to the horn and allowing the animal freedom to swim. As he had learned to do so many times in the last three years, he depended on the big horse to get him out of trouble.

The stallion stretched its neck forward and with powerful strokes of its long legs soon found the muddy bottom. Clint walked out behind, with a death grip on the reins. The palomino shook like a dog while Clint wiped water from his own hair and eyes.

"Eye, yi, yi!" Sancho yelled from nearby. "The Sacramento, she is cold for summertime."

Clint mounted and waited for Sancho and Enrico, who looked like drowned kittens with their dark hair matted to their bean-brown faces as they rode up beside him.

"We ride, Lazo, to hot coffee and tortillas," Sancho said. Without awaiting an answer, he spurred his horse into the darkness. Clint followed at a lope, barely able to see the trail in the moonlight. They rode for an hour before Sancho drew rein, setting the bay back on its haunches.

In the distance a light glowed.

"It is the hacienda, amigo," he said to Clint. "It is only a few more minutes."

As they neared they passed through a vineyard,

and Clint could make out the whitewashed walls of a big adobe in the moonglow. Through a tall arched gate in the wall, they came into a courtyard. A boy hurried to take their horses, and Clint reluctantly handed his over. It had been a hard ride and he was concerned about the palomino.

Sancho sensed his reluctance. "He will be well cared for, Lazo."

Their roweled spurs rang as they made their way to the big carved door, which swung aside before they reached it. Wall sconces holding a dozen candles each lit the entry, and the tall well-dressed don extended his hand to Clint.

"El Lazo," he said as Clint shook. "I am Don Carlos Vega. Welcome to Rancho del Rio Ancho."

The distinguished man led Clint into a huge dim living room with a wide fireplace at one end. Another man sat in one of four chairs, his legs splayed in front of him, a crystal snifter cradled in one hand.

As they approached, Don Carlos made the introduction. "Lazo, this is my daughter's betrothed, Don Gaspar Cota."

The man rose and extended his hand, but his look was doubtful and hard. He sported a thin mustache, lost in his wide round face. Clint attempted a smile, but was unsuccessful. The man's grip was like shaking one of the salted cod that had been barreled on board the scow they had just left—dry and lifeless.

"I must be frank, Señor Lazo," Gaspar Cota said as he collapsed back into the chair. "You are invited here over my objection. This is a matter best handled by the Vegas and the Cotas."

"What matter?" Clint asked.

"Please be seated." Don Vega motioned him to a chair. "Sancho, please bring another snifter for Señor Lazo . . . and pour one for Enrico and yourself before you leave."

Clint found a seat in one of the high-backed leather chairs, nodded his thanks to Sancho for the brandy, and waited.

Don Vega leaned against the fireplace, staring into its low flames. It crackled and spat a few sparks out onto the smooth well-packed earthen floor. The don ignored them. The small fire was the only light in the room other than a pair of candlesticks on a table lining the wall. The don remained silent until he heard the door close, signaling his vaqueros' retreat.

"How is the brandy?" he asked, but didn't wait for an answer. "We make it right here on the rancho. I have heard a great deal about you, Señor Lazo. I feel fortunate that you were seen near Monterey on your way to San Francisco. We had a most unfortunate occurrence only yesterday. My daughter, Gaspar's betrothed, was abducted."

"By whom?" Clint asked.

"We know very little. She was riding, as she did every day. She was miles from the hacienda near the river, being watched, as is our custom, by her *dueña* and her driver in a buggy."

"And?"

"She was dragged from her horse by four Chinese. José, the driver, attempted to go to her rescue, but he was shot. He died only a few hours ago. But he was able to tell us that it was Chinese who did this thing."

"I am surprised, Don Vega. I have known many Chinese, sailed with them on a number of vessels. I even speak a little of their language. They respect and fear the law . . . more than most."

"These obviously did not," Gaspar said coldly. "Had you Anglos not brought those heathens to our shores—"

Don Vega interrupted him. "You are an Anglo, Lazo, but have the reputation of being a friend to those of us who once ruled California." Don Vega took a sip of his brandy, studying Clint's reaction.

"Like most men, I have many friends and a few enemies, Don Vega. If I can be of service to you, I would be pleased."

"The Ortiz and the Padilla families have daughters missing also. And the wife of Don Robles has disappeared. At first I thought these girls merely ran away, probably with Anglos whose pockets were packed with gold. I would have understood why Don Robles's wife might have fled him. But now . . . now I think there is some plot at hand. All of them live near San Francisco on San Pablo Bay, so the water seems to be a common thread . . . if there is one." He again looked into the fire, the reflection of the flames dancing in his eyes. "I would go myself, but English is now the language of preference there; I speak little of it and, of course, no Chinese. And San Francisco is a quandary to me, Señor." For the first time the old don began to show his frustration.

"Things are not the same as they were before you Anglos came. Killings, robberies . . . and now kidnappings." He raised his eyes from the fire, and Clint realized Don Carlos was pleading. It was not a thing the proud man seemed accustomed to. "Would you please find my daughter, and return her to me?"

"Have you contacted the law?" Clint asked.

"Ha!" Gaspar said, tossing the last of his drink down his throat.

"The law, Señor," the old don said with derision, "is only for the Anglo. The Californio is only laughed at and ridiculed and treated like an interloper in his own land if he appeals to the law. You may talk to the law if you wish. Maybe they will listen to an Anglo. For us, it is fruitless."

Clint quietly digested that. He had seen the attitude of many Anglos, particularly those who had arrived as a result of the gold rush. Just as Don Carlos said, they treated the Mexicans as if they were the foreigners. Hell, Mexican miners even had to pay a thirty-dollar-a-year mining tax—a foreigner's tax—to mine land they had occupied for two hundred years. It was easy to understand Don Vega's distrust and disrespect for the Anglo law.

"I will do what I can," Clint offered reluctantly. What he really wanted to find out was how to go about getting title to the Kaweah ranch. But the land would be there when he found the time.

"And I will ride with you," Gaspar said. Standing, he tucked his chin back and puffed up like a ruffled grouse strutting before a hen.

Clint eyed the rather pudgy, round-faced Californio don with the finely trimmed narrow mustache, and did not picture him as a great deal of help in any endeavor. More importantly, he sensed that this would be work for one man working alone. The less dust raised, the better.

Ignoring the man's offer, which had more the inflection of a command, Clint turned his attention back to Don Vega. "Why are you convinced they are in San Francisco?"

"Their tracks led downriver, at least for a few hundred yards, where they boarded a small boat." Frustration rang in his voice. "I know it is very little, Lazo. But it is all the information we have. I will pay you well if you succeed. There is little gold, but I have some of the finest horseflesh in California. Purebred Andalusians."

Clint's ears perked up. "Just how many horses would you consider fair, if I returned your daughter safely?"

The old don hesitated a minute before he answered. "Forty head?"

"Forty head of my choice?" Clint asked.

"Any among the four hundred or so on the ranch, with the exception of our personal riding stock."

Clint extended his hand and shook with the old man.

"Then we ride!" Gaspar said. "First thing in the morning."

"I'll be going alone," Clint said, his gaze finding the small dark eyes of Gaspar Cota.

"No!" Gaspar slammed a fist on the arm of the chair. "This is my fiancée, and I and my vaqueros will ride with you. There were many Chinese, and one man—"

"Don Vega," Clint said, ignoring Gaspar. "I ride alone. As you said, this is a job for an Anglo."

"Carlos," Gaspar sputtered, his jowls shaking, "I told you it was unnecessary for you to call this . . . this Anglo."

Clint gave his back to Gaspar, facing the old don. "I will leave now, Don Vega, if you would be so kind as to have some tortillas and meat packed, and to describe your daughter to me while I saddle up."

"*Momentito*," Don Vega said, and walked to the table holding the two candles. With reverence he picked up a small framed object from between the candles, walked back, and handed it to Clint.

"She is beautiful," Clint said respectfully, studying the tiny daguerreotype. "May I keep this?"

"Of course. . . ." Don Vega's voice wavered. "But I want it back, no matter what."

Clint nodded, then started for the door, with Don Vega close behind.

"If you will not accompany me, I will search without you," Gaspar yelled from behind.

Don Vega stopped; his shoulders straightened as he turned back. "Don Cota, Apolonia was my daughter long before she became your betrothed, and she is your betrothed only at my bequest. You may search the hills of Rancho del Rio Ancho or the Cota rancho or even Sacramento City all you wish." His voice hardened. "But stay away from San Francisco and allow Señor Lazo to do what I am paying him to do. Mexican Californios are not among San Francisco's most admired citizens at the moment. You will do more harm than good there and possibly get yourself killed." He glared at Gaspar. "And I would find that difficult to explain to your father."

Gaspar Cota sputtered, but was unable to say anything more. Don Vega yelled some instructions down a hallway, then slammed the big carved door and followed Clint across the wide courtyard to the barn. While they walked, the don described Apolonia Vega's size, voice, and manner.

Clint led the palomino, now grained and watered, outside, and was met by an Indian woman with a muslin sack full of food.

He thanked her and tied it on the back of the saddle.

The don laid a slender hand on Clint's shoulder. "I am sorry there is no more gold to pay you, El Lazo—"

"I would help even if there were no horses, Don Vega."

"Horses we have. The finest in California. I will give them willingly."

"Five stallions, thirty-five mares," Clint said, mounting.

"Willingly," the old man said. "You must want to become a breeder. You can do no better than Rancho del Rio Ancho stock." He paused, and Clint caught the glimmer of wetness in his old eyes in the dim moonlight. "I would give all to have my Apolonia back. Her mother is gone, and she is the last of the Vegas."

"Even though boats leave no tracks, I will find her, Don Vega."

"Vaya con Dios." The old man raised his arm and waved as Clint loped his palomino out of the courtyard and then gave the animal its head. The horse would have to find the trail back to the river, which Clint knew it would do with no problem. Then it was up to Clint.

He hoped his task would prove only a hundred times as difficult.

He feared it might be a million or more.

CHAPTER
FIVE

CLINT HAD TO RIDE ALONG THE RIVER ALL THE way to Benicia before he was able to catch a morning boat and return to San Francisco. Benicia, with its wide back bay and tidal estuary, reminded him of Mystic, Connecticut, where as a young boy he had been indentured to a tanner.

During the long voyage from Ireland, Clint's parents and sister had died from the dreaded cholera—when he was but seven years old. His time in Mystic, as an indentured servant, had not been pleasant, but he had learned a trade and how to work—and when he ran away to sea it had been easier for him than it might have been for a wet-behind-the-ears country boy.

The sun was straight overhead by the time the scow pulled alongside the old iron revenue steamer *James K. Polk,* now high and dry and used as a wharf. An irate landing agent started to berate Clint when he led the palomino onto the gangplank and crossed the deck of the *Polk.* A sharp look at the man quelled his ardor, and Clint reached the hundred-yard-long pier that had been constructed from the landward rail of the *Polk* across the tide-out mud flats.

When Clint and his palomino clomped off the pier onto the sand, he mounted, rode a few steps to another beached ship, the *Apollo,* and tied his horse to a rail outside. The *Apollo* lay buried six feet deep in the sand. Six-by-six-inch posts at forty-five-degree angles buttressed her hull and gave the impression of a ship under construction on the ways. But she would never feel the sea under her bow again. Her hold now housed a plank bar and tables—and over fifty drinking and gambling men. Her inner bulkheads had been torn away to open her up. Ports covered with waxed paper to let in the light but keep out the kelp flies were cut into her hull well below what would have been the waterline.

Clint figured this was as good a place as any to begin his quest. At least a few hours listening to the scuttlebutt on the waterfront was the best way to start.

He sipped a beer, ate a couple of pickled eggs for his lunch, and moved from table to table, where he found nothing but newly arrived men awaiting transportation up the river to the gold fields. One thing he did discover was that the day before, over a thousand Chinese had arrived aboard five different ships. Maybe circulating among the city's permanent residents would turn up something more.

As Clint started up Montgomery Street, he passed two other wooden ships, each rapidly becoming a skeleton of ribs as workmen stripped away their rigging, planking, line, and canvas for use in constructing more permanent structures—permanent at least until the next fire swept through the town. He had overheard an ex-captain at the *Apollo* brag that he had gotten more for his ship as building supplies in San Francisco than he could have sold her for as a working vessel in New York.

Before Clint had made his way for one block through the workmen and drays and crowds of miners, the sand street gave way to boards, and Diablo's hooves clattered hollowly. The tents and clapboards gave way to wood-frame and even a few brick-and-metal-shuttered buildings. He glanced at one of the only canvas-covered businesses on this block and decided to stop. If anyone in San Francisco, or any other town, knew what was going on, it would be a barber.

PHILAS PHISTER'S TONSORIAL PALACE AND BATH EMPORIUM, as foot-high red letters on a canvas banner proclaimed, was hardly as big as its name. A canvas roof stretched across a twenty-foot lot between two permanent two-story buildings. Half the frontage was occupied by two tall stools and a brick fire pit. The pit, billowing black smoke and obviously constructed from scraps and broken bricks left over from the construction of its neighbors, roared with flame. The other half of the frontage was enclosed by a ten-by-ten-foot tent ensuring the relative privacy of two leather tubs.

A one-eyed Chinaman, not more than four feet tall, with a braided queue protruding from under a skullcap and dangling to below his rump, carried buckets from a copper boiler on the fire pit into the bathing tent, where curses and yowls were emitted each time he filled the occupied tubs with boiling water.

Two barbers, each perfectly coifed and sporting upturned mustaches that would shame a Turk, worked away at the stools, clipping and combing a line of men that stretched across the boardwalk and into the board street.

Around each stool lay a foot-deep semicircle of variegated hair.

Clint didn't want to waste time in line, but the surest way to pushing up daisies was to crowd in front of mud-soaked placer miners eyeing a hot bath—unless, of course, it was crowding into the line across the street under the golden-lettered sign which read, MADAM DUPRE'S FRENCH SUPPER HOUSE AND ENTERTAINMENT EMPORIUM.

It seemed Montgomery Street had an undeclared battle under way for the longest-named emporium and gaudiest sign. This one, Clint had heard, was the finest brothel on the newly christened Barbary Coast, and the only one that bragged a white woman, though she had never been seen outside the front door. The only way it could be proven was by paying up. The establishment's name was only slightly longer than Phister's, but its line was four times as long—even though the rumor was that the shortest time a man could spend upstairs at Madam Dupre's cost five ounces of gold.

Clint tied Diablo to a hitching rail and stepped

to the end of the barber's line. His own sandy locks hung to his shoulders; the sight of his ears was a memory. The barber would provide more than much-needed information. Clint waited, and visited with the men in line as he did so, but learned nothing of value.

It took him an hour to reach the stool.

"How long is it gonna be afore you get back to see us?" the barber asked as he stropped the razor he had used to shave the last man.

"Trim 'er down and lay on the foo-foo so I can find my ears and turn a few ladies' heads," Clint said, returning the barber's smile.

"That's a laugh, friend. Hell, I ain't seen a woman, at least not a white one, since I left Philadelphia almost a year ago."

The man introduced himself and draped Clint in a soggy, spotted cloth. Clint was pleased to learn that he had landed in the chair of Philas Phister himself. While Philas lathered him up for the shave, Clint managed to pose one two-part question.

"Just what is the lady situation hereabouts, and what the hell do all these Chinese do for women?"

As barbers are so adept at doing, Philas talked the whole time he shaved and trimmed Clint. Three of the man's nonstop sentences stayed with Clint, whose ears were now plainly visible.

"The newest feature in town, the Barracoon, is the only place for a man to find a woman, at least for a keeper, if he can't find an Indian girl to entice away from her brave with a poke full of gold, and you can't find one there at the Barracoon least for a few days," was the first.

"There are no white women who show their faces on the streets, except for Sultana Mulvany, and I've yet to have the pleasure of seeing her," was the second.

"Tok Wu 'Huly Up' Hong is the man to ask if you want to know anything, and I mean anything, about the Chinese, 'cause he is one of the few John Chinamen who speaks any English a-tall," was the third.

Clint gladly paid the two dollars and fifty cents for what would have cost two bits in ordinary times. The information was well worth it.

Smelling so good he could hardly stand himself, he left Philas and set out to find Huly Up Hong. Even Diablo turned his head and eyed Clint, as if wondering if he had been loaded with a bushel of lilacs.

Telegraph Hill rose over the bay between the foot of Montgomery Street, where the majority of the waterfront activity took place, and the distant narrow opening to the Pacific, christened the Golden Gate by John Freemont. The early settlers of Yerba Buena and, later, San Francisco, had scrambled up the hill to watch ships entering the harbor—but that was a thing of the past. The west side of Telegraph sported hundreds of Chinese shacks and the east side half as many Italian shanties—with a no-man's land in-between. It was rapidly becoming the worst section of San Francisco, other than Clark's Point, where the waterfront degenerated into the worst nest of shanghaiers, thieves, and murderers on the Barbary Coast. None of the thirty San Francisco city marshal's deputies would venture into the area without a number of their mates watching their backs.

Clint left the board-covered streets and followed a winding road, Calle de Fundación. Most of China-town teemed with shacks constructed from every imaginable scrap, but a few buildings were of lumber. Men in black cotton pants and long-sleeved coats or robes hurried about, each as if he had a mission. Few horses were in the streets, but small cages of ducks, chickens, pigeons, and an occasional pig or goat occupied every crack and cranny around the crowded tents and shacks.

Every available spot of earth not used for a dwelling or road or cage was growing something. The permanent buildings had window boxes at each opening, and each had a well-tended herb garden. An occasional flash of color marked a spot where hunger or flavor gave way to beauty, and a flower grew.

Paper lanterns hung from the front of every

shanty. Chinatown, when the Chinese wanted it to be, was better lit than any other section of the city.

Clint had spent enough time aboard ships with Chinese crew members to know that crowded conditions did not daunt them. Where other sailors might have messy bunks and chests in which nothing could be found, the Chinese, always relegated to the smallest and most confined of the fo'c'sle bunks, were a picture of order and—if it could be said about a fo'c'sle—beauty. A Chinese could dump a bucket of cod, a cork float, and a piece of seaweed on the deck, and within seconds it would be arranged as a still life worthy of the walls of a cathedral. A Chinese bunk always held some decoration, if only a paper design along the bulkhead or a hanging decoration that swayed with the roll of the ship. The Chinamen had gained Clint's respect, and he had become fast friends with a number of them during his seafaring days.

Clint dismounted in front of a shack, made from a rusted-out boiler and several partially rotted hull planks, that served as an eating establishment, and found a seat at one of two tables in front of it. Two Chinese at the other table glanced at him nervously, finished their bowls of rice and their cups of tea, and hurried into the dirt street.

An old man stuck his head out of the rusted boiler section and eyed Clint with suspicion. Obviously he got few white customers. Clint reached to the other table, picked up a handleless teacup, and motioned to him. The man disappeared and quickly reappeared with a teapot and spotlessly clean cup, then filled it for Clint.

"Tok Wu Hong?" Clint asked the man, who shrugged his shoulders. Clint reached into his pocket and removed a tiny one-dollar gold piece and placed it on the table. "Tok Wu Hong," he repeated, pointing to the tiny gold piece, then to the old man.

A hint of a smile tugged at the corners of the old man's mouth and he disappeared into the boiler. Clint was startled as a small boy bolted past him, then disappeared down the street.

Before Clint had finished his third cup of tea, the boy returned, with a squat square-shouldered man following. The man, unremarkable in his plain black robes, bowed politely in front of Clint.

"I am Tok Wu Hong," he said, finding Clint's eyes for only a fraction of a second. His own black eyes continually worked the street, the small yard where the tables sat, the sky, and every other conceivable target.

"You're the man known as Huly Up Hong."

He bowed. "Your humble servant, honorable one."

Clint motioned him to sit, and he did. The old man refilled Clint's cup and poured one for Hong. Clint waited until the old man shuffled back inside the boiler. "I need information about some Chinese."

Hong's dark eyes quickly found Clint's, then cut away.

"And why do you seek these men? A man's life would be of no value if he gave information about his own that might lead to their injury."

"If these men were stopped, it would be for the good of all honorable Chinese. They have taken a girl. Maybe more than one. All of California will soon rise up against the Chinese if these men are not found and this girl returned."

Hong studied him. "It would be a terrible thing for the wrath of the white devils to fall upon the Celestials. There is only one man who can speak of this with you."

"And who might that be?"

"You are willing to go alone to see him?"

"I came alone to see you."

"Are you willing to pay Tok Wu ten dollars in gold?"

"I would pay one dollar."

"I thought you wished badly to see this man."

"I thought you believed it would be a terrible thing for the wrath of the white devils to fall upon the Celestials."

"I think it would be maybe five dollars worth of terrible."

"Fine. I wish to see this man five dollars worth."

Hong rose and stuck his head into the boiler shack. He spoke rapidly; then the boy ran out and around Clint and down the street again. Hong strode past Clint. "Have your five dollars in hand. Follow me, huly up, huly up, prease," Hong instructed, and was half a block down the road, living up to his nickname, before Clint was mounted and following.

Hong walked deeper into Chinatown, Clint following on Diablo. By the time they had covered three blocks, the boy approached and spoke to Hong, who looked up at Clint and extended the flat of his palm.

Clint dropped a five-dollar gold piece into Hong's hand. Hong bit it, testing its validity, then smiled briefly.

"Zhang Ho will see you. I am surprised." He hurried on, and Clint nudged the palomino after him.

One block of structures was better constructed than the others, and Hong stopped in front of the only two-story brick building Clint had noticed in all of Chinatown. It stood without adornment, with board shutters covering the windows.

Hong climbed the four steps to the stoop and rapped sharply on the plain-paneled door while Clint dismounted and tied Diablo to a single wrought-iron post with a ring in it. By the time Clint had loosened Diablo's cinch and started for the door, Hong was descending the stairs.

"I am not needed here," he said, and disappeared down the street.

The door creaked open and a boy of no more than ten, barefoot and dressed in ragged cotton pants and shirt, bowed when he saw Clint.

"Zhang Ho, please," Clint said, and the boy opened the door wider and stepped aside. Clint crossed the threshold and waited for his eyes to adjust to the darkness. He made out a man sitting in a corner on the floor. A frayed mat in front of him held a cup and a bowl half filled with a meager portion of rice and some scraps of meat, and a wooden cane topped by a carved dragon's head lay on the floor next to him. A wisp of pure white hair stuck out from a hooded cloak that covered his old head, in contrast to a pure black mustache that hung a foot down on either side of his tightly drawn mouth. His ragged cloak hung past his shoulders to the floor.

The boy quietly disappeared out the front door, pulling it shut behind him. The room reeked of cheap incense and the smoke of a single candle, which also rested on the floor of the barren room in one far corner.

"You seek Ho?" Though the old man managed to raise his head, he seemed almost too feeble to talk.

"Yes. I understand he will speak to me of a problem that threatens both your people and mine."

"A thousand pardons, sir, but problems of *bai* not business of Celestials. It better to remain so." Clint had to strain to hear the old man. He moved closer.

"*Wan ri shenti, laodaye,*" Clint began, wishing him ten thousand years of health and calling him by the respectful term *old grandfather*. Then he smiled. "*Kai wanxiao,*" "You make a joke," Clint said, insisting that the problems of the whites in California must be the problems of the Chinese. He spoke slowly, haltingly, remembering all that his shipboard friends had taught him.

The old man had looked up in surprise when Clint offered his first words in Chinese, then regained his composure. He, too, changed to Chinese, but also spoke deliberately and slowly. "You speak the honorable language of Han."

"I am an ignorant man, old grandfather. I speak the Celestials' language only a little, but I come on an important mission that the honorable Zhang Ho must hear of."

The old man studied him carefully, then picked up his cane and labored to his feet. Clint moved forward, put his hand under the old man's arm to steady him, and helped him up.

An inner door separated the room from what lay

beyond, and the stooped old man creaked his way toward it. He stopped before he reached for the knob. "You are friend to Chinese?"

"I am a friend to any man who's a friend to me."

The old man studied him, then appeared satisfied with the answer. He turned the knob, and light flooded the room. Clint waited until the old man shuffled through, then followed. He stared at the great room, at least six times as large as the entry. The incense that graced the room wafted to him like a fresh high-mountain meadow. Colorful paneled screens adorned the walls—scenes of ancient China, intricate paintings of gardens and birds. A carved mahogany screen stood nearby—a dozen Chinese warriors doing battle with a great fire-breathing dragon.

Clint shook his head in wonder, but was even more amazed when the old man straightened and shed the ragged cloak he wore. He ran his hand through his hair, putting the wisp of white back into place. He seemed to lose twenty years with the cloak and gain twenty pounds as his shoulders squared and his spine straightened. Another Chinese hurried forward and held a fine embroidered black and red silk robe for him. He donned it and extended his hand to Clint.

"I am Zhang Ho," he said from under a full head of black hair, the single streak of white tucked carefully into place. "What do you wish of the Fu Sang Tong?"

CHAPTER
SIX

CLINT ALMOST CHUCKLED OVER THE RUSE, BUT didn't.

"Would you like to take tea while you tell me of this 'mutual problem'?" Ho asked politely as they moved across the room and reclined on silk pillows, separated by a low carved table. As soon as Clint was settled, the servant returned with a pot of mint-scented tea and two fine porcelain cups.

Anticipating Clint's question, Ho spoke first—in precise English. "I am sorry for the deception, Señor Lazo, but a Celestial cannot be too careful in these trying times. I presume you are here in regard to the missing Californio ladies?"

"You know who I am and why I've come?"

"I have heard of you and of your mission. At the risk of seeming less than humble, there is little that goes on, on the river, the bay, or in San Francisco, that I do not hear of. Members of our humble tong are everywhere there are Chinese. The Chinese are already the muscle of California, Señor Lazo. They have ears and many Californio friends among the working class."

"Then you already know why I have come?"

"Yes, and I, too, am concerned with the deception someone has played on both of us. Let me assure you, the Chinese, and certainly those of the Fu Sang Tong, had nothing to do with this."

"How can you be so sure?" Clint settled back in the pillows and sipped the excellent green tea.

"I would swear on the spirits of my ancestors that

no Fu Sang member is involved. I would be forever
shamed if it were any Chinese, and would wager all
the gold of the *gum san* against a farthing that it is
not."

"It seems to me that thousands of men without
women might have a few among them who would
resort to anything—even kidnapping." Clint drained
the rest of his tea. "The Anglos will not stand for John
Chinaman breaking the law."

"Please do not be offended, Señor Lazo, but I
must tell you. You may know something of our language, but you know little about the Celestials."

"Then enlighten me."

Ho stood up and began to pace as he talked. "Do
you know why our tong is named Fu Sang?" He didn't
wait for an answer. "In your year four hundred and
ninety nine, the Buddhist priest Hui Shen, along with
other priests, came to the shores of what we Celestials
now call *gum san*, the gold mountain. What you Anglos call California." He smiled wryly at Clint. "That,
if my history is correct, was long before the Spanish
or the Mexicans and was while you Anglos still herded
goats in Europe. Hui Shen reported back to the Im-
perial Court that there was a wondrous tree here, and
named the land for that tree, Fu Sang. Its fruit was
said to be like pears, its fibers like iron, its root edible.
Pins and needles were made from its thorns, paper
from its bark, and liquor from its juices."

Clint wondered if he was being fooled. "I know
of no tree like that."

"Really?" Ho said, flashing another polite smile.
"You've never seen the maguey of Mexico?

"Each year for over a hundred, the Celestials
came to the Fu Sang, before we lost interest in a land
with no treasure or history, and peopled only by the
heathen. If Hui Shen and those who followed him had
only gone inland and found the true *gum san*, you,
not we, might now be the guest in Fu Sang."

"Hell, maybe the Chinese were here a thousand
years before the Spanish. I am a Celt, Zhang Ho, and
the Celts, if you know your European history, did

more than herd goats. But what does any of this have to do with the problem at hand?"

"I tell you only so you know that the Fu Sang is an old and honorable name, representing an old and honorable people who accomplished much. Still, we know we are here as guests." His tone hardened. "Even though we were here long before the Anglo. We do not complain when you Anglos pass the foreign miner's tax and each Chinese must pay thirty dollars a year to work in the gold fields. We do not complain when you drink your whiskey, act the heathen, and dishonor us by cutting off our queues."

He folded his hands behind his back. "We ship most of what we make back to China, where we all plan to return. The *gum san* is not our home, and as you know, no Chinese wishes to become a citizen of your California. China is our land, as it is the land of our ancestors." He returned to his seat.

"No Chinese did this thing you speak of. The Chinese would not dishonor their homeland, nor their ancestors, by doing such a thing . . . nor would they risk being thrown out of the gold fields."

That made sense to Clint.

Ho sipped the last of his tea. "No, Señor Lazo, the men who did this were not Celestials. All know of the Barracoon. The news flew through California on falcon's wings. Only two weeks ago, the first shipload of *mui gai* arrived. Even now they are overcoming the rigors of the voyage, and within the week will be auctioned off. Soon there will be plenty of Chinese women in San Francisco."

"The Barracoon? *Mui gai?*"

"The Barracoon is the humble place where we, the Fu Sang, will offer indentured Chinese girls, *mui gai,* to any who wish to bid."

"Bid? What the hell is that, Ho? This is a free state."

"It is not slavery, honorable Lazo. It is only the free trading of indentured servants."

"I was indentured, Ho. I know how free an indentured servant is." Clint stood, his fists balled at his sides.

"This sounds like a sham for a slave market to me. The good men of San Francisco will not stand for it."

Ho ignored Clint's remark. "So you see, Señor Lazo, we have no need to abduct Californio women. We will be able to bid for our own very shortly."

Clint walked to the door and pulled it open, but hesitated a moment. "I don't mean to be rude, honorable Ho. You have been very helpful. I don't think this Barracoon will be the answer to the Celestials' problem. I fear, from what little I know, that it may be just the beginning of a new one. If you hear anything that will help me find the Chi—the abductors of that girl, please contact me."

"It was not the Chinese, honorable Lazo. Look elsewhere. The expensive silk purse sometimes holds the fewest jewels. Look where it is not so obvious. Besides"—Zhang Ho smiled—"if they were Chinese, they would have been clever enough to dress like white devils."

"I'll think on that. Thanks for your help." Clint pulled the door shut, then made his way through the dimly lit barren anteroom and into the street.

He now believed that the abductors were not Chinese. What he knew of Celestials had already given him doubt. And what Zhang Ho had said made sense. If Chinese women were coming to California, or already were there, there would be little reason for the Chinese to risk the wrath of Californians by committing a crime—and it was just not like them. They respected the law.

But still, he felt they were making a mistake with the Barracoon.

CHAPTER
SEVEN

"I DON'T WANT TO MOVE TO ANOTHER ROOM. I want to go home!" Apolonia shouted, and stomped her foot.

Abner Baggs stepped back, hands extended, palms out. "Now, missy, if'n you give me trouble, I'll have to call for some help."

"When do I get to go home?"

"The cap'n will have to talk to you of that. Now, you come on along." He turned and backed down the passageway until he reached the ladder, then pulled a key ring from his belt and worked at the brass lock on a door.

Apolonia eyed the sunlit ladderway behind the old man and wondered if she could manage to run past him; but barefoot, wearing only a smock and not knowing if the ship she was on was at sea or anchored, she hesitated until his attention turned back to her.

"Come on, missy." He pushed open the door, squinted, and searched the inside until he was satisfied where the others were. "The rest of you step back. Go on, get away from the door." He motioned Apolonia inside, and when she complied, slammed the door behind her. She cringed as she heard the key rattle and the lock being turned.

Relief flooded her as she looked at the others, also barefoot and clad in smocks, in the long, narrow, eight-bunk room. Five other women, three of whom she knew well. Maria Carranda, Helena Obregon, and

Señora Juanita Robles rose from their bunks and rushed to her side.

They all began to question her at once, until Juanita Robles hushed them. "Stop it! Stop chattering like barnyard hens." They quieted. Juanita took Apolonia's nervous cold hands. "Are you all right, *niña*? Did they hurt you?"

"I am fine, Señora Robles. My jaw is sore where one of those brutes slapped me . . . an ugly man with a big mustache—"

"Stoddard," Juanita confirmed. "The worst of them."

"And my back and sides are sore. But it is nothing, really. Can you tell me what we are doing here?"

"We know nothing. We hoped you might know what is happening."

For the first time since she had been abducted, Apolonia allowed someone else to see her true feelings. "I am so frightened. . . ." She sank to her knees and began to sob into her hands.

Juanita knelt beside her. "Don't cry, little one. So far, none of us has been hurt . . . or touched in any way."

Apolonia glanced up at Juanita. The thought hadn't yet dawned on her that she might lose her honor. She glanced at the women in the room and realized that they were all beautiful—some of the most beautiful women in northern California—and sobbed even louder.

Juanita rose. "Apolonia Vega, stop crying right this instant," she demanded. Apolonia stopped immediately and looked up at her older friend. She nodded. She would cry no more. Juanita helped her to her feet.

"Either of those top two bunks on the end are yours. The chamber pots are under the lower bunks and there is water in that pitcher."

"How long have you been here?" Apolonia asked, looking from girl to girl, each dressed in a simple straight smock.

"Sarena Gutierez has been here the longest. Almost a week. The rest of us arrived on almost a daily basis."

"Why are we here?" Apolonia's tone rose, and she fought to hold back the tears.

"We just don't know," Juanita said. "Now, kneel with us, and we will pray for guidance."

They sank to their knees and Juanita led them in prayer.

But Apolonia's thoughts were of more immediate problems.

Escape. Somehow they must escape.

Captain Isaac Banyon backed away from the borehole on the wall opposite the one he had used to peek in on Apolonia Vega, and cursed his luck—all of the women were clad. This Vega girl was the most beautiful and the most modest of the women, never removing her smock for any reason. And her modesty caused his neck to tickle with prickly heat and his thick thighs to roast. *Damn her infernal pride.*

Now he had had her placed with the other women. Damnation, he wished they would do something that would give him the excuse to bring them out and punish the papist whores. A sound lashing on their bare backs would serve them. It would break their spirit and their hope for escape, he told himself.

He wished he spoke Spanish. Maybe he would overhear something that would give him the excuse to thrash them. He had some crew members on board who did speak the Mexican tongue, but none of them was among the only five other men who knew of the women.

The sailors had had no problem bringing the *mui gai* from China—willing or unwilling—but they might have a problem concerning the Californio girls, who were clearly opposed to their fate. Some of the sailors on board were probably papists themselves— Banyon had Portuguese and Italians and a Chilean among the crew.

Banyon climbed up the ladder, replaced the floorboards, and stepped out of the closet into his cabin. Lucretia had been taken onshore by his first mate, Stoddard, for some last-minute purchases before they sailed, and would soon return. It wouldn't do to have his wife discover him checking the rudder gear again. She was becoming even more of a problem than usual. He had made a terrible mistake bringing her on this voyage. He brushed the mildewed splinters away from his coat and trousers.

Soon. Soon, he promised himself, he would be able to lay the leather to those comely bare brown backs. Just as he had to a few of those of the heathen litchi-nut-colored China Marys on the trip over. But not so hard as to mark them permanently. Then they would not bring so good a price. Just enough to make them wither and pray to the Lord God Jehova for forgiveness. Wither, and squirm, and kneel before him.

Before Captain Isaac Banyon, and God Jehova.

Clint stopped by the old man's rusted-out boiler shack, left another gold piece, and asked him to find Huly Up Hong. He carefully explained where he would be for the next couple of hours, then worked his way down Calle de Fundación out of Chinatown.

He noted a livery, Hardy's, not far from the saloon he was headed for, and stopped there. He had a belt full of money, but planned to hang on to it. It was for the Kaweah ranch—and San Francisco hotel rates were higher than a cat's back.

"Need a stall for this stallion and a place to bed down, myself," he told the stocky man who met him at the wide doors.

"You're in luck, friend," the man said, extending his hand and introducing himself. He motioned into the darkness of the barn, where a man was saddling a hammer-headed black mule. "That fella is just ridin' out. Normally we're full up."

"I'm real partial to this palomino, Mr. Hardy," Clint cautioned. "See he gets a couple of handfuls of grain a day and a forkful of clean hay. I'd take it

personal if I came around and his water bucket was
empty."

"We know our job, but I appreciate your concern. That's a fine-lookin' animal," Hardy said in a
businesslike manner. "Your tack and anything else you
want to leave will be under lock and key. We don't
take responsibility for your goods, but we do our best."
He motioned to a walled-in stall with a big brass padlock on it. "Paco!" he yelled to a brown-skinned boy,
who ran forward and took Diablo's reins. Then the
stocky man strode away toward the rear, with Clint
following. "Come on out back and I'll show you a
spot."

Clint followed Hardy to the rear of the stable and
to a row of rooms that seemed to have been built up
against the wall as an afterthought. Each tiny cubicle,
half the size of the horse stalls, held a rope-strung log-
framed bunk with just enough room beside it to stand
and dress.

"You supply your own candle," the stocky man
said, "and be damn careful with it. Water is at the
trough. Privy is there," and he pointed to an outhouse
against a corral fence in the very rear. "Half dollar a
day for you and a half dollar for the horse. If your
stallion kicks my stalls out or you kick up hell, you're
out of here faster than a stump-tailed horse flicks it in
flytime."

"Damn." Clint moaned, still trying to reconcile
the price.

"If the price or the terms are too steep, there's a
hundred or so who don't think so."

"It'll do," Clint said quickly, knowing he was fortunate to find anything in San Francisco. He handed
the man a five-dollar gold piece and gave Paco a few
more instructions before he strode out.

"We do a little shoein'," he heard Hardy call after him. "Four bits a shoe with no guarantees." Clint
waved over his shoulder.

On the boardwalk in front of the El Dorado, two
men leaned against the porch rails, the shorter man
reading a newspaper. They straightened as Clint ap-

proached, and Clint recognized the redheaded deputy marshal. He searched the man's gaze for any threat, but the green eyes betrayed nothing.

"Hold up a minute, Lazo," the deputy said, his tone, as usual, less than friendly.

"I got a minute, McPherson, but just." Clint's voice was light with a nonchalance he did not really feel.

"This is City Marshal Larson." McPherson motioned to the stocky potbellied man next to him. Two long nine cigars extended out of a pocket of his fancy waistcoat—more that of a gambler than a marshal, Clint thought.

Clint nodded, as the man made no effort to shake. "Did you catch up with that fella who shot the Frenchman?" Clint asked, hoping that was the reason he had been summoned.

Larson pulled out one of his cigars and shoved it in his mouth. McPherson snatched a match from his own pocket and lit his boss's long nine. Larson blew a cloud of smoke before he answered for his deputy.

"We caught up with him, and he and six other witnesses testified it was a fair fight. You and that Negra gonna find any fault with that?"

"Not really my business," Clint said. "Can't speak for Mr. LaMont, but it'd be my guess he's got other rows to hoe."

"Good thing," Larson said smugly. "I'd hate for the newspaper"—he shook a rolled-up copy of the *San Francisco Call* at Clint—"to get the wrong impression about the way we handle our business. The *Call* is itchin' to find some dirt to kick up."

" 'Course, nobody would pay no mind to what that Negro said anyways," McPherson said. "That's all, Lazo." The deputy turned his back on Clint.

"Not quite all." Clint fished into his pocket and came up with the picture of Apolonia Vega. "This young lady is missing and her father has asked me to make the law aware of it."

"Right good-lookin' woman, for a greaser," Larson said, a slow smile curling his lips and puffing the cheeks of his round face. McPherson reached for the picture, but Clint repocketed it. He fought an impulse to shove the cigar down the potbellied marshal's throat.

"She's missing"—Clint managed to keep his voice steady—"and I understand a number of other California girls are too."

"I've had two families in my office expecting me to search for these women." Larson took a deep draw on his cigar and exhaled. "We got no time to look for runaway girls. That's a family matter."

"Runaway? Apolonia Vega was abducted. Carried off by the Chinese, or at least by men dressed as Chinese. Eyewitness said so."

"The Vega place is way up the river, ain't it, Ryan?" the marshal snapped.

"Halfway to Sacramento City," McPherson chimed in.

"Way out of my jurisdiction," the marshal said with a politician's smile. "I've got enough trouble right here in San Francisco. Don't have to go lookin' for other people's, particularly foreigners'."

How right you are, Don Vega, Clint thought. "If you happen to hear of anything, I would appreciate knowing about it," Clint said, still fighting to keep his temper.

"You some kind of lawman?" McPherson asked, raising an eyebrow.

"Nope," Clint said quickly. "Family asked me to see if I can locate their daughter."

"Keeping an eye out is one thing," Larson said. "Trying to play lawman is another. Don't you be breaking the law while you're sticking your nose into the law's business. We're trying to keep the peace with the Chinese, and we don't need strangers coming around stirrin' things up."

"If the law took this Vega matter on as their business, the Vegas wouldn't have to hire someone," Clint snapped.

"I offered that as a suggestion," Larson said. He took a half step forward, all trace of a smile gone from his face. "Now take it as a warning, Lazo, if that's really your name. Don't break the law, or the law'll break you."

"I wouldn't think of it, Marshal," Clint said, his voice steady and assured, but his blood boiling. Clint tipped his hat, trying to convert the smirk on his face into a smile, but it didn't quite work. He turned on his heel, headed away, and shoved through the bat-wing doors.

Larson stared after him, gnawing on the long nine. "I don't much like that som'bitch," he said, more to himself than to his deputy. He glanced at McPherson. "You nose around and find out what you can about this Lazo. That's a funny handle for a man who sounds like he's from New England."

Clint shoved through the crowd in the El Dorado. It was strangely silent. Then he realized why. Ostrich-feathered bulging-bodiced Sultana Mulvany had taken the stage.

A pianoforte player with a head as white and clean of hair as his ivory keys sat at an upright just below the stage. Where a New York pianist might have his sheet music, a sawed-off scattergun rested in a buckhorn rack. Clint smiled, figuring the cigar-smoking ivory tinkler had duties other than his music—such as keeping the rowdy bunch from laying their hands on Sultry, the Barbary Warbler, as she was rapidly becoming known.

The room fell so silent Clint could hear beer-foam bubbles bursting in the mugs. The first notes of "My Old Kentucky Home" brought cheers from half a dozen in the room, but they were quickly quelled by threats of lost life from those who wanted to hear every tone and inflection of the feminine voice. The men stood in respectful silence until she finished. Then the place rocked and dust rose with foot-stomping hand-pounding enthusiasm.

During the uproar, Clint elbowed his way to the bar and muscled in between a miner and a black-suited high-hatted Negro dude. He smiled as he noted that the suit had been let out with inset swatches of bright red cloth. A four-inch-wide patch ran down the middle of the back of the coat, and two-inch stripes down the outside of each leg converged in the seat of the pants and ran upward to the waist. A gold-handled walking stick hung from the brass-edged bar.

"By the saints!" Clint exclaimed when he focused on the man's dusky face. "If it isn't Gideon LaMont."

Turning his eyes from the stage, where Sultry was waving as she left and the piano player was scrambling around gathering tossed gold coins, Gideon flashed a grin and extended his large, rosy-palmed hand. "At your service, sir."

Clint pumped it.

"I'd be proud to buy you a drink, Mr. Ryan." Gideon quietly motioned the barman over.

"I would accept, sir," Clint said, still amused at the costume. "I see you decided not to bury your unfortunate friend in his city suit."

"No sense in soiling such a fine piece of goods when I could find a talented Chinaman to resurrect it." Gideon placed a gold piece on the bar and paid for Clint's whiskey. "Unfortunately"—Gideon smiled playfully—"he had no black cloth."

"It appears you have prospered since I last saw you," Clint said with a wry smile as Gideon swept his change from the bar.

Gideon leaned closer to Clint and spoke in low tones. "It seems that Henri LaMont carried a money belt with a considerable amount of gold. I would not have found it, had I not decided that he would no longer be in need of the suit. I relieved him of what I felt was a fair wage, after found, for thirty-three years of service, and entrusted Adam's Express Company with the balance."

He took a deep draw on his flavored soda water. "It, and a note informing them that I consider myself a freedman, since California is surely coming into the Union as a free state, is even now on its way to New Orleans and the LaMont family."

"Sounds fair enough to me," Clint said, but he couldn't contain a chuckle.

"Quiet!" The miner on the other side of him cautioned with a hard tone when Sultry returned to the stage. The piano tinkled and she began to work her way through a lively "Camptown Races."

She finished her number and fled the stage. Gold and silver coins rained down on it from the enthusiastic crowd. The pianoforte player/bodyguard scrambled over the stage collecting the money. The place resumed its midrange roar. Men returned to gambling, drinking, laughing, and telling lies about the amount of gold in the hills—but a few of them proved it by the number of nuggets they piled on the gambling tables.

Clint quietly related his business to Gideon, who listened with interest.

"This Barracoon," Gideon said, his face strained and distant, "sounds no better than the slave auctions of the South."

"I agree," Clint said. "But it appears this, too, is legal. Indenture contracts have long been bought and sold . . . even in the free states."

"Doesn't make it right. Do you think it has anything to do with the missing Californio girl?"

"I don't know. But rotten apples tend to rest in the same barrel, and dealers of women . . . Hell, I'm just guessing, but I don't have anything else to go on. Those women could be somewhere in the Sierras by now, or on their way to Mexico, or the territories, or who knows where."

"So what now?"

"I'm waiting for a man who can help me find this Barracoon. I'm gonna see for myself what it's all about."

He had just finished his statement when someone tapped his shoulder. He turned to look down into the wide face of Huly Up Hong.

Clint dug into his pocket, found a couple of silver pesos, and placed them in Hong's palm. "This is for finding Mr. Ho for me. And this"—he flashed another five-dollar gold piece—"is for taking me to the Barracoon and getting me inside."

Huly Up's eyes flared, and he glanced quickly around. He shook his head, and his long black queue, protruding through a black skullcap, danced. "No do. Not possible. No."

Clint eyed him and the men around them, standing almost shoulder to shoulder. "Come on outside. We'll talk there."

Gideon drained his mug of soda water and followed.

They walked outside, now in darkness, and Clint led the way to a nearby alley. "Now, why the hell can't you take me to the Barracoon?"

"General Zhang Ho cut my throat if interfere in his business."

"General? Ho is a general?"

"He led revolt against emperor. He is vely powerful man in China. Vely powerful man here in *gum san*."

"Come on, Hong, no one will know if you just show me where it is."

"Everyone know soon. In two days, auction."

"I want to know now. Five dollars gold."

Huly Up's eyes narrowed. "You tell no one?"

"Not even my sainted mother." Clint smiled.

"Midnight. I take you there midnight."

"You'll take *us* there," Gideon said, speaking for the first time.

"Ten dollar, take two."

"Is it farther if you take two?" Gideon asked with a hard look.

"More risk."

"Not with me." Gideon grinned wryly. "Can't see me in the dark."

Clint smiled, but Hong obviously didn't see the humor.

"White devil mad at John Chinaman," Hong said with a grimace, "then Chinaman lose honorable queue. Chinaman mad at Chinaman, then Chinaman lose queue and head 'long with it. Seven dollar fifty cent," he offered.

"Six dollars even," Gideon said, not losing his

grin. To Clint's surprise he pulled the walking stick open slightly, exposing a gleaming blade hidden in its shaft.

"Six dollar," Hong agreed quickly, "but no wait to show you way back."

"I've never been anywhere I couldn't find my way back from," Gideon said, and winked at Clint.

"Be here, midnight, no wait. Huly Up always on time." Hong shuffled away and disappeared down the alley.

CHAPTER EIGHT

"I'LL HANG THOSE BLOODY FOOLS UNTIL THE gulls pick their bones clean!" Isaac Banyon roared. Harlan Stoddard took a step back, his large bulk cowering before the verbal onslaught. "Had ye been minding the quarterdeck as ye should, 'twould not have happened."

"Those gold-hungry fools must have gone down the forward anchor rode, Cap'n." Harlan nervously smoothed down his thick mustache with the palm of his hand. "Prob'ly had a boat waitin'. I was alert, sir. But a man can't be everywhere."

"Five men. Five experienced crewmen we have to replace. Hear me, Harlan Stoddard. You'll be a common seaman again if ye don't get me a full crew in less than a week. We sail then, and by the gods of the sea, you'll be pullin' double shifts on the yardarms if ye don't have those men replaced."

Stoddard's gut ached from the captain's harangue. How the hell could he be expected to watch the whole damned crew? More than eight hundred ships lay at anchor in San Francisco Harbor, each shy of sailors, each swaying on the tide, her fo'c'sle empty, her men in the Sierras seeking the golden metal that had brought their ships there in the first place.

"We'll do well not to lose more afore we sail, Cap'n Banyon," Stoddard said quietly, steeling his resolve not to take all the blame for the desertion.

"Belay that!" Banyon shouted, spittle flying. "Shanghai me a crew, or we'll sail shorthanded and I'll put the papist wenches on the ratlines with you."

"I'll do me best," Stoddard said, "but it'll not be easy. Every bloody man in San Francisco is armed to the teeth, and there be few drunks. They come, provision up, and set off for the mountains."

"White, yellow, brown, or black, Stoddard. A crew. A full crew in five days or I'll feed your mate's papers to the fishes."

"You'll have your crew, Cap'n," Stoddard agreed, but as he turned and descended the ladder off the dark quarterdeck, he wondered how the hell he would accomplish such an impossible task. If he didn't have a crew in five days, he decided, he would join the other men in the Sierras. Hell, who needed the abuse of this crazy captain? Who needed first mate's papers if he had his pockets full of gold?

With gold, he could buy his own bloody ship. The harbor was full of them.

Clint reached over, plucked Gideon's pocket watch from his waistcoat, and checked the time. In half an hour they were to meet Huly Up. Clint had sipped only beer while they waited, wanting to be alert when he visited the Barracoon. He had no idea what he would find, or really even why he thought he should go there. It was merely his hunter's instinct, but he had learned to follow it.

"Are you headin' for the gold fields, mate?" A thin-faced man no taller than Clint's shoulder asked as he elbowed his way to the bar next to him.

"Thought I might, in a few days," Clint answered.

"Then I'm just the bloke you need." He smiled a crooked grin and focused both a good and a wandering eye on Clint.

"I didn't know I needed a bloke." Clint instinctively rested his hand on the pouch of gold he carried laced through his gun belt. He had heard about the Sydney Ducks, and this man's accent identified him as one. On the Barbary Coast, they were among the most feared of all the ethnic groups.

"It's not a man you need, mate, but a map. I've

been to the fields, mate, and made me poke . . . enough to last me the rest of me life. I'm headin' out for home on the first outbound vessel. You look like a good enough sort, and I'll not be needing me mountain of gold any longer. I've got more'n a man can carry." He glanced from side to side to make sure no one was listening.

"Reginald Shaddock's me handle." He extended a thin hand, and Clint felt as if he were about to have his pocket picked, but he shook and introduced himself. "Are you in the market for a map to a hill o' gold?" Shaddock continued.

"I thought you said a mountain." Clint couldn't help but smile.

"Hill, mountain, who's to quibble? It's more than either of us could spend if we lived five lifetimes. That's the reason I've left it and headed home. Got more'n I can spend."

A few steps away, Gideon turned from the faro game he was watching and stepped over beside Clint. "Fish, Mr. Ryan is a friend of mine and knows California from the sea to the desert. Sell your maps to the pilgrims."

"Well, if it isn't me abo mate, Gideon." Reginald "Fish" Shaddock managed to focus both eyes on Gideon. "Since you're not in the market for the opportunity of a lifetime, how 'bout standing a mate to a mug?"

Clint laughed and Gideon motioned to the bartender for a beer. For a man with a mountain of gold, this Sydney Duck was quick to skate a drink.

The same bulldog bartender who had given Clint a bad time the first time he was in the El Dorado slammed the mug of Dog's Head bass ale down in front of the Australian.

"Drink your Dog's Head, Fish, and keep your hands in your own pockets. I'll be having no trouble tonight."

Fish nodded. "You'll have no trouble from me, Luther Baggs," he said, and drained the mug in one long gulping swallow. He backhanded the foam from his mouth and turned back to Clint. "So you're a native?"

"Compared to most. I've been here over three years."

"I know a body in need of a guide and a bodyguard, if you be handy with those weapons." The Aussie glanced at the Colt revolver at Clint's waist and the rifle leaning against the bar.

"Handy enough."

"Would there be a commission in it for an agent who brought you a job—say, ten percent?" Fish's eye wandered, giving him the wary look of a darting haddock who kept a constant bulging eye out for the shark.

"I guess, Mr. Fish, if I took a job I'd be happy to pay a commission," Clint agreed, though he had no intention of taking one.

"Good enough," Shaddock said, and disappeared into the crowd.

Gideon rested a hand on Clint's shoulder. "He's a slippery one, that Fish. He'd snatch the pennies off a dead man's eyes."

"I'll keep mine open," Clint said. Gideon nodded, then returned to watching the game.

Fish returned almost as quickly as he had disappeared, with the bald-headed piano player in tow. "Now, you two blokes don't be forgettin' that I'm in this for a commission."

Ignoring Fish, the bald-headed man, whose eyebrows were bushy enough to make up for his clean pate, removed a stubby cigar from his scowling mouth, spat a chunk at a nearby spittoon, missed, and extended his hand to Clint.

"Jasper Henry," he said, and Clint shook with him, noting with amazement his stubby fingers and thick hands. He got the impression that even the knots on his bald head were muscles. "Fish tells me you're a man who knows every nook and cranny of California and can hit a gnat at a hundred yards with that Colt's."

"The only thing Fish knows about me is that I'm not in the market for his gold mountain map."

"Then he's wasting our time." Jasper Henry shoved the cigar stub back in his mouth and turned to leave.

"Wait, now," Fish said, seeing his commission flying away. "I'm as good a judge of character as any man. Can you?" he asked.

"Can I what?" Clint smiled.

"Can you hit a gnat at a hundred yards with that fancy revolving Colt's?" Jasper eyed Clint's Californio clothes and awaited the answer with furrowed eyebrows.

"I doubt a gnat. Maybe a big green horsefly," Clint said, "if you mean on the wing." He laughed heartily.

"See, I told you, Jasper. And he knows every rock and tree in California."

"Is that true?"

"I know southern California and the coast south of San Francisco. I've been up the Kaweah into the Sierras, but those mountains are big enough it would take a man a lifetime to know them. I've been through the Ton Tache, but no white man knows it well."

"How about the gold country?" Jasper asked anxiously.

"Never had the pleasure," Clint answered honestly.

Gideon, bored with the faro game, turned to listen in.

"Then you're no good to me," Jasper said gruffly.

Clint was becoming a little irritated with the man's manner. "I never said I was *anything* to you, friend."

Fish stepped between the two men. "You'll not find a man around here who knows much about the gold country, Jasper. Hell, the ones what found gold are still there and the ones what didn't are pushin' on, still lookin'. You need a man that knows his way around, and this here's your bloke. Right, Ryan?"

"I've never been anywhere I couldn't find my way

back from," Clint said. He winked at Gideon, who chuckled.

"You might just do. I'll talk to my boss." Jasper started to turn just as the crowd behind him parted and Sultry Mulvany floated up. Clint snatched his broad-brimmed, sand-colored hat off his head and Gideon had his narrow-brimmed high hat in hand as quickly.

"This is Miss Sultana Mulvany," Jasper said. Clint bowed slightly.

"And this is my friend, Gideon LaMont," Clint said.

"Pleased, I'm sure," she said, extending her hand. Gideon bowed deeply, a little surprised at the white woman's reaction. He accepted the hand and brushed it near his lips.

"*Enchanté, Mademoiselle*," Gideon said in perfect French. Sultana beamed.

"Why, it's so nice to meet a true gentleman," she said, and Gideon's status in San Francisco was elevated to the zenith. The nearby crowd buzzed.

"I've been speaking to Mr. Ryan about employment," Jasper said, stepping between Gideon and his employer, obviously irritated by her reaction to the black man.

"Are you considering joining us on our trek to the gold country, Mr. Ryan?" Her voice rang as only a trained singer's would.

"You're to become an argonaut, too, Miss Mulvany?"

"No, sir." She laughed, and the sound of it enchanted those in the room close enough to hear. "I'm only going to mine the miners, so to speak. Singing is my business, and the whole world is my stage. I plan to have a traveling road show."

"I'm afraid I'm currently employed. And soon, with luck, I'll have a herd of horses to drive south."

"Damn," Fish muttered under his breath. He looked accusingly at a miner nearby as if he had been the one disrespectful enough to mutter a curse in front of Sultana Mulvany.

"I'm sorry to hear that," she said, looking Clint up and down with obvious admiration. "I don't doubt your qualifications, and am in need of a skilled guide and guard."

"Maybe next time," Clint said, and every man within earshot moaned.

"It's been a pleasure," she said. Clint sensed a hint of disappointment as her liquid blue eyes darkened for a second. "Gentlemen." She flashed a brilliant smile and turned. The crowd parted as she moved away, and both Clint and Gideon returned their hats to their heads.

"Damned fool," Clint heard a man exclaim, and several more agreed.

Sensing there was no money to be made, and seeing no purses easily lifted, Fish slipped off into the crowd.

"As God is my witness," Gideon said with conviction, "that's the most beautiful creature on this earth. Her hand was like a feather in mine. Hair like corn silk, eyes as blue as the Caribbean, and skin as smooth and clean as crystal glass."

"Never truer words," Clint said as he watched her ascend the stairs next to the stage and disappear behind the curtain. Following his employer, Jasper Henry paused and glared back at Clint. Clint held his gaze until Jasper turned and disappeared behind the curtain.

"What time is it, Gideon?" Clint asked.

The broad-shouldered man checked his pocket watch.

"It's almost midnight."

"Then let's go find Huly Up."

They elbowed their way out of the El Dorado.

CHAPTER NINE

TRUE TO HIS WORD AND THE SIX DOLLARS IN GOLD, Huly Up Hong waited in the alley.

"How far?" Clint asked.

"Few blocks. Near bottom of Telegraph Hill." Huly Up trudged off, his black pants flapping, his sandals slapping callused heels, and his long queue bouncing. Clint toted the Colt's revolving rifle and followed behind Gideon and Huly Up. He would rather carry the long gun than trust anyone with it. He had seen too many admiring glances since he had been in San Francisco.

Soon the planked streets gave way to dirt, and lantern-lit windows to dark shuttered ones. He remembered thinking that Chinatown must be the best-lit place in the city with all the paper lanterns. He was wrong, for though there were many lanterns, only very few were lit. Huly Up's pace slowed and soon he was walking a few steps and stopping to glance in each nook and alleyway.

"It would not do to be seen," he whispered. On a dark street lined with shanties, he stopped at an alleyway. "Alley only go partway. At end is door to Barracoon. Guard at door, guard at windows on side street."

Clint dug in his pocket and fished out the five-dollar gold piece and a one-dollar one and handed it to the Chinese.

"I pay my own way," Gideon whispered.

"You buy the drinks when we get back to the El

Dorado," Clint said, and caught the flash of Gideon's smile.

"Hope you get back," Huly Up whispered, then turned and disappeared down the street.

Clint and Gideon crossed the alley, carefully surveying it, but it was too dark to see. They rounded the corner, walking with a purposeful stride, as if they had a destination. A guard rose as they neared, backed into a deep doorway, and gripped a long tong ax. They ignored him and hurried on.

The Barracoon was a two-story clapboard building set exactly in the middle of the block. It extended to one side street, was lined with closed shops on the opposite street, and the alley dead-ended into it front and back.

"How many of these China girls do they have in that place?" Gideon asked.

"I have no idea, but if they're going to have an auction, there must be plenty."

"You gonna knock on the door, or do you have something else in mind?"

"By the scowl on that guard's face, I don't think knocking on the door in the dark of night is exactly the right approach." Clint scanned the dark street. The fog was beginning to settle in, so he could only see a half block in the darkness. "If we wait awhile, this fog may cover anything we want to do. If we climb to the roof of these shops, I bet we'll find a way into the second story."

"Makes sense to me. And odds are, the later we wait, the more chance of the guards dozin' off."

They settled back against a shuttered shack and waited. By the end of the first half hour, the fog was so thick Clint could barely see the foresights of the Colt's rifle if he held it out in front of him. They crossed the street and found a likely porch fronting one of the more permanent shops. Linking his fingers, Gideon boosted Clint up, then handed up his rifle. Clint reached down and clasped wrists with Gideon, hoisting him up. In a moment they were creeping across the flat *brea*-mopped roof of a Chinese shop.

They came upon the second-story wall of the Barra-coon almost before they saw it.

Clint felt his way to a rough wooden shutter. He leaned his Colt's rifle against the wall, unsheathed a short-bladed knife and ran the blade up and down between the center crack until he found the latch, and tripped the simple mechanism. The shutter swung outward. The room was dark as a foot up a bull's backside, and smelled somewhat worse. Clint swung over the sill and entered. He drew a sulfurhead across the horn shank of his knife and it flared, lighting the room with a dull flickering glow.

"A storage room," he whispered, and Gideon followed him inside. Clint moved across the room, its shelves filled with cartons and bales and bottles of exotic substances that Clint had never seen. Each was identified with Chinese characters.

Quietly, a quarter inch at a time, he opened the door.

Voices startled him. The building was open in the center, the roof in that area two stories high. Surrounding the fifty-by-fifty-foot center court was a railed walkway with rooms off it. In the open area below, on a raised platform two feet higher than the rest of the floor, several Chinese surrounded a table lit by a single whale-oil lantern. Long-handled tong hatchets hung from their waists or leaned against chairs. One man wore a broad-bladed sword that caught the light of the lantern. They shouted and moaned as they played fan-tan.

The raised area must be the auction floor, Clint thought as he moved quietly down the walkway. *It would make a good place to show off the goods*. It was almost pitch-dark above the hooded lantern and if he made no noise there was no reason the nine men he counted below would know of his presence. The first door he came to was barred from the outside. It wouldn't be, he reasoned, unless they wanted to keep something in. He carefully worked the bar away, just as Gideon caught up with him.

With a loud squeak, the door opened. The noise

from the men below quieted. Neither Clint nor Gideon breathed as they awaited footfalls on the stairway leading to the walkway. But they didn't come. The men returned to their game, their singsong chatter reassuring.

Clint eased inside and Gideon followed, leaving the door slightly ajar so they might have a chance of hearing approaching footsteps. They stood perfectly still, waiting for eyes to adjust.

A fine ray of light filtered through the crack in the open door, and Clint could make out the open, fear-filled eyes of a girl lying in a bunk, staring back.

He sensed that there were other girls in the room, but could only make out what appeared to be built-in bunks. He moved forward to the girl, who whimpered something in Chinese that Clint didn't understand. He knelt beside the bed. "I'm not going to hurt you," he said, dredging up his best Chinese.

She gaped at him in surprise, then swung her feet out of the bunk and stood. Clint rose to face her. Her hair was intricately braided and piled on top of her head, making her almost as tall as Clint. He couldn't help but glance down—even in the darkness he could make out the proud breasts that pushed against the silk wrapper she wore.

"You speak the language of the Celestials?" she asked.

"I am an ignorant man, beautiful girl, but I try," he said with his finest Chinese humility.

"Why are you here?"

"To see that everything is all right with the China girls." He smiled.

Her eyes cut to the doorway. "Do they know you are here?"

"No. I have come without their knowledge." Clint struggled with the words, but she understood.

She stepped forward, stumbled, and caught herself against his chest. Only then did Clint realize that her feet had been bound, allowed to grow into little more than stubs on the ends of her slender legs. He had seen it before on a Chinese girl in the Sandwich

Islands and knew that the Celestials found it beautiful. He found it barbaric.

"You will buy Su Chin?"

Slightly taken aback, Clint changed the subject. "Are there other girls here? Mexican girls?"

"What is Mexican?" she asked.

"Are there girls here who are not Chinese?"

"Only China girls, and Su Chin is the most beautiful."

Looking at her, Clint had no reason to doubt her words, nor the quiet desperation with which they were offered.

"You buy Su Chin's contract?" she pressed.

"You will bring a very high price," Clint complimented her. She smiled slightly, but sadly, he thought.

"I hate this." Gideon spoke for the first time. "Let's herd these women out of here and turn them loose."

"Hell, Gideon, I don't even know if they want to be turned loose, and in case you didn't notice, there's about two thousand pounds of Chinese-mean down below. Let's get the hell out of here. I've learned what I came to learn."

Gideon began to pull the door open, but heard the approach of footsteps. Pausing only an instant, he opened it wider and snatched up the two-by-four used to bar it. The burly guard's eyes flared in surprise at the tall black man in the patched city suit whose hat barely cleared the doorway.

He who hesitates is lost, Gideon figured, and drove the end of the two-by-four deep into the man's midsection.

The man *oofed* loudly and doubled.

"Come on!" Gideon yelled, and brought the other end of the bar across the back of the man's head, felling him.

"Please buy Su Chin," the girl called after Clint, who scrambled through the door and followed Gideon down the walkway at a pounding run.

Gideon darted through the storeroom door before Clint reached it. Realizing a half dozen men were almost to the top of the stairs, Clint took two quick steps in their direction and planted a booted foot in the chest of the first man to top the stairs and kicked hard.

The guard threw up his arms and tumbled, gathering the others as he fell. They went down the stairway in a screaming pile. Clint scrambled through the storeroom and dived out the window, where Gideon pulled him to his feet. He grabbed his rifle from its resting place, and they flew off the rooftop onto the porch roof and hit the ground at a run. It was so dark and foggy they could have hidden five feet from their pursuers and not have been seen.

Instead, they ran for half a block, then began to walk.

"Where the hell are we?" Clint asked, puffing, his breath short in the cold night air and from the rush of excitement.

"Be damned if I know," Gideon said, also puffing.

"Hell," Clint said, "and you're the fellow who can find his way back from anywhere he's been?"

"I can, and I will, as soon as this soup clears."

"It would take a ship's compass to get us home," Clint grumbled.

"Then let's find a place to curl up and lay low."

"I think I'd rather be curled up in that room full of China Marys."

"As would I, my friend," Gideon agreed, "but only if they were free. I'd as soon lay with a goat than with a woman who was not there of her own free will."

"Well said, my friend, and I agree."

"Good. Now let's find a hole for a while."

CHAPTER
TEN

GASPAR COTA REINED THE BIG BAY STALLION sharply around and impatiently awaited his three vaqueros.

The waterfront street teemed with work wagons loaded with lumber and produce, argonauts and Chinese just off the ships and still agog at the hustle and bustle—or staring at the road, expecting to pick up nuggets of gold—and a few workmen who had not yet earned their stake so they could leave for the diggin's. Trace chains clanked and wheels and axles creaked as whips cracked their twenty-foot braided rawhide namesakes and cursed their stock. Creaking along, a *careta* filled with stiff cowhides and pulled by two lumbering oxen paused before a herd of swine. The pigs squealed and snorted and rooted in the road while a pair of homespun-clad boys moved them along with the help of stout willow switches and a yapping yellow dog. A farmer in a wide-brimmed straw hat shouted orders to them from astride a deep-chested roman-nosed dray horse while trying to keep the two dozen, slaughterhouse-bound, black and white hogs from being scattered in the traffic. The farmer tipped his straw to the Californio in the *careta*, who doffed his sombrero in return.

But one ingredient necessary to make the burgeoning town into a city was painfully absent from the scene—women. Not one skirt—just a smattering of long robes worn by some male Chinese immigrants.

The vaqueros caught up with their patron's son.

Although each of the other vaqueros had some silver trim on his tack, Gaspar was a picture of the fancy Californio don, with silver conchas covering headstall, martingale, and saddle. The fenders and tapaderos of the high-canted saddle were completely layered with two-inch-square engraved silver plates that caught the sun and announced his arrival with glittering magnificence, and Gaspar, in wide embroidered sombrero, silver concha-festooned vest, and fancy *calzonevas*, drew the attention of every Sydney Duck in this section of the Barbary Coast.

Fish Shaddock leaned on a rough adz-hewn oak hitching post among five of his fellow Australians, eyeing the riders, mentally calculating the weight of the silver trim along with the horses' value. The four Californios worked their way out of the clatter of drays and wagons.

"Have ya ever seen such a fancy bloke?" Fish murmured, a slow smile curling one side of his mouth as he crammed a cigarillo into the other.

"Never in all my days," Booker Whittle's gravelly voice reverberated behind Fish. He wheezed as he sucked in a breath.

As the gods tend to be, they had been unfair when they had divided the attributes between these two men. Where Fish lacked size and power, Booker more than made up for it, with arms the size of most men's thighs and a neck like a bull. Where Booker lacked brains and cunning, Fish was more than adequate. Together, they were a dangerous pair.

"Shall I bang their heads together, Fish?" Booker asked with considerable enthusiasm. He spat a stream of tobacco juice into the dust, dug into his pocket, and gnawed another chaw from a twist.

Fish turned and eyed his barrel-chested companion, who looked as if his face had been used as a butcher's block. Eyebrows sagged from going unstitched after being battered, giving the big man a constant glaring grimace. Cauliflowered ears bulged from a too-round head and framed a pudgy face scarred and mangled from a hundred fights in as many waterfront taverns all over the Pacific. Booker had a habit of running his tongue through the gap left when a front and canine tooth had succumbed to a belaying pin during a shipboard brawl.

He wheezed when he spoke, as air no longer traversed his bent and angled nose, flattened to twice its original width. All of it combined to give Booker Whittle the glowering look and sound of a mastiff, and he imparted the same powerful presence when he was in a room. More so in the back alleys he and Fish frequented.

"Let's sit a bit and see what they're up to, mate," Fish said as he watched the vaqueros approach.

Gaspar's mount pranced and sidestepped as he reined up in front of the Outback Roo, the waterfront Australian hangout, and dismounted. His vaqueros aligned their stallions at the rail, then followed their patron's son through the batwing doors of the clapboard building. The Roo's entrance featured carved kangaroos decorating the jambs on either side. Its two tall thin windows, bracketing the batwings, faced the daytime hustle and bustle and nighttime threat of Front Street, and its rear door rested well out upon Peabody's Wharf—far enough into the bay that the Roo boasted indoor privies which deposited processed beer directly into the surging bay twenty feet below.

The Roo was the thirteenth saloon Gaspar and his vaqueros had visited in the two days they had been in San Francisco, but so far they had learned nothing about Californio girls being abducted by Chinese. Worse, their meanderings through Chinatown were a study in frustration, since none of them spoke Chinese, and none of the Chinese they met spoke Spanish. Smiles and polite nods were the best they had gotten.

Gaspar was a little drunk, somewhat frustrated, and a whole lot angry. As he led his men inside the saloon, his nose twitched in rebellion at the odor of sweaty men and cigar smoke. He kicked through sawdust and peanut shells, his big roweled spurs clanking, and made his way up to the bar.

"A gift from the gods, mate," Fish said, flipping his cigar butt in the dust and leading Booker into the saloon behind the four vaqueros. "A bloody gift from the gods."

Fish quickly surveyed the twenty or so occupants of the dim smoke-filled establishment. By far the majority of the customers were other Australians, men who would have been on their way to the diggin's if they had not been without the money to buy grub and picks and shovels. Men who would do almost anything to get those necessities. Most of them drank little due to their economic situation—dead broke. They just sat and groused about their fate and awaited an opportunity to change it.

Satisfied that he was among friends and possible coconspirators, and followed by the toughest of all the Ducks, Fish moved confidently alongside the vaqueros who stood side by side at the long plank bar. Mugs of *aguardiente* sat in front of the men.

"Beer, mate," Fish instructed the bartender.

"I thought you said you were shy of money," Booker complained, looking accusingly at his slight friend and running his tongue in and out of the space between his teeth.

"Out of knock-about money, mate. This is business." Satisfied with that, Booker upended his beer mug, leaving a dollop of foam adorning his bent nose. Fish let his mug rest on the bar and nudged the vaquero next to him. "What brings you fellows down out of the bush?" he asked, a crocodile smile curving his mouth.

The vaquero looked at him coldly, then said something in Spanish to the fancily dressed dude who had ridden the silver-studded saddle, and stepped aside to let his *jefe*, his boss, speak to Fish.

"Have you been here long, amigo?" Gaspar asked in English while he tried to decide which of Fish's eyes to focus on.

"Here? Here in the Roo?" Fish asked in return.

"Here in San Francisco." Gaspar's tone was short, his attitude superior.

I'll soon cure the fancy-pants dude of his snotty airs, Fish thought, but did not misplace his smile. "I've been in Frisco since the beginning, mate," he said proudly. "Ol' Fish knows every nook and cranny, every back alley and Barbary Coast brothel. You fellas here looking to take a meander up cock alley?"

Gaspar ignored the question and eyed the little Sydney Duck as if he were a rat in the kitchen grain bin. The pox was the last thing he wanted, and the only brothels on the waterfront were full of pox-ridden Peruvian girls. Even they were in such demand that the lines extended for a block.

"Since the beginning!" Gaspar retorted with a smirk. "You were here when Mission Dolores began a hundred years ago?"

"No, friend, when the rush began." Fish's lips curled again in a smile, but his eyes held contempt. "When the real Frisco began. Are ya looking to find a little recreation?"

"I am seeking information."

"Then you come to the right place, friend."

"How do you know that, when you don't know what it is I seek?" Gaspar glared down at the smaller man.

"Just tell ol' Fish your problem, and I guarantee I'm your man."

Gaspar's knuckles tightened on the mug. Had it been another time and place, he would have had this runt of a man horsewhipped for his audacity, but Gaspar had a family matter to solve, a matter of pride.

"I seek information. We have had a señorita abducted and a vaquero killed by some Chinese scum. I will pay in gold coin"—he tapped a pocket—"to find them so they can be punished, and even more to find Señorita Apolonia Vega."

A gift from the gods, Fish thought. "Best we take a seat at a table away from the rest. As I said, I'm your man. Ol' Fish knows the Chine'e like the back of his hand."

For the first time in two days, Gaspar felt a glimmer of hope. He managed a knife-edged smile and turned to a slender vaquero at the bar.

"Be alert, Chato. This is a place to watch your back." Chato Juarez, Gaspar's head vaquero, merely nodded, and continued his vigil and his drink.

Gaspar moved away to a vacant table. Fish lingered to give quiet instructions to Booker, repeated them to make sure he had them, then flashed his crocodile grin at Gaspar and trailed him across the sawdust floor.

As Gaspar and Fish talked quietly, Booker moved to the end of the bar to whisper with the bartender. Then from table to table he quietly negotiated in his no-choice manner with the Sydney Ducks seated there.

To the vaqueros' pleasant surprise, Fish graciously paid for the next round of *aguardiente*. Gaspar drank and told his tale and had almost decided he had been mistaken about the little man when he realized he was becoming dizzy. The Ducks didn't wait for the drinks to take their full effect. As Gaspar rose unsteadily from his chair and called out to his vaqueros, the Aussies fell upon them.

The drugged and dazed vaqueros were no match for the twenty Ducks. Mugs and fists crashed against heads, and sombreros rolled into the sawdust. A few well-placed blows and Gaspar and his men, beaten into unconsciousness, sprawled on the floor, trussed, gagged, and blindfolded. Passersby glanced inside but made no effort to interfere in what was a common occurrence on the Barbary Coast. With a smile of triumph, Fish dug into Gaspar's pocket and found his poke full of gold and silver coin and distributed the money among the Ducks—with three shares going to the bartender, whose laudanum had been used.

Booker flung Gaspar over his shoulder while

other Ducks dragged his three vaqueros to the rear of the saloon. Booker creaked open a gaping trap-door in the plank floor. The longboat heaving in the waves below would hold eight men comfortably.

With little ceremony the vaqueros were roughly lowered and loaded like so many trussed goats on their way to market.

CHAPTER ELEVEN

CLINT AND GIDEON SPENT THE MORNING IN Chinatown. They moved from shop to shop, asking questions. Even though Clint spoke enough of the language to get by, he remained frustrated by his lack of progress. The Chinese seemed appalled by the news of the abduction, the possible involvement of their brethren, and more so by the possible reprisals that would fall upon their community.

Clint knew without a doubt a major confrontation could result from the spreading news of the abductions. Even though the argonauts liked the Californios little more than they did the Chinese, they seemed to relish any excuse to fall upon the "yellow infestation," as the newspaper writers enjoyed labeling the Chinatown occupants.

"The chances of finding that girl diminish drastically as each day passes," Clint groused to Gideon as they walked back to the El Dorado. "I wish to hell something would turn up."

"Don't give up hope, my friend," Gideon said, laying a hand on Clint's shoulder. "Perseverance and patience pay."

"Unless we turn up some kind of lead, I can't help but think maybe I should be hunting in Sacramento City or the gold country, rather than here."

"Ah, but San Francisco is the obvious first place to look. If the girl was taken inland, you have time to follow. If she's to be transported by ship, then time may be of the essence. You chose correctly."

"I hope so. I have refused the possibility that she

may not be alive. For her sake, and her father's, I hope so." They shoved through the batwing doors of the El Dorado.

Luther Baggs set a beer in front of Clint and a flavored soda water in front of Gideon without being asked. He swiped Gideon's money from the bar.

Clint took a deep draw and looked into the mirrors over the backbar, speaking his thoughts aloud. "I gotta figure the Barracoon is involved in the abduction of Apolonia Vega . . . in some way. Still, Zhang Ho was convincing that the Chinese had nothing to do with it."

"It's an evil place," Gideon said quietly. "The skin color is different where I come from, but the purpose is the same. The girl you spoke to seemed cheerful enough. I don't think she understands her fate . . . but I do, too well."

Clint took another deep draw on his beer and wiped the foam away with one of the towels that hung under the bar at six-foot intervals. "True enough. No telling what those women were told in order to get them here. They think they're going to find husbands, or honorable households to work in. I would guess their fates are far worse."

"Knowing men as I do, I agree." Gideon looked around him. His face was expressionless but his eyes spoke of sadness and frustration. He studied the men in the room. "Kindness seems against the nature of man."

"Everything is better in California," Clint said, his tone more hopeful than convinced.

"Men are men, my friend."

"You doubt their ability to change?"

"Have you noticed in your many travels how the good Lord has designed his creatures?" Clint didn't answer. Rather, he waited to see where Gideon was going with this.

"The great cats, the lion, tiger, the wolves, and the raptors . . . eagle, hawk, even the sharks," Gideon continued, a slightly sardonic smile on his face. "All of them have their eyes in the front of their heads.

They look forward—the chase is the thing with the predator." Gideon sipped his soda. "The deer, the antelope, the small birds, the little fishes . . . all the creatures preyed upon have their eyes on the sides of their heads. They must watch in all directions. Surviving the predator is the uppermost thing in their lives."

"Is there a point to this?" Clint asked.

"Look around you."

Clint glanced around the room, still not getting Gideon's intent.

"All of them . . . the humans . . . the harbingers of peace on earth, goodwill to men! Those who believe they are made in the very image of God. Eyes in the fronts of their heads, my friend. Predators, each and every one, by their own and God's will. It is their nature." Gideon shook his head in disgust. "As much as it is the nature of the jaguar. Only their fangs and claws are the Colt's, the Bowie, and the lash."

Clint glanced at the people around him—the Chinese, the Peruvian, the Chilean, the Australian, the American. He sipped his beer quietly and thought about Gideon's observation.

Maybe it was the nature of man, even though he was supposedly civilized, to prey on his fellow man.

Clint drank quietly, but his enjoyment was gone. For some reason, the beer tasted bitter.

Yawning, more from frustration than exhaustion, he downed the last of his drink. "I'm going to check on my horse," he said, waving to Gideon and heading for the door.

Outside, he came face-to-face with Don Carlos Vega as he cleared the batwing doors.

"I was told I could find you here," Don Carlos said, a disappointed look on his face.

"Here, Chinatown, the waterfront," Clint said, a little defensively.

"May we talk?" Don Carlos asked.

"Of course." Clint began walking away from the saloon, noticing the five mounted vaqueros who discreetly followed at a distance.

They walked half a block before Don Carlos spoke. "You have had no success?"

"Not enough to speak about yet, Don Carlos. It is very soon. I have met with the Chinese and have talked with the city marshal—"

"And that did no good, I suppose?"

"You were one hundred percent right about the law."

"As I knew." He folded his hands behind his back. "Gaspar Cota and his vaqueros have come to San Francisco to search. He thinks you are a meddling young Anglo fool and that I'm just an old fool."

"I wish him luck. I have no problem with that so long as he doesn't get in my way."

The old don paused before the window of a mercantile. It was filled with all kinds of goods, mostly for the miner. "Ah . . . San Francisco has changed so much. I fear I will never see my daughter again." His eyes looked deep and hollow and his voice wavered.

"I'll find her, if she's in San Francisco."

"Not in some saloon!" the don snapped, his voice suddenly stronger.

"It is a center of information, Don Carlos. You and your men hunt in your way. Let Gaspar hunt in his. I will hunt in mine. If I do not succeed, I do not get paid. I truly hope one of us finds her soon, and I don't care which of us."

"Thank you," Don Carlos said, his voice weak again. He waved at his vaqueros and they spurred their mounts and trotted up, one of them leading the don's horse.

He mounted with an easy swing up into the saddle, belying his age.

"Find my daughter," he said, his voice strong and cold, "and you shall have your horses. If she is not found soon, I fear it will be never."

"If she's in San Francisco, I'll find her," Clint said.

The don nodded, swung his horse, and led his men away at a gallop.

Clint watched him go. Frustrated when he left

the El Dorado, now he felt doubly so. He wished he were truly as sure of his success as he had tried to make Don Carlos Vega believe.

He feared the old don was right.

Soon, or never.

Captain Isaac Banyon stood at the taffrail watching the approaching shore boat being sculled alongside. A single black-clad skull-capped oarsman stood in the rear of the little boat. In her prow reclined Isaac's partner, General Zhang Ho.

"I do not like that Chinaman." Lucretia's voice grated at Isaac from over his shoulder.

"Damn ye, woman, how many times must I tell ye not to slip up on me like that?"

"And how many times must I ask you not to curse, Isaac Banyon?"

Isaac took a deep breath. God, if only he had left his wife behind in Philadelphia. "Get ye below, and ye won't have to deal with the heathen. I like him little more than ye, but business is business."

"It's Satan's business ye do," she muttered, but he could hear her move away to the ladder. He yelled to the cook's helper, Willie Boy Wong, to stand by to assist the general, then strode aft to greet his guest.

Atop the quarterdeck, Stoddard, the first mate, directed two hands to drop a block and tackle line, rigged from a spanker boom with a sling, over to the waiting boat. General Zhang Ho adjusted the sling under his backside while his oarsman held the little boat steady. The men above hauled away, then swung the boom and the general amidships. In a moment, with Willie Boy's help, Zhang Ho stood before the captain, the first mate, and the supercargo, Abner Baggs.

"What brings ye here, General Ho?" Isaac asked. "No problems with the sale, I hope."

"No, Captain. Everything progresses well. There is one small thing, however. . . ." He watched as the captain winced, anticipating more negotiating. "There has been a man named Ryan asking questions

regarding the abduction of some Californio women.
He and another violated our privacy and the women's
quarters at the Barracoon, obviously looking for these
women." Ho waited for Banyon's reaction. He got
none. "Do you know anything of these abductions?"

Banyon cleared his throat. "Nothing. Is the sale
of the women on schedule?"

General Ho refused to be detoured from the matter at hand. "It is very important that we Chinese
maintain good relations in this country. We are guests
here, as you know, Captain Banyon. We would be
very unhappy if anything were to upset our peaceful
coexistence. And, of course, our ability to do business. . . . We wouldn't want our partners to suffer
along with us." General Ho offered a slight but def-
erential bow, though his eyes glowed with suspicion.

Banyon perceived Ho's statement as a veiled
threat, but did not react. "I understand," he said.
"Now, is the auction on schedule? I will not sail until
I have my half of the proceeds, plus the cost of the
voyage, General. The faster I sail, the faster we will
have another load of . . . merchandise to sell."

"We are on schedule. Tomorrow at break of day
the buyers will begin inspecting the goods. By nightfall, when they have had plenty of time to admire the
quality of the merchandise and to drink enough liquor
to loosen their purse strings, the sale will begin."

"Good," Isaac said, and smiled for the first time
since General Ho had arrived.

The general bowed slightly and moved back to
the rail. Willie Boy helped him into the sling and Ho
spoke to him in rapid Chinese. "I want to talk with
you. Come to the Barracoon tonight."

"I do not have leave," Willie stammered.

"Come tonight, or join your ancestors," Ho said,
his tone as cold and relentless as a Manchurian winter
wind. "My boat will await you at the aft anchor rode
at midnight."

"Tonight," Willie quickly agreed, his mouth dry.

They slung Ho up and over the side.

"What did he say?" Captain Banyon asked Willie.

"Nothing, sir," Willie said, not meeting his eyes.

"The hell you say, boy. I have ears."

"He said only to be careful with the sling, sir. If he dropped into the sea, I would meet my ancestors."

Banyon guffawed. He might come to like this General Ho after all. At least he would like him a lot more if the take from the sale of the indenture contracts was large enough to fill another small chest with gold to join those he had hidden in the rudder gear well.

The captain rested a hand on his supercargo's shoulder. "Abner, it's time we took on fresh supplies, replenished the vegetables and chicken and pig pens. If all's well, we'll sail day after tomorrow. I want to go ashore with you. Then we'll stop by the El Dorado so you can bid farewell to your son."

"Aye, Cap'n." Abner's eyes lit up.

"And Stoddard," Banyon continued, "you'll come along. I want to find out who this Ryan is, and why he's interested in our business. Luther Baggs knows more about what's going on in this town than any man I know. I smell a foul wind blowin'."

"Should I bring some men?" Stoddard asked.

"Aye. This Ryan might make a good hand, but it might take a few of us to convince him to sign on. If not him, we still need half a dozen hands."

Stoddard laughed, and even Isaac smiled.

During the long trip from Macao, Su Chin had become the undisputed leader of the more than fifty girls who had been quartered in the cold, damp holds of the *Amnity*, and the go-between with the captain and crew.

The regal status of her bound feet assured her position among the women. Their deference to her and her unusual beauty assured her the attention of the captain and his men.

Su Chin was convinced that the sickness and deprivation of the long trip was taking her to a better life—the violent snowstorm before the blossoming spring.

The daughter of a simple farmer and farsighted mother who was a forceful woman in her own right— at least in the eyes of her husband—Su Chin had been lucky. Her mother had insisted upon keeping her daughter, not drowning her in the Yangtze, as was the fate of many girl babies, and of binding her feet in the regal manner.

"Su Chin will marry well and bring fortune to our family," her mother had insisted. And she proved to be right . . . at least for a short time. Due to the efforts of a marriage broker who was bribed with her mother's meager savings, Su Chin was selected as the fifth wife of a young but powerful warlord. But shortly after joining her husband's household, the young leader became involved in a territorial dispute and fell victim to the swords of another's warriors. Along with other booty, Su Chin became the sixteenth concubine in a far-off household of women who despised her for her height and beauty and fullness of breast, and did everything they could to make her miserable.

But Su Chin was not one to turn the other cheek. She fought fire with fire and with her clever planting of gossip caused infighting and backbiting among the women—more than had happened in the old lord's court in all the years he had had wives and concubines. When he discovered the root of the continuous bickering and dissension, he immediately ordered her sold.

Captain Isaac Banyon, in the right port at the right time, took one look at her and paid handsomely.

After a fortnight in the hold, Su Chin was given the run of the decks of the *Amnity* and, during the last half of the voyage, the use of the private cabin below the captain and his wife. Su Chin believed she was given this special status because of her bound feet, and the fact that she, of all the girls, could cause little trouble. She had enough trouble just getting around.

She was well into the trip when she discovered the peephole.

After carefully considering her options, and being the clever girl she was, she decided not to stuff a rag into the hole, as was her first impulse, but rather used it, in a most seductive and teasing manner, to display her many charms. By the end of the trip, she knew she had driven Captain Banyon wild.

But no wilder than she intended. Only once in the night had she heard the latch on the door being tried. She had no way of knowing if it was the big, dreadful-looking captain who had been testing for the invitation of an unlocked door. Both the chair under the knob and the latch she had devised discouraged the intruder. The next day, fearing she might have teased too much, she had fetched Willie and, in the presence of the captain's wife, complained about someone trying to enter her quarters.

Later that night she heard the captain's wife screeching in the cabin above.

Her latch never rattled in the night again, though the sound of heavy breathing continued behind the peephole.

Su Chin was happy that the auction was near. She was convinced that she and the other girls would soon be the treasured and revered wives of the white devils—some of whom she had come to know and like on the trip.

They were not the eaters of babies that she had been led to believe. They were polite and admiring, and like all men, malleable in the hands of a clever girl.

Su Chin hobbled from room to room along the walkway above the auction floor, talking with the girls.

"Prepare yourselves," she advised. "Brush your hair with a thousand strokes to make it shine like ebony. Stand your tallest and throw your shoulders back so the richness of your womanhood draws the glances of every potential husband or kindly master."

The girls giggled and laughed, most of them now having fully regained their health and vigor.

"Remember to color your cheeks and lips." As soon as she had arrived at the Barracoon, Su Chin had convinced the general to provide them with more blankets and a better variety of food, as well as a few bolts of silk so they could sew properly enticing gowns for those who didn't have anything but peasant clothes. And, as important, abundant face paint—a variety of powders and coloring and scents—as she had convinced him it would greatly increase the return on his investment. Reluctantly, and with some difficulty, he had provided it.

Yes, Su Chin was very happy to be here. It was the beginning of a new life. She hoped the handsome white devil, or his dark friend, surely a rich and respected Javanese or South Pacific islander, would be among the bidders for her contract, or her hand. They were certainly potential bidders, for hadn't they been so anxious to see the China Marys that they had risked the wrath of General Ho's guards to do so?

Either man, or any of a thousand others, would suit her well—if he was rich, and clean, and kind.

CHAPTER
TWELVE

CLINT CROSSED MONTGOMERY STREET DODGING drays and horsebackers just as the shadows lengthened to envelop it. He entered Mariano's Cold Day Tavern, dragged up a chair, and ordered a beefsteak.

"Rare, and top it with a couple of cackleberries," he instructed the rotund proprietor.

"Cackleberries?" Mariano looked puzzled.

"Eggs, friend." Clint managed a smile, even though frustration gnawed at his gut more than his hunger.

"The only eggs I've seen in a week are duck eggs," the Italian said. "Every farmer is on his way to the gold fields, and they must have taken their hens with them."

"Then whatever you've got." Clint extended his coffee mug, then grimaced as the stream of *brea*-black appeared from the snout of the granite pot Mariano carried. The Italian motioned at a sugar bowl as if it were a requirement for the black syrup, and hurried away. Clint abstained from the sugar, but was pleasantly surprised at the rich flavor of the brew. Mariano's coffee was real, not laced with scorched pinto beans or any of the other fillers that some of the restaurants used.

In moments, Mariano, who also served as cook, bartender, and waiter, returned from the steamy nook that passed for a kitchen. He placed the platter in front of Clint without comment.

After sawing at it with the dull-bladed knife provided by the establishment, Clint drew his own small-bladed skinning knife and carved off a bite of the onion-disguised chunk of rump. *Beef, hell*, he thought. He knew mule when he tasted it—but he had eaten mule before, and at only fifty cents for a meal that included noddles with an Italian name he couldn't pronounce, beans, bread, and coffee, he decided not to complain.

Besides, the bread was hot and fresh out of the oven, and it alone was worth the price of the meal. Though twice the cost of what it had been a year before, the food was still less than most of the eateries in San Francisco.

Clint managed to gnaw the mule into submission, sop up the last of the beans and red sauce with the tender but hard-crusted bread, and was downing the last of his cold coffee when Tok Wu "Huly Up" Hong entered. Since he had sent for him over an hour before, Clint had begun to believe Hong wasn't coming.

Hong pulled up a chair across the rough-hewn table.

"I still have need of information, Huly Up," Clint said, studying the short, wide-shouldered Chinese.

"And Tok Wu have need of money, Mr. Ryan, but have no information about Californio girl for you."

"How about the Barracoon?"

"You not satisfied last night? I understand you foolish enough to break in. It now common knowledge in Chinatown."

"And General Ho?"

"General Ho know everything go on in Chinatown, Mr. Ryan. Some thing he know before Chinatown know."

"Does he know you led us to the Barracoon?"

Hong's head snapped up in alarm. "No, Mr. Ryan, my life not worth duck dung if he find out." He glanced about nervously. "You say nothing?"

"Not a word. What will Ho do if Gideon and I show up at the auction?"

"Nothing. If harmed nothing during your 'visit' to Barracoon, and if bring pouch full money."

"I have no use for a China Mary. I'm only going because I'm interested in the proceedings."

"I think best you bid, even if drop out early."

Clint smiled; then his look turned hard. "You're sure you know of no connection between the Barracoon and General Ho and the missing Californio señoritas?"

"Absolutely not," Hong said with such conviction, and such concise English, Clint believed him.

"Thank you for coming," Clint said as Hong rose to leave.

Damn the flies, Clint thought. *I guess I'll have to go on to Sacramento City and see what I can turn up there. All I'm doin' is suckin' my teeth around here.* Just as Hong reached the door, Clint had another thought. "Huly Up, who else is involved in the Barracoon?"

Hong glanced around, but there was only one other customer in the place, and his head rested on the table next to an empty jug of wine. Mariano was working in the back, banging pots and pans and singing an aria of some seemingly one-note opera. Still, Hong shuffled back to the table before he answered.

"Again, Mr. Ryan, I be killed if General Ho think I talk of Fu Sang Tong business."

Clint reached deep into his pocket reluctantly, dug out another five-dollar gold piece, and placed it on the table.

"Not even to 'sainted mother'?" Hong pressed, darting his eyes around.

Clint nodded and pushed the gold piece across the table.

Hong eyed it nervously, but picked it up. "You are vely persuasive man, Mr. Ryan. General Ho's partner white devil." He looked slightly embarrassed at using the term, but Clint merely nodded his encouragement. "The captain of *Amnity,* ship that brought China Marys across Pacific, said to be honorable partner."

"Thank you, Huly Up. That is interesting news."

Hong hurried to the door and was gone. Wanting

to shout a hooray, Clint instead left a generous tip for the Italian—even if the beefsteak was mule.

"Hurry up, Willie Boy," Abner Baggs chided the Chinese cook's helper as they descended the ladder to the rooms below the captain's cabin. Abner set his bowls down on the floor and fumbled with his keys, while Willie balanced two of the hot receptacles on each arm. Abner had enlisted Willie's help so he would not have to make two trips.

"Now, Willie, like I told you, don't be saying nothing to no one about these here señoritas. If'n I wasn't in such a hurry to go ashore with the captain, I wouldn't be lettin' you see."

"Happy help, Mista Baggs, sir."

"If'n we weren't sailing day after tomorrow, I wouldn't dare let you in on this. But the cap'n says we'll be out with the tide then."

Abner gave the boy his sternest eye, and Willie grinned widely, nodding until his short queue bobbed.

Abner swung the door aside and led Willie Boy in. The women were each in their respective bunks. Abner set the bowls of gruel, each with a wooden spoon, chunk of salt pork, and dollop of molasses, on the deck, and Willie Boy followed suit. The Chinese boy stared wide-eyed from bunk to bunk, saying nothing.

Señora Juanita Robles swung her legs out of the low bunk and rose, her voice shaking. "Señor Baggs, surely it is not that loathsome gruel again."

"Don't be complainin', Señorita!" Abner scowled.

"It is Señora, Mr. Baggs, not Señorita. I am a married woman, one who wants to return to her husband!" This elicited no response out of the old man. "We are out of candles again, and the chamber pots are in need of emptying. We must launder these terrible smocks, and we need more towels."

"It'll be morning afore we get to any of it."

"But we must have candles—"

Ignoring her requests, Abner pushed Willie out the door in front of him.

"And the chamber pots!" Juanita Robles yelled, and began to beat on the door. Apolonia rose and hurried to her. Tears were pouring out of Juanita's eyes and she was trembling uncontrollably.

"Why are they keeping us here?" Juanita sobbed, finally breaking down after a week's imprisonment on gruel, salt pork, molasses, and water.

Apolonia held her until she quieted, then looked her directly in the eye. "Now, do you see the futility in waiting? We *must* escape. No one has come to our aid, and no one will, for they do not know where we are. It is up to us. Only us."

Juanita, who until this instant had been so strong, looked hopeless. Then her tears stopped and her eyes steeled. She lifted her chin, but her hands still trembled. "As you say, it is up to us."

The other girls rose and hurried to join them, a group now united by a common purpose. Each looked at the other, awaiting a plan. Awaiting a leader.

A week ago she would not have had the courage, but now Apolonia decided she had no choice.

Clint walked to the waterfront and stood on the wharf. With the help of a dockworker, he picked out the packet ship *Amnity*, moored a little over two cable lengths out in the harbor. She lay quiet, with little activity on deck. Her anchor lantern was lit, but few other lights glowed through her ports. Convinced by the inactivity that she was not sailing tonight nor on the morning's tide, he returned to the El Dorado.

Having retired to the room he had rented for some much-needed sleep, Gideon was nowhere in sight. Clint bulled his way to the bar and ordered a beer. The saloon was its usual rowdy din, but, as usual, quieted when Sultry took the stage.

By the time she had finished her third song and the bald-headed pianoforte player had begun gathering the coins and nuggets from the stage floor, Clint felt a tap on his shoulder.

"Ye be Clint Ryan?" Clint turned to face a man

of equal height, but thicker than Clint, with a full gray beard spread across his chest.

Clint hesitated a moment, for he was still a wanted man for his "malfeasance" aboard ship, and this man was clearly an officer of the sea even though he carried no braid or insignia on his well-tailored black suit. But if the man sought him for the problems of the *Savannah*, he would hardly tap him on the shoulder.

"Yes, I'm Clint Ryan."

The man extended his hand in a businesslike manner, and Clint shook as Captain Isaac Banyon introduced himself. Clint, slightly taken aback, held his tongue. This was the man who captained the only ship in a harbor of eight hundred that Clint wanted to board.

"Can I buy you a drink, Captain?" Clint offered, signaling the bartender for another mug of Dog's Head ale.

"Demon rum is the devil's own, Mr. Ryan. I will partake of a glass of clean water, or cool cow's or goat's milk, if available."

Luther Baggs delivered Captain Banyon a glass of water without argument, then took up a friendly animated conversation with the man who accompanied the captain.

"How is it you know me, Captain Banyon?" Clint asked, carefully sipping his beer.

"I make it my business to know every able-bodied man in the harbors I visit, Mr. Ryan, and you look able-bodied enough. We need hands, sir. We sail on the tide, day after tomorrow. Would ye be interested in signing aboard the finest packet ship in the Pacific?"

It must be quite a task to know every able-bodied man among more than twenty thousand, Clint thought, wondering what was the true reason the captain had sought him out. "What cargo are you hauling, Captain?"

"The usual, lumber and iron to China, silk and china and fancy doodads to tempt the ladies of New

England in return." Banyon cut his eyes away, a dead giveaway for a lie, Clint surmised.

"I'm currently employed, Captain Banyon. Otherwise I'd be proud to serve on a fine ship. I spent many years at sea and, if I may say so, I am a skilled mariner."

"As I suspected, Mr. Ryan. I can always spot a man of the sea." The big captain made an attempt at a smile, then took a drink of his water. He backhanded drops from his beard. "That is unfortunate, for the *Amnity* not only is a fine ship, but she's a friendship—a percent of the voyage's profits fall to even the common sailor." Banyon's eyes narrowed. "And, if I may ask, what is your current employment, Mr. Ryan?"

Caution waved a flag and Clint hesitated before answering. There was no sense in alarming a man he had already perceived as an enemy. "I've taken a job as a guide for the one and only Sultana Mulvany."

"You'd work for a woman?" The captain's bushy eyebrows narrowed until they touched.

"Not merely a woman, Captain. The most beautiful woman ever to bless the stage—hell, maybe the country. And she needs a guide."

"Well, if that be ye choice." The captain turned his back on Clint. "We be on our way, Abner Baggs. Say your good-byes to Luther."

Clint watched as the older man shook with the bulldog bartender. Luther Baggs knew exactly what Clint was about, and he was obviously related to a sailor on the *Amnity*.

This should teach you to keep the slack out of your tongue, Clint chided himself, knowing that everything Luther Baggs had overheard him say had been told to the *Amnity*. And the *Amnity* crew and her captain were now far too interested in what Clint was up to.

And if the captain had sought him out, then the captain must have something to hide. He wanted to be on board the *Amnity*, but he would be damned if he would do so by signing aboard. No, there had to be another way to get on board the ship, and now that he knew when she planned to sail, he knew just how to go about it.

Clint studied the broad-shouldered captain as he left, noticing that five other men, obviously sailors, from their duck pants and striped shirts, followed. One man, particularly big and sporting a soup-strainer mustache, locked gazes with Clint until he passed through the door. The captain had come in force.

Maybe for a last drink for the crew . . . or maybe for something else?

Clint wondered if he was that something else.

CHAPTER
THIRTEEN

CLINT SIPPED HIS BEER SLOWLY AND GLANCED AT
Luther Baggs out of the corner of his eye. The potato-
faced bartender moved up and down the bar, wiping
with a wet cloth, picking up mugs and glasses. Finally
Clint waved him over.

"You related to the man with Captain Banyon?"

"My pa. The supercargo of a full-rigged packet
ship and the best at his trade." Baggs swiped at the
polished planks with a towel.

"And he's off again to the Orient?"

"Aye. Day after tomorrow."

"Did you come here on the *Amnity*?"

"As a working passenger. She brought a load of
argonauts on her last voyage from Philadelphia, like
every other vessel from the East."

"And she seeks more crew?"

Baggs stopped and looked up from his work. "Are
you writing a journal, Clint Ryan?"

Clint flashed a knife-edged smile. "No, but I find
it a bit strange that the captain sought me out. Did
you mention me to him?"

Baggs went back to his wiping. "I tell my father
of any able-bodied man who might be tempted to sign
on. I may have mentioned you."

"What cargo has your father been gathering for
the crossing?"

Baggs turned his back on Clint and began shining
glasses. "The usual—iron, tools, manufactured goods
. . . though it's difficult, as all the goods in San Francisco are in demand."

"I'd like to speak with your pa, Luther. Could you arrange it? I might be able to help him locate some cargo." Clint paused. "No one knows California better than I."

Luther turned from his work. A slow smile crept across his face. "My pa is always anxious to find another agent who'd bring him some cargo. I could arrange a meeting this very night if you think you might help him . . . and yourse'f, a'course."

"Then do it." Clint managed a smile, but feared it was as hollow as the one returned by the bartender.

"Don't go away."

Clint nodded and tipped up his mug.

Luther chuckled to himself as he made his way down the long bar. His father had instructed him to pour generous drinks for Clint Ryan. Stoddard and Captain Banyon had plans for him, so Luther had laced the last two beers with a shot of powerful rum. But this would be better and faster, for the fool had actually asked to meet with his pa.

After finding his way through the storage room to the side door of the saloon, Luther pulled it open and checked up and down the dark alley before he ventured out. The fog had begun to crawl into the city. Even the areas normally lit by the upstairs windows of the El Dorado lay hidden. It wouldn't do for him to be shanghaied by another ship's crew or any of the roving bands who found an easy living performing that function. He was supposed to be helping his father fill the crew of the *Amnity*.

Quickly Luther worked his way along the narrow cleft between the two-story buildings to the alley entrance, where he could see the silhouette of several lingering men.

"Stoddard!" Luther called out to the distinctive broad-shouldered image that loomed near the alley opening.

The massive form rolled away from the wall and settled into an arms-at-the-ready, legs-spread stance and his mates arranged themselves behind him as Luther approached—happy that he wasn't the man they truly awaited.

"Where's my pa?" Luther demanded.

Stoddard recognized him, then looked disappointed that he was not a prospect. "He's off with the captain. They said for us to wait here, just in case Ryan left the saloon afore they returned."

"Well—" Luther managed a chuckle, "the fool's asked to meet with Pa. Send a man to fetch him. Pa will talk with him outside, then you can knot his noggin and tote him away."

"I don't know where they be," Stoddard said, scratching his lip under the thick mustache. "But it's no matter. Tell Ryan your father waits in the alley."

"He's not fool enough to wander into a dark alley. And I hear tell that he's handy with that Colt's rifle and handgun. You best send for Pa and the captain."

Stoddard's shoulders hulked and his chin thrust forward. Even as alleywise and handy with his fists as Baggs was, he slinked before the powerful first mate. "I said tell Ryan your father waits in the alley. Do it."

Baggs nodded quickly and worked his way back down the mist-occluded alley to the bar's rear door. He paused before entering the safety of the saloon and called back.

"I'll tell'm, but don't blame me if he don't come." Baggs disappeared into the El Dorado's alley door.

As Luther made his way through the storeroom and opened the door to the smoky saloon full of shouting and laughing men, his gut relaxed. He moved down the bar, convinced that he knew a way to get Ryan into the alley and to keep his pa out of it. Though a common practice, shanghaiing was against one of the many new city ordinances in San Francisco.

He waved Ryan over to the bar, and the man bulled his way through the crowd.

"I couldn't find my pa, but your Ethiopian friend . . . Gideon LaMont . . ."

Clint riveted his attention on the bartender.

"He's out in the alley. Seems his big black ass has finally had a little too much to drink. You better see to him afore the shanghaiers find the easy pickin's."

Clint brought his ever-present Colt's rifle up, spun on his heel, and used its muzzle to get through the crowd. The men parted easily as the rifle's cold threat worked it steely way between them.

Gideon had been sober and on his way to his room, Clint remembered as he made his way out of the El Dorado. This smelled as fishy as the hold of the cod-bank schooner Clint had worked on when he first went to sea.

Clint paused on the boardwalk in the light of one of the El Dorado's tall windows, checked the loads in his Colt's rifle and revolving breech pistol, then moved to the opening of the alley.

No one was in sight down its dark length—but half a dozen eight-hundred-pound grizzlies could easily be waiting among the many crates and barrels and deep-shadowed doorways.

He surveyed the street, which was quieter than earlier but still far from vacant. Figures moved in and out of the patchy fog and a few wagons still plodded along. Then he turned to the alley. It felt like worms gnawed at his vitals and his eyes, cold and gray as the night fog, darted at every hiding place. His calloused thumb found the iron hammer of the rifle. Pausing, he allowed his eyes to adjust to the dank darkness. Then he started forward.

The gravel alley crunched underfoot. Lights from windows on the second story of the El Dorado cast deep shadows near the middle of the pathway, and the street at the far end was only slightly less black than the alley itself. Clint stiffened, hearing a scratching sound. He put it off as the scurrying of a rat.

He caught a movement out of the corner of his eye and a swinging piece of lumber flashed out of the shadows, crashing into the barrel of his rifle. Clint swung the heavy muzzle upward, slamming it under his attacker's chin. The man's head snapped backward and Clint caught the flash of the whites of his eyes.

Then powerful arms enveloped him and a blow racked the side of his head.

Clint dropped to his knees and rolled out of the grasp of the man, kicking his legs out from under him. The man crashed heavily to the gravel with an *oooff*.

A club slammed into Clint's shoulder and he felt his Colt's rifle being wrenched away by another attacker who had climbed out of the pile of barrels and boxes.

Instinctively Clint scrambled to get his back to the wall. At the same time he pawed for his Colt's revolver—and found the holster empty.

He tensed for the next attack as the four men left standing formed up in front of him.

Sultry Mulvany sat at her dressing table, redoing her makeup. She heard the muffled sounds of blows and the clatter of boxes in the alley below her window. Against her better judgment she rose and walked to the tall narrow glass and peered down at the dark shadowy alley below.

One man lay unmoving, sprawled in the alley, and four burly men surrounded another with his back to the wall. The men held clubs and Sultry caught the reflection of light from a gun barrel. The man with his back to the wall kicked out and caught one of his attackers in the belly as he charged, driving back and doubling the man, but another swung his bludgeon and drove the attacked man to his knees, knocking his hat flying. Sultry caught a flash of color and recognized the sandy hair.

She ran to the door and shouted down the stairs.

Jasper Henry was relaxing in a chair near the stage door, his feet propped up, his slouch hat covering his bald head and pulled low over his eyes. He almost fell from his roost at the high-pitched urgency of her voice.

"Help that man in the alley!"

He stepped to the curtain and yelled to the six

burly bartenders before venturing out the stage door. Thinking that Sultry had a problem, they came at a run.

Clint's head swam and one arm and leg were pinned by two sailors, but still he pummeled with his free fist. He could taste the blood in his mouth and feel the hot rush that poured over his face from a gash in his head.

His head crashed against a brick wall, crushed between the heavy men and the bricks. He clawed, momentarily cheered as he felt his thumb plunge deep into an eye socket, but then a club flashed and again his head snapped backward. Blows rained over him, so many they were indistinguishable.

Clint fought to retain consciousness, but reeled deeper and deeper into blackness. He couldn't feel or hear the club as it smacked into flesh and crunched into bone.

The fog enveloped him, and with it a vision of a terrible storm he had fought at Tierra del Fuego. He was hanging in the ice-covered shrouds, his hands frozen, unable to move.

CHAPTER
FOURTEEN

WILLIE BOY WONG SWUNG HIS LEGS OUT OF HIS bunk in the fo'c'sle and padded to the ladder, carrying his low-heeled leather boots so as not to disturb the other sleeping crewmen. He mounted the ladder and paused on the holystoned pine deck to pull on the boots as he scanned the dark decks of the *Amnity* for signs of the anchor watch. Marvin Vandersteldt, the second mate, stood at the wheel on the aft quarterdeck. Willie could see the flare of his cigar. He knew Marvin would be armed to the teeth and instructed to shoot to kill any man attempting to jump ship.

With the deckhouse concealing him from Vandersteldt, Willie crept forward. He was in a terrible quandary. The anchor watch stood near the wheel, on the aft of the ship, and General Ho had said his boat would wait at the aft anchor rode. It would be very difficult—impossible—for Willie to climb down the aft anchor rode without being seen by the watch.

Unless he could entice the man forward or below decks.

As he neared the forward ladder, he heard a quiet pounding from deep in the bowels of the ship. He craned his neck so he could make out the man at the wheel, and wondered if he, too, could hear the noise from below—but Marvin made no move. Willie descended the half ladder to the deck accommodating the captain's cabin and officer's mess, then descended the full ladder below to the passenger's quarters, where he knew the women were kept.

The pounding was coming from inside the women's door. He paused and leaned close. "What ladies want?"

Apolonia stopped pounding, her hold growing tight on the chamber pot she held. This could be their chance. "Get ready," she commanded in a harsh whisper to the others. "Someone is here."

She leaned close to the door. "Please, Señor. Señora Robles is very ill. Open the door."

Juanita Robles took her place on the deck in the center of the cabin, held her stomach with both hands, and began to moan softly. The other girls assumed their places on either side of the door. A teak stanchion, worked carefully from one of the bunks by the combined efforts of all of them, and Apolonia's chamber pot, would serve as clubs.

"What kind sick?" Willie asked through the door.

"I don't know, but she needs a *médico*."

Apolonia leaned hopefully against the jamb, silently praying that the man outside would open the lock and offer them their chance. Then she heard his footfalls padding away. Crestfallen, she turned to the others. "He's leaving."

They made their way back to their bunks, and Juanita Robles rose from the floor. As Apolonia sank into her narrow cubicle, she heard the quiet sobs of one of the girls. It only steeled her resolve.

She had hardly settled into her narrow berth when she heard the footfalls of someone returning, the clinking of a key in the lock, and the tumblers being turned. With a rush, the women returned to their places.

Willie Boy Wong stepped into the dark room, and Apolonia brought the crockery chamber pot across his head. Shards scattered over the room. The little Chinese collapsed to the deck beside the feigning Juanita as if his legs were chopped off at the knees.

"What the devil!" Marvin Vandersteldt charged

into the doorway and grabbed Apolonia's wrist, wrenching the remains of the pot away.

Apolonia screamed in pain, and Juanita lurched forward, wrapping her arms around Marvin's legs and sinking her teeth deeply into his calf.

He yelled and kicked her loose, but the stanchion flashed out of the darkness and caught him flush on the forehead, tumbling him into a black corner of the room.

"Run, girls, run!" Juanita yelled, stepping over Willie Boy on her way out. She dashed for the ladder, with Apolonia and the others close behind, shouting their encouragement.

As they topped the ladder, Lucretia Banyon opened her own cabin door and, Bible in hand, watched them ascend the half ladder to the main deck.

"May God have mercy on your soul, Isaac Banyon," Lucretia murmured, hugging the Bible to her chest. She closed and locked the captain's cabin door and returned to her rocking chair.

The women, smocked and barefoot, gathered together on the deck, clinging to one another for reassurance.

The *Amnity* lay in the quiet of high tide, her furled topgallants obscured by the night fog. Cold enveloped Apolonia, and her bones suddenly felt like spikes of ice. She shivered uncontrollably. The lights of the city in the distance came and went like distant fireflies behind gray gauze curtains.

"We must find a boat!" Apolonia whispered harshly, forcing her shaking to stop and breaking the clasp of fear that bound the women to silence. She climbed up on the quarterdeck and spotted the small six-man captain's boat in its davits.

"Here!" she called, motioning to the others, who gathered at the ladder to join her. They began to claw at the lines at each davit, pulling and tugging to release the boat—but the strength of the sailors' routine knots was too much for them.

Apolonia pushed the others aside and began to work on the knot binding the aft line, carefully studying it as she pulled on this end, then that, then at a tuck in the knot. Juanita worked on the bow.

"It's coming!" Juanita cried out.

"Mine too." Apolonia's voice shook with the glimmer of hope, real hope, for the first time.

Juanita's attempts were successful a split second before Apolonia's and the bow of the little boat began to fall toward the black sea below.

"Oh, no!" Juanita cried, as Apolonia's side began to drop. Apolonia and Juanita both grasped for the lines, but Juanita's had begun to run and it jerked her hands upward into the block, tearing the flesh from her palm. She yelped in pain and jerked away, closing her eyes and bringing her bleeding hand to her mouth. But Apolonia was successful in bringing her end to a halt—which was exactly the wrong thing to do.

The bow dropped and the full weight of the vessel came to bear on the aft line, jerking the rope from Apolonia's hand. With the whine of free-falling hemp and spinning blocks, the little boat plunged bow first into the sea. The women stared in horror as their hopes of escape floundered below, then floated to the surface filled to the gunwales with water.

"Who goes there?" The shout rang out of the fog. The longboat, with the captain, first mate, supercargo, and four crew members appeared out of the fog, followed by another longboat full to her gunwales with trussed men. "Belay that, ye papist wench," Isaac Banyon yelled, and the oarsmen pulled with added vigor to bring the longboat alongside.

"Run! Hide!" Apolonia cried in desperation, and plunged for the ladder to the main deck. She reached it just as Marvin Vandersteldt topped the rail and grabbed for her, ripping the front of her smock away.

"No!" she yelled, fighting for her modesty. The other women ran in every direction. Willie Boy Wong topped the ladder behind Vandersteldt, who shoved Apolonia into Willie's arms and ran in pursuit of another of the fleeing women.

Banyon and the longboat reached the ship, and

men began climbing up the rope ladder left hanging for their return.

Willie Boy held tightly to one of Apolonia's arms and watched Vandersteldt chase one of the women across the deck while the others searched for recesses and shadows in which to hide. Seeing his distraction, Apolonia raked the nails of her free hand across his face.

He screamed and shoved her away. She ran for the rail, stared into the blackness, and cursed herself for not knowing how to swim. Frantically she looked for a hiding place. She scampered down the ladder to the main deck and ran forward just as the yellow-toothed first mate leaped over the rail. Fear flooded her. She tried to stop but panicked. Her feet became tangled and she tumbled head over heels to the deck. Stoddard reached down and jerked her to her feet, spinning her around and holding both her arms behind her. She tried to kick backward at him, but he pulled her close and his powerful callused fingers dug deeply into her arms. The pain stopped her cold.

"Now, Polly," he said, bending his head over her shoulder, close enough that his mustache tickled her cheek and she recoiled at his rancid breath. "Don't ye be makin' it harder on ye'sef than already 'tis."

Captain Isaac Banyon reached the taffrail and leapt over it to face her. Seeing his bulging stare, she realized that her smock hung open.

Her face flushed crimson. "Please, let me cover myself," she pleaded.

"You have no rights aboard this vessel," Banyon spat, but his eyes would not meet hers. His were fixed on the sight of the helpless woman in front of him, and what her torn smock revealed.

"Let that girl go, you evil men." The sound of Lucretia's voice rang with righteous indignation across the deck.

The captain instructed Stoddard to release her, but he already had. Apolonia sank to her knees and pulled her smock closed, holding it in front of her with both hands, her head bowed, fighting to keep the tears from falling in front of her captors.

All over the deck, surprised men chased the other women.

The women were collected, kicking and screaming curses in Spanish, and were dragged below.

But Lucretia Banyon crossed the deck and protectively cradled the kneeling Apolonia's head against her skirt. She could feel the child sobbing, but the girl kept it quietly to herself.

The crew dropped a line overboard from the aft spanker boom and began loading the trussed bundles from the second longboat.

"Come on, child. I'll take you below and mend the rips in your smock."

Apolonia climbed to her feet wearily, and meekly followed Lucretia Banyon to the rear ladder. She stopped just before she reached it and looked back, wide-eyed, with a combination of hope and disbelief.

The load the sailors hoisted was the bundled, slightly rotund Gaspar Cota. He was gagged, but his eyes glared wild as a caged cougar. The sailors swung him over the taffrail and he caught Apolonia's gaze for a fleeting second while spinning on the end of the mizzen halyard.

"Get ye below!" Banyon's voice startled her, and his rough hand shoved her along to the ladder.

No longer able to see her betrothed, but for the first time *pleased* to see him, she quickly followed Lucretia Banyon into the captain's cabin.

Before anyone returned to the anchor watch, Willie Boy Wong, dead aft behind the wheel, looked down into the murky blackness, searching for General Ho's boat. A trickle of blood found its way out of Willie's hairline, where the girl's chamber pot had found its mark, and lined his cheek.

"Dive in the water." A voice, speaking Chinese in a harsh whisper, rose from the deep shadow of the hull.

"I cannot swim," Willie answered, his voice an octave higher than usual.

"I said dive in," the voice repeated.

Willie glanced over his shoulder, making sure no one watched, stepped to the top of the rail, held his nose with one hand and his aching forehead with the other hand, looked upward and silently advised his ancestors that he was sure to be with them soon, then leapt out into the darkness.

Clint tried to roll over as he awoke, but firm hands restrained him. He lashed out.

"Whoa there, Ryan!" Jasper Henry stepped out of Clint's reach. Clint's eyes finally converted the blurs to recognizable figures, and he was glad they did, for Sultry Mulvany, an image of beauty except for the bloody wet rag in her hand, stood near Jasper Henry.

The room was small, but papered from an oak chair rail to the ceiling, and carpeted expensively. A crystal chandelier hung from the ceiling and refracted light in dancing rainbow spots on the room's rose-colored walls. A dressing table with graceful Queen Anne legs and loaded with small bottles, jars, and tortoiseshell brushes and combs rested under a large mirror lined with polished silver whale-oil lamps. The settee and three cherry-wood straight-backed chairs with brocaded green fabric seats finished off the feminine decor. The door stood ajar, and Clint made out Sultana Mulvany's name in gold letters.

"The battle's over, Mr. Ryan," she said. She stepped forward and lightly sat on the edge of the settee he rested on. "Let me get the rest of your face cleaned up."

"Who won?" he asked, trying to smile, but his mouth would not quite function.

"Looked like a draw to me," Sultry said. "At least until Jasper and the boys got there. Then the riffraff decided on a strategic retreat and carried off their wounded."

"You was a cooked goose when we got there, and they was ready to spit out the bones," Jasper said.

"There were two down and three to go." Sultry smiled and laid a soft reassuring hand on his arm. "Given the odds, I'd say you did real well."

"I thought you could hit a bluetail fly on the wing with that Colt," Jasper chided.

This time Clint managed a smile. "That was a green horsefly, Jasper . . . and these bugs got behind me. Thanks for the help. I owe you a bottle of Noble's Finest."

"Humph," he grumbled.

Sultry leaned down and her blond hair cascaded over her shoulder, covering half the swell of her breasts, where Clint's eyes seemed to stray. The stage dress was red satin trimmed with black lace and wide with petticoats. Clint caught the delicate odor of lilac water as her gentle touch worked at a cut in his hairline.

It was almost worth the beating.

Lying back, he relaxed as best he could, every movement an exercise in which joint or bruise hurt the most. But his limbs seemed to be functioning. At least nothing was broken. And his eyes worked fine. He tried to keep them on hers, but they kept falling to a tiny heart-shaped mole on the inner cleft of her ample left breast.

"That should have a stitch or at least some plaster," Sultry told him with concern, dabbing at his head.

"I'll heal without." Clint's gaze found her eyes and he got a smile for his trouble. Sultry rose, wadded up the rag, and tossed it to Jasper Henry. She returned to her dressing table.

Clint suddenly realized he didn't have the Colts. "My guns?"

"They're under the settee." Jasper motioned. "Those boys was lucky to get away with their hides."

Just as Clint remembered why he had been in the alley in the first place, Gideon LaMont rapped on the open door to Sultry's dressing room with the gold handle of his walking stick.

"Come in, Mr. LaMont," Sultry said, seeing his image in her mirror. Gideon snatched the high hat off his head and entered.

He took in his beaten and reclining friend with a sweep of his dark eyes. "I understand you took on half the crew of the *Amnity*." Gideon crossed the room, his lips curling in a smile but his eyes reflecting his worry.

"The *Amnity*?" The vision of the granite-shouldered, mustached man that Clint had locked eyes with as Banyon left the El Dorado flashed into his mind and came together with the man he had seen in the alley.

Clint tried to rise, then decided to wait awhile before attempting the maneuver.

"The *Amnity*," Gideon repeated. "One of the bartenders knew half those boys in the alley. Seems they're a bit short of crew and must have thought you'd make a hand."

"That son of a bitch." Clint swung his booted feet to the floor. Sultry glanced back at him from her dresser. "I'm sorry, Miss Mulvany. It's that bartender of yours. Baggs. He told me Gideon was in the alley, liquored up and near passed out. I went looking for him and found the crew of his father's ship."

"Don't blame Baggs on me, Mr. Ryan. Luther Baggs works for the El Dorado, just as I do."

Clint struggled to his feet. "I need to have a chat with Luther."

Sultry crossed the room and placed her hands softly on his shoulders, pushing him gently but firmly back on the settee. Clint winced, but sank back down willingly.

"That'll wait until tomorrow or the next day. You need to rest. I've got two more shows. Then I'll fetch you some soup."

Jasper Henry's jaw tightened and he frowned, but he said nothing.

Sultry returned to her mirror and talked as she

applied some color to her cheeks. "You can sleep right there on the settee."

"Sultry—" Jasper growled.

"Right there on the settee, and I'll get you some soup after my last appearance. By then I'll be ready for something to eat myself." She rose and her red satin skirts reflected the light from the whale-oil lamps as she moved to the door. "Don't you go away, Mr. Ryan. Come on, Jasper." She nodded politely to Gideon and was gone in a whirl of petticoats, with Jasper hulking along behind, scratching his gleaming bald head and scowling.

Clint looked at Gideon, feeling a little bit foolish. "He said you were drunk and lying out in the alley."

"That happened when I was twelve. My friend and I snuck some of the LaMonts' rum." Gideon pulled one of the straight-backed chairs over and sat astride it. "My head hurt for a week and my backside for a month . . . after my daddy got through whippin' on it. We were lucky it was daddy who found us, for the LaMonts might have done a lot worse. Liquor is a horsewhippin' offense for a slave. And though a freedman, I don't think it wise for me to be uninhibited by the effects of the demon rum. It's hard enough for a body to get along in this world. I appreciate the worry, but don't fall for that again."

"I'm damn lucky to be here to get that lecture."

"I agree."

The raucous sounds of the saloon quieted, the piano tinkled, and they heard Sultry begin the strains of "Greensleeves."

Gideon rose and returned his hat to his head. "Lucky to be here—and extra lucky to have the self-appointed nurse you do. I'm going back to the saloon to admire her, then to the faro table. I won't be far. I think that beautiful lady has taken a real shine to you. You rest."

"A shine? Don't count on that. I've never had much of a way with the ladies."

"And I've found that it's the ladies who let us know if we have a way with them or not. If they take a shine to you, you got a way. If not, you've lost your way. You rest."

"Yes, sir." Clint had his eyes closed by the time Gideon reached the door.

Gideon hesitated in the doorway, his voice rumbling low. "Clint . . . thanks for worryin' about me."

Clint said nothing. As far as Gideon knew, he was already asleep.

CHAPTER FIFTEEN

GENERAL ZHANG HO, RESPLENDENT IN A BLACK robe with a yellow bird of paradise embroidered on it, reclined in a pillow-lined, carved mahogany chair, his slender well-manicured hands draped casually over the dragon heads that graced the arms. He splayed his fingers through his black hair, smoothing the slash of white that highlighted it on one side, and studied the shivering figure who knelt on the floor in front of him. Two thick-chested, full-bellied guards flanked him, paying little heed to the water-soaked rat of a man who awaited his questions.

Ho slowly stroked each foot-long tail of his dangling mustache, then stepped forward and motioned to one of the guards. "Bring him some tea and a robe."

Willie Boy nodded a thank you and managed a wan smile.

"Rise and take a seat, Wong," Ho instructed, and Willie hurried to one of three smaller chairs that faced Ho's. He did not sit down, but stood beside it, awaiting the general's return to his own seat. The general fluffed his pillows before he sat, then reclined into them. Willie sat rigidly on the edge of his straight-backed chair.

"I have come as you ordered, honorable Ho."

"You have come even though the white devils you work for would not approve. You are a wise young man. In fact, wise beyond your years, and I wish you a long life . . . that is, if you will truthfully answer a few questions."

"My truths are no more a test of my obedience

than my coming here, honorable Ho. Did I not jump into the cold dragon-filled waters of the hostile sea at the order of the Fu Sang Tong?"

Ho stifled a smile at the eloquence of this young man, even though the quiet bay was far from a "hostile sea."

"Then tell me, what cargo does the captain who brought the *mui gai* here plan to carry on his return?"

"There is much pig iron in the holds, and also iron tools."

"And?"

"That is all I have seen."

"And passengers?"

"There are women, but I do not understand their position. They are kept under lock and key, and not treated as passengers."

"Chinese women?"

"No, honorable Ho, Californio women."

Zhang Ho stroked his long mustache. It was as he suspected. The captain had assembled a cargo of women for the return trip, probably to sell to the same brokers and warlords who provided the *mui gai*. To Ho, Californio girls were large and clumsy, but they seemed beautiful in their cowlike way, and they would be an oddity in the courts of China. Yes, they would bring a high price— a price Captain Banyon had no intention of sharing with his partner. A price, and a cargo, that would reflect badly on all Celestials in the *gum san*.

Zhang Ho understood that the Celestials had already been blamed for the abductions, for were the abductors not dressed as Chinese? Yes, perhaps Captain Isaac Banyon was also a student of Sun Tzu and the ancient art of war. Divide and confuse the enemy. But not a good enough student, for Sun Tzu did not teach doing so at the expense of valued friends.

It was imperative, even as valuable as Captain Isaac Banyon and the *Amnity* were to the tong, that he not be allowed to bring the wrath of the white devils down upon the Celestials.

Ho returned his attention to Willie. "When does the captain plan to sail?"

"I have been told that we sail day after tomorrow."

But not without his money, Zhang Ho knew. *Not without his half of the proceeds from the sale of the* mui gai *contracts. No, he will not sail until I pay. That will give me time to make sure the Californio women are released.*

The best of all possible solutions would be to have Captain Banyon believe someone else caused their escape, so the tong could retain his goodwill and the use of his ship. But at all costs they must be set free.

Zhang rose as one of the *mui gai,* whose services he had decided to use until the sale, returned with the tea. "My men will return you to the ship after you've finished your tea," he told Willie. "Do not be caught climbing back on board. Tell no one of your visit with me. I will call upon you again before you sail and your help will not be forgotten by the Fu Sang."

"Thank you, General Ho," Willie said, jumping to his feet as the general rose. "I will await your summons . . . and possibly, someday, Willie Wong might enjoy the comradeship of the Fu Sang as a member."

"Possibly," Ho said.

Zhang left the meeting room for his private quarters to reflect upon what he'd learned. But he knew one thing for sure: the white devil, Clint Ryan, who came to him seeking news of the Californio girls, could be the solution to his problem.

Clint awoke to the odor of beef stew and freshly baked bread. Sultry had her back to him dishing up the stew from a crock on her dressing table. She'd changed out of her red satin stage dress into a black silk wrapper. The whale-oil lamps surrounding her mirror showed off the soft curves of her body and highlighted her long blond hair. The pattern of her black silk stockings showed beneath her flimsy wrap, and her trim ankles and small feet were bare except for the fancy stockings.

She must have sensed his eyes on her.

"I've got coffee or wine," she said without turning.

"Wine now, coffee later."

She turned and brought him a bowl and spoon. The V in her wrapper showed enough cleavage that his favorite mole was exposed, and below it, a red silk flower on the tightly fitting corset that thrust her breasts up and sucked her waist into two hand-spans. She set the soup down and went back to fill a mug with rich red wine from a carafe.

Clint took a mouthful of the stew and realized how hungry he was. Sultry handed him a mug and seated herself. She held her glass out and toasted him, her countenance serious but her blue eyes laughing.

"Here's to not taking any unplanned ocean voyages."

"I'll drink to that."

They drank, and Clint studied her carefully as she picked at her food. "You've been awfully kind to a stranger, ma'am."

"Not a stranger. We were properly introduced by my friend Jasper Henry."

"Friend?"

"Yes, Mr. Ryan. Friend. Jasper is my employee and traveling companion."

"Nothing else?"

She watched him a moment. Then she smiled softly. "If you're going to ask such forward questions, Mr. Ryan, perhaps we should be on a first-name basis. My friends call me Sultry."

"Sultry. Clint, please. Jasper didn't seem too happy that you allowed me to rest here."

"He's neither father, brother, nor chaperon, Clint. I'm my own woman."

"That you are, ma'am—and all woman at that, if you don't mind me saying so."

Sultry took a sip of her wine, but her eyes never left Clint's. She dabbed at her mouth. "Would you care to see why Jasper was upset with your being here, Clint?"

"I'd care to see anything you'd care to show me, Miss Sultry."

She crossed the small room and opened the only other door in the room. It appeared to be a closet. She pushed the clothes aside, and Clint could see a door behind them. Sultry opened it, and Clint could make out a larger room beyond, and a canopied bed.

"My personal living quarters while I'm here at the El Dorado. We felt it too dangerous, even with Jasper as my bodyguard, to go back and forth to a hotel, since San Francisco is as it is. The two-way closet is a convenience."

"So I see."

"Would you care to take your coffee in there?"

Clint was amazed at how little he noticed his bumps and bruises as he crossed the room and followed Sultry into a satin, lace, and pillowed room that was about as pretty as anything Clint had ever seen—except for the woman who turned to face him, letting her wrap slide to the floor in a pile. Her black stockings and the corset with the red silk flower were barely visible in the dimly lit room.

Clint took a tentative step toward her, then stopped as she held out a hand.

"I want you to know that, though I have a number of men friends, Clint, none of them are allowed in here." She searched his eyes for understanding.

"I'm privileged," he managed.

Accepting that, she reclined across the soft down-filled counterpane, patting the place beside her.

"You are discreet? It's difficult enough for a woman who works in a man's world to keep her reputation. And I'd only allow a man here who would defend mine with his life."

"I won't say a word, even to my sainted mother."

Sultry smiled. "I should hope not." She reached to the bedside table and turned the lamp wick even lower.

She heard the thump of a boot hit the floor in the darkness.

"Tomorrow, when you have time to think on it, I'd like you to reconsider going to the gold country with me."

"That's for tomorrow," he said, and let the other boot fall to the floor.

CHAPTER SIXTEEN

LUCRETIA BANYON SAT IN HER ROCKER, SEWING up the rips in the girl's smock with practiced hands. Apolonia rested on the edge of the Banyons' bed, wrapped in a blanket. The door creaked open and Captain Isaac Banyon strode in.

"Are ye about finished with this foolishness, woman?"

"It is not foolishness for this girl to be properly clothed. If you will leave us, I'll be finished in short order."

Apolonia tucked even her bare feet up under the blanket and kept her eyes turned away from the captain. Grumbling, he closed the door, and she heard his footfalls moving away.

"Please, Señora Banyon, can you tell me why we are here?"

"Women are the evil business of this ship," Lucretia offered, not looking up from her sewing.

"I don't understand."

"This ship trades in women." Lucretia paused in her sewing, then stabbed fiercely into the ugly brown fabric. "Buys and sells them, like cattle or swine."

"And you . . . you condone this?"

Lucretia's voice softened. "I think it is the devil's work. It is an evil that begets evil." She bit off the remnants of a thread, then rose and crossed the room. "Here. I'm finished." Lucretia turned her back while Apolonia slipped the simple brown dress back over her head.

"Then will you help us escape?" Apolonia pleaded.

Lucretia looked away. "I would be going against my husband if I helped you."

Apolonia sank to her knees and took Lucretia's hand in hers, pulling it to her cheek. "If you are a Christian woman, you'll help us in the name of Christ. If you are not, you will help us because we are fellow women."

Lucretia jerked her hand away, but her voice caught in a sob. "I *am* a Christian woman. A woman who vowed to love, respect, and obey her husband. A holy vow in a Christian church, obeying God, not a papist edict from Rome."

Lucretia opened the door and shouted for her husband. Apolonia's hope waned as she heard his heavy footfalls in the passageway, then disappeared when the door opened and Banyon's frame filled the hatchway.

Captain Banyon clasped her wrist in an iron hand and began to lead her out. "We all worship the same God," she pleaded, her voice ringing down the hall. "All of us are made in His image. Help us, for the love of God."

Isaac Banyon worked the key in the padlock. "I should lash ye all for what ye've done," he said, and thought, *And I would, if it were not for my prying wife who awaits my return.*

Apolonia shivered, but said no more. The captain shoved the door open.

"Captain," she pressed, gaining enough courage to ask the question that had been burning in her. "You brought some men aboard? Men who were bound and gagged?"

"Not your business."

"But why are they here?"

Her voice sounded vulnerable and pleading, and so feminine. He thought of the girl's smooth bare breasts, and knew that he could never look at her again without remembering what he had seen. One answer would do no harm.

"They're conscripts. They've been brought aboard to fill out the crew." He shoved the door open and motioned her inside. "Now, ye best not cause any more trouble or ye'll taste the lash."

He slammed the door and moved back up to his cabin. Lucretia awaited him. She said nothing until he was seated and pulling off his boots.

"I will no longer be a part of this." She stood rigidly, her voice low, but her tone firm.

"I beg ye pardon, Madam?" Isaac paused, one boot in hand, one still on, and looked at her in astonishment.

"I have decided I will go ashore here in San Francisco and take a house. You will make this trip without me."

It was the answer to his prayers, but he knew better than to seem pleased. "Ye are sure this is what ye want?"

"Tomorrow we will go ashore and find a house."

"If it's what ye wish," he mumbled. "I may have to put my departure off a day to accommodate ye. But whatever makes ye happy, my dear." He did his best to sound as if she had just told him he was condemned to the gallows while fighting to hide the smile on his face. He removed the second boot and wanted to do a jig in his stockinged feet, but he restrained himself.

Gaspar Cota rested in the aft end of the ship, but his quarters were not as comfortable as even Apolonia's and the other women's. He and his three vaqueros lay chained in the stench of the dark bilge below Apolonia's room—a space tall enough only to crouch in. With the quiet roll of the ship, brackish bilge water, littered with the ship's refuse and an occasional floating dead rodent, lapped at their feet and legs.

They had not eaten in two days, not since they had been struck down and bound and gagged by the Sydney Ducks. Now, for the first time, they were ungagged and could at least talk among themselves.

"I know it was she," Gaspar lamented to Chato, his head vaquero and the *segundo* of the Cota rancho.

"But why would Apolonia Vega be on board a sailing ship?"

"Why was she abducted in the first place?" Gaspar snapped. "Tell me that, and I'll tell you why she's here."

Chato jerked on his chains for the hundredth time since they had been clasped on his wrists and ankles. "Well, *jefe,* now that we've come to her aid, maybe we can enlist hers."

"We will get off of this scum bucket," Gaspar said. "And we will take Apolonia with us."

By the time the sun warmed the streets, Gideon was already drinking his second cup of strong black coffee and awaiting his breakfast in the crowded Mariano's Cold Day Tavern. He squinted at the figure crossing the board-covered street outside, then chuckled as Clint came in. Leaning his Colt's rifle against the wall, he jauntily seated himself across the table.

"Top of the morning," Clint said.

"You're full of vim and vigor for a man who looks as if he was run over by a team of four and a beer wagon."

Clint self-consciously touched a bruise on his cheek, then smiled. "Nothing that a plate of Mariano's cackleberries won't cure."

"He's out of eggs again, but looks like he got a good do on the biscuits."

The fat Italian stuck his head out the door and looked questioningly at Clint.

"Ham, biscuits, gravy—" Clint said. "Hell, anything you got that won't bite back."

"Been bit enough, have you?" Gideon teased.

"Those boys weren't so tough."

"I wasn't talkin' about those boys." Gideon didn't smile, but his eyes took on a mischievous glint.

"How's a fella get a cup of coffee around here?"

Clint got up and fetched his own, ignoring Gideon's subtle inquiry, then returned to his seat. "Today's the big doin's at the Barracoon. You goin' over there with me to see the festivities?"

"I'm goin', but *festivities* isn't the word I'd choose." Gideon waited as Mariano set their plates in front of them and waddled back to the kitchen. "I know what it's like, being on the auction block. It's no fiesta."

"That girl, Su Chin, seemed eager to be sold."

"That girl has no idea what she's in for."

"After we've finished, let's go see for ourselves." Clint sopped at his gravy with a biscuit. "I've got all day to kill."

"Then what?"

"Then I'm paying a return visit to the crew of the *Amnity*."

"You're a glutton for punishment."

"Those boys took an unusual interest in me . . . and I think it's because I've been asking around about the missing Californio girls."

"That seems a long shot."

Clint took a draw on his coffee, draining it. "It would be, if the *Amnity* wasn't the ship that brought the China Marys here. A ship about to return to China, and I think her intent is to return with another load of women. Looks to me like Captain Isaac Banyon thinks he can conscript women with the same impunity he conscripts San Francisco drunks." Clint finished the last of his breakfast while Gideon mentally chewed on what he had been told. "I've got to take a look on board before she sails, and the dark of night would be the best time." Clint shoved back his chair. "You coming along to San Francisco's newest form of entertainment?"

Gideon pushed away his plate, leaving a good portion. "You couldn't keep me away with a team of draft horses."

Fifty China Marys stood on the raised platform in the center of the Barracoon. Though it was early morning and the auction didn't begin until nightfall, the place was already teeming with men eager to preview the goods.

For the first time, Su Chin began to feel like she had absolutely no control over her future. Her stomach seemed to house a thousand crawling scratchy-footed beetles and she trembled from her well-coiffed hair down to her silk-bound feet. Already she had been poked and prodded and commented about, as if she were not there, by dozens of leering, ugly, foul-smelling men.

Su Chin looked out over the crowd, her eyes searching for even one man she would consider a fit master. She had a mental picture of an eagerly bidding fine Chinese gentleman who needed someone to run his *gum san* household, or at worst, a wealthy white devil who would cherish an almond-eyed beauty and take her into his home and show her off like the treasure she was. Instead she looked out over a crowd of rowdy miners in calf-high boots, stained canvas pants, and rough shirts of jersey or homespun.

They milled around, made lewd remarks, spat vile gobs of tobacco juice on the floor, and eyed the women with hungry looks that would chill the stoutest heart. The Chinese who moved among them appeared no better. Fat, grasping, greedy-eyed men she feared would use the girls for far less noble means than running a household, or even serving as an honored concubine.

The men laughed, drank from one of the four bars centered on each wall of the big room, and commented on the cluster of women who stood on the platform, appraising them like sides of beef.

Scattered throughout the crowd was a select group of a dozen of General Zhang Ho's finest, largest, and best-trained Fu Sang Tong members. Big barrel-chested men dressed in black robes. All but one huge guard displaying no weapons other than ham-sized hands, they moved quietly through the growing crowd. A wide thick-bladed sword with a two-handed hilt was carried casually by the huge guard. Its hilt was wrapped in red silk, and Su Chin knew, and feared its significance—the executioner's sword. She had seen, in China, many heads lopped off with a single swing of the heavy blades.

The last thing the general wanted was for his guards to be forced into using the tong hatchets or thin daggers each carried concealed under his robe.

Ho expected the preview and the auction to be carried out without any problem, and he'd instructed his guards to use the greatest discretion, especially with the white devils. He wanted no trouble with them; he wanted their gold.

As added insurance, he had hired ten white devils to also act as guards. Men specifically recommended to him by the city marshal's office, in addition to four deputy marshals the Fu Sang Tong had paid Marshal Larson to provide. The white devil guards were prominently displayed at each doorway and flanking the bars—and each carried a shotgun and wore a sidearm. They were identified with wide arm bands of white silk with an intricate *B* for *Barracoon* embroidered in bright Chinese red.

By the time Clint and Gideon had walked the several blocks to the Barracoon, the long alley that ended at the front door of the big clapboard building was filled with men, and the street outside was crowded four deep with men watching a fistfight between two burly teamsters who bludgeoned each other over a place in line.

Clint and Gideon glanced at each other. Gideon shook his head. "What do you think Miss Su Chin thinks of being sold now?"

"Come on." Clint motioned him to the side street. "The hell with this line. We know a better way inside."

They circled the block, mounted the roof of the shop that backed up to the Barracoon, and pried the second-story shutter away. The building was so crowded that no one noticed when two men appeared out of the storeroom on the walkway above. All eyes were on the women.

As Clint and Gideon reached the bottom of the stairs, a lantern-jawed cigar-chewing guard at the end of the bar noticed them and walked over, his shotgun cradled comfortably in one arm. "No one is allowed upstairs."

"Suits me," Clint said, nodding politely to the man.

"What a bunch of vultures," Gideon said, looking out over the milling, leering crowd.

"Let's get a little closer." Clint began elbowing his way through the men, and Gideon stayed close behind. A rope had been strung between four-foot pedestals to keep the crowd out of grasping range of the women—though the men continued to broach it. It took several minutes, but finally Clint and Gideon reached the taut rope.

Su Chin saw them almost immediately. "You buy Su Chin . . . please?"

Before Clint could speak, a miner ducked under the rope and mounted the platform. With burly arms, he circled the shoulders of two of the girls. Standing between them, he smiled at his friends in the crowd, but two guards reached him and pulled him away from the women. They shoved through the crowd, pushing him toward the door. "I got money," he complained drunkenly, shaking his poke at them. "I got plenty of money and I aim to buy me a China girl."

The guards moved him to the door and outside.

"This could become a Donnybrook Fair," Clint cautioned while the crowd hooted and hollered after the man.

"Or worse," Gideon said quietly. "Much worse."

CHAPTER
SEVENTEEN

THE CROWD SETTLED. CLINT TURNED HIS ATTEN-
tion back to Su Chin, who still watched them carefully.

Gideon shook his head slowly. "As beautiful as
she is, that girl and this circus are the most pitiful
things I've seen since I left Louisiana."

A group of men on Clint's right got into a shoving
match over a table and chairs, and the guards yelled
at them, pushing their way through the crowd. Clint
moved away toward the wall. "Let's get off to the side
and out of this gaggle."

As they passed the bar, Clint paused and ordered
himself a beer and Gideon a soda water.

"I got no soda water," the bartender snapped. "I
got some of this newfangled ginger ale . . . but it'll
cost you same as if it had whiskey in it."

"Gimme the whiskey on the side," Clint said.

Clint turned to a miner leaning on the bar, passed
him the whiskey, and received a tip of the hat in
thanks. They moved on.

"You two are in the wrong part of town." The
gruff voice stopped Clint short. "You remember me.
I'm Vester Grumbles." The solidly built man sneered
at them.

It was the man who had shot Henri LaMont. He
held a shotgun in both hands, its barrels close to being
leveled on Gideon. The muscles in Clint's shoulders
bunched. Beside him he sensed Gideon about to move
on Grumbles. Clint rested a hand on Gideon's fore-

arm. The business end of a scattergun was nothing to trifle with.

"I didn't see a sign outside that said 'the wrong part of town,' " Clint said. "You saying we're not welcome here?"

Before Grumbles could answer, another man, dressed in a black robe and flanked by two thickset bodyguards, stepped in front of him.

"If you have gold in your pocket, Mr. Ryan, you're more than welcome here." Zhang Ho turned and said something under his breath to Vester Grumbles, who curled his lip at Gideon but turned and melded with the crowd.

The general returned his attention to Clint. "I'm glad you have come, Mr. Ryan. I wish to talk with you in private, if you have time."

"I've got time," Clint said, glancing from Ho to his guards and wondering just what it was Ho wanted. He had thought about just what Ho's reaction would be to his showing up at the auction, after his uninvited visit.

Ho turned and headed for the stairway.

"You want me along?" Gideon asked.

"Damn right," Clint said without looking back.

Gideon followed Ho and the guards, who cut a wide path through the crowd.

Ho moved up the stairs and all the way down the walkway to the last door, where he motioned to his guards to wait outside. Clint followed Ho inside, but Gideon folded his arms and leaned against the rail. His brown eyes began a stare-down with the bodyguards.

Zhang Ho walked around to the back of a small oak desk centered in the barren corner office.

"You still seek the Californio women?" Ho asked.

"Yes. I have been employed to do so."

"By whom?"

Clint studied the man for a moment. He was the keeper of the Barracoon, and Captain Isaac Banyon's partner—but he was the only man who had ever

mentioned the Californio girls without being prodded.

"I was hired by the family of one of the girls."

"I know where they are."

"On board the *Amnity*," Clint said quietly.

"You know?" Even Ho's inscrutable face regis-
tered some surprise.

"I guessed. I would have known soon."

"I will help you free them, Mr. Ryan. On two
conditions."

"And those are?"

"It is imperative that the Chinese be cleared of
any suspicion in these abductions, and almost as important to the Fu Sang Tong, it is imperative that
Captain Banyon know nothing of my helping you."

"You're walking a fine line."

"Yes, but it's a path I must walk. It is critical to
the future of the Celestials in the *gum san* that no one
believe they are involved in such a thing. And you
must relate to the authorities, and to the newspapers,
that we were not. It is also critical to the tong that
we maintain our partnership with Captain Banyon."

"How can you help me, then?" Clint sat on the
edge of the desk.

"We will talk again tonight, after the auction."

"Good enough," Clint said, extending his hand
and shaking with Ho.

For the first time he had a real break. Elated, he
followed Zhang out the door. Gideon unfolded his
arms and moved from his position on the rail.

The post next to him exploded in a shower of
splinters and the room below reverberated with stac-
cato gunfire.

Gideon dove forward into the bodyguards, who
shoved him away. All of them realized at the same
moment that the gunfire was not directed at them,
and looked over the rail to the crowd below as it
erupted in a clamorous riot.

Chairs and tables flew, bottles crashed, men
cursed, and *mui gai* shrieked in terror. Knives flashed
and guns roared.

Clint and Gideon charged down the stairs behind the bodyguards, but Ho cautiously backed into the office doorway, where he could watch in relative safety. He wrung his hands, fearing his business and profits were flowing away with the beer and blood below.

Clint jumped the last four stairs to the floor, where a burly cigar-chewing miner locked gazes with him and clawed for the pistol in his belt. The barrel of the Colt's flashed and thumped into the side of the man's head, the cigar flew, and he hit the floor.

Gideon spotted Su Chin on the platform among a group of grasping miners and screaming girls, her eyes wide with fear as a bearded miner reached for her. Gideon crossed the distance in three bounds. He poleaxed the man with a smashing right that knocked him out from under his slouch hat and sent him sprawling across the platform.

Gideon reached for Su Chin just as both barrels of a shotgun went off next to him. Stunned by the blast, he reeled, but the shot wasn't meant for him. A miner staggered on his heels, then fell like a timber near Su Chin's silk-bound feet, a knife still in his hand, but most of his chest blown away. Blood splattered across Su Chin's breast and she wiped madly at splotches on her cheek. Staring in revulsion at her bloodied hand, she wondered if it portended her future.

Gideon grasped her wrist and pulled her across his shoulder, then charged for the stairway, battering his way through the fighting men. His hat flew off and rolled away.

Clint and a teamster who held the jagged remains of a mug in his hand circled each other until Clint switched ends of the Colt's and used the butt on the side of the man's head. With a resounding thump, the teamster's eyes rolled back and he crashed unmoving to the floor.

Clint cut a path through the crowd toward Gideon. Using the barrel of the Colt's as a scythe, he led Gideon and his wide-eyed load to the stairs. They ascended halfway and Gideon set Su Chin down. He and Clint turned and started back into the melee.

They had moved only a few steps when the crowd quieted.

The huge Chinese guard had caught the attention of all by swinging the executioner's sword. It whistled through the air. When all turned to watch its fearful arcs, he brought it across a thick table, severing it like butter. It sobered every man in the crowd.

The guards had formed a line and moved into the crowd with shotguns leveled.

"Enough!" Zhang Ho shouted from the railing above. "You have seen enough of the girls. The auction will begin at sundown. Come back. Bring gold."

Grumbling, the men began to filter out. Deputy Thad McPherson and two other deputies, stars gleaming on their chests, burst in. Men holding bloody noses and knotted heads, carrying or allowing friends to lean on them, moved out into the alley.

Five men lay sprawled on the floor of the big room. One, whose chest was blown away, exposing his vitals, was obviously fodder for the undertaker. Another sat on the floor, leaning on one arm while his other hand grasped at his chest, where pink frothy blood bubbled from a knife wound. He moaned quietly, calling the name of some faraway loved one, though his throat gurgled blood. He would not live to see the auction.

Clint glanced upward to make sure that Su Chin was all right. Then he and Gideon began to move toward the door.

"You buy Su Chin, please, Javanese man?" she called down from the stairs.

Clint caught the look on Gideon's face—a grab bag of mixed emotions. He pulled his friend to the door.

Vester Grumbles stood close by, using the scattergun to prod the men along. "This yours?" he asked, and extended Gideon's high hat, smashed flat and covered with beer and mud. Grumbles snickered, but

Gideon accepted it, popped it back into its proper shape, and fitted it in place on his head.

"Boss said to put the garbage out." Vester curled a lip. Reaching out with the shotgun, he poked Gideon in the ribs. "Outside," he managed, before Gideon wrenched the double barrel out of his hands and slammed it across his throat, pinning him to the wall.

Another guard, blond-headed and blotchy-faced, leapt forward, only to find the cold barrel of the Colt's rifle shoved under his wispy whiskered chin.

"Stay out of this," Clint warned, his eyes as cold and blue as new pond ice.

"You've pointed a gun at a LaMont for the last time," Gideon growled, nose to nose with the red-faced Grumbles.

Grumbles clawed for his sidearm, but Gideon slung the scattergun away, dropping a hand and catching Grumbles's wrist in a vise grip. Gideon brought his knee up with a crunching blow.

Vester lurched six inches up the wall. His red face went green, and his sidearm clattered to the floor. Gideon released him, and he slid slowly down the wall, grasping his groin with both hands. Gideon kicked the pistol away and it spun into the crowd.

Gideon snatched up the scattergun and the crowd reeled back as he swung it like a bat, bending the barrels across a post. He dropped it nonchalantly beside a retching Vester Grumbles, who had managed to get to his knees but was bent over, puddling the floor between his hands.

Gideon ambled past Clint and made for the door.

"We're going on outside now," Clint cautioned the blond-headed guard.

"Fine with me, friend," the guard replied, but his eyes were fixed on his fallen friend.

Clint caught up with Gideon, who took a deep cleansing breath as he stepped out into the crowded alley.

"I hate that place," Gideon said.

"And I get the impression you don't much like ol'

Vester Grumbles," Clint said, a slight smile crossing his face.

"In a way that man did me a favor, shootin' Henri LaMont and setting me free, and he talks right about slavery." Gideon's look hardened. "But I can't abide a coward, and a backshooter is the worst kind. And that man even looks stupid."

For the first time since they had arrived at the Barracoon, Clint laughed out loud.

"I can't come back here, Clint," Gideon said, his eyes distant.

"Why not? So far you've cut a wide swath."

Gideon turned to him. "If I'm here, I'll spend every dime I've got to buy that girl."

"A fella could blow his money in worse ways."

"Maybe, but can you imagine me owning someone?"

Clint wanted to smile, but the anguished look on Gideon's face wouldn't allow it.

Instead he told him of his meeting. "Well, I've got to come back. Zhang Ho says the Californio women are aboard the *Amnity* and he'll help me get them off. On the condition that no one knows. I've got to meet with him again."

"Then I'm coming back with you. I'll just ignore the auction."

"I'm sure you won't have to worry about it. Those women are going to go for big money."

Gideon didn't respond. He just kept walking.

CHAPTER EIGHTEEN

"I THINK IT'S BEGINNING TO WIDEN," CHATO whispered to Gaspar through gritted teeth.

He'd been jerking on the chain binding his right arm since the deck hatch to the bilge had been closed the night before. His wrist was gouged and bleeding. Still he jerked. The last length in the chain was slowly widening, an infinitesimal amount with each pull.

Suddenly he stopped. A shaft of light split the dank space and a voice echoed. "The captain said to bring you some gruel." Legs appeared at a deck hatch, and an old man dropped into the bilge, followed by another, younger form carrying a lantern in one hand and a bludgeon in the other.

The older man reached up through the opening and someone handed him a pot, some bowls and spoons, and a bucket. Then, awkwardly, he made his way across the ship's wooden ribs to the prisoners. The other man, a young Chinese, stayed well out of reach of the vaqueros, holding the lantern so the old man could work and a heavy belaying pin so he would be unmolested.

"I'm Abner Baggs, the supercargo of this fine ship and your jailer . . . until you take up your duties."

"How long are we to be kept in chains?" Gaspar asked.

"One of your hands will be released so you can relieve yourself and eat. Then you'll be chained again. You'll be set free after we're well out to sea. Then you'll take up the duties of a common sailor."

"When do we get out of this stinkin' bilge? Forcing a man to wallow in his own filth like a pig is inhuman."

"The bilge gets worse than yer paltry leavin's." Abner laughed. "We pump her clean every fortnight, less'n there be a storm at sea—then the pumps run day and night. But you'll soon enough have your turn at the pump handle."

Abner bent over Gaspar. "I'll be removin' the bolt from your right hand manacle. A slap at me'll cost you your grub and a kick—an' ol' Abner kicks like an Erie Canal mule. Any other tricks will cost you a knot on the head from Willie's belayin' pin." Abner began working at the bolt with a wide-mouthed wrench. "As you can see, these bolts is mighty tight and you'll never loosen one with yer hand. With Willie near, you'd have a head knotted like you stuck it in a hornet's nest long afore you ever got loose."

Gaspar merely grunted. He sighed in relief as the clasp clanked open, and he rubbed his wrist on his pants—but didn't get it near the other restraint. Abner began to work on Chato's clasp. Gaspar got to his knees, fumbled with his pants one-handed, and relieved himself into the bilge water.

"Look at that wrist, you fool." Abner chastised Chato as he worked on his bolt. "You can jerk against this chain like a coon in a trap until you tear that hand off, then Captain Banyon will feed it to the sharks and work you like you had two."

It was all Chato could do not to grab the old man by the throat and jerk his Adam's apple out. The old man hadn't noticed the link beginning to part.

Baggs released the other vaqueros, dipped up the gruel, and added a piece of salt pork to each bowl. The men ate in greedy silence. After drinking their fill from a bucket of water passed from man to man, they extended their wrists and the old man replaced the clasp bolts.

Isaac Banyon had risen with the sun as usual. His night's rest had not been good and, even though elated with his wife's decision to remain in San Francisco, he was troubled. He would have to spend the afternoon and the evening at the Barracoon, protecting his interest and making sure he received his fair share of the profits. Consequently, he could not personally supervise the course of action he had decided upon during his night's tossing and turning.

Even though his first mate, Stoddard, had failed miserably in abducting Ryan, he was more than capable of the chore Banyon had in mind. A sea chore. Banyon spent the early morning hours carefully going over his instructions with Stoddard.

Lucretia also rose early. She had attended to her toilet and was dressed by the time Isaac left the room.

"I'll get my things together. When will we go ashore?" she asked calmly.

"Midmorning, if ye can be ready by then, dear."

"I'll be ready. I want to say good-bye to Mr. Stoddard and to Mr. Baggs and Mr. Docker."

"Mr. Baggs is going to accompany us into town. He has a few more supplies to gather. When ye are ready, come topside and ye can say your farewells while we load ye things."

She smiled tightly and nodded, and Isaac left. Immediately she went to Isaac's small rolltop desk, opened one of the tiny compartment doors, and removed a key. She didn't bother to put on her cloak. She hurried out, pausing to listen at the half ladder that led to the deck. Hearing nothing, she descended to the deck below and went straight to the women's door.

She knocked and heard the footfalls of someone hurrying to answer. "Yes."

"I want to talk to the young girl whose smock I sewed."

In a moment she heard Apolonia's voice. "Yes, Mrs. Banyon?"

"I'm going to open the door and I want you to step outside. Tell the other ladies to step back and give me no misery."

"They're back," Apolonia said anxiously.

The tumblers fell and the door creaked open. Cautiously, Apolonia stepped out.

Lucretia held the key between two fingers. "I want ye sworn promise that ye'll tell no one how ye got this."

"I swear."

"Ye must leave tonight. The *Amnity* will be at sea tomorrow or, at the latest, the next day. Then it will be too late for ye."

"Thank you." Apolonia hugged the key to her breast with both hands. Lucretia spun on her heel and made her way to the ladder. "God bless you," Apolonia called after her, staring at the small brass symbol of freedom as Lucretia's skirts disappeared up the ladder. She stepped inside the room and relocked the door.

By the time Isaac had returned from his meeting with Stoddard and his morning ship's rounds, Lucretia was packed. Two huge trunks and the rocker were tightly grouped in the center of the captain's cabin.

"Are ye ready, woman?"

"I'm ready, Isaac. I've made my peace." Isaac eyed her strangely, not sure what she meant.

But lately he was used to that.

Clint and Gideon stopped at Hardy's Livery on their way back to the El Dorado, where they had decided to wait until the Barracoon reopened. Clint looked Diablo over. The big horse reared and stomped and spun in the tight confines of the stall. He was either getting barn sour and didn't want to leave his stall, or there was a mare on the wind.

To make sure he would be well cared for, Clint tipped the stable hand, then spoke to the hostler, Hardy, about an extra ration of grain. Clint instructed him to have the stable boy exercise the big horse, agreed to an extra dime a day, then he and Gideon walked the next two blocks to the saloon.

The saloon, as usual, was packed. Clint strode to the bar, purposefully selecting the section where Luther Baggs worked.

"Mr. Baggs," Clint said, the sarcasm clear in his tone, "you need to treat your customers with a little more care."

"What's that supposed to mean?"

"That's supposed to mean . . ." Clint almost lost his temper, but didn't want to start trouble in the El Dorado. "That means you owe Gideon and me a drink."

"What the hell are you talking about?" Luther's bulldog brow crinkled as if he didn't understand.

Clint cut his wolf loose. He leaned forward, snatched Luther by the collar, and dragged him halfway across the bar. When he was nose to nose with the bartender, Clint's voice rang low and slow. "I got a passel of knots on my head on account of you lying about my friend here being drunk in the alley. Now, you can buy us that drink, or you can step out in the alley with us and we'll take turns teachin' you how to speak truthful."

Baggs grabbed Clint's wrist with one hand. His droopy eyes wide with fear, he cut them to Gideon, then back to Clint's steely gaze.

"I was only trying to help my pa," he mumbled.

Clint shoved him back across the bar. "While you're pourin' me three fingers of Noble's Finest whiskey, I'll tell you a story." Baggs hurried to get the backbar ladder so he could reach the highly placed bottle. Gideon and two strangers leaning on the bar listened with interest as Clint talked.

"An old farmer bought himself a mail-order bride. He took a mule-drawn buggy to pick her up, got hitched, and started back to his farm.

"That old mule acted up, and the farmer whipped him with a buggy whip, and said, 'That's one.'"

As Clint talked, Baggs poured him a generous glassful of the expensive whiskey and poured Gideon a soda water.

"Gideon will have a ginger ale," Clint instructed Baggs, then continued. "They went aways and the mule acted up again. The farmer climbed out of the buggy and hit that mule between the eyes with the butt of his rifle, and said, 'That's two.' His new bride looked at him with a jaundiced eye, but said nothing.

"The mule acted up one more time just as they turned into the farmer's gate. He jerked his rifle and shot the mule dead in his traces, and said, "That's three.'

"The woman jumped up and said that was the dumbest thing she ever saw a human do. The farmer stared at her a minute, then said, real quiet like, 'That's one.' "

Gideon and the two other fellows at the bar began to chuckle, but Luther looked puzzled. "What's that all supposed to mean?"

"Well, Luther, when you sent me out to the alley," Clint said, leaning across the bar, "that was one."

Luther blanched. Gideon picked up his ginger ale and toasted Clint. "Providential, Mr. Ryan." Then he turned to Baggs. "I hope you heard good."

"Good enough," Baggs managed sheepishly. He snatched up the bottle and topped Clint's whiskey off again. "On the house," he said.

The saloon quieted and Clint turned to the batwing doors. Sultry Mulvany, dressed in pink silk with a pink-feathered hat and matching Jenny Lind parasol, pushed through the doors. A few steps behind stalked Jasper Henry.

Sultry spotted Clint and the crowd parted as she walked to the bar. "Good afternoon, Mr. Ryan, Mr. LaMont."

"Ma'am." Clint took his hat off and smiled, feeling a warm pleasure at seeing her.

"I trust you two are having a pleasant morning?" As friendly as Sultry's smile was, Jasper Henry's frown more than offset it.

"We are now," Clint said, and the compliment caused Sultry's smile to widen even more.

"I'll see you later, Mr. Ryan." She spun her parasol over her head and moved away toward the stage. Jasper caught Clint's gaze and held it just a moment more than was polite.

"Good morning, Jasper," Clint said.

"Not to my way a thinkin'," Jasper said, his eyes searing into Clint. He spun on his heel and stomped after his employer.

After Jasper moved out of earshot, Gideon sidled up to Clint. "You've rubbed the salt in that ol' boy's scrapes about as deep as you should."

"I mean no insult to Jasper. In fact, I owe him a bottle of Noble's."

"Sometimes just being in the same state seems an insult to some men. Just watch out for him. He follows that woman like a dog, and there's nothing like a case of lace and lilac poisoning to make a dog go rabid."

"You fellas want another?" Luther interrupted.

"Yeah, a bottle," Clint said, and pointed at the Noble's. Luther produced it and Clint paid him. "Take it to Jasper. Tell him I appreciated the help. Can you handle that, Baggs?"

Luther nodded.

"Let's get something to eat," Gideon advised. "It may be a long night."

"Thank you, Mr. Baggs," Clint said politely, as if nothing had transpired between them.

They turned and left for Mariano's.

CHAPTER NINETEEN

CLINT AND GIDEON STOOD IN THE LONG ALLEY line to get into the Barracoon, for the word had been passed that no weapons were allowed inside; they would have to be checked with the guards at the door. The crowd, many of whom displayed the wounds of their earlier encounter, was subdued compared to the morning.

Clint handed over his Colt's rifle and pistol, a bit uncomfortable that the guards, including Vester Grumbles, still carried their scatterguns. Grumbles gave them a hard look but cut his eyes away when Gideon stared him down.

Four marshal's deputies, badges plainly displayed, were in attendance, including Thad McPherson, who caught Clint's eye and gave him a smile resembling one that a cat might give a cornered mouse. Clint tipped his hat.

The blood, beer and broken glasses, smashed chairs, and tables, had been mopped up and removed. An auctioneer's podium rested on one end of the raised platform, and a roped-off walkway led to the stairs from there. A sign hanging near the entry door announcing CASH, GOLD, OR DRAFTS ON LOCAL BANKS ONLY was repeated in squiggly Chinese characters.

Clint spotted General Zhang Ho and approached him immediately. "Can we talk now?"

"After the auction, Mr. Ryan." Ho avoided meeting Clint's eyes. "We must not be seen talking. Meet me in the corner office after everything has quieted down."

Turning to go back to where Gideon had captured two chairs for them, Clint saw the reason for Ho's reluctance to talk. Captain Isaac Banyon stood against a wall, watching the growing crowd with interest.

Clint walked straight to him. "Captain Banyon, I believe."

"Mr. Ryan, isn't it?" Banyon's eyes narrowed, but he extended a sun-reddened hand that met Clint's.

"Are you bidding?" Clint asked, flashing a razor-thin smile.

"Hardly. I am owed a little money by the yellow devil who runs this affair. Are ye a buyer, Mr. Ryan?"

Clint ignored the question. "The rumor is that you're a partner in this meat market."

Banyon's jaw knotted. "That is a dirty lie. I'm an honest seafaring man."

Clint worried it like a cat with a near-dead mouse. "I may bid, but I prefer my women taller, and my Spanish is much better than my Chinese. You don't perhaps have any Californio girls coming under the gavel?"

Banyon's hands balled into fists, and his knuckles whitened. "Zhang Ho is the proprietor here. Ask him." Banyon spun on his heel, gave Clint his broad back, and shoved his way through the crowd.

Clint started back to his seat, but Thad McPherson stepped into his path, his gangly scarecrow body blocking the way. "Lazo, eh? I hear you go by Clint Ryan."

"I used to, before I came to California years ago. Now I use my Calfornio name, Lazo. Some still prefer Clint."

"You tried to cause trouble for a friend of mine—"

"I don't call many backshooters friends," Clint snapped.

McPherson colored, his face almost the same red cast as his rumpled hair. He snarled, "You didn't come here on a brig called the *Savannah*, perchance?"

"I knew of her. Word was she went down with all hands near Santa Barbara," Clint said, purposefully evading the question.

"Not all hands. Among other survivors, a fella name of Ryan, John Ryan, is still being sought in connection with the sinking. That fella wouldn't be you, now, would it?"

"My name is Lazo. It used to be Clint Ryan." Clint laughed and shrugged. "There must be ten thousand Ryans and Rileys and Kellys in the States from County Kilkenny alone."

"Well, Mr. Californio Lazo." McPherson's voice rang with sarcasm. "I haven't had a chance to sit down with Marshal Larson with this info yet, but I wouldn't be a damn bit surprised but what you'll have some real hard questions to answer, once I do."

"I'm not going anywhere," Clint said, "except over there to join my friend and watch these proceedings." Clint touched the brim of his hat and brushed past McPherson. As he crossed the room, he wondered how long it would take them to tie him together with John Ryan . . . John Clinton Ryan, his whole name. His time in San Francisco might be cut short. Wishing he had Apolonia Vega home and was on his way south to the shores of the Kaweah River, he found his seat.

"Well, look who's here," Gideon said, his eyes on the platform.

Clint glanced up to the podium, where Huly Up Hong stood next to the auctioneer. Dressed in black pants that matched the black collar and pocket trim on his bright red coat, the auctioneer rapped a highly polished cherry-wood gavel, quieting the crowd, then began to read out the rules of the auction. Hong translated into Chinese.

Not to be outdone, Hong wielded a gleaming

black wooden striker and, leaning over a two-foot polished brass gong suspended from a mahogany frame in front of the podium, struck with abandon, gaining the total attention of the room. The second the room quieted, he began a slow repetitive beat and the first of the girls stepped out of a room above onto the walkway.

With the peculiar shuffling half walk, half trot of the Chinese, the girl descended the stairs and took the podium. Nervous, her eyes remained fixed on the floor. She was short, even for a Chinese, and her face shone almost white, with the help of zinc powder, and she was moon-faced—which was in proper proportion to her ample body. The auctioneer stepped toward her with a proud smile. Reaching out, he raised her chin like a father would show off a cherubic child.

"Pretty and chaste as the day she was born. And strong enough to launder and clean and"—his eyes took on a lecherous gleam—"strong enough to satisfy all the other household needs . . . all night long, if necessary."

That drew an appreciative laugh from most of the men. Gideon fidgeted in his chair and looked at everything in the room but the now-quaking girl.

"Wish they would stop that damned dirge," he complained quietly to Clint, referring to the gong.

"Now, gentlemen, let the bidding begin." The auctioneer chattered and chided and worked the crowd, and to Clint's surprise, at the strike of the gavel, even this homely girl sold for a thousand dollars in gold. The slender hawk-faced man who purchased her had been pointed out to Clint before—he owned one of the worst pox-ridden brothels in town, and his face reflected the pocked memory of some dreaded disease. The girl would soon be ensconced alongside her Peruvian sisters.

The man paid in gold nuggets, and Zhang Ho carefully worked a fine set of glass-enclosed scales while Isaac Banyon stood a few feet away, pretending to watch the auction. Actually he was carefully noting each transaction on a piece of paper.

The bidding faltered for some of the girls who took the podium, going as little as four hundred for one who was butterball fat and sported a thumbnail-sized wart on her chin with inch-long black hairs dangling from it. But it mattered little to the fat Chinaman who bought her contract. He looked a little like a yellow warthog, shuffling and snorting as he excitedly paid for her with a melon-sized mound of silver Mexican pesos.

Gideon grew more taut as the bidding wore on, mopping his brow, grinding his jaw, shifting in his seat. Clint kept watch around the room. Thad Mc-Pherson leaned on a bar, his green eyes growing more the color of muddy pond water as he continued to knock down the free drinks the deputies had been allowed. Clint glanced to where Captain Banyon leaned against a wall, making copious notes. The wider Banyon's smile grew with the sales, the more furious Clint became, until a slow fire simmered in his gut. *The self-satisfied son of a bitch,* Clint thought to himself. Maybe he'd just scuttle the tub Banyon owned after he got the girls off.

Clint turned his attention back to the podium.

"Now we have the prize of the auction," the auctioneer began. "From the harem of a king." Hong did a roll on the gong that would be the envy of a fife and drum corp. All eyes turned to the smoke-hazed walkway, and whistles and cheers arose. Perched on a chair festooned with silk banners and affixed to two long poles, Su Chin was carried down the stairs by two of Ho's strongest guards, and the huge guard, displaying the executioner's sword, followed.

With regal aplomb, she was placed upon the platform and the red-coated auctioneer approached and gave her his hand. "An Oriental beauty of rare quality. A bird of paradise too beautiful to touch." He led her around the platform, demonstrating that she was mobile, even if only barely so on her bound feet. "The Chinese consider the binding of feet to be the ultimate in beautification.

"As you can plainly see, she can attend to all household duties." He cackled and the crowd came to life, whistling and shouting and stomping the floor until the dust rose.

He led her back to the chair, seated her, and stood in staged amazement at her beauty. Su Chin looked as if she were about to be cast into the lion's den.

He returned to his podium as Hong beat the gong. Su Chin kept her head lowered, her eyes searching the crowd with desperation.

"Now, gentlemen—and we would only allow this orchid to be sold to a gentleman." He paused. "But of course, the true measure of a gentleman is the size of his purse!" Clint scowled as this brought a laugh from every other man in the crowd, save Gideon, who mopped his brow and refused to catch the searching gaze of Su Chin.

"Now, who offers two thousand dollars to begin the competition?" The auctioneer waved his gavel around the room. He was asking for five hundred more than the top price of the day. For a moment Zhang Ho feared that all the high bidders had spent their gold and that he should have offered her early in the evening. Then the pock-faced Peruvian rose. "One thousand five hundred dollars."

The room buzzed. Then the noise increased as a tall, thin, graying Chinese, his silver queue extending from a high hat matching Gideon's, rose and spoke in singsong Chinese. Hong repeated. "One thousand six hundred."

"Another brothel owner?" Gideon asked with a low moan.

"I've never seen the man," Clint said. "But any man who put her in a brothel in San Francisco would have to buy a mule to carry his gold by the end of the first night."

Gideon looked ill.

"One thousand seven hundred fifty," the Peruvian shouted as soon as the room quieted enough so he could be heard.

Gideon stared across the room at the man, who looked like the grim reaper himself. "One thousand eight hundred dollars," Gideon called out, coming to his feet.

The room quieted. Then whispers blended and increased in volume like a beehive stirred with a stick, and quieted again. The auctioneer glared at Gideon. Finally he spoke. "You have the gold to meet such a bid?"

"I bid, didn't I?" Gideon's voice cut like sheet ice.

The bid by a black man seemed to encourage some and anger others. Within seconds the price rose to two thousand two hundred dollars. Then the bidding faltered.

The Peruvian stood and his eyes roamed the room. "Nothing but the best for my customers." He paused as dramatically as a Shakespearean actor. "Two thousand four hundred dollars." He sat back down casually, looking convinced that his jump would settle the matter.

Gideon rose again. "Two thousand five hundred dollars."

The Peruvian jumped to his feet, shouting over the clamor in the room. "I insist you make this man show you his gold."

The auctioneer looked at Gideon questioningly, but Gideon's eyes burned across the room to where the Peruvian stood.

"My mouth doesn't outweigh my purse, sir," Gideon stated flatly. "And any man who thinks it does better have fists like sledgehammers, or his blade sharp and his powder dry."

The Peruvian recanted his challenge by turning back to the podium. "Two thousand six hundred dollars." He grinned ghoulishly, as if the matter were finally settled, and took his seat. Noting the look on Gideon's face, the auctioneer seemed to agree.

"Going once." He raised his gavel.

With quiet desperation, Gideon whispered to Clint. "Do you have five hundred dollars?"

Clint still had not recovered from the fact that Gideon was bidding in the first place. "Five hundred dollars? You'll have me sleeping in the streets."

"Going twice," the auctioneer yelled over the din.

"Do you want to see Su Chin rot away with the hunk?" Gideon asked, the question punctuated by the most agonized look Clint had ever seen.

"No, I don't, and yes, I got five hundred, but we'll both be out robbin' Chinese of their rice and fish heads tomorrow."

"Three thousand!" Gideon shouted triumphantly, and the room fell so deathly silent you could hear Zhang Ho rubbing his palms together.

"Damn," uttered the Peruvian.

Even the auctioneer gasped in shocked surprise.

"Three thousand?" the red-coated man repeated, recovering his composure. "Any other bidders?" With an anticlimactic plop of the gavel, he mumbled, "Sold. To the Ethiopian gentleman in the high hat and fancy suit."

Su Chin sagged in relief, closed her eyes, and sank into the festooned chair.

Gideon turned to Clint. "I hope you have that five hundred on you."

"I had five hundred," Clint corrected. "If my mathematics is correct, we paid about a month's wages per pound. I now own one sixth of a clubfooted China Mary. If I figure right, that entitles me to a leg and a rump."

For the first time since they had reentered the Barracoon, Gideon smiled.

"But not for long, my friend," Gideon said as he made his way past Clint and headed for Ho's scales. "Not for long."

Slightly confused by Gideon's statement, Clint followed along behind. Gideon's smile was only outshone by the normally inscrutable Ho's. Clint and Gideon untucked their shirts and removed money belts. Clint's Spanish reals joined Gideon's much larger pile of double eagles on the scale plate.

Clint wondered what Gideon had meant by "not for long," but now nothing Gideon would do could surprise him.

CHAPTER TWENTY

After Ho completed assigning Su Chin's indenture contract to Gideon and Clint, they headed for the platform, where Su Chin remained seated. Behind them the crowd of men filed out of the Barracoon—a few of them smiling, with *mui gai* in tow.

Clint and Gideon made their way under the rope and stood before her. She glanced up at Gideon, then bowed her head. "I your servant."

"Only until we can find a lawyer," he said gently. She looked up in surprise.

"What mean?"

"I will set you free of your contract. Maybe someday you'll be able to repay Mr. Ryan and myself the money we *loaned* you."

Clint was not surprised. He said nothing, just watched quietly.

"How Su Chin get along?" she asked, her face a jumble of mixed emotions.

"Su Chin is a clever and beautiful girl," Gideon said softly. "I too was chattel, and I'm doing fine as a freedman. You will find a way. I have a few more dollars to advance you until you figure out how to get by."

"Hell, I've got fifty more," Clint said, seeing how frightened the girl was. "You can borrow half of it."

Gideon flashed him a grateful smile. "Then you'll have almost a hundred dollars. If you're careful, you can live for three months on a hundred dollars, even at San Francisco prices. That'll give you a good start."

"When must Su Chin repay? What interest?" she asked quickly.

"When you can. I want no interest," Gideon said, glancing at Clint for confirmation. Clint shrugged his shoulders.

"Not fair," she said. "Four percent per month?" her face faded to the cunning blankness of a natural-born negotiator.

"It's not necessary," Gideon said.

"Four percent?" she repeated. That was less than half what the market would bear in San Francisco.

Gideon glanced at Clint and again received only a shrug of the shoulders. He turned back to her. "If you insist. I'll have the note drawn at four percent."

Clint watched the girl and suddenly felt at ease. He had already written the five hundred off as a cost of friendship, but now had no doubt that he would be repaid in full, with interest.

Su Chin extended her hand to seal the bargain. Gideon took the slender soft palm and smiled broadly. A tear glazed her cheek, leaving a track in the zinc powder she had used to whiten it. Knowing it was a tear of joy, Clint chuckled until Gideon turned to him.

"I don't know what the hell I'm laughing about," Clint growled. "We'll all be sleeping in the stall with Diablo tonight."

"You and I, maybe. She'll have a room and a bed and no by-God keepers chaining her to it while some pox-ridden sailor passes Satan's burden on to her."

"That sounds right to me," Clint said. He noticed Captain Isaac Banyon crossing the almost vacant Barracoon to where Zhang Ho and his Fu Sang guards were bagging the money in three heavy canvas sacks, each of which would have held twenty pounds of grain. Clint moved to where three miners stood finishing their drinks. Acting as if he were part of the miners' conversation, he listened to Ho and Banyon.

". . . and by the gods, that wasn't the bargain," Banyon was saying, his face slightly red.

"I will make the settlement in the morning, Captain," Ho said placatingly, backed up by several of his guards. "I must have time to account for all of the expenses. Then we will split the proceeds as agreed. You are welcome to remain here in the Barracoon with the money and my guards if you so desire."

"I will sail, with my share of the gold, on the afternoon tide tomorrow. Do ye understand?"

"I assure you, the accounts will be complete long before you raise another." Ho's tone left no doubt that he meant what he said. "And you will have your half as agreed."

"I'll be here at first light, and the money had best be here, too, or I'll track ye heathen hide to the ends of the earth. My crew will be usin' yellow skin to scour the decks." Banyon spun on his heel and stomped for the alley door.

Clint immediately went to the stairway and made his way up, catching Ho's eye as he did so. Ho nodded in acknowledgment. After giving the guards instructions, Ho ascended the stairs, with one of his burly guards close behind. The hired white guards and the two remaining marshal's deputies filtered back into the Barracoon from the alley.

Clint followed Ho into the office, while the guard waited outside.

On the platform below, Gideon glanced uneasily at the way the twelve white guards were dispersing themselves around the room.

Vester Grumbles stood beside Thad McPherson and another deputy, chatting and laughing. Still, the way two of the white guards approached the deputies from the rear made Gideon tense. Then the pieces fell in place. He jumped up and yelled, "Look out!"

But it was already too late. One of the white guards clubbed McPherson from behind with the butt of his shotgun. McPherson slammed to the floor. Grumbles shoved his shotgun into the belly of the second deputy. Another guard slammed a gun butt into the back of the deputy's head, and the deputy joined McPherson out cold on the floor.

The Chinese guards, at first confused, drew their hatchets from under their robes, and the huge guard with the executioner's sword stood in front of all of them, its arcs whistling a warning.

Grumbles glanced over at Gideon. "I'll get to you later." He laughed aloud and joined his shotgun-toting companions, who closed in on the Chinese. Like a stand of black oak tree trunks, the Chinese gathered around the sacks of gold in a semicircle. The white guards stopped a dozen steps from them.

"Now, what do you Chine'e boys think you're gonna do with those little excuses for axes an that meat cleaver?" Grumbles said with a sardonic laugh. "Let me show you what a real weapon will do." The shotgun bucked and spat flame, and the largest of the Fu Sang guards flew back against the wall, his arms and legs splayed out, his chest a pattern of bloody slug holes, and the executioner's sword spun away uselessly. He slowly slid down the wall, leaving a smear of blood.

Clint and Ho, deep in conversation behind the closed office door, hoped the shot they heard had come from outside. When they realized it hadn't, Clint scrambled for the door.

Gideon scooped up Su Chin and placed her behind the low platform, out of Grumbles's line of fire. "Don't move," he cautioned her. His right hand snaked behind his back, under his coat, and reappeared with Grumbles's own Root's Patent Model. Shoving both hands in his coat pockets, the Root out of sight, he climbed back up on the platform, an interested nonparticipating observer.

Clint flung the door open and took in the scene at a glance. His jaw clamped—his Colt's rifle and pistol were checked at the door below.

He glanced around the office for a weapon, any kind of a weapon. From the desk drawer, Ho drew two of the prettiest nickel-plated Patterson Colts's

Clint had ever seen. Ho tossed them both to him. "They are loaded, but I have never fired them," he said.

Clint stepped out of the door and caught the glint of the hatchet held by the guard who had followed Ho upstairs. The white guards below moved forward, gesturing with the scatterguns, and the Fu Sang retreated from the money bags. The guard on the walkway swung his hatchet in a full arc and flung it. Clint stood hypnotized by its keening whistle, watching the blade spiral end over end, then slam into the back of one of the white guards below.

The response was instantaneous. Half a dozen shotguns cut loose at the walkway above. The big Chinese slammed against the wall with half a hundred pellets in his chest, with such force that he bounced back over the railing and spun head over heels to the floor below.

Clint dove back in the office. The white guards fired at him and splinters from the doorjambs splattered through the room.

"Jesus," Clint swore.

He cocked both Colt's and leaned through the doorway, snapping off two shots before the wall exploded with a burst of splinters again.

Three of the white guards hefted the money bags, and Grumbles yelled to the others to keep Clint in the office. He followed the three carrying the money toward the door, then realized that Gideon stood on the platform, taking it all in as if watching a stage show.

Vester Grumbles paused at the edge of the platform, a sadistic smile curling the corners of his mouth. "I shouldn't waste one of these loads on your black ass, but then again, why not?" He raised the shotgun just as Gideon's coat pocket pointed at him and exploded. Grumbles's eyes stared vacantly when he hit the floor, a perfect round .31-caliber hole between them.

Gideon dove off the platform and covered Su Chin with his body, pressing her to the floor. The edge of the platform and the chairs behind where they hid were blown apart. The room roared with shotgun fire.

With the distraction, Clint dropped to the floor of the walkway and began firing both Colt's alternately. Four of the white guards sprawled on the floor, but the three with the money reached the doorway. One of them did a forward somersault and dropped his money bag, a .31-caliber hole in his spine. Five of the guards, empty-handed, reached the rear door of the Barracoon, but two of them fell to Fu Sang Tong hatchets before they made it out.

The last of the guards, only one load in his shotgun, ran past Thad McPherson, who, groggy from the blows, struggled for his revolver. The guard gave him the remaining load, blowing away McPherson's face as he passed.

Clint tracked the guard with the Colt's in his right hand. The gun bucked, and the man spun. Another shot from Gideon's .31 took him in the throat.

But two bags of money were gone.

The room hung heavy with the smell of gunpowder. Clint panned the Colt's, seeking another target. Moving down the walkway, he descended the stairs to where Gideon was rising from behind the shelter of the platform. Su Chin wisely made no move to get up.

Ho reached the bottom of the stairway just behind Clint and looked around at the carnage. Four of his guards lay on the floor holding ugly gaping shotgun wounds. One lay dead, his chest raw meat and shattered bone. Eight white devil guards sprawled around the room, along with two marshal's deputies. Clint and Gideon moved from guard to guard, making sure that those who were only wounded had no weapons. Low moans filled the room.

Su Chin looked up at Gideon as he reached down for her. He had decided to get her out of the blood-splattered room—at least as far as the alleyway. "Can go now?" she asked, her eyes wide.

"We can go outside, Su Chin, but we can't

leave quite yet," Gideon said, a gentle smile on his face. "We'd better wait there for the marshal. He'll want some answers. Then we'll get you to a hotel."

"As wish," she said, and managed to pick herself up off the floor onto the edge of the platform.

Clint walked over to where Ho stood, wringing his hands. "They got away with two bags of money."

"This is terrible," Ho said. "As part of our bargain, I was responsible for the girls after they arrived—for their safety, and for the money's. There will be enough to pay Captain Banyon for his share of the profit. The loss will be ours. We must get our money back."

He waved what was left of the Fu Sang guards over and gave them quick instructions in Chinese. They disappeared out the door, one remaining behind and taking up a watchful position near Ho.

"Can you help us get the money back?" Ho asked. "I will pay handsomely."

"I've got a job to finish first. Then I can," Clint assured him. "I'll be back as soon as I finish with the *Amnity*."

"Of course. Do your job . . . but you could be of service to the Fu Sang while you are at it. If Captain Banyon were to die, that, too, would be to the tong's benefit, under the present circumstances."

"Not my line of work," Clint snapped.

"Still, you will help recover the money?"

"I'll come back, and we'll talk about it."

"Don't you think we should wait for Marshal Larson?" Gideon asked.

"No time," Clint said. "You can, but I'm gonna make this thing with the Californio women end."

Gideon turned to Su Chin, loaned her an arm, and guided her to the door.

Clint recovered his own weapons from a closet used as a checkroom, and followed out the door into the darkness.

"You never mentioned that nasty little belt gun,"

Clint chided Gideon as they moved down the dark alley.

"Never felt the need to. Never thought I'd have to pull it. 'Sides"—Gideon smiled in the darkness—"I didn't have much time to practice and you shouldn't depend on a fella who's not much of a shot."

"Yeah, I noticed that," Clint said facetiously. "You blew a hole in a good suit."

After a few steps, Gideon realized they would be half the night walking at Su Chin's pace. With a broad smile, he swept her up into his arms and followed Clint's brisk stride.

Within the hour they had Su Chin situated in a room—Sultry Mulvany's. She agreed to let the girl stay until they could find a house for her the next day.

While they headed for the wharf and the *Amnity*, Clint explained to Gideon what information he had received from Ho during their short meeting before the shooting had started. Willie Boy Wong was to be their contact on board the ship. If they could find him before the other sailors discovered them, he would help them locate the women.

The two men made their way through the quieting late-night streets of the city. Around them, men without rooms camped in the streets, fires burning near their bedrolls, stock tethered nearby. They walked to Front Street, then to the end of Long Wharf, where the quiet was interrupted by a group of men enjoying a song played on pan pipes and a fiddle, and stared out into the bay.

At first Clint thought his eyes were deceiving him. Then he walked over to the group of sailors who warmed their hands at a small fire built in a whaling ship's try-pot, only one of the thousands of nautical items—coiled line, ricking, rigging, and sails—that cluttered the wharf.

"Where's the *Amnity*?" he asked. The players laid their instruments aside and one of the listeners glanced up. "The *Amnity*?" Clint repeated. "She was anchored out there." He pointed to the vacant spot among the many ships.

"She moved out on the afternoon tide," the sailor muttered, returning his attention to the fire.

Clint's mouth went dry. Beside him, the men took up a lively chanty.

CHAPTER
TWENTY-ONE

THE AFTERNOON TIDE, THE MAN HAD SAID.

Clint stayed silent as he and Gideon made the dark climb through the quiet streets back up from the bay to the El Dorado. The *Amnity* sure as hell didn't leave without her captain. And Banyon had been at the Barracoon until well into the night. No, she was still in San Francisco Bay. But where? The bay, including its sister bay, San Pablo, lay over fifty miles long and ten miles wide in spots. There were over a hundred and fifty miles of shoreline, not to speak of the three major islands lying inside the Golden Gate. He cursed himself for not acting sooner. She could be anywhere.

The *Amnity* had to leave via the narrow Golden Gate, but standing on Telegraph Hill watching her leave would do him little good. All he could do was wave good-bye—good-bye to the Californio girls and any hope of returning Don Vega's daughter to him. Good-bye to the promised Andalusian brood stock. And probably good-bye to his hopes for a ranch.

Clint shoved open the batwing doors to the El Dorado, and he and Gideon shouldered their way through the crowd. Luther Baggs leaned against the bar, on the customer side, talking to his father, Abner Baggs—the supercargo of the *Amnity*.

"The saints are smiling upon me," Clint said, half under his breath. He and Gideon bellied up to the bar beside the two men.

"Your night off, Luther?" Clint asked with a smile. "I owe you a drink."

Luther eyed him suspiciously when Clint waved the bartender over, ordered a Dog's Head ale and a ginger ale, and told him to bring Luther and Abner whatever they were drinking. He flinched as the man took the five-dollar gold piece he handed him and returned him only three dollars. The twenty-five dollars he had left after Gideon's experiment in emancipation was already down to twenty-three, and that would go fast at this rate.

"Luther tells me you're serving aboard the *Amnity*?"

"Aye, and a fine vessel she is."

"I noticed she's hauled anchor. I'm surprised to see you here."

"She's not far, friend. Thanks for the drink." Abner toasted Clint, then gave him his back and continued his conversation with his son.

"Why'd she move?" Clint pressed.

Abner glanced over his shoulder. " 'Cause Captain Banyon ordered it. Are you with the newfangled city harbor commission, lad?"

"Hardly," Clint said with a feigned laugh. "Just interested."

"Well, to tell the truth, I don't know where she lies at the moment. I'm waiting for her master. Then we'll be off to the *Amnity*, and off to the shores of the Orient."

"To a good voyage!" Clint raised his glass. When the old man resumed his conversation with Luther, Clint whispered to Gideon. "We'll find her soon enough, if we can stay close to this old salt."

"Best we not be afoot," Gideon advised. "I'll fetch your horse and rent myself one while you keep an eye out." He upended his drink and left the bar at a brisk stride.

Clint moved away from Luther and the old man and found a spot near Jasper's pianoforte where he could listen to the bald-headed man's rambunctious pounding, but still see his quarry.

Jasper didn't take time from his playing to thank

Clint for the bottle of Noble's, but did manage to shoot him a baleful glance.

It was a good thing Gideon left in a hurry, for shortly after he had gone, Isaac Banyon's ample frame entered the saloon. Clint glanced away as Banyon surveyed the room. If Banyon noticed Clint across the smoky distance among the hundred or more customers, he gave no indication. Rather, he moved directly to the bar. Clint hoped he'd pause long enough for a last drink before he headed out to the ship, but he didn't. Instead he spoke sharply to Abner, who quickly shook hands with his son. Then the two sailors strode out the door.

Clint hustled to the batwings, ignoring the insults of the men he elbowed aside, in time to see the two climb into a poor copy of a hansom-style cab with a shimmering whale-oil cut-glass lamp on either sidewall, pulled by a big dappled gray horse. The driver sat at the rear and above the body of the cab, overlooking it and the animal. Behind and below his perch, demonstrating frontier practicality, hung a low leather boot for luggage.

Clint squinted into the darkness, hoping to see Gideon and the horses. Then the cabby cracked his whip over the gray and the carriage started away—with Clint's hopes.

Clint ran for the cab, caught the leather straps of the boot with both hands, and managed to swing his feet under and rest them on the single axle. It was uncomfortable and straining, but as long as he wasn't seen by the driver, he could hold on for a short trip.

The handler whipped the gray into a trot. A group of boys in the light of a shop window pointed at Clint and laughed as the carriage clattered past on the board-covered street, but the driver paid them no mind. Clint wound his arms into the straps, giving himself a firmer grip. The cabby had to rein up to allow a dray through an intersection.

"Here, now!" a voice rang out from the boardwalk as the cab clattered by a whale-oil streetlamp.

"Driver," the meddlesome voice shouted. "You've got a freeloader!"

Clint cringed when the cabby looked over his shoulder, but apparently seeing nothing awry, he went back to his job. Clint could see the back of the man's head and the tail of his whip on its backstroke.

The cabby must have had an afterthought. He leaned back and looked down. Before Clint could unwind his forearms and avoid the cabby's wrath, the whip lashed down and caught him across the face. He dropped away, skittered across the boards and rolled into the gutter, hearing the curse of the cabby, who shook his fist and disappeared into the darkness. Clint's stomach churned. The cab and his hopes for Apolonia Vega and the ranch disappeared into the darkness.

Apolonia and the girls had been ecstatic when Lucretia Banyon had brought them the key. They planned carefully, assessed their mistakes from the earlier attempt, and decided upon the course of action that they would take just as soon as it was dark.

Then they had heard the capstan being manned by six able sailors, and the anchor chain clattering aboard. The women stared at each other in panic in the dimness of their little room and wondered if they had waited too long.

"Should we run on deck and jump into the water?" one of the girls asked.

"Don't be silly," Juanita Robles snapped. "None of us can swim and we would only drown or these brutes would hook us out of the water like fishes."

"Then what do we do?"

"You will wait here," Apolonia said. "I will sneak out and try to find our men."

"No," Juanita said sharply. "Not until it's dark. If they find you, they will want to know how you got out of the room, and that key and surprise are our only hopes."

"Then I will go when it is night."

After several hours, just about the time it was

good and dark outside, they again heard the clattering of anchor chains and felt the ship come to a shuddering halt.

They looked at each other in relief.

"How far do you think we've gone?" Apolonia asked.

"A few hours only. I would guess we are still in the bay."

"Good. Then we still have a chance. If only I can find where they have kept Gaspar and the others, we will soon be free."

Harlan Stoddard liked the feel of being the master of the ship, at least as long as Banyon was gone. He was pleased with his relocation of the *Amnity* to Hunter's Point. No one could have done it better. In fact, he thought, as the anchor chains were secured and he released the men from duty, he was so pleased that he would treat Mr. Vandersteldt to a drink.

He headed for the officer's galley, aft on the same level as the captain's cabin, and yelled at the second mate, Vandersteldt, to join him.

Yes, it had been a fine sail, if a short one. And it would be a fine voyage, now that Lucretia Banyon was ashore. Stoddard had never approved of having a woman aboard a vessel. A hen ship, the *Amnity* was known as while she had a woman aboard. It was demeaning.

A drink would suit him fine, in celebration of his flawless command of the ship and of Banyon's getting rid of the pious woman. Hell, Banyon might even be fit to live with now.

"Damn the flies," Clint grumbled, climbing to his feet and brushing himself off, wondering if he could possibly keep up on foot.

"Mount up!" Gideon shouted, galloping out of the darkness, leading Diablo. "I tried to stay far enough back so they wouldn't see."

A resurgence of hope rushed through Clint. He slapped Diablo on the rump and mounted, swinging into the saddle without the use of the stirrups. Within seconds they had the side lamps of the carriage in sight.

They crossed Market Street, passed through the residential area south of it, and were soon out of town on the wagon road south to San Jose.

"It was a damn good thing you caught up," Clint said to Gideon, who trotted his buckskin alongside on the wide rutted road. "They're turning."

He could see the flickering lights of the carriage leave the road. They slowed, giving the cab time to get well into the grove of sandpaper oaks, then followed a narrow wagon path east. The night was starlit, with the hint of a fingernail moon just appearing across the bay. They cleared the oaks and crested a sand dune. A village of a few Chinese huts lay near the water. They reined up and watched as the cabby drew rein and stopped near one of the hovels.

Beyond the village, a quarter mile out into the bay, the *Amnity*, only one anchor lantern glowing, lay dead still in the quiet water.

Clint exhaled a sigh of relief, then realized his problems were just beginning.

CHAPTER
TWENTY-TWO

APOLONIA EASED THE CABIN DOOR OPEN AND stood listening to the silence in the lower passageway. She stepped out, closed the door, and locked it behind her. She knelt and searched her garment until she found a loose stitch, then hid the key in the hem of her smock. Making her way carefully along the passageway, she felt her way along, arms spread from wall to wall. Pausing, she listened at two other doors, tried the locked handles, and whispered, "Gaspar!"

Nothing.

She saw no light from the rooms, nor heard any sounds.

Starlight filtered from the deck hatchway on the level above and offered some light, but little comfort. She looked upward, her palms cold and wet, her mouth dry.

Taking a deep breath, she calmed herself and mounted the ladder. She climbed until she could peek into the level above. Lantern light filtered out of a louvered door into the passageway. She topped the ladder, then tiptoed forward.

Gruff laughter hit her and she reeled back, almost stumbling, but she made little noise and the laughter continued. Trying to be silent, she took several deep breaths until her heart stopped pounding so hard. She moved deeper into the passageway and paused at a second door, across and farther aft. No light came through its louvers, but someone might be sleeping inside.

Her hand found the cold brass handle. It opened.

The door behind her creaked and light flooded the hallway. With a leap she darted inside the dark room and shoved the door shut. More noises outside, then quiet. When she peeked out the door, the flood of light was gone. Her chest beat like a kettle drum, and her ears rang with the pounding.

She surveyed the room. Two large portholes graced the large cabin. *This must be the captain's*, she thought. She made a mental note of its contents—a four-poster bed, a desk with brass lamp and chair. She moved to the desk and, unable to make out the items on the top, rifled her hands over it. She tried the drawers and felt around for a weapon. Nothing. Then something sharp pricked her finger and she pulled a foot-long wooden instrument out and examined it while she sucked at the tiny wound. The wooden arms of the device were connected by a wing nut at one end and needle-sharp two-inch metal points at the other. Points sharp and long enough to serve as a weapon.

She hurried back to the door, found the cold brass again, and eased out. Stepping onto the ladder to move up to the deck, she caught a glimmer out of the corner of her eye. The laughter from the lighted room had become an argument. She was afraid they would leave the room again.

She ascended the half ladder to the deck on cat's paws, clasping the weapon tightly, then stepped out into the night. A gentle breeze caressed her cheek and she realized how much she hated being locked up below. Light threw flickering shadows from a lantern on the quarterdeck over the aft end of the ship. She could hear singing and instruments being played somewhere forward, where she guessed the crew must sleep. A lively sea chanty rang from their quarters.

At another time and place, she might have enjoyed it.

Where would Gaspar and the others be? She heard a man cough, near where the light came from, and she ducked back out of sight. She moved quickly down the ladders to the lower level and stood in the dark passageway, searching her mind.

The men had come aboard bound. They were prisoners. Male prisoners would not be treated nearly as well as the women. They would most likely be locked up somewhere. The hold? But how to get into the hold? She knew it must be the greatest portion of the ship. The massive center area between the captain's and officer's cabins aft and the fo'c'sle forward. She also knew that the deck of a ship she had visited long ago had huge hatchways located in the main deck itself that opened into the hold.

But she could never manage to move one of those big, heavy hatches.

There must be another way.

As her eyes adjusted to the almost total darkness of the passageway, she caught a faint glint from the wall forward of the ladder. Since the hallway stopped there, the hold must be beyond. She ran her hand up and down the bulkhead and felt the coldness of brass in two spots. Hinges? She moved her hand away from them an adequate distance and felt a rush of hope. A let-in metal latch! Fumbling with it, she moved it, and the cover swung in.

She ducked inside. Though it was totally dark in the space she entered, she pushed the cover closed behind her. Dropping to her hands and knees, she felt along the rough unfinished deck to determine the size of the space. The area was cold and dank, and a shiver racked her. She crawled faster, the space being larger than she had imagined. Then her hand shot into an opening where the deck should have been and she fell heavily to her chest.

"Who's there?" a voice called out in Spanish.

She collected herself and listened, but heard no more. Finally she gathered her courage and ventured a reply.

"Apolonia Vega."

"Thank God. You are all right?"

"Gaspar . . . Gaspar Cota?"

"Yes. We are chained in the bottom of the hold.

You are above, on a sort of balcony overlooking the main hold. Do not try to come down. It is too dangerous in the darkness. We need a tool, a wrench, in order to loosen our manacles."

"I have a tool . . . a sort of spreading tool with sharp points. I found it on the captain's desk."

"They are dividers, used for measuring distance on charts. Useless. We need a wrench for loosening bolts."

"Where would I find such a tool?"

"I don't know. Chato has freed one hand. He can work the wrench and we can all be free, if only you can find one."

"I will try," Apolonia said, her voice wavering. Somehow the sound of a familiar voice made her feel suddenly vulnerable and helpless and very, very frightened.

"I will try," she repeated. *I must try*, she convinced herself, bolstering her courage. She turned to crawl back to the cover. In a few seconds she found it, and her strength and bravado returned with the dim light of the passageway.

Now to find a tool.

Clint and Gideon sat astride their horses, watching the carriage deposit the captain and his supercargo. Banyon paid the driver and the cab wheeled around. Clint reined away from the road and led Gideon over a sand dune. They waited until the cab passed, then reined nearer to the Chinese hovels.

The moonlight glimmered across half a dozen mud and pole shacks, which squatted just above the bay's high tide line. Nets and cork floats hung drying, draped across the rounded huts. An interwoven willow-pole rack, eight feet square and high, arched over a two-foot-deep pit smoldering with glowing ash. The rack was shingled with hundreds of flat round petrale sole absorbing the rising smoke and emanating an oily haze that permeated the night air.

Clint could see Banyon near the open door of one of the shacks, backlit by a lantern, negotiating with a Chinese fisherman. Soon the man led him and Baggs to a small fishing boat among several that had been dragged high up on the mud flat. All three of them fought to get the boat into the water.

"If we got rid of those two now, we wouldn't have to deal with them later," Gideon advised.

"True enough, but the shooting would alert those on board. I think it's better we wait and catch them all unawares."

"We might not have to shoot."

"But then again, we might, or they might. Not worth the risk."

They waited patiently while the Chinese sculled the little boat out to the *Amnity*, then sculled back. The night was clear, but mist was beginning to rise from the mud flats and soon, Clint hoped, it would be foggy. Clint approached the Chinese fisherman at the beach while Gideon hid the horses among the sandpaper oaks. Clint stopped the fisherman before he could drag the boat out onto the mud. Another quick negotiation, aided by Clint's ability to speak some Chinese, and Clint and Gideon were aboard the tiny catboat.

Harlan Stoddard, in the officers' mess, sat back in his ladder-back chair and glared at Vandersteldt, who with a pained look on his face rubbed his right bicep, then the burned back of his hand.

"You'll never beat Stoddard of the steel arm," Stoddard chided the Dutchman he had just mercilessly bested at arm wrestling. To make things interesting, he had placed candles where the loser would snuff the flame with the back of his hand. Stoddard had sadistically held Vandersteldt's hand over the candle when he could have easily driven it down and ended the contest.

The door to the officers' mess burst open. Captain Isaac Banyon filled it, eyes wide, nostrils flaring. Behind him Abner Baggs stood on tiptoe to look over his shoulder. Harlan Stoddard, a half-empty mug in his hands, faced Marvin Vandersteldt across the table. Both men were obviously in their cups.

"Damn ye, Harlan Stoddard," Isaac spat. "I cannot leave ye for a day without ye gettin' into the grog."

"You weren't due back until dawn," Stoddard growled back, his words slurred.

"Aye, but that damnable woman of mine wanted to spend the nighttime hours reading me the Scriptures, rather than the way a woman should treat a man about to set sail on a long voyage."

"But we've seen the last of her," Stoddard said with a tone that irritated Banyon. Even more irritating was his question. "Did it go well at the Barracoon?"

"We're heading back in the morning. You and half the crew to accompany me—well armed and ready to burn the damnable place if I'm not satisfied with the divvy."

"That crafty Chinaman cheated you, did he?" Stoddard grinned drunkenly.

Isaac Banyon's face reddened and, rattler-quick, he leapt the distance to the table. With a sweeping motion he slung Stoddard's drink in his face. "Don't ye be drinking a drop without my permission, and don't be thinking any heathen be man enough to cheat Captain Isaac Banyon."

Stoddard swayed and tottered slowly to his feet, his jaw set tight, drops of grog forming along its hard line. He didn't bother to wipe them away. "A man might cross me once too often," he muttered through clenched teeth.

"Then let this be the time." Banyon stepped even closer to the first mate. "I'll have no insubordination aboard my ship, and if you're not tucked into your bunk singing lullabies by the count of ten, I'll chuck your sogger hide overboard without your cut of the *mui gai* money, and ye can find a new berth."

The muscles in Stoddard's shoulders and arms knotted, but he made no move toward the big captain, nor even one to wipe the grog away as it formed another drop on the end of his nose.

Banyon held his gaze, steely-eyed, until Stoddard calmed down and looked away. Then the captain stepped aside and, fists balled at his sides, allowed Stoddard to pass. Banyon reached down and caught Vandersteldt by the collar. "And ye'll stand extra watch for a week, Dutchman."

"But Stoddard broke out the grog, sir."

"For a week, extra watch, starting now. Now get ye gear and get up and relieve the anchor watch."

Vandersteldt said nothing, just hurried out and headed for the fo'c'sle and his coat.

"It's a bloody shame you can't get decent sailing men," Abner grumbled. Banyon shot him a look that would curdle milk. "Would you like a cup of tea afore you turn in, Captain?" Abner asked quickly.

"I'd like one man aboard this vessel who does his task," Banyon snapped. His movements stiff, he left the room.

Abner listened to the captain stomp down the passageway and slam his door. He decided that he would have a cup of tea, laced with the grog left in Vandersteldt's cup. Since the captain had retired for the night, why let it go to waste? He smiled to himself. A man needs some comfort after standing to Isaac Banyon's insults.

Clint shushed the Chinese fisherman with a finger to his lips as they neared the *Amnity*, and the man complied by barely moving his oar. Pointing to the forward anchor rode, Clint leaned far out and caught it. He steadied the boat under the rode, passed the fisherman a gold piece, shoved his Colt's rifle deep into his belt at the back of his pants, and began a hand-over-hand climb up the rode. He reached the chain scupper, managed to get a foot in the opening, and stood high enough that he could see over the rail. There was no sound on the forward deck, only the quiet singing of a sailor, his tenor voice relishing a trip back to O' Virginny, in the fo'c'sle below. Clint leapt up over the rail and waved to Gideon, who followed his example up the rode. In a second they stood side by side, watching the Chinese scull away.

"There should be a man standing anchor watch aft," Clint whispered. "The Chinese who's supposed to help us will be in the fo'c'sle, unless he's on watch."

"So do we check aft, or the fo'c'sle?"

"Aft. Someone's still awake forward."

Clint crept along the rail in the darkness, his long time at sea a godsend as he wove through the fixed gear, ventilators, and lines on the foredeck. Gideon stumbled along behind, as out of place as a feathered and fluffed whore in a Sunday service.

Clint moved across the main deck and crouched behind a six-pound waist cannon, then again at the raised quarterdeck. The man standing anchor watch sat on a ventilator, quietly enjoying the calm sea, smoking.

"Can't tell if he's Chinese in the dim light," Clint whispered when Gideon joined him in a crouch.

"Then let's walk up and find out," Gideon said, standing upright.

"I'll go first. There may not be any dark-skinned men aboard. Chances are he'll mistake me for one of the crew."

Gideon waved him on. Clint climbed the short ladder, leaned his rifle against a scuttlebutt, and shoved his revolver and holster around behind his hip so they were hidden. He moved aft with the rolling gait of a sailor.

"A quiet night for it," Clint called out. He was not a Chinese, Clint decided as the man looked up. The anchor watch, a swarthy dark-skinned Portuguese, glanced at his visitor with little concern, then looked out over the sea and took a deep draw on his pipe.

He expelled a roiling puff of smoke. "Near the

last of the quiet nights, I suspect. We'll be well west of the Farallons in blue water by this time tomorrow." He glanced back at Clint. "You just sign on?"

Before Clint could answer, Gideon, who had approached the man from the other side of the mizzenmast, raised his belt gun and slapped it across the man's temple. The pipe flew, showering dottle and sparks across the holystoned deck. The man sagged without a moan or kick.

"He wasn't a Chinaman," Gideon commented, staring down at the fallen anchor watch.

Clint smiled at his friend's cold efficiency. "Tomorrow his aching head will wish he had been," Clint said, then grabbed the tail of a halyard and began binding the man. Gideon helped Clint back him up against the mizzenmast, and they tied him in a sitting position. Gideon tore away a long piece of the man's shirttail and gagged him.

Clint turned down the hanging anchor lantern so it would cast even less light across the deck, then started around to the entrance to the fo'c'sle. The singing had stopped and no light escaped from the fo'c'sle hatch.

Clint reached for the latch just as the door jerked open.

"Who the hell are you?" a ruddy-faced man asked. He was only one man, but twenty-eight sleeping men lay behind him.

CHAPTER
TWENTY-THREE

APOLONIA HESITATED OUTSIDE THE COVER TO THE hold where Gaspar and the men were imprisoned. She wondered where in the world she could possibly find a tool such as Gaspar wanted. The ship was a maze of rooms and storage areas and chests. She could search for a month if she wasn't lucky—and if she didn't get caught.

She slowly started up the ladder. She felt like a small rabbit coming out of its hole to face a pack of dogs. When her head cleared the deck above, she hesitated and listened. The light was still on in the cabin where she had heard men earlier, but it was silent now. She had not searched the small empty cabin nearest the ladder. Maybe she could find a tool there.

She moved to the door and found the cold brass handle. A tremor raced up her backbone, cautioning her—but she didn't heed it. She conquered it and ever so slowly worked the latch. The door swung wide and she stepped in.

A ham-sized hand snaked out of the darkness and closed over her throat. She felt herself being lifted off the deck and plunged into a narrow bunk, where she could barely move. She tried to scream, but the hand clasped so tightly she was afraid she would suffocate.

She tried to kick, but the man smothered her with his body, forcing himself between her legs.

"Polly, my little Mexican lass," the gruff voice said, "don't you be fightin', now. If you scream or say a word, the captain'll know ye are sneaking about the boat, and he'll chain ye in the hold for the rats to nibble on."

Fear numbed her limbs. But the thought of even that fate was not as terrible as what was happening to her. Stoddard's hand found its way along her leg and under her smock. She tried to get a knee between his, but his hold tightened even more.

She was afraid she would pass out. Even if she were unconscious, she knew this brute of a man would have his way with her. As fear flooded her, the bile rose in her throat, and her heart hammered in fear.

Clint stared at the square-jawed ruddy-faced sailor who blocked his way into the fo'c'sle.

"Who the hell am I?" Clint repeated, stalling for time. "Who the hell am I?" he said, this time in indignation. "I'm the by-God San Francisco harbor commissioner, that's who the hell I am! What the hell is this ship doing anchored in an unauthorized area? And who the hell are you?"

"Vandersteldt . . . second mate," he mumbled, a puzzled look on his face. He stepped out of the fo'c'sle and turned to pull the door closed. Gideon didn't wait. This time he brought a belaying pin across the man's head. The crunch made Clint wince.

The Dutchman fell like a timber, the thump echoing across the silent deck.

Clint stepped back so he could get a good swing with the butt of his Colt's at anyone who came out of the fo'c'sle to see what the commotion was. But it was unnecessary. No sounds came from inside. He motioned for Gideon to tie the ruddy-faced man up and, as he set about the task, Clint slipped inside the crew's quarters.

He found a candle where one always rested on shipboard—in a sconce mounted on the base of the foremast where it passed through the fo'c'sle—and lit it. His muscles bunched when the lucifer flared, but no one moved. The quiet coughing and snoring of sleeping men were the only sounds in the low-ceiling, three-cornered room.

Knowing the pecking order of ships, Clint quickly made his way to the most forward bunks, the smallest and tightest of those in the fo'c'sle. Odds were, a Chinese on board would not have his pick of the better locations.

In the last bunk forward, he spied an Oriental face. Quickly checking the other forward bunks to make sure there was not more than one, Clint clamped his hand firmly over the man's mouth. Willie's eyes snapped open, wide with fear. Clint bent low and whispered, "Zhang Ho sent me, Willie." Willie's eyes signaled recognition of the name.

Slowly Clint released the little man, who quietly moved his covers aside. Willie found the pair of trousers rolled up at the foot of his bunk and pulled them on under his nightshirt.

Clint headed out and Willie followed without bothering to pull on his boots.

They reached the deck and Clint extended his hand. As Willie Boy shook, he glanced down at the fallen, now-bound second mate, then craned his neck to locate the anchor watch.

"He's tied up too," Clint offered.

Gideon stepped forward. "Where are the women?"

"They aft, below officers' mess, in passenger quarters."

"Locked in?" Clint asked.

Without answering, Willie Boy dug in his trousers pocket and produced a key with a satisfied smile.

Clint snatched it out of his hand. "You lower the captain's boat for us, then go back to your bunk." Willie nodded his head and smiled gratefully—his participation was to be over quickly. He hurried aft to the quarterdeck to lower the tender. Clint and Gideon followed, but then headed to the hatchway below.

They checked their weapons at the hatch, then quietly descended the half ladder. Clint motioned to Gideon, making sure he saw the light coming from the officers' mess just as Gideon caught a muffled sound from the closest door off the passageway.

The quiet cry was little more than a gurgled moan, but it sounded panicked and female. Gideon put his ear to the door and heard another keening whimper, followed by a choking sob. It steeled his resolve.

He cocked a foot and kicked the door so hard it flew off its hinges and slammed against the bulkhead across the little cabin. Storming in, he caught the white reflection of Stoddard's buttocks, his belted pants being shoved below them with a gnarled hand.

In a step, Gideon's booted foot found the target and he kicked, propelling Stoddard forward. The man's face crashed into the bulkhead at the end of the bunk.

A muffled scream from the girl who still lay pinned below Stoddard angered Gideon even more, but the man spun out of the bunk and sprang to his feet before Gideon had a chance to kick him again.

Stoddard, his pants at his knees, feigned a punch, then ducked and dove across the room, burying his burly head in Gideon's midsection. Clint tried to get into the room, but Gideon's body crashed out into the passageway. Stoddard followed, bellowing and clawing to pull on his trousers.

Clint sidestepped. Stoddard leapt on Gideon, who had backstepped a foot into the ladder well and fallen. His massive attacker pummeled his face.

Clint could not get a clear swing at the first mate's head, for the fighting men rolled under the half ladder. Instead he slammed the Colt's butt into Stoddard's ribs again and again, beating the breath from him and dislodging him from atop Gideon.

Apolonia suddenly appeared in the doorway, her face ashen.

"We're from your father!" Clint said quickly, recognizing her from her picture. Before she could respond, Stoddard knocked her back into the cabin in an effort to get to his feet. He spun to face Clint in a half crouch, but a well-placed kick from Gideon sent him sprawling back into the cabin after Apolonia.

In a bounce the man reappeared, a half scowl, half grin on his face--and an ugly long-bladed knife in his hand. This time Clint had a clear swing and the butt of the Colt's crunched into the side of his head. The big man merely bounced against the bulkhead and glared, if a bit cockeyed, at Clint. The butt of the Colt's slammed into the man again, this time splattering his nose across his face, blood across the bulkhead, and dropping him.

Stoddard collapsed heavily on his back across the ladder well to the deck below. A well-placed stomp from Gideon, who had regained his feet, and Stoddard folded and clattered down the ladder.

Apolonia made her way back into the doorway. Clint reached for her, but she screamed and pointed over his shoulder.

Gideon charged past Clint in the narrow passageway, knocking him aside and sending his rifle spinning down the hall. Gideon met the bellowing charge of the captain head-on. The clash straightened both of them, and the blast of a pistol filled the narrow way with flame and acrid smoke. Gideon reeled away.

Clint dove into Isaac Banyon, driving him back into his cabin. The reflection on the gun barrel in the captain's hand brought a rush to Clint, and he pummeled the man's face with both fists, snapping his head back, forcing him deeper into the room.

Banyon tried to raise his pistol, but Clint found the barrel and they struggled.

Fighting chest to chest, they seemed stalemated. Then the captain grimaced over his full beard and ever so slowly the barrel inched up.

Like a wildcat protecting a den of kittens, Apolonia Vega raced across the room and drove the sharp metal points of the dividers deep into the captain's shoulder. He growled and his eyes filled with pain, but still he managed to lift the muzzle another few inches. Apolonia uttered a primal snarl, jerked the dividers out, and struck again and again with the needle-sharp ends.

The pistol clattered to the floor and Banyon clawed at his injured shoulder and collapsed. Clint kicked the pistol away, grabbed Apolonia's arm, and guided her out of the room.

Gideon stood in the passageway, his face slack, one arm hanging limply, dripping blood. Realizing his friend had taken the captain's bullet, Clint shouted at him, "Can you make it up the ladder?"

"I think so." Gideon turned to the ladder. Clint gave him a shove up behind Apolonia. They hesitated on the deck.

"What about the other women, and Gaspar?" Apolonia asked. When Clint did not answer, she tried to run back into the hatch. Clint caught her waist with his hands and picked her up. He hauled her, kicking and screaming, to the rail and dropped her over. *That Chinaman had better have done what I told him to do*, Clint thought as he turned to help Gideon, but his friend was already on the rail. He jumped and Clint followed.

Clint dove, plunging deep into the murky water, and surfaced to the sound of a choking and spitting Apolonia Vega.

"I . . . can't . . . swim," she sputtered between gags.

His eyes searched the ship's waterline and, proof of Willie's loyalty, Clint saw the captain's boat bobbing where Willie had lowered it. Clint swam to the girl, gathered the back of her smock in a hand, and dragged her to the boat. As soon as she had a hold on its gunwales, he turned back to try to find Gideon.

He was nowhere to be seen.

CHAPTER TWENTY-FOUR

FOUR WHITE DEVIL GUARDS MADE IT OUT OF THE Barracoon with two sacks full of gold. Their waiting horses took them south, the only way other than the sea that they could get out of San Francisco.

As soon as Zhang Ho's guards had discovered their route of escape, he and his guards boarded the *Fei Dao*, a slender sailing sloop with eight oars whose name meant "Swift Knife." Properly manned, she was the fastest boat in the harbor. With the wind at their back and the help of the powerful guards who served as oarsmen, she averaged fourteen knots on her trip down the bay.

She passed the new mooring place of the *Amnity* well before Clint and Gideon arrived, and reached Palo Alto, a place the Mexicans had named for its tall timber. Ho and the guards disembarked and by midnight had made their way inland to wait in the trees, and the darkness, along the roadside. Their patience was rewarded when the white guards, still wearing their Barracoon arm bands, galloped into the waiting hatchets of the Celestials. The white guards were taken by complete surprise. The battle lasted only seconds.

The horses were set free, the arm bands stripped away so the bodies would have no connection with the Barracoon, and the dead guards were dragged into the brush and left stripped and unburied for the coyotes, crows, and gulls.

Even though he sailed against the wind, taking

much more time, the trip home was a joy to Zhang Ho—he was content.

With rapid strokes Clint swam to the spot where Gideon had hit the water. Taking a deep breath, he dove and stroked down, down until his hands hit the muddy bottom. He searched frantically, but found nothing. His lungs crying for relief, he kicked off the bottom and shot to the surface, finding himself alongside the hull. The tide was coming in and the current increasing. He heard a slapping sound, then a cough in the darkness, and followed it.

Gideon, too, was alongside the *Amnity*, desperately clinging, trying to find a handhold on her slimy barnacled side.

Clint grabbed Gideon's collar from behind and kicked off the ship's rough side. "Kick your feet . . . don't move your arms."

"Can't move one," Gideon confided calmly.

Gideon's upper body went limp in Clint's grasp, but his legs took up a rhythmic kicking. By the time they reached the side of the captain's shore boat, Apolonia had managed to get her upper body over the gunwales. Gideon grasped the boat and Clint put a hand under Apolonia's bottom and shoved. She flew into the boat.

"Unhook the lines," Clint instructed her, glancing up at the *Amnity*'s rail, fearing disaster. He moved to boost Gideon. Apolonia, completing the task of casting off the block and tackle, helped the big black man aboard, then collapsed in exhaustion. Clint hoisted himself into the rocking boat, positioned himself on the rowing thwart, fixed the oars in the oarlocks, and pulled for the shore.

"There! There they be!" he heard a shout ring from the deck of the *Amnity*. He pulled oar as he never had.

Luckily a low haze lay over the water and the sliver of a moon offered little light.

"Get down," Clint cautioned as the boat cut through the water. Almost before he finished, a lead ball cut the air with a deadly whistle across the bow of the little boat and he saw the flash of a musket at the taffrail of the ship.

"Bloodly hell," Clint swore, realizing he had left the rifle behind on the ship. That rifle meant a lot to him.

Behind them the ominous silhouettes at the rail faded out of sight in the fog, and Clint slowed his pace. They would make it.

Two more wild shots hummed a frustrated note nearby after Clint worked the left oar and changed his path of flight.

"See if you can stop his bleeding," Clint instructed Apolonia, who carefully tore away the ragged bloodstained shirt at Gideon's left shoulder.

She checked the wound carefully, then began to tear away the hem of her smock. "This will hurt," she said. Without hesitation and with deft hands, she packed the gaping hole.

"You're right," Gideon calmly agreed. "It hurts. But thank you." He glanced up at Clint. "Will they follow?"

"I'm sure they're launching the longboat now. But they'll never catch up."

"My friends are aboard that ship," Apolonia said.

"More Californio women?" Clint asked between strokes with the oars.

"Five other señoritas and Gaspar Cota and three of his vaqueros."

"I'm sorry we can't help," Clint said, his tone cold, his mind on the Kaweah ranch. "But my job was to get you home safely. We'll report the other women, and maybe, with your testimony, the authorities will do something about them. As far as I'm concerned, Gaspar can shovel his own stall."

Apolonia fell suddenly silent, but she looked in the direction of the ship until the little boat grounded against the mud flat.

The horses were tied and waiting where Gideon had left them. Clint mounted Diablo, swinging up behind Apolonia, and they were off well before the crew of the *Amnity* was able to get the longboat ashore. Clint had to stop and tie Gideon to the saddle before they got back to Hardy's. Apolonia stayed with Gideon while Clint fetched a doctor, who arrived quickly to tend Gideon's wound.

"Through and through," Doc Baxter said as he dressed the wound in Gideon's shoulder. "But he's lucky. It missed the bone. The bleeding has almost stopped and I won't have to cauterize it. Rest and care and good food is the order of the day." The doctor led Clint outside. "If it goes green, call me and I'll load him up with laudanum and cut away the bad flesh."

"Thank you." Clint paid Baxter with one of the few gold coins he had left. "Stay with him," Clint instructed Apolonia, "while I fetch him a nurse."

Clint trotted the two blocks and entered the El Dorado. Pushing his way through the crowd, while Sultry was singing, he made his way to her rooms to get Su Chin. Then they exited through the alley door. Impatient with her hobble, Clint carried her back to the livery and deposited her in Gideon's room.

Then he returned to the El Dorado with Apolonia in tow and entered via the alley. They were waiting when Sultry returned from the stage.

"Where's Su Chin?" Sultry asked as she swished into the room. She sat at her dressing table and, in the mirror, noticed the beautiful Californio girl on the settee. She began to remove her heavy makeup without greeting the señorita.

Clint cleared his throat. "This is Apolonia Vega. With your permission, your new guest. Gideon took a ball through the shoulder and is flat on his back. I took Su Chin to Hardy's to nurse him."

Sultry spun on her stool to face Clint. "Is he all right?"

"He'll be all right, with rest and barring any infection."

She looked Apolonia up and down. "I swear, Clint Ryan, the Mexicans gave you the right handle. You lasso these women in like a Texican after longhorns."

"Then she can stay? It's just until tomorrow. I promised her a visit to the marshal's office before I take her home. And I sure as hell can't have her stay with me. Her father might not think that's rescuin'."

"Then when you get the señorita home, your job is finished and you can head for the gold country?"

"I never said I'd take your nursemaid job."

"But you're about to." She flashed him a smug smile. "After all, fair is fair. You haven't had any compunction about asking me to take *your* nursemaid jobs."

He looked around in frustration. "After I get her home, I'll have a herd of horses to drive south." But if Apolonia didn't have a safe place to stay he might not have a herd of horses to worry about, and with Jasper and the bevy of bartenders acting like Sultry was their chaste younger sister, backstage at the El Dorado was the safest place he knew of. And as Sultry pointed out, fair was fair.

Besides, he was bone-aching tired and needed the rest and didn't have the energy to argue.

Sultry fluttered her eyes at him. "The new fields at Sonoma are south of here, like this ranch you talk about. You can drive your herd as far as there. I'll begin and end my tour there, then you can pick them up again when I've finished and drive them to hell, for all I care." *By that time*, she vowed, *you won't want to leave me for ten thousand horses.*

"Twenty dollars a day and found against ten percent of your take," Clint said, knowing that that would bust the deal.

"And Gideon will go along?"

"I can't speak for Gideon," Clint said, wondering if his alligator mouth had overloaded his hummingbird backside.

"Done." Sultry rose, her look triumphant, and extended her hand.

"Done," Clint said quietly. With reluctance and a deep sigh, he accepted her soft handshake. She had roped him in and hog-tied him with far more skill than the Texicans she spoke about.

Clint sat down on the settee beside Apolonia and took her hand in his. "I'll see you at daybreak."

Sparks flew from Sultry's eyes, but she didn't say what she was thinking. Instead she instructed, "Don't wake me at that obscene time of day."

"No, ma'am," Clint said, and headed for the door. "Or should I say, no, boss man?"

"Only if you want to join Gideon in the recovery bed." She shot Clint a killing glance and a smile as thin as the fingernail she had begun to file.

Clint hurried back to Hardy's to check on Gideon once more. Content that Su Chin was watching him with studied care, he fell into his own narrow bed.

He was asleep in half a heartbeat, but he tossed and turned. The thought of the other Californio girls at the mercy of Harlan Stoddard and Isaac Banyon gnawed at him like a starving dog on a new bone.

If he saved him from a few months in the yard-arms, he might even get to see Gaspar Cota's flapping jaw shut for more than a second.

But he doubted it.

CHAPTER
TWENTY-FIVE

APOLONIA WAS BEAUTIFUL, WEARING ONE OF Sultry's most conservative dresses. Still the sleek black gown showed off Apolonia's ripe figure as if she, too, were a showgirl. She and Clint stood in Portsmouth Square, near the squat Mission Delores in the oldest part of the city, and awaited the arrival of Marshal Larson at his office. Clint had thought long and hard about risking a visit to the marshal's office—but Thad McPherson was dead, and he had said he had not had a chance to talk to Larson about "John Ryan."

They saw Larson at the end of the block and waited patiently as he glad-handed each of the merchants between there and his office.

"Well, howdy there," he said, exhibiting his politician's smile and snatching off his hat with his left hand while extending his right to Clint. It wasn't the kind of greeting a man with a warrant for your arrest would extend. With new confidence, Clint launched into the reason for his visit.

"Marshal, this is Apolonia Vega, the girl I was telling you about."

The marshal nodded. He opened his door and stepped aside, ushering Clint and Apolonia ahead of him.

"I'm glad you showed up, Ryan. Saves me from having to come and find you. I need a statement from you and from that darkie friend of yours about that shindig at the Barracoon." His brows furrowed like a peach pit. "Folks don't much cater to a Negra being involved in a shootin'."

He politely pulled a chair in front of his broad oak desk and seated Apolonia, then took his own chair as Clint dragged one up.

Marshal Larson snaked a cigar out of the desk drawer, leaned back and lit up, and put a foot up while he enjoyed the first draw. He exhaled a cloud of smoke.

"I see she's all right, just as I suspected." He wore a smug look and laughed gruffly. "Run off with one of those fancy-dan Mexican lads—" He frowned at Apolonia. "Having a little jollification, were you, girl?"

"No," Apolonia said coldly. "I was taken prisoner."

"Taken prisoner!" Larson repeated, his voice laced with skepticism.

"Taken prisoner," Clint snapped. "Gideon La-Mont and I boarded the *Amnity* last night and found her here."

"Boarded? Without Captain Banyon's permission? It's a wonder you aren't hanging from his yard-arm right now." He turned to Apolonia. "Captain Banyon is a well-respected man. This sounds a little farfetched. Were you locked up or chained?" Larson asked.

"She wasn't at the time. She was being accosted—" Clint glanced at her, concerned that she would be embarrassed, but her look remained hard and intense, "by the first mate, Stoddard, in his cabin."

"Sometimes," Larson said with a snicker, "with these dark-skinned girls, it's hard to tell bein' accosted from bein' pleasured." A slow smile crept across Larson's mouth. "Are you sure you didn't like that, girly?"

Clint was on his feet before Larson finished his insulting question. He leaned forward, both hands on Larson's desk.

"You know, Larson, you're as insulting as you are ignorant." Larson jumped to his feet also, but Clint continued. "I've brought you proof that the *Amnity* and her captain are behind these abductions, and all you want to do is insult this girl who's spent a week locked up on a slave ship that masquerades as a freighter. Are you going to go down there and get the other girls off her or not?"

Larson's face was as red as Apolonia's lips. "Down where?" he snapped, gnawing on his cigar.

"Hunter's Point," Clint fired back.

The marshal's side door opened, and one of Larson's deputies looked in, wondering what the raised voices were all about. Larson relaxed back in his chair and plopped his feet back up on the desk.

"I'm going to overlook your crack about ignorant, Ryan, 'cause my jail is full up from last night. As for insulting . . . these so-called Californios bring the insults on themselves." A wry smile crossed his face. "Besides, Hunter's Point is also out of my jurisdiction."

Clint's fists balled at his sides, but he could do little good for the girls still on board the *Amnity* if he was cooling his heels in Larson's filthy jail.

Without speaking, he spun on his heel and led Apolonia out of the office.

"You get back here afore the week's out and give me a statement about that mess at the Barracoon," Larson called after him, but the slamming door shut him off.

"What are we going to do?" Apolonia asked, trotting along to keep pace with his brisk stride.

"You're going to go back to Sultry's and stay out of sight. I'm going to get some help and resolve your problem."

"My problem?"

"Those other girls and Gaspar Cota are sure as hell not my problem," he snapped. Then his scowl faded. "Pardon my French."

"French?" she asked.

"Just a figure of speech. Hurry up!"

She trotted along beside him, sleek and beautiful, as he headed back to the El Dorado.

While Clint had been arguing with Larson, Isaac Banyon, Harlan Stoddard, and ten of the crew of the

Amnity arrived at the Barracoon, all armed with muskets, sidearms, and blades. Zhang Ho and his guards were not back from chasing the thieves.

Banyon, his arm and shoulder bandaged and in a sling from Apolonia's well-placed strokes with the dividers, roared at the little Chinese man who served as the Barracoon's swamper and watchman, and who had just told him about the robbery.

"By the devil's eyes, I'll draw and quarter the heathen bastard and feed his offal to the hogs, and ye, too, if ye lie to me."

"I told you,"—the little man quaked—"honorable Ho seeks men who robbed gold. He said you wait here. He has your share."

With his good right arm, Banyon snatched the man up by the front of his robe, lifting him clear off the floor. "And I'm to cool my heels here while he gets farther and farther away? The hell I will. How did the yellow scum go? By land or sea?"

"By sea, on the boat *Fei Dao*."

Banyon stormed outside and reboarded the wagon he had rented from the Chinese fishing village. Harlan Stoddard, his nose grotesquely swollen and his eyes raccoon black, whipped up the broken-down horse and they lumbered off toward the wharves.

With Apolonia back safe at the El Dorado, Clint was on his way to the wharves also. Mounted on Diablo, he reined up and watched Banyon's wagon approach. Clint hoisted his Colt's revolver an inch, just to make sure it rode free and easy in its holster, and locked eyes with Stoddard, then Banyon, who also rode in the driver's seat. Stoddard pulled rein.

Clint spoke quietly. "You've got more Californio ladies aboard that scow of yours, Banyon. You'll not get out of the harbor with them."

"I should shoot you down right here," Banyon roared, and the sailors in the rear of the wagon started to bring their weapons up.

Leather whispered, and Clint held the cocked

Colt's in hand, its deadly eye staring at the surprised sea captain.

"Any man who cocks one of those old pieces of junk will wear this bastard's brains."

Not a man twitched.

Banyon's eyes never left the end of the Colt's muzzle, which was not three feet from his face. "Whip up this wagon, Stoddard," Banyon commanded coldly.

Carefully Harlan tapped the old mare's flank with the buggy whip, and the horse began to clomp away. The Colt's tracked the wagon as it rolled by, and none of the men in the back took their eyes off it or moved.

"I'll see you long before you pass through the Golden Gate," Clint called after them.

"I'll rein up as soon as we get out of pistol range and shoot that son of a bitch with his own rifle," Stoddard offered quietly, toeing Clint's Colt's rifle, which rode in the floorboards under Stoddard's feet, stained across the butt with Stoddard's own blood.

"Not here, but you may get your chance," Banyon growled. "He's a brazen bastard, and I expect he'll do just as he says."

"Let him come," Stoddard wheezed, for he couldn't breath through his swollen nose. "I'll be ready for him this time."

"That would be a pleasant change, Mr. Stoddard." Banyon glanced at his first mate and shook his head in disgust. "But far more important than Clint Ryan and your pride is Zhang Ho and my money. We'll check the waterfront, and if we don't spot the *Fei Dao*, I must presume he's run for it. The *Amnity* will chase that sloop and the yellow scum down, and I'll see him swinging at the end of my halyards.

"Hurry this nag up," Banyon snapped.

Clint needed help, and it was now plain that he wasn't going to get any from the law.

But he thought he knew where he might buy some loyalty, even if only for a short time. Even if he would have to watch his back.

For over an hour he searched the Barbary Coast,

looking for the guns he needed, before he reined Diablo up in front of the Outback Roo. He dismounted and tied the big palomino where he could watch it from inside the batwing doors, and entered. As he had hoped, he spotted Fish Shaddock and his big friend, Booker Whittle, standing at the bar among another half dozen Sydney Ducks.

Clint boldly pushed his way through the men, faced Fish, and got right to the point. "I need to hire you men for a day's honest work."

Most of them looked at him like he'd lost his mind, but Fish immediately responded. "I act as the agent here, mate. You talk with me if you want help from the Ducks."

"Yeah," Booker agreed. His scarred face broke with a snaggletoothed grin "Fish is boss."

"Come over to my office," Fish said, motioning Clint to a table. Booker loitered nearby, but stayed just out of earshot.

"What's the work?" Fish asked.

"Pistol and rifle work. Settin' some conscripts loose from the *Amnity.*"

Fish laughed and slapped his thigh. "That's a by-Christ lark. We'll be gettin' paid comin' and goin'." His laugh faded. "What's the pay, mate?"

"Twenty dollars a man for the try, win or lose, and twenty dollars a head bonus for every conscript freed."

"How many?"

"Nine, by my count."

"In gold?" Fish's voice dropped, and he bent closer.

"Gold," Clint assured him.

"You got that much gold on you now?" Fish asked, glancing at Booker.

"You might be crazy, Fish"—Clint smiled—"but don't take me for a fool."

"Then how do I know we get paid?"

Clint reached into his pocket and pulled his last five-dollar gold pieces out. He slapped them on the table. "This'll seal the bargain. You get the rest when the work's done."

Fish swiped the money off the table and pocketed it, then extended his slender hand, and they shook. Clint started to get up. "Wait," Fish said, and motioned him closer. "No need for the boys to know about the bonus. Let's keep that 'tween you and me," he said, his look hopeful and his tone conspiratorial.

"Just you and me, Fish," Clint assured him. He didn't give a damn how the money was split; he was more concerned with where he would get it and what these Ducks would do if he could not produce at the end of the day.

"Get your boys outside," Clint instructed. "And Fish—let them know that I'm running this operation. They take orders from me."

"Your gold, your orders," Fish agreed, then moved away to the bar to strike his own bargain with the Ducks.

CHAPTER
TWENTY-SIX

CLINT MOUNTED DIABLO AND WONDERED HOW he was going to get eight men back to the *Amnity*. He had no money left and he sure as hell couldn't give the Ducks even a hint of that fact. He glanced to where they stood on the boardwalk, awaiting his orders.

Hardy would give him credit for horses for the day, he thought. Then he looked out on the wharf and saw Zhang Ho and the guards disembarking the *Fei Dao*.

Maybe things are going my way, he decided, and called to Fish, "I'll be right back."

Spurring Diablo, he galloped through the piles of goods, Diablo's pounding hooves making a hollow drumming ring on the wooden planks, out to where the little sloop had tied up alongside Long Wharf.

Pulling rein, Clint dismounted before Diablo came to a complete stop. The guards surrounded Zhang Ho protectively, but relaxed when they saw who the rider was.

"Ho, I need your help to get those girls off the *Amnity* before she sails. Do this for me and I'll help you recover the money the guards stole."

"That problem is resolved, honorable friend. I can offer money, I can offer men if I have time to hire those who Banyon cannot identify with the Barracoon or the tong, but as I told you, I cannot be tied to the effort."

"Have you given Banyon his cut yet?"

"No. I expect he'll be waiting at the Barracoon."

"Banyon was heading away from the Barracoon the last time I saw him, looking mad as a stepped-on rattler and twice as nasty. But I hope he is going back there to wait for you." *That'll mean fewer men to face aboard the Amnity*, Clint thought. "Money I'll need," he told Ho, "and that boat."

"You can sail her?"

"Like I built her," Clint said.

Ho thoughtfully stroked the tails of his long mustache, then smiled. "If it comes to it, I will say you have stolen her."

"That'll work," Clint agreed. He called down the wharf and waved to his new gang of Ducks. Tying Diablo's reins to the saddle horn, he slapped him on the rump and sent him running, knowing he would go straight back to the livery and that Hardy would care for him.

"May your ancestors remember you fondly," Zhang Ho said, then hurried his men away, including the one who served as captain of the *Fei Dao*.

By the time the Ducks got alongside, the jib was tied off and Clint was running up the main sail of the sloop. He waved them down and they took up positions at the oar thwarts.

"I get seasick," Fish said sheepishly, "and these boys ain't partial to rowing."

"God willing, the wind'll do the work," Clint said just as the sail billowed and he cast off the dock line. He took the tiller and swung the quick little sloop away from the wharf.

"Maybe the work, but how about me belly?"

They had been under way for almost two hours when they made out the *Amnity* under full sail and heading northerly, the direction of the Golden Gate and open sea. She heeled in the brisk wind less than two miles away from them, on a diagonal course—a course Clint did not believe he could intercept.

"Damn," Clint grumbled under his breath. Fish looked up from the bottom of the *Fei Dao*, where he'd been since he'd finished chumming with the contents of his stomach.

"What?" Fish asked, moaning quietly.

"The *Amnity*. She's under full sail and heading for the China Sea."

"We still get the money. Win or lose, you said."

"With a little luck, I can cut across her bow." Clint spoke more to himself than to the Ducks, but as soon as he adjusted the sloop's course and trimmed her sails, the *Amnity* pointed even closer to the wind as if she were attempting to bear down on the sloop.

Clint quickly made a mental note of the armaments on board the packet ship. She was no cruiser, but he remembered a small six-pound waist gun amidships on each side, and an even smaller three-pound swivel gun mounted on her aft rail.

The sloop, too, was armed. A little two pound swivel gun rested on her bow.

"Do you know how to load that gun?" Clint called to Booker, who sat at a forward thwart.

Booker examined the two-foot iron cannon with slow but studied thoroughness. "Can't be much of a chore," he finally said.

The bow of the sloop was decked-over three feet back. Booker searched under the cover and came up with a two-inch-bore cannon and a small keg of powder.

"Don't bother with the ball. Load her with five ounces of powder and two dozen pistol balls." Booker looked at Clint for a moment, studying the suggestion. "We can't do a damn bit of harm to the hull," Clint ordered. "It's the men we're after."

Booker nodded, and set about the task as the *Amnity* closed to within half a mile.

He rammed the small swabber home, ready to fire, but the *Amnity* swung away, her course perpendicular to the *Fei Dao*. "Damn," Clint cursed under his breath, thinking that she was tacking, running for the open sea. But suddenly the sailors in her shrouds began to gather sail when she luffed in the turn, and she slowed.

"I'll be . . . she's heaving to—" before he finished, the six-pounder on her starboard amidships spat a bellow of fire and smoke.

"Duck!" Clint yelled, but rather than hitting the deck, each of the Sydney Ducks turned to see who Clint was yelling at.

Two of the men on the second thwart were blown overboard and the mainsail was holed as some of the grapeshot found its target.

"Jesus!" Booker yelled. Wide-eyed, he swung the bow gun on target. Leaning far back, he snatched a cigar out of the hand of the Duck who sat on the thwart behind him, puffed it with a long draw, and held it to the cannon's touch hole.

The sloop rattled with the recoil of the swivel gun and Clint got a moment's satisfaction when the men amidships on board the *Amnity* dove for cover. But the little gun only bought he and his men a moment.

One more shot from the six-pounder and the *Fei Dao* would be out of business. He swung the tiller and headed the sloop for the bowsprit of the ship, where a webbing of line formed a net of last resort for any man who tumbled overboard, and where a bowsprit stay ran from the end low to the hull. Either of those could be handholds, and a path to the deck.

"She'll crush us," Booker warned.

Fish raised his head just over the gunwale, looking even sicker. He buried his face in his hands and hugged the bottom of the sloop.

"No, she won't," Clint said. "Get ready to jump for those lines. We'll climb up onto the bow!"

The Ducks stared at him as if he'd completely lost his mind.

Clint slid his Colt's from its holster. "Any man who doesn't make the jump will face the six-pounder on her far side, and that shot will be point-blank."

He didn't have to say any more as the men fixed their eyes on the bow of the *Amnity*, closing less than thirty yards ahead. Clint took a turn about the tiller with a dock line and fixed her course. Then he scrambled forward. Passing the mast, he threw the halyards off their cleats and the sails dropped, slowing the vessel.

At the last moment, Clint snatched up the keg of powder and tucked it under his arm. Only four of them made the jump. Two others fell back onto the *Fei Dao*, and one fell into the water. Fish didn't make the attempt, he was so sick. He elected to take his chances against the larboard six-pounder. The bow of the ship caught the aft of the sloop. With a sickening scrape, the sloop slammed against the hull of the ship and slid alongside, undamaged, but so close the starboard gunners had no shot.

The four from the *Fei Dao* made the deck, hidden by the three slack jib sails forward of the mizzenmast. They moved forward, seen only by the ship's crewmen high above tending the shrouds, and none of those men were armed. A man yelled a warning to the deck crew, who had gathered at the larboard rail, hoping to see the sloop destroyed by the six-pounder. Eight men, Banyon and Stoddard among them, looked overboard at the sloop scraping alongside the *Amnity*.

Clint, Booker, and the other two Ducks began a barrage of fire into the men.

Two men dropped immediately. Others dove away in confusion. Banyon and Stoddard headed for the cover of the aft passageway, jumping down the half ladder.

"Booker, come with me!" Clint yelled. "You two keep those men in the shrouds. If a man from above tries to make the deck, shoot him. Keep those forward in the fo'c'sle."

The men above heard the order and headed up into the cover of the canvas and line.

Clint and Booker ran for the aft passageway. Two crewmen, one wounded, raised their hands in surrender.

"I want only Banyon and Stoddard," Clint yelled.

"They're all yours," one of the sailors told him.

A muzzle flashed in the darkness of the passageway, and Clint dove for the deck, the powder keg under one arm. The ball sliced his back, burning like a hot poker.

"Just a crease," Booker called from his position on the other side of the entrance.

Clint snapped off two shots into the darkness and heard a man scream. He rolled to the side and made the quarterdeck, out of sight of the passageway.

"I'm hit, Captain," he heard Stoddard shout.

"Stop ye whining, ye sogger," Banyon said. "Get up on deck and put the lead in that bastard Ryan."

"Get up there yourself!" Stoddard's voice had lost its power. Clint heard a cabin door slam, and he knew he had Banyon. Like a rat in a trap. He moved aft on the quarterdeck to a ventilator, studying it for a second. It looked big enough for what he had in mind. He went to the mizzenmast and jerked the anchor lantern down. With his belt knife he cut away a piece of line from a halyard, unraveled a third of it, and poured whale oil on it, soaking it.

He stuffed the homemade fuse into the bunghole of the gallon-sized powder keg and moved back to the ventilator.

"Do you have a lucifer?" he asked Booker, who stood forward, guarding the passageway from above.

Booker made his way aft to where Clint worked with the keg. "I believe I do," he said, a slow smile crossing his face.

Clint situated the keg in the ventilator. It would not drop all the way into the captain's cabin, for there were flutes to carry away seawater in case the deck was awash, but the opening it did have would be enough.

Clint dragged Booker's match across the bottom of the lantern, touched it to the fuse, and ran for the mizzenmast. Booker dove behind a deck box.

The blast rocked the ship and sent splinters whistling across the deck and smoke and fire billowing up into the shrouds.

Clint rose, his ears ringing and his eyes watering from the noise and acrid smoke.

"That should do it," Clint said.

Booker gave him a wide snaggletoothed grin. "I believe that was one of the least neighborly things I ever saw done, mate."

"Let's go below and see if we did our task in a good and workmanlike manner." Clint jumped cautiously to the main deck and peered into the passageway. The door to the captain's cabin had been split in half and blown away.

"I'm hit already," Stoddard moaned from behind his closed door. "Please don't blow me up. I'm gut shot." His voice rang hollow with fear.

Clint palmed his Colt's and moved carefully past Stoddard's door to the rear, passing the door to the officers' mess. An Aston pistol lay on the floor. Stoddard's? Or Banyon's?

He stepped over half the door that blocked his way.

"Ye bastard!" The words came from behind him. The mess door crashed aside and powerful arms closed around his. "I'll kill ye with my own bare hands."

Clint tried to bring the pistol to bear, but Banyon, having shed the sling, held him in a crushing bear hug from behind.

"With my own hands," Banyon snarled. Clint could feel the man's beard on the side of his neck and smell his rancid breath. The ironlike arms forced Clint's ribs into his lungs.

"No, you won't." Booker's quiet voice wheezed though his many-times broken nose.

The roar of the pistol was so close to Clint's ear that its flame singed his hair. He dropped to the ground, but the captain fell on top of him. He turned to fight, his mind reeling from the shock of the blast, and kicked free. Glancing at Banyon, he realized half the man's head had been blown away.

"Jesus," Clint managed.

"You would have blown him all over the back of the ship," Booker said, umbrage on his scarred and bent face.

"True enough." Clint smiled and came to his feet.

"True enough, indeed, mate. I thank you. At least I will when my ears stop ringing."

"Say nothing of it." Booker's twisted grin returned.

"Now, let's see to Mr. Stoddard and the ladies—"

"Ladies?" Booker's scarred eyebrows raised.

"Some of the conscripts are ladies, mate. But don't worry about it. You fellows will still get your full share."

"I'll be damned," Booker mumbled.

"You get Stoddard's gun, and I'll get down below to free the women and their men. Then we'll get this scow back to San Francisco."

When Booker kicked open the first mate's door, Stoddard made no complaint. He never would again.

Clint smashed in the door to the passengers' cabin and found the women cowering together in a corner.

"You're free," he said simply.

"We were afraid that terrible explosion would sink the ship," Juanita Robles said. Then she realized what the man had said. "Free?"

"Free," he repeated. "Compliments of Don Carlos Vega."

The women crossed themselves, then sank to their knees to thank God and Don Carlos and the sandy-haired man who had kicked in their door.

It took Clint a while to locate Gaspar and the vaqueros, still chained and shackled in the hold.

He held a lantern in front of him and walked the ribs.

"You," Gaspar moaned. "You are the bastard behind this."

"Hardly, Cota. I'm the *gentleman* who's come to free you."

Gaspar glared in silence, reconciling in his mind that he was about to be freed by the Anglo. "You were paid well," Gaspar exclaimed with a haughty glance.

"You weren't part of the deal," Clint said.

"Don Cota," Chato snapped, "this man has been wounded trying to set us free."

Clint glanced down and saw the blood from the wound in his back had soaked his pants.

"You are a miserable whelp," Chato said, glaring at Gaspar, "and I will whip you one-handed if you don't tuck your flapping tongue back in your mouth—that is, if this gentleman will set us free." He glanced up at Clint. "I, for one, would be forever indebted if you would find a wrench and remove these cursed manacles."

"With pleasure," Clint said. "And you will be first, amigo."

Gaspar remained silent.

CHAPTER TWENTY-SEVEN

CLINT MADE HIS PEACE WITH SULTRY, TELLING her he would meet her and Jasper in Stockton in a week. From there, they would go on to Sonora together. He was surprised to learn when he returned to Hardy's that Su Chin had left Gideon in the care of a young Chinese man.

"Where'd she go, Gideon?" Clint asked his friend, who was sitting up, eating some Chinese vegetable concoction with enthusiasm.

"Don't know," he answered between bites. "She said this young man would lead me to her when I got well enough to worry about it."

"When do you think that's going to be?"

"Doc was here this morning. Said I could get up and around day after tomorrow."

"I've got to take Apolonia back to her father. I would have taken her today, but I had to make my peace with Marshal Larson and see to the *Amnity*. Seems Banyon has a wife who owns her now that he's met his maker. I've already sent word to Apolonia's father that she's all right, but I know he's anxious to have her home."

"I'd like to go along," Gideon said, "if you can wait until I can travel."

"I can wait, but I don't know if Sultry can stand Apolonia's company for that long. She looked at me like a bull at a bastard calf when I asked her if Apolonia could stay there awhile longer."

"Somehow," Gideon said with a knowing grin,

"I think Sultry would keep a grizzly bear in her room if you asked."

"You've got more faith in my persuasive abilities than I have," Clint said with a laugh.

The next day Gideon convinced Clint that he could accompany him to find Su Chin. They took it slow and easy, and rested when Gideon began to tire. But they followed the Chinese boy down to the waterfront until he pointed ahead. "Su Chin house," he said, smiling proudly.

A long line of men, all shapes and sizes and colors, stretched for a block away from a small clapboard house.

"This Su Chin line," the boy said in his broken English.

Clint and Gideon looked at each other, each face reflecting the other's disappointment.

"I had hoped . . ." Clint started to say.

"Me too," Gideon agreed. "But I'll be damned if I'll wait in any consarned line when all I want to do is pay my respects."

They moved down the block, passing the group of men, and mounted the four steps in front of the house. The men in the front of the line gave them a hard look, but Gideon's sling and Clint's gift with the blarney got them by. "I'm with the city's new building and construction and pest inspection and—" Two massive guards met them in the tiny living room, making it clear that the two newcomers would wait their turn.

"Su Chin," Gideon shouted past the burly guards, who prepared to toss him and Clint out the door.

She hobbled to the kitchen door before the confrontation came to a head. "Wait, wait," she commanded the guards. "These are my partners."

She motioned the two of them in. Her dress was the finest green silk and she wore no jewelry, except a single red stone the size of Clint's thumb that hung at the end of a gold chain around her neck.

"Partner, hell," Clint grumbled. "I'm no purveyor of women."

"Come in, prease." She hobbled away.

Clint and Gideon moved around the guards, giving them a conquering look. Su Chin reclined on a pillow on the kitchen floor. A grizzled full-bearded miner sat across from her—sipping tea.

"You no mind, Mr. Johnston?" Su Chin sweetly asked the man. "Only two more minutes. If you get back to end of line, I give you ten minutes free next time."

"Surely, ma'am. Don't mind if I do." The man scrambled to his feet and, hat in hand, backed out of the kitchen. "I'll be back, as soon as I get through the line again."

Clint's face still wore a look of disappointment, if a somewhat confused one. "What are you doing, Su Chin?"

"Name now Ruby Su Chin," she answered, looking a little embarrassed. "Su Chin work to repay loan." She smiled demurely.

"Why do you call yourself Ruby?" Gideon asked.

"First customer cheat Su Chin. Give me red glass. Say is ruby." She blushed. "Su Chin now have name to remind her not to be cheated again."

"But you didn't have to . . . to . . ." Clint wanted to tell her that an honest job would have gotten the money back soon enough, but he couldn't find just the right words.

"I think you no understan', honorable Clint." She bowed, then giggled. "Miner pay one ounce gold to have tea with Su Chin for ten minute . . . then maybe two ounce if Su Chin show honorable feet."

"Feet?" Gideon worked to keep his chin from dropping to his chest.

She turned and pulled a small box from under the pillow. Opening it, she offered it to Clint, who took it out of her hands. "Please to apply to loan," she said.

"There's over a hundred dollars in gold here," Clint stammered. "You couldn't have been at this for more than a day."

"Su Chin start ten o'clock this morning. Will have rest of money by end of week."

Gideon glanced at Clint. "We're in the wrong by-God business."

They visited awhile longer, taking up valuable time, until the clamor outside the door began to worry the guards.

Clint and Gideon rested on the top rail of Don Vega's corral fence, admiring the forty head of Andalusian horses—five stallions and thirty-five mares, some of them already with foal—that Clint and Sancho, the Vega's head vaquero, had cut out of the huge herd that roamed the Rancho Del Rio Ancho.

Apolonia Vega and her father stood a few steps away, arguing for the tenth time that morning.

"I'll not marry a man who's not of my choosing, Father."

"You'll do as I say," he snapped, his tone as adamant as hers.

"Never, never, never," she vowed. Tears forming in her eyes, she turned and ran for the hacienda.

"Women." Don Vega moaned. Walking over, he mounted the corral rail and sat next to Clint.

Apolonia stopped midway to the house. With a secret smile she turned and walked back to where her father, Clint, and Gideon sat.

"I cannot marry Gaspar Cota," Apolonia announced from behind the three men, who repositioned themselves on the rail to face her.

"Apolonia, we have been over and over this," Don Vega said, his voice ringing with frustration.

"No, we haven't, Father. Tell him, Mr. LaMont."

"I beg your pardon?"

"Tell him about Stoddard."

"What about Stoddard?" Don Vega said, and Gideon and Clint began to worry.

"He took my honor."

"What?" her father roared.

"It is true," Apolonia said, relief in her voice. "Tell him, Mr. LaMont."

Don Vega stared into Gideon's dark face, his look pleading for reassurance that it wasn't so.

"I don't know," Gideon said truthfully.

"And just what do you think he was doing, Mr. LaMont?" Apolonia asked.

"Well, it was dark, and I couldn't see real well."

Clint could have sworn Gideon was beginning to blush, but Clint was beginning to see what Apolonia was trying to accomplish, and he decided to help her.

"He was surely in a position—"

"*Mi Dios!*" Don Vega looked crestfallen. "The Cota family will never allow it."

"But we don't have to let anyone know, Father." Apolonia laid a hand on her father's arm, placating him with her soft voice. "Just tell the Cotas that the wedding is off."

"If they don't have to know . . ." His voice rang with hope. "Surely you women have ways . . . ways to fool a man." He glanced at Clint and Gideon. It was his turn to color.

"I would not know, Father. But this woman will tell the Cotas, if you attempt to force this wedding."

Don Vega dismounted from the rail, his head hanging. He made his way to the hacienda, Clint, Gideon, and Apolonia staring after him.

"He'll get over it," she finally said.

"Stoddard didn't really . . . he didn't . . ." Gideon's jaw tightened at the thought that he hadn't been in time to prevent Stoddard from having his way.

Apolonia flashed him a sly grin, winked at him, and with ladylike grace walked after her father.

"I'll never understand women," Clint said.

"I'm not sure I want to."

They readjusted their positions on the top rail and looked over the small herd of horses.

"I'm gonna need some help driving these animals to Sonora. How about coming along?" Clint asked.

Gideon tipped his top hat. "I believe I've taken to the city life." That drew a smile from Clint.

"Hasn't it been about long enough for the La-Monts to have gotten your letter, and couldn't they be on their way to San Francisco by now? How many of them did you say there were?"

"Henri had two brothers and an uncle with four grown sons." Gideon arched an eyebrow, beginning to see what Clint was driving at.

"All duelers and dead shots, I believe you said."

"You're cagey as those cotton-pickin' women, Clint Ryan."

"If you don't want to risk being back pickin' cotton, maybe you'd like a job driving horses. Doesn't pay much, but it beats gettin' beat." Clint jumped off the rail into the corral.

"I'll have you know I held a position in the stable caring for the family's best stock. Then I became Henri LaMont's personal man." Gideon's look changed to one of compliance. "Maybe a little time in the gold country wouldn't be so bad after all." Gideon tipped his high hat again. "Think I can trade this for a sombrero?"

"Pick yourself out a cayuse, cowhand." Clint laughed and shook out his reata.

If you enjoyed THE DEVIL'S BOUNTY
by Larry Jay Martin, you will be thrilled
by his next novel for Bantam.
History comes to life as never before in:

RUSH
TO
DESTINY

Here is an exciting preview of this new
novelization of the life of Edward Fitzgerald Beale,
a true hero of the West, to be published in 1992.
It will be available wherever Bantam Books are sold.

Turn the page for a preview of
RUSH TO DESTINY, by Larry Jay Martin.

The afternoon of the next day, Navy lieutenant Ned Beale, his black-Indian companion Jourdan, Marine Major Archibald Gillespie, Scout Alexis Godey, the deserter Machado, and twenty-five San Diego volunteers loped into Warner's rancho and dismounted in front of a squat wide-shouldered General Kearny and his exhausted and trail-worn dragoon officers.

Kearny's men were enjoying the first meal of fresh beef in over six weeks, a change from the "Missouri elk"—mule—they had been relegated to eating.

Ned introduced himself and handed the parchment to Kearny, who wrinkled his brow and motioned for Ned and Gillespie to follow him into his tent.

The general whipped his hat off and wiped the water from his face with a kerchief, then unfolded the parchment. He read silently, grunted, and flung the parchment aside unceremoniously.

"This commodore, Stockton, has declared himself king of California?"

Ned cleared his throat. "Commodore Stockton and the Navy have been at this for some time, General. It was necessary for him to establish some command for the Californios to look up to."

"Fill me in, gentlemen." Kearny motioned for the two officers to take seats in folding chairs surrounding a small map table, and sat down. "I'd offer coffee, but we've been out for three weeks."

Ned rose and stuck his head out the tent flap to yell at Jourdan. "Break out the coffee. These men look as if they could use some."

The other dragoon officers who had gathered outside the tent smiled at the thought of hot coffee, their breath white in the cold as they blew into cupped hands. Ned returned to his chair.

"I notice your stock is broken down and sorry-looking."

"It's been a rough trip, on men and stock," Kearny agreed. Then a short man in buckskins and fur hat stuck his head in the door.

"Kit!" Ned said. He and Gillespie rose and extended hands. "I thought you'd be in Washington."

"General Kearny here turned me 'round in New Mexico. Ol' Broken Hand Fitzpatrick carried the commodore's packet on. I'm sure its been a-gatherin' dust in Polk's office for several days. . . . I just wanted to howdy you boys." He nodded and backed out of the tent after an uncharacteristic full paragraph of speech—it was normally yea and nay with Kit Carson, and little more.

"We'll come jaw with you as soon as General Kearny's through with us," Ned called after him, then turned his attention back to Kearny, and was surprised to note the general's obvious antagonism toward Kit Carson.

"The man actually had the effrontery to argue with me regarding leading me back here," the general groused.

"He's an independent sort," Ned said, not bothering to inform the general of a fact he already knew, that Carson was beholding to no man or army. He was an independent contractor.

Gillespie and Ned filled the general in on the past few months' activities in California, including the news that Pico and his soldados were rumored to be nearby—just outside of San Pasqual. When Ned related Fremont's appointment as provisional governor, Ned could see the general's hackles rise.

"Governor! A shavetail *colonel* in the topographical corps. And a colonel by the grace of a Navy commodore. A commodore who only yesterday signed a dispatch as 'governor.' Pardon me gentlemen, but this whole thing's a laugh." But he was not laughing.

"I'm sure the commodore did what he thought was right, and, General, he was acting on the orders of the Secretary of the Navy," Ned managed, as the general reached over and pulled a slightly damp cigar out of Gillespie's pocket.

"You don't mind," the general said. Oblivious to whether Gillespie minded or not, he bit the end off and spit it on the dirt floor. He lit the cigar, having to work at it to quell the dampness, and puffed a few times, seemingly in deep thought. Then he rose.

"And I am operating on the direct orders of the president of the United States. You're dismissed, gentlemen," he brayed. "The Army is here now, and I'm acting on the orders of the *president* to establish a civil government, and things will soon be under control. What's past is past. The commodore's *attempts* will be noted and appreciated . . . such as they were."

Ned and Gillespie rose as Kearny walked out into the rain, then followed. Kearny turned to his men.

"Pack up, gentlemen. Sleep in your slickers tonight, ready to ride before dawn. We've got word of a considerable force of Californios nearby." Kearny yawned and stretched nonchalantly. "And we're going to rout the bastards."

Kearny called to one of his lieutenants. The man walked over, his eyes ringed with dark exhaustion. But he nodded enthusiastically at Kearny's order.

"Mr. Hammond, find the Mexican camp, without being found out, and get back here well before dawn."

Beale stepped forward. "I know something of the country, General. I'd be happy to accompany the lieutenant."

Kearny looked Beale up and down and clamped his teeth on the stub of the cigar. "We don't need any more damned Navy interference."

Without the formality of a salute, Ned spun on his heel and stomped away. Kit Carson rose from a nearby fire and joined him.

"He's mule-headed," Kit said, his short legs working to keep up with Ned.

Ned strode to the shelter of a yawning live oak before he paused. His jaws muscles worked.

Kit stood a minute, smiling. "I don't figure you got any chewin' backy?"

"Not a chewin' man, Kit. Sorry."

"Been outta chaw most of a month." He studied Ned with a glint of humor in his eye. "You're gonna wear your chompers down like a twenty-year mule, you keep a-gnashin' 'em thataway."

Ned, realizing he was working his jaw like a dog worrying a bone, gave Kit a tight smile. "You've been putting up with the general for two months. Is he always this hardheaded?"

"One thing I've learnt 'bout Kearny . . . he's seldom wrong."

Ned snapped his head up, then realized Carson was being sarcastic.

"I notice the more brass a man totes, the righter he is," Carson added.

Ned clapped the little scout on the back. "Let's go find Godey. He's got a chaw for you."

"I don't imagine ol' Alex might have a dollop of cactus juice?"

"I wouldn't be a damn bit surprised, Kit. Not a damn bit." They turned their collars up against the cold and rain, strode out from under the cover of the oak into a heavy rainfall, and went hunting Alex Godey.

Kearny, dreary-eyed and open-collared, stood warming his hands outside his tent where his orderly had a fire going. Lieutenant Thomas Hammond, soaking wet from his night's foray, stood erect at the general's side, his voice ringing with excitement.

"I found them, General. Must be most of a hundred of them."

"And did they find *you*, Lieutenant?"

"I'm not positive," he said, uncertainty ringing in his voice. "A sentry challenged us, and we turned tail.

I'd guess they figured we were unfriendly, the way we lit outta there."

"Still, there's a good chance . . ." Kearny folded his hands behind his back and paced.

Rolled in his oilcloth nearby, Ned, with a group including Carson, Godey, and Jourdan, watched and listened as the general turned to his orderly.

"Have reveille sounded. We ride out in twenty minutes."

Long before dawn, the column formed up.

Dragoon Captain Abraham Robinson Johnston, with an advance guard of twelve, rode in the lead. Kearny rode close behind with Lieutenant William Hemsley Emory of the topographical engineers and five other surveyors, and with Lieutenant William Horace Warner. Captain Benjamin D. Moore and Lieutenant Hammond followed with fifty dragoons.

Another fifty followed in no particular order, some riding with the baggage, some forming up with friends, whether in their particular unit or not. When Kearny had met up with Carson, he'd had more than four hundred men with him. But hearing that the California situation was well in hand, he had sent the majority of his men on to Mexico to help with the war effort there.

At Kearny's direct orders, Ned trailed far in the rear with Major Thomas Swords and the baggage—and Kearny must have considered the cannon baggage, since the four pieces—including the small four-pounder Gillespie had dragged from San Diego, and which had earlier been hauled all the way from Sutter's Fort—were spaced among the pack mules. Jourdan had elected to ride with Ned rather than with the other volunteers.

The column, decrepit horses and mules hanging their heads in exhaustion, began to string out almost immediately after leaving Warner's rancho, and Captain Henry Smith Turner, on a fresh mount obtained at Warner's, continually rode back and forth trying the keep the ranks closed up. The rain pounded down, hampering horses and men and causing the cannon to slip and slide on the narrow road, a road not much more than wagon tracks, and often much less.

After a few hours on the trail, Ned unrolled his oilcloth and rode along under the protection of its cover, reloading the Allen's revolver with dry powder from the cotton sacks that it had been tightly rolled in it. He carried his saber, his single-shot muzzle-loading cap-and-ball carbines hanging from a saddle ring, and his Allen's. He knew neither firearm was worth a tinker's damn if the powder was wet. Jourdan also carried a carbine and Allen's, but no cutlass.

Reholstering his revolver, Ned commented to Major Swords, "Shouldn't the order be given to have these men recharge their weapons?"

Swords cast Ned a sideways glance. "You want to ride forward and suggest to General Kearny that he may have forgotten something so basic?"

Ned would have laughed if it wasn't so important. "Your good general suggested I keep my position here with the baggage. It might come better from you."

"General only listen to general," Jourdan quietly put in.

Swords ignored the zambo's remark. "Suggestions, in this outfit, originate from the general, *as undisputable orders.*" Swords shook his head, seemingly in disgust, but as a good officer he would not directly condemn his superior. Nevertheless, Ned saw that Swords promptly pulled his own revolver and, without further comment, began recharging it. Jourdan followed suit.

"The hell with it," Ned said, spurring his horse out and around the column. He knew that just ahead the road forked, and with the condition of these men and their animals, he decided he had to put his two bits in with Kearny. As he passed Gillespie, the major, too, spurred his horse and followed.

They reined up beside the general.

"Something the matter in the rear, Lieutenant?" Kearny snapped to Ned, who now rode directly beside him.

"No, sir," Ned answered as politely as he could manage. "The road forks just ahead, General. If we take the left, we bypass San Pasqual. These Mexicans will be mounted on fresh stock. The finest horses I've ever seen, ridden by the finest horsemen in the world—"

"Poppycock. I don't suppose you've ever seen the Apache ride?"

"No, sir," Ned admitted. "Still, all in all, I'd say the Californio is among the finest."

"And I concur," Gillespie offered. To Ned's surprise, the Marine agreed with his conservative approach.

"So what are you suggesting?"

"I'm suggesting that we avoid San Pasqual, give your men and animals a chance to recover from the desert crossing and get their strength back, and give us a chance to provide the men with fresh mounts."

"You have fresh mounts at San Diego?" Kearny asked, obviously already tired of Ned's suggestions.

"Possibly, by now. We brought in a herd of horses, and even now they're being broken."

"So you want me to avoid a contact with the enemy in order to obtain horses that are unbroken . . . or at best green. That's good Navy reasoning, I suppose." Kearny shook his head in disgust. "I suggest you return to the rear of the column, and don't move forward again unless ordered."

"Yes, sir." Ned saluted without enthusiasm. He started to spin his horse, then hesitated. "My own powder was getting damp, General. Shouldn't you have your men—"

"By God, man, you can be infuriating!" Kearny brayed, red in the face. Ned gave the spurs to the horse. Gillespie stayed beside the general for a moment, but he did not gain even a glance from the thickset man. Finally the major quietly reined his animal around and returned to his Marines.

Ned reined up between Jourdan and Swords. They did not bother to ask him about his success with Kearny—the look on his face was enough.

They rode in silence for another half hour, the rain now a drizzle but still dampening the men's interest in conversation. Faces remained buried as deeply as possible in upturned collars. On the crest of a rise up ahead, the forward section of the column halted.

"What's up?" Swords asked.

"San Pasqual is just over that rise." Ned pointed. The mountains, climbing steep on either side and covered with chaparral, were clouded in mist, their tops not visible. Ned saw Kearny, over a quarter mile ahead of him, raise his cutlass in the air in an enthusiastic motion, and saw the small troop—Captain Johnston's lead guard—joined by a number of surveyors, spur their horses and disappear over the rise.

Unable to contain himself, Ned dug heels to his own horse. He was damned if he would be caught guarding a bunch of pack mules if the action was about to begin. Besides, he knew he was one of the few men well-enough mounted to do any good against the Mexicans. Swords stayed with his cannon, but Jourdan galloped close behind. By the time they reached the head of the column, which had crested the rise, Ned could see the troop strung out in front of him, including Kit Carson and some of the San Diego volunteers who had left Gillespie's band—and a group of Mexican soldados, thirty strong, riding easily away in front of them. A few straggled shots echoed up the canyon when the dragoons fired after the soldados.

As Ned passed Kearny, he heard the general shout after him, victory ringing in his voice. "Avoid this, eh, Beale? It's a rout . . . a bloody rout, you Navy slacker!"

But as far ahead as the men rode, Ned could see that the Mexicans were not earnestly riding away. If they had been they would have quickly outdistanced the dragoons.

Apprehension flooded Ned, and almost instantly he saw another group of lancers sweep down onto the trail out of the deep chaparral—behind the strung-out dragoons. Reatas sung in the air and the men were jerked out of their saddles. Many were able to unsheath their heavy cutlasses, but they were no match for the long lances of the mounted soldados when carbines misfired from damp powder.

Ahead, Carson and the volunteers caught up with the uneven fight, but Kit's horse stumbled and the little scout flew forward, rolling deftly into the chaparral. Ned saw him rise and pick up his carbine—broken in half at the breech. As Ned and Jourdan pounded by, Ned unclipped his own carbine, yelled "Carson!" and flung it to Kit, who caught it on the fly and turned to make his way up into the chaparral where he could find a vantage point

His cutlass unsheathed and in his left hand, Ned began firing his Allen's from his right when he got within range. His chest surged with anger when he saw the numbers of dragoons lanced and dying on the canyon floor.

He sensed something to his right, and ducked just as Jourdan yelled a warning and the loop of a reata whistled its deadly song over his head. Dropping low in the saddle, he reined the mustang and faced two soldados, charging down on him with lances at the ready. The Allen's bucked in his hand and one of the men grimaced and grabbed his side, dropping the lance. But the other came on. Before Ned could recock, a lance ripped across his right side. He swung the cutlass from low on his left and caught the surprised Mexican a glancing blow across the head. The cutlass buried itself in the horse's neck just in front of the Mexican's saddle pommel and was almost jerked from Ned's grip when the horse wildly plunged away.

Ned took a fleeting second to survey the scene around him and saw Gillespie and his Marines charging into the fray. Gillespie rode well in the lead of his men, and directly into a group of five soldados. Even over the roar of battle, Ned could hear the Mexicans calling out Gillespie's name in anger. They fell on him when his carbine misfired. His cutlass flashed, knocking lances aside.

Ignoring the pain in his side, Ned hunkered low in the saddle, driving his mustang forward and into the nearest of the mounted soldados just as another's lance drove into Gillespie's face, knocking the Marine from the horse. Ned kicked free of his horse and a Mexican also went to the ground—but Ned landed on top. He smashed the hand guard of his cutlass repeatedly into the Mexican's face, leaving him covered with blood and unmoving, then spun to find Gillespie.

Ned fired into the mass of men surrounding the Marine, and swung his cutlass, beating his way through. He heard Jourdan's shouted warning and turned to see a Mexican flying out of the saddle, a victim of Jourdan's empty swinging carbine.

A barrel-shaped soldado, his broken lance held like a sword, lunged at Ned, who turned aside at the last desperate moment. The lance pierced his tunic and he smashed the heavy Allen's against the man's head. The Mexican's eyes rolled up and he went down in a heap.

Gillespie staggered out of the crowd of men, his teeth smashed out and his lips flinging blood. He was screaming in anger at his enemies, cutlass waving in one hand, holding his chest with the other where a gaping wound lay open under the sliced uniform.

The Mexicans suddenly retreated, and Ned glanced over his shoulder to see Kearny and fifty of the dragoons gallop into the battle. They flashed past Ned, who madly searched for his horse. He had to get Gillespie to the rear, if the mortally wounded man was to have any chance at all.

Ned watched Kearny gallop by, the Mexicans fleeing in front of the onslaught. Ned caught his horse's reins and, with Jourdan's help, pushed Gillespie into the saddle. Then, realizing the Marine was about to lose consciousness, Ned climbed on behind him and urged the horse to the rear at a gallop. Jourdan followed, turning in the saddle and firing at two pursuing soldados who had come out of the undergrowth swinging reatas.

Ned reached the rise where Swords aligned the

cannon, and shoved Gillespie out into the major's arms. Swords caug ered him gently to the ground.

"Get him some help!" Ned yelled, g. the mustang again.

By the time he had covered the quarter n he could see that Kearny and his dragoo. charged into the jaws of hell. The Mexicans had the same trick as earlier, allowing the dragoons string out deeper into the canyon, then circling bac. again.

Trick me once, you're a fool. Trick me twice, I'm a fool, Ned thought in anger as he looked for the general.

Jourdan, galloping behind, screamed at him, "Reload, while time." Ned reined up and reloaded the Allen's. He could see Carson on the hillside, picking targets carefully, but almost every time he tried to shoot, the carbine misfired. Again Ned gave heels to the mustang and charged into the battle. Kearny was surrounded by soldados, and Ned saw one of them drive his lance deeply into the general's broad backside.

With the irony of men in battle, Ned laughed. *If he or any of them lives through this, the general will carry a scar he cannot show to his grandchildren.* Ned carefully picked targets, nudging the mustang forward, Jourdan by his side doing the same—driving the Mexicans away from the general. Kearny, suddenly finding himself out of it, staggered around, his hands hanging at his sides. Then he dropped to his knees.

At the roar of Swords's cannons, the Mexicans swung their horses away and retreated at a dead run.

The hillsides above the battle exploded with the four- and six-pound shells. Ned, his battle-weary horse heaving in exhaustion, saw the general being picked up by his men and hoisted onto a horse. Ned looked back up the rise to see a group of Mexicans weaving through the chaparral on the hillside, pounding down on the cannons and their few defenders. Now it was

...rdan, who stood gazing into the
...for a target. Ned caught his atten-
...d the lathered mustang back up the
...e passed, he hooked elbows with Kit,
...ved back to the road, dragging Kit up
...dle behind him. Before they reached the
...position, Ned's stomach filled with dread.
...s afraid all would be lost, as the cannoneers
...t in hand-to-hand desperation, surrounded by
...ce-armed Mexicans.

To Ned's surprise, Archibald Gillespie was back
on his feet, long cannon swab in hand, manning his
little four-pounder when not using the swab to
parry the thrust of a mounted soldado. Another
group of twenty soldados who had circled back
were descending the hill at full charge, weaving
through the heavy brush to join those already at-
tacking the cannoneers.

Alone, Gillespie calmly adjusted the cannon to
meet the Mexicans' charge. At less than twenty
yards, he touched off the load of grapeshot. Smoke
and fire billowed from the four-pounder, and horses
and riders tumbled end over end down the slope,
almost rolling into their own fighting soldados and
cannoneers—and that cannon shot seemed to break
the spirit of the Mexicans. Those still mounted
reined away from the battle and back up into the
chaparral. Ned and Carson leapt from the saddle
to help Gillespie reload while Jourdan recharged
both his and Ned's revolvers, firing with either hand
when groups of Mexican riders challenged from the
hillsides. Again Jourdan reloaded, and flipped
Ned's revolver back to him just in time to meet another charge brought on when the cannon's wet
powder misfired. Two lancers galloped into them,
and Jourdan sidestepped one when his revolvers,
charged with the same powder used for the cannon, misfired. When a soldado's horse reared, Jourdan managed to jerk the lance out of the man's
hands, but not before he had taken its blade across
his shoulder.

Ned's pistol fired and h゜ jerk. After reining away in des⸜ slid from the saddle, his mustang seeking the solace of the heavily brush゜ the battle continued to roil around th゜ scrambled forward and with Jourdan's h゜ the wounded Mexican soldier back and bound゜ oners might come in handy, Ned figured. The゜ loaded and awaited another attack.

. story of America's last great frontier
from one of our most powerful writers.

EL LAZO
by Larry Jay Martin

In the 1840s Alta California is on the verge of revolution.
The Mexicans are struggling to keep their gracious life-
style intact. The Indians have sworn to defend their
tribal heritage against all invaders. Both are doomed by
the inevitable war with the colossus to the east: an
America determined to expand to the shores of the
Pacific. To this land of transition and turmoil comes
John Clinton Ryan, an adventurer, a seaman by trade,
stranded and alone. To survive in his thrilling and
dangerous new home, Clint must learn the skills of the
proud vaqueros. For only then will he have a chance
against the cruel Mexican soldados, and a brutal
American sea captain who has sworn to see him hang.

On sale now wherever Bantam Domain Books are sold.

AN240 -- 5/91

A Proud People In a Hars...

THE SPANISH BIT

Set on the Great Plains of America in the early 16th ...
Coldsmith's acclaimed series recreates a time, a place an...
that have been nearly lost to history. With the adven...
Spaniards, the horse culture came to the people of the Plains. ...
is history in the making through the eyes of the proud Nat...
Americans who lived it.

☐	BOOK 1: TRAIL OF THE SPANISH BIT	26397-8	$3.50
☐	BOOK 2: THE ELK-DOG HERITAGE	26412-5	$3.50
☐	BOOK 3: FOLLOW THE WIND	26806-6	$3.50
☐	BOOK 4: BUFFALO MEDICINE	26938-0	$3.50
☐	BOOK 5: MAN OF THE SHADOWS	27067-2	$3.50
☐	BOOK 6: DAUGHTER OF THE EAGLE	27209-8	$3.50
☐	BOOK 7: MOON OF THE THUNDER	27344-2	$3.50
☐	BOOK 8: SACRED HILLS	27460-0	$3.50
☐	BOOK 9: PALE STAR	27604-2	$3.50
☐	BOOK 10: RIVER OF SWANS	27708-1	$3.50
☐	BOOK 11: RETURN TO THE RIVER	28163-1	$3.50
☐	BOOK 12: THE MEDICINE KNIFE	28318-9	$3.50
☐	BOOK 13: THE FLOWER IN THE MOUNTAINS	28538-6	$3.50
☐	BOOK 14: TRAIL FROM TAOS	28760-5	$3.50
☐	SUPER: THE CHANGING WIND	28334-0	$3.95

In the tradition of Wagons West
and the Spanish Bit Saga Comes:

RIVERS WEST

- ☐ 27401-5 **The Yellowstone #1**
  Winfred Blevins $4.50
- ☐ 28012-0 **Smokey Hill #2**
  Don Coldsmith $4.50
- ☐ 28451-7 **The Colorado #3**
  Gary McCarthy $4.50
- ☐ 28538-1 **The Powder River #4**
  Winfred Blevins $4.50
- ☐ 28844-X **The Russian River #5**
  Gary McCarthy $4.50

Buy them at your local bookstore or use this handy page for ordering:

Bantam Books, Dept. RW, 414 East Golf Road, Des Plaines, IL 60016

Please send me the items I have checked above. I am enclosing $_____
(please add $2.50 to cover postage and handling). Send check or money
order, no cash or C.O.D.s please.

Mr/Ms _____

Address _____

City/State _____ Zip _____

RW–6/91

Please allow four to six weeks for delivery.
Prices and availability subject to change without notice.

Acclaim for
SPEED WEEK

"The Chamber of Commerce should hate it, which is the highest possible compliment for any Florida novel."
—Carl Hiaasen

"Babes, bikers, and a bad-ass shark in Daytona Beach. I love it!"
—Les Standiford

"Dark suspense and dark comedy . . . This one has more turns than the Daytona 500."
—*The Buffalo News*

"S. V. Date is a graduate of the Carl Hiaasen School of Florida Novel Writing, and *Speed Week* suggests he's among the star pupils. The plot charges like one of those Daytona racers, and Date has the kind of warped sense of humor required to bring Daytona to tacky life."
— *St. Petersburg Times*

"Date makes each attempted hit a humorous study in criminal incompetence . . . *Speed Week* is one book you'll be tempted to race through on a rainy spring afternoon."
—*Chicago Tribune*

"Revels in the sleaze and greed of wacky nincompoops driven mad by the Florida sun."
—*Kirkus Reviews*

SPEED
WEEK

S. V. DATE

BERKLEY PRIME CRIME, NEW YORK

SPEED WEEK

A Berkley Prime Crime Book / published by arrangement with
G. P. Putnam's Sons, a division of Penguin Putnam, Inc.

PRINTING HISTORY
G. P. Putnam's Sons hardcover edition / May 1999
Berkley Prime Crime mass-market edition / October 2001

Visit our website at
www.penguinputnam.com

ISBN: 0-425-18222-3

Berkley Prime Crime Books are published
by The Berkley Publishing Group,
a division of Penguin Putnam Inc.,
375 Hudson Street, New York, New York 10014.
The name BERKLEY PRIME CRIME and the
BERKLEY PRIME CRIME design
are trademarks belong to Penguin Putnam Inc.

PRINTED IN THE UNITED STATES OF AMERICA

10 9 8 7 6 5 4 3 2 1

For Mary Beth

Many thanks to Craig Quintana for a critical eye,

■

Daniel Zitin for encouraging words,

■

Neil Nyren for his confidence,

■

Edee Dalke for insights into a bizarre world,

■

and as always, Mary Beth for her boundless enthusiasm.

SPEED WEEK
...

ONE

...

Circuit Court Judge Anthony Antoon, Civil Part, Volusia County, Florida, pushed his bifocals toward the end of a long thin nose, carefully pulled open the Ziploc bag on his desk and gingerly withdrew Plaintiff's Exhibit F from its bubble wrapping. Slowly he raised it toward the recessed lights high above in the vaulted ceiling.

With a wrinkled, liver-spotted hand, he spun it around twice clockwise, then stopped, turned it the other way. Still with the one hand, he flipped it end for end and spun it around once more.

"What in hell is this?" he growled finally.

Nolin and the other lawyers behind the railing in the brand-new, faux nineteenth-century courtroom slunk even lower and buried themselves in suddenly fascinating legal briefs. No one dared a smile, let alone a laugh. Judge Antoon held a powerful sense of decorum about Judge Antoon's courtroom. Judge Antoon also held a grudge.

The lawyers on the other side of the rail weren't so fortunate. They looked at each other helplessly. Finally, the plaintiff's attorney cleared his throat. It was, there was no getting around it, his exhibit.

"An egg, Your Honor."

A couple of snickers erupted from the rear of the gallery. Antoon extinguished them with a death glare.

"Counselor, Justice may be blind, but I'm not. Why is it in my courtroom?"

Nolin bit his tongue, bit hard, until he tasted blood. His case was next, his client an irredeemable weasel, but a rich irredeemable weasel. One he couldn't afford to lose. And Antoon was still mad at him from a case a month ago. If his stony mask crumbled, he was finished.

"Well, sir," the plaintiff's lawyer began again. "It's one of 1,559 eggs found this morning at thirty-six sites between the Seabreeze Boulevard and Raceway Avenue access ramps in Daytona Beach. That's the portion of the beach we maintain has suffered the most adverse impact from beach driving, sir. Where the traffic volume and the associated pollutants, motor oil, antifreeze—"

"I've heard it before, counselor," Antoon intoned heavily. "Automobile traffic on the sandy beach has curtailed the nesting of green, hawksbill and leatherback sea turtles on Volusia County's shore, blah, blah, blah, in contravention to the federal Endangered Species Act, yaddah, yaddah. Such is your client's position. So how do you explain thirty-six nests in the most heavily driven strip of beach?"

"I apologize, Your Honor. I was returning to the coincidence of thirty-six so-called nests, where none has been found for the last dozen years, appearing just in time for today's hearing."

"Vile subterfuge. So you allege." Antoon lifted the egg toward the light again. "And how do you know that thirty-six actual turtles didn't crawl up the sand last night and lay them?"

"They couldn't have, Your Honor. What you have in your hand is a *chicken* egg. Actual turtle eggs are smaller, like Ping-Pong balls, and have a leathery shell. In addition, sir, whoever planted the eggs didn't know that turtles drag themselves along the sand and leave a long trench. These nests all had prints leading to and from the water, sir. My biologist examined them and determined they came from the front paws of a five- to six-foot male alligator."

Antoon's brow visibly darkened, a gathering storm. "They brought an alligator to the beach?"

"No, Your Honor. Just its paws. Just its front paws."

Nolin looked up. This was a new one, even by Daytona standards. He allowed himself a smile.

"It appears that the perpetrators of this hoax didn't do their homework, sir," the plaintiff's lawyer said, more confident now. "I guess they figured eggs were eggs."

Antoon stared down the plaintiff's lawyer until he had stopped beaming and dropped his eyes to the floor. "I find no humor in perpetrating a hoax on this court, counselor. Do you?"

"No, Your Honor." The plaintiff's lawyer retreated to the safety of his table where he shuffled some papers.

Antoon turned toward the defendant's table. "And I assume Volusia County has no knowledge of any of this? That the county attorney, working *hand in glove* with the Hotel-Motel Association, the Tourism Board, the Chamber of Commerce and Daytona Raceway, has no *earthly* idea how a thousand chicken eggs showed up on the beach?"

Nolin heard a muffled gasp behind him, saw a pale, bearded man in dark glasses slouch into the collar of a plaid sportcoat. He turned back to watch the county attorney shift his weight from one foot to the other.

"For the record, Your Honor, it's more like sixteen hundred eggs," the plaintiff's lawyer offered helpfully before catching Antoon's glare again.

Within a few seconds, though, Antoon's eyes had returned to the defense table. The county attorney could stall no longer. "Your Honor makes an excellent point," he began cautiously in a thick, north Florida drawl. "A purposeful effort to subvert the will of this court would indeed be a terrible and dishonorable thing. Something that my office, indeed, the entire county would condemn in the strongest possible terms. But might I suggest, Your Honor, that there is a perfectly plausible explanation for the, ah, seemingly implausible situation with the eggs. To wit, sir, upon information and belief, there may have been, and in an abundance of caution, I want to emphasize 'may have been.' We're still working to confirm this: There *may have been* a group of poultry farmers traveling from a convention in Fort Lauderdale back to their homes in Georgia, and at least some of the hens *may have escaped* and, confronted with unfamiliar . . ."

This time Nolin bit his lip, but couldn't keep his stomach muscles from convulsing. On the bench, Antoon hadn't blinked, but his tongue started moving inside his mouth, as if trying to escape a foul taste.

The county attorney glanced up, recognized the look and scrambled for an escape. "But of course, Your Honor doesn't want to deal in conjecture, but in hard, cold facts. Let me assure you that my office and I will work hand in glove with the Beach Patrol, with plaintiff's counsel and Save Our Turtles, and with any and all appropriate authorities to make certain that something like this never—"

"Counselor."

"Yes, Your Honor."

"Shut up."

"Of course, Your Honor."

Nolin wiped the smirk away and sat up straight. His case, he reminded himself, was next.

"We've already wasted more time on this . . . chickenshit than we should have." Antoon leaned over the desk toward his stenographer. "Strike 'chickenshit' from the record, would you, Sandy dear?"

Sandy nodded, tapped at her keypad.

"The next time I see you two, you *will* be prepared to pick a jury and proceed. I've blocked out two days for this trial. It won't go a minute longer. Is that clear?"

Both tables nodded enthusiastically.

"Good. Now, as to the chicken and egg question." Antoon chuckled to himself. The lawyers looked at each other, nervously began grins.

"The matter will be noted in the record without prejudice to either side. But let me add here for the county attorney's benefit: Yes, it's true I've grown up right here in Daytona Beach. I've raced hot rods on this beach. I've screwed girls in the backseat of my car on this beach. I happen to like driving on the beach. But if someone fucks with my court again, I'll rule this beach a state conservation area and clear all cars *and* all humans, and that includes tourists foolish enough to come here instead of a decent beach, from every inch of shoreline between Cape Canaveral and the Flagler line. I hope I make myself clear."

He banged his gavel on his desk, then leaned over it again. "Sandy, strike 'screw' and 'fuck' from the record, if you would, please. Next case."

Both tables hurriedly packed up their papers as the bailiff called out "Emerson versus Emerson." Nolin stood, heard the courtroom door slam shut behind him. He glanced back, noticed idly that the man in the plaid jacket was gone.

The diver kicked his feet slowly, giving a slight boost to the propulsion pack he held before him. As usual the visibility was lousy, about twenty feet, tops, and he suppressed a wave of panic that he'd missed it.

Steady, steady; anxiety sped up the heart. That would increase respiration and therefore cut bottom time. He looked over the compass on the console and kept kicking. He'd measured it all out: With the pack on low speed and a slow kick, he moved at three knots. He'd entered the water exactly one nautical mile away, so it would take him twenty minutes. He had been swimming for eighteen. Unless there was a crosscurrent . . .

He forced himself to count breaths. Long, slow inhale. Long, slow exhale until, there: Dead ahead, out of the gloom, he saw it. He flicked off the propulsion pack and released it. Because he had balanced it that morning for a fifteen-foot depth, it stayed right where he left it, neutrally buoyant.

He glided over the shiny box, sliding his fingers over the rubber seam between sides and lid. Perfect: no leaks. He swam around to the shoreward side and gently untwisted the plastic tie he'd used to hold the coils of wire together overnight. It was gossamer thin, and he had worried it would break if subjected that long to waves and tide. Breaking wasn't an option. It had to work perfectly. Hence the long, risky underwater swim to set it.

From the pocket of his buoyancy compensator he pulled a small, Styrofoam ball and gently pushed two feet of wire through its center. Where it emerged, he twisted the tip into a loose knot until he was satisfied it wouldn't pull back through. Then he let the ball drift upward, pulling out loops of wire as it went, until finally it was within a foot of the surface. It undulated with the waves, but never broke through. The wire itself would be invisible from shore. He had tested that himself, using high-powered binoculars.

Satisfied with the placement, he retied the remaining coils of wire, checked dive watch and pressure gauge. Twenty-six minutes and more than half a tank remaining. Right on the money. He patted the box once and swam over to the propulsion pack. He flicked it on, checked his heading and began kicking.

All that was left was to stow his gear on the bottom, swim back to shore, change and then hang around the beach for a few hours. That would be distasteful, what with the cars and the music and the butt-thong-clad groupies and the crowd . . .

Still it would be worth it, in the end. He noticed a shadow, turned to see a pair of blacktips swimming in formation. Mouths slightly agape, tails swishing silently through the water. Simple perfection. With luck they'd be around in a few hours. The more the merrier.

Sweat beaded Madame Rosa Castilla Murdo as she hunched over her glass ball, peering intently through at the black "antiqued" table beneath. Once again the air conditioning was on the fritz, and, though only February, the fans were no match for the heat.

"Maybe you should take off your shawl, Rosa," Barbie offered.

Rosa looked up with a glare before letting loose a Spanish-tinged tirade. "Meesez Van Horne, thees is how my mother taught me, and her mother before her taught her. Thees is how we do it in Andalusia. Maybe you like somebody else? Maybe someone with the incense and the music and the leetle crystals? Maybe you like that?"

Barbie sighed. Rosa had long ago copped an attitude about the New Age psychics at Cassadaga. Dilettantes, they were. Unschooled. Ill-mannered. Crooks. "No, Rosa, of course not. It's just that, well, it's hot." She pulled at her green tank top. "Even I'm hot, and I'm only wearing this."

Rosa leaned back. A woolen shawl covered jet-black hair. Another draped over her shoulders. Beneath it she wore a long, sequined red gown. From Sevilla, she had told her. Like all her clothes.

"Pardon me for saying, but where I come from, Meesez Van Horne, ladies do not go out in public wearing"—she waved a long, red-nailed finger at Barbie's chest—"that. It is indecent. But, your ways are deeferent. So. Tell me again your troubles. Today, I have the deeficulty seeing into your eyes."

Barbie studied Rosa's eyes. They were a bright blue, all the more stunning because of the dark skin and black, black hair. She looked around at the dingy walls, decorated with the trappings of classical Spain, or at least the sort of kitschy Spain that sold for inflated prices at Epcot. Scarves, castanets, a matador's cloak, a bullfighter's killing sword.

Someday she'd travel to Spain, travel the back roads, visit the quaint fishing villages, climb the rugged Pyrenees. Someday. Someday when she had her act together, figured out who she was, where she was going and how she was getting there. Yet thoughts of the indeterminate future invariably brought up the recent past, replete with foolish choices and wasted time. How many years had she lost? Four? Five? Six, depending on how you counted? And for what: to change him? Make him grow up?

Against her better instincts, she wished again now as she frequently did that she'd taken the money and run. She had, after all, earned every penny. He'd been a jerk, but a rich jerk, and she could have taken what she needed and left him with enough that he'd never have thought to complain.

Instead she'd sworn to make it on her own. To prove to him, to *all* of them, what she was made of. Well, here she was: on the edge of depression, with nothing left but an unpopular, costly crusade that she could no longer afford but didn't have the heart to abandon. Even her morning in court, her best shot at victory, her lawyer had promised, had withered to nothing when the judge decided the other side would not be punished.

"Tell me about the turtles again, Rosa," she asked finally.

"Ah, *las tortugas, sí.*" Rosa leaned back suddenly in her straight-backed chair, her extra chins shuddering from the jolt. Her eyes fell closed. "It is as I told you, Meesez Van Horne. You, and the turtles, you are *familia*. Many years ago, in many previous memories, you swim in the deep, blue sea. And every other spring, you climb up on the beach and lay your babies in the sand, and crawl back to Mother Ocean. Thees is you, Meesez Van Horne. Thees is your soul. As free and wonderful as the mother turtle. And also as full of love and duty. Why, Meesez Van Horne? Why do you ask Rosa?"

Barbie sighed again. "Because, Rosa. I tried to help them. But it wasn't enough."

"You help them plenty, Meesez Van Horne," Rosa said quickly, wondering what the hell Barbie was talking about. "You help them plenty. And they know, and they love you."

"But it's not going to be enough, is it? And now that they really need my help, I'm going to have to give up."

Barbie laid her long, bony hands on the table. "So tell me, Rosa. What happens to them? And what happens to me?"

Rosa swallowed softly, cupped her hands over the crystal ball and closed her eyes. "I see hardship, Meesez Van Horne. Much hardship and much sorrow. But, in the end, I see much joy. And in the end, you will prevail."

Barbie looked at Rosa hopefully. "So I'll find another lawyer?"

"Another lawyer?" Rosa blinked slowly, then stared straight into Barbie's pale green eyes for a long minute. "*Sí!* A *very* good lawyer. He will be everything you need."

J. Robert "Nick" Van Horne III leaned back against the wall, hands thrust in his trouser pockets, chin on chest. It was his usual pose of excruciating boredom as he waited for Joanna's attention to fall, eventually, finally, his way.

"J. R., does this midnight blue work?" She held a slinky, full-length evening gown against a no-longer-slinky figure. "Or is this better?"

It was a curse, being born a Van Horne. The richest family in stock car racing, the apex of the Daytona Beach social pyramid, yet still snubbed by the old money in Long Island, Charleston, even Palm Beach. Sure, they owned cottages in all three places. But they couldn't make the "A" list. Not even, frankly, the "B" list, and it made his stepmother crazy.

He smiled to himself, remembering the previous summer when Joanna had decided to crash the Worthingtons' ball in East Hampton. Because it was a charity affair, no one had thrown them out. But no one had talked to them either. He had cheered inwardly when they finally left after an hour of standing by themselves next to a Greek statue.

She had replaced the blue gown with a shorter, strapless black dress. She turned her back to Nick and alternated dresses before the three-part ceiling-to-floor mirror. "Black gets *so* tiresome. Don't you think? Perhaps I have time for a quickie down to Palm Beach. Oh, I *do* get tired of living in a town without a Lord and Taylor's."

Nick groaned. It had become her favorite complaint: the trials of holding a formal in a town so gauche that men actually wore *rented* tuxedos. He had come to dread talking to her. A lecture or a scolding—it was always one or the other, and that only after a prolonged recounting of her latest tribulation. He wondered again what it might've been like to have been born a normal guy with a normal job—timeshare salesman, or maybe a strip-joint manager. He'd have done great at either, he knew. And then he remembered the little Lotus coupe in the garage and the way the expensive, high-class debs fawned over him. Being the grandson of James Van Horne, né Jim Bob Horn, he had to admit, did have its advantages.

"You haven't heard a word I've said, have you?" he whined finally.

She kept her attention on the mirrors. "Of course I have, dear. The judge was very upset about the chicken eggs. Explain again, dear, why you used them? I'm still having a little trouble with that."

He swallowed hard. It was a subject he'd hoped to avoid. He decided to go on the offensive. "Chrissakes, Joanna, how the hell were we supposed to know? I mean, did *you* know turtle eggs don't look like chicken eggs? Gimme a break!" He spoke to the back of her neck. "What were we *supposed* to do? You said make turtle nests. You didn't tell us where to get turtle eggs."

"Do you read at all? Ever? It's in the paper just about every day. There are thousands of sea-turtle nests south of the Brevard County line, thousands of sea-turtle nests north of the Flagler line. That's why your slut wife is suing *our* county, remember?" Joanna peeled the straps of her sundress off her shoulders and pushed the black gown up to her chest, draping strands of bleached blond hair down over the fabric. "Now. If there were thousands of sea-turtle eggs a few miles north, thousands more a few miles south, explain why it seemed a good idea to use chicken eggs. Is my hair too light for this dress?"

"You didn't tell me any of that yesterday," Nick complained. He continued addressing the back of her head. "The judge knows we did it, Joanna! He's gonna rule against us!"

She hung both gowns on the rack, smoothed the yellow sundress and walked to the edge of her bed. The pink sheets crinkled as she sat down and crossed her legs, pointing a perfectly pedicured big toe at her stepson.

"How many times, Robert, have I told you never to call me Joanna?"

Nick groaned. "Come on, Joanna, I feel stupid calling you Mom. You're younger than me."

She nodded. "A technicality. It's also a technicality that I control your father's trust fund, and the foundation, and the business. So, technically, if I wanted you to call me the Queen of Sheba, it technically would be in your interest to do so." She smiled brightly. "Don't you agree?"

Nick dropped his head and sighed. "Yes . . . Mom."

Joanna wagged her bare foot, admiring the bright red nail polish. "So explain. Tell me *why* you picked chicken eggs, although I suppose I should count my blessings you didn't use ostrich eggs or robin eggs or Egg McMuffins. After all, I didn't tell you not to use any of those, either."

More than anything, he loathed the smug sarcasm. "Me and the Ramseys got way behind schedule when that turtle bit off Tony's little finger."

Joanna didn't even flinch. "Of course. What turtle would that be?"

"We needed to make tracks. You know, from the nests down to the water? So we needed a turtle. So Tony and Toby and me drove up to Reptile Kingdom in Saint Augustine." Nick lowered his eyes. "I *told* them not to take a snapper. Anyway, by the time we got out of the emergency room, it was almost light. It was too late to find a turtle, so we figured we could make do with gator tracks, seeing as how we already had those gator-claw back scratchers in the office."

Joanna continued wagging her foot. "Of course. Gator back scratchers."

"*You* remember," he sniffed. "The Chamber sent them out as publicity for Crother's airboat rides?"

Joanna cocked her head forty-five degrees, as if a fresh angle might clarify everything. "And you made alligator tracks leading to sea-turtle nests because . . ."

"*Jeez*, Joanna, how the hell were we supposed to know they'd have such different feet? The Ramseys saw this sign at Reptile Kingdom that said gators and turtles were cousins." Nick pouted. "Sure, it's easy to criticize now, in hindsight. *You* weren't there . . ."

"We keep coming back to the Ramseys. The Ramseys this. The Ramseys that. Perhaps you've forgotten? The Ramseys are half-wits? We employ them to stack heavy things on top of other heavy things? And even *then* they need close direction? Yet now they're reptile experts?" She sighed, shook her head sadly. "Go on."

"So they figured out they weren't real turtle nests when some kids got into an egg fight this morning. Some smart-ass tourist looked at one and called the lifeguard. The lifeguard called the Beach Patrol, the Beach Patrol called Barbie."

Joanna stared icily, and Nick shuddered. For a short, on-the-dumpy-side, middle-aged lady with rounded cheeks, too much makeup and platinum hair, Joanna had a terrible stare. It gave him the willies.

"This isn't what I had in mind."

Nick snorted. "No shit, Jo—"

She lunged forward with an open hand. "You watch your mouth. A gentleman doesn't use that kind of language."

Nick opened his mouth to argue, saw her glare, shut it again. She stood and walked back to continue her inspection of her closet. "Do you have any idea what I had to go through to take us public? Do you know what's involved in lining up state funding for a project this size? We won't see a penny of it if this turtle nonsense continues. John Robert, I've devoted too much time and energy to this to let Barbie screw it up."

Nick swallowed. "Yes, Mom."

"We need to move to the next level, Robert."

"Yes, Mom," he said automatically while wondering: *What next level?*

Joanna slid gown after gown down the rack, stopped at a spaghetti-strapped creation of purple crepe. "We need to stop this lawsuit at the source."

"We already tried the lawyer, Mom. There was nothing there. The bastard pays his taxes, cuts his lawn, doesn't cheat on his wife or beat his dog."

Joanna passed on the purple and flipped more rapidly. "I said at the *source*, Robert."

Nick's eyes brightened. "You mean I can divorce her?"

She turned, aghast. "At the start of the spring season? How would that look? And with the public offering next month. No, I said the *source*."

He looked at her helplessly. "I don't follow . . ."

Joanna picked out a shimmering, semi-sheer, ankle-length gown. "You remember that lunch with the

Teasdales, a couple of months ago? It was right after they took Floyd away?"

He thought back to the lunch, a three-hour ordeal with all of Joanna's gossipy friends to leak word about Raceway Enterprises' coming public offering. Their news had been overshadowed by the arrest of Floyd Chappel, of Chappel Chevrolet Buick, for hiring his gardener to kill his wife. A dimmer switch slowly turned inside Nick's head.

"You mean I should . . . kill her?" he whispered.

"Gentlemen don't kill their wives," Joanna said, untying the strap to her sundress and stepping out of it. She lifted the shimmering gown over her head and tugged it downward over various bulges. "Gentlemen have them killed. Quietly."

She turned back to the mirror. "Can you see my underthings through this?" She pulled the fabric tight over her breasts. "I might have to wear it without them."

Amee Mosher sipped her drink and watched the cue ball bounce off the cushion and roll across the table before coming to a stop. Perfect, right in front of her Joe. She put down her drink, picked up the chalk and, though she still had no idea why, rubbed it purposefully onto the end of her cuestick.

She sashayed around to the cue ball, squeezed between the table and the T-shirted tourist who held the other stick. He had pressed himself flat against the wall, but she made sure to brush heavily against him as she passed.

"Excuse me." She smiled, then leaned over the table, unnaturally and unnecessarily lifting one leg to knock the cue ball against the solid blue while simultaneously providing her opponent an opportunity to inspect the strip of swimsuit that ran between her thighs.

The blue fell into the corner pocket and the cue ball came to a stop directly across the table from her Joe: her other favorite position. She wandered around the table, sipped her drink and bent over, leisurely lining up her shot while giving her customer a nice, long view down her cleavage. She jiggled a little to swing in unison, then shot her opponent a smile and the eight ball into the side pocket. Game.

The T-shirted tourist laid down the cuestick and rooted through his Day-Glo orange fanny pack for a five-dollar bill. "You shoot a nice game of pool," he said with a strong midwestern accent.

Amee took the five and stuck it in her own fanny pack, cherry red to match the triangles of Lycra covering her nipples and groin. In the back were just thin red strings. "You shoot a good game yourself, Fred. Maybe you'll come back for another before you head home to Akron?"

"How about right now?" He dug a pudgy hand back into the fanny pack. "I'm goin' to the time trials tomorrow, and the wife wants to do Disney on Wednesday."

Amee smiled broadly, big white teeth gleaming despite the pool hall's dingy fluorescent tubes. "Can't right now, sport. Gotta take a break. But I'll be here all afternoon." She smiled at him again, studied his sunburned features. Oh, what the hell. He'd dropped $25 on her in just over twenty minutes. She stood on tiptoe to kiss him on the cheek.

"You come back to say 'bye before you leave Daytona," she warned as he stumbled through the door. "And bring your wife, next time." She walked through the passageway into the bar, where another rumrunner awaited in a big plastic tumbler.

"Thanks, Rick," she called out as she popped herself onto a stool, leaned forward to take a big slug from the tumbler. It was a Chamber of Commerce giveaway with drawings of large-bosomed women playing beach volley-ball on one side and stock cars on the other. The slogan "Daytona Is *My* Beach" ran all the way around it.

"Havin' a good day, Cherry?" Rick had returned from the back room and was clearing empties off the bar.

"Same old, same old," Amee said between gulps of the bubblegum-colored drink. She unzipped her fanny pack, pulled out a fistful of bills and began sorting: two twen-ties, one ten and three fives. And it was barely noon. She would do even better come evening, when passersby on the Boardwalk could see in through the plate-glass win-dows and watch her dance around the pool table wearing only a thong, a wisp of a top, an ankle bracelet and a navel ring. She usually took in $100 to $150 a night, more dur-ing the prime tourist season of Speed Week, Bike Week and Spring Break, though the college students were noto-riously tight with tips.

Her game had actually gotten pretty good, and she could usually polish off a Joe within five minutes. She would always break: Ladies first, she would tell them. Sometimes she would run the table without the customer ever getting a shot. At $5 a game—she was always a player; the rare win by the customer only earned him the right to an immediate rematch—it was pretty easy money. A hell of a lot easier than the street stuff she'd done in her younger years, back when she still called herself "Cherry on Top," back before that November five years earlier when she'd finally hitched her way down from Erie.

Now, at age nineteen, with chest and hips fully filled in, Amee Mosher had hit her prime in a town that fully appreciated her talents. She struck a match from one of the cardboard books at the end of the bar and lit a crumpled cigarette from her fanny pack. "Gimme another, Ricky-Boy," she called.

Rick poured a pink mixture into the blender, splashed

in some Bacardi and flipped the switch. "You'd better watch yourself with all that cash," he warned, nodding at the pile of bills on the bar. "People here kill for less."

She nodded and smiled. "I know. Isn't this a great town?"

It was the lunch hour, the most likely time for customers until the true tourist season began, yet not even a single window-shopper roamed the street.

Barbie Baxter laid the library book on the migratory patterns of green and leatherback turtles on the counter, wedged open the front door and moved onto the sidewalk to smile at passersby. With her runway-model legs and exotic bone structure, she was Harmonic Age's best advertisement, and she certainly wasn't bringing in any customers sitting on a stool behind the cash register.

She stood with the model's permanent half-smile, but continued worrying about finances. Without $50,000 to pay her lawyer, he would drop the case just as it was going to trial. Not that she could blame him. His business had suffered already for taking on such an unpopular cause. Daytona was known the world over as the place you could drive on the beach, and here she was trying to get rid of it.

But she was right and she knew it. Ancient species that scientists knew almost nothing about were becoming extinct before her eyes. How many hatchlings had been crushed under the wheels of cars cruising the sand? How many more had been poisoned by motor oil and antifreeze drippings? The county didn't know. Because they were in Joanna Van Horne's pocket, they didn't care, either.

She sighed, wished again she'd cleaned out half the joint account when she'd had the chance. That would have paid the legal fees and then some. But no, she'd had her pride, and had wanted to walk away with no more than she'd brought in.

The decision had cost her dearly. The store that had done so well when New Age was the latest fad now barely held its own. She'd been late a couple of times on the mortgage, and the bank had threatened to call the note, which, if they'd followed through, would have finished her. And all of *that* was before she founded Save Our Turtles and took on the city, the county, the Van Hornes and pretty much everybody else who mattered in northeast Florida.

She sighed again and crossed the sidewalk to lean against the lamppost. The unseasonably warm February sun was generating a sea breeze off the cool Atlantic four blocks away, and Barbie rubbed her upper arms to smooth away the goose bumps. She'd always been sensitive to the cold, and two decades in Florida had thinned her blood even further. She would have preferred a sweater over the white cotton minidress, and sneakers instead of the white leather sandals, but she didn't sell sweaters and she didn't sell sneakers.

If customers liked what they saw on her, and they almost always did, then she wanted to be sure they could find it on her racks. Today she had chosen a white coral necklace and matching bracelets and earrings to complete the ensemble. With her golden complexion and long brown hair, the effect was, as intended, stunning.

She turned west toward the river and noticed a bohemian couple strolling hand in hand. Both were decked out in the latest salute to the seventies: tie-dyed shirts, neckerchiefs, Birkenstocks. Barbie flashed them her best smile and smoothed out her dress. The long-haired boy grinned back sheepishly, while the short-haired girl dragged him to the window display of amethyst jewelry.

Barbie always put out that month's birthstone in a prominent location, and the display usually brought in more than its share of customers. She was about to ask if she could help them find anything when the girl tugged the boy's hand and started down the street again, telling him they had to hurry or they wouldn't get a good spot for the race. The boy raised his eyebrows and smiled at Barbie—you know how women are!—and let himself be dragged away.

Bewildered, Barbie could only shake her head. Since when did kids who dressed like hippies care about Jet Skis, for God's sake? She watched them as they walked away and noticed the glint of gold around the girl's ankle. She examined her own unadorned feet and wondered whether she should finally give in and start wearing an ankle bracelet. She'd always considered them the mark of wild teenagers and horny divorcees, the sign of a true slut, willing to do just about anything with just about anyone.

Lately, though, she'd noticed them on all kinds of women: lawyers, dental assistants and bank officers as well as the waitresses, hotel managers and salesclerks who had worn them for years. Maybe they were more respectable now. Or maybe they were only respectable in Daytona. Maybe, she sighed, it was time she learned to go along to get along.

She stepped back through the doorway and noticed the crystal wall clock was almost at one, almost time for the races. With no customers in sight, and as much as she hated to, she realized she might as well head down to the beach. She needed to keep current, and in a town that lived and breathed racing, that meant knowing who won and why.

She grabbed her book and keys, flipped the OPEN sign to CLOSED and stepped back outside to lock up.

• • •

The radio blasted out "Fun, fun, fun" and Nick snapped his fingers to the beat. Ordinarily he would have switched stations on subject matter alone, but nothing could dampen his day now. Not even the fact that he was driving the hideous green Monte Carlo he hated but had to pretend to love because Chevrolet had given it to him and Chevrolet was a major sponsor. It had bugged him for years. Why the hell couldn't Ferrari be a NASCAR sponsor? Or Aston Martin? James Bond didn't have to drive a Monte Carlo; why the hell did he?

Yet even that chronic complaint was set aside for the moment as he savored his good fortune: He would be free! And no long, drawn-out divorce, no papers, no *alimony*! Just a quick, one-time payment and that was that. Joanna had simply cut him a $50,000 check and told him to take care of it!

He came to a stop and returned the wave from the car beside him. He had no idea who the man was. A banker maybe. Or insurance agent. One of the many smarmy hangers-on who made their living off his inheritance. Someday, it occurred to him, when he was running things, he might have to pay attention to names and faces and the like. He glanced back at the vaguely familiar face and decided: no, he wouldn't. No, he was going to be *so* damn rich that he'd be as rude and inconsiderate as he wanted and people would *still* have to be nice to him.

The light turned green, Nick pushed the accelerator and the Monte Carlo surged forward as Nick held the wheel steady. Big, dumb, American muscle car. Wanted to go anywhere but straight. Ah, the hell with it. When he was boss, he would end the stupid charade and buy himself a Beemer. If GM and Ford didn't like it, well, they could go piss up a tree. They could go find some other car-racing circuit with NASCAR's numbers.

Come to think of it, he might even sell the whole works

and live off the proceeds. *That* would be nice: no more pre-dawn Rotary breakfasts, no more interminable Halifax Club lunches, no more mind-numbing trips to Talladega or Bristol or Darlington. Best of all, no more races! Ever! No more obligatory visits to the grimy pits, no more ringing in his ears for hours afterward, no more inane conversations with backwoods drivers.

Nick sighed in anticipation. Patience. All that would have to wait. First things first: find someone to do Barbie. He smiled again at the $50,000 in his pocket, equal to half his yearly allowance. In fact, he'd never had so much money on him in his life. The thought made him dizzy, and without warning the light in his head came on, full and dazzlingly bright: Why did he have to spend it *all* on Barbie? Surely it wouldn't require the entire fifty grand! Whatever was left could go straight into his pocket, and Joanna would never be the wiser. He smiled to himself, wondering how to spend a $25,000 windfall. Or $35,000. Or $45,000.

God, he wished now he'd paid more attention when Floyd Chappel had been arrested for hiring his gardener. How much had Floyd paid? Surely not more than $10,000. And was that all up front? Or half now, half on delivery? What if the guy failed? Was there a refund? And what about weapons? Was that the responsibility of the customer? Or the contractor?

So many questions . . . He wished he could talk to Floyd. Well, maybe he could! Maybe he could run down to the county jail and visit him, ask him about how he'd gone about looking for someone, how he'd settled on his gardener, if he had any advice . . .

In a flash, Nick's smile vanished. Floyd was in *jail*! He had killed his wife, and now he would fry in the electric chair! Christ, what the hell was he thinking? *Visiting* him?

He slowed down, took a deep breath and calmed himself. Lots of guys had their wives killed. It was on the news all the time. Only the dumb ones got caught. He wouldn't be dumb, that's all. And on second thought, he didn't *care* what Floyd did. Floyd got caught. Floyd was dumb. *Floyd* was not a good person to emulate. He would be careful, Nick decided. He would wear his disguise when he met with prospects. He would never use his real name.

Besides. Most guys who had their wives killed didn't have the local police chief in their pocket. The smile returned. Nick turned up the radio and stepped on the gas.

Out on the river a flotilla of sailboats headed south, fore-sails flying in the afternoon breeze. The lead boat was a classic old yawl with a long, graceful sheer, with a mid-dle-aged woman moving forward to remove the mainsail cover. Long black hair shimmered in the bright sun as she peeled off the blue canvas and walked barefoot back to the cockpit.

Nolin sighed and pulled himself from the window. The view only depressed him, and too many briefs lay piled on his desk awaiting his attention. He locked his eyes onto the top page of the top folder, but his mind wandered back to the yawl and her crew. Middle-aged, he'd thought when he saw her. Middle-aged, with long thin legs, a terrific tan and able to wear shorts and a T-shirt every day.

Middle-aged. But then what the hell was he? A year away from forty, never married, no children. In another few years or two or one, he'd be middle-aged, too, and what would he have accomplished? A struggling law prac-tice in a tawdry little town, that's what. A tawdry little town he'd sworn he'd leave as soon as his old man died, when there would be nothing left tying him down. That had been three years ago and, wonder of wonders, here he was still.

He stood and returned back to the big, wood-framed window looking out on the river. There had been a time when the house itself kept his attention. Big and old, with enough space for a two-room office in front and three bedrooms, kitchen and den around and above. He'd loved restoring it, replacing rotten timbers, installing new wiring, painting, staining, polishing. And then it was done, and he'd spent an ever increasing amount of time gazing at his dock that jutted out into the Halifax, with the little Boston Whaler that sat tied to the end.

He'd thought perhaps it was the location that was driving him antsy, and he'd sunk a good year's profits into a ramshackle beach house not far north of the inlet. The energy had returned as he went back to work with hammer and crowbar. He'd come to realize, though, that the only thing that would change was his view. Instead of looking out across the river at the other shore, he would look out across the ocean and think of Africa.

The last of the boats disappeared beyond the bend in the channel and he returned to his chair, once more picking up the brief at the top of the pile and throwing his long legs over the corner of the desk, the only patch remaining uncluttered by paper. Oh, what the hell. He had most of the drywall up and had already bought the tile; he might as well finish. It was grunt work, but he enjoyed it. And he knew he could sell the finished product for at least twice what he'd paid. It really wasn't a bad gig: one house to live in, one to fix up. Meanwhile, the occasional divorce case paid the bills.

Behind him he heard the car pull into the driveway that connected Riverside with 10th. He dropped the file back on top of the pile, waited for the doorbell and rose to answer it.

A soft, doughy face peered through the glass panels beside the door. Short arms rose to adjust a tie. Nolin pulled the door open, and the visitor quickly stepped past him into the foyer.

"Big fancy lawyer answering his own door now?"

Nolin remembered the face, but couldn't attach the name. "I'm between receptionists," he answered pleasantly. He glanced at the necktie, noticed the red-and-white stock cars and it came to him. "What can I help you with, Mr. Van Horne?"

Nick looked out from under lazy eyelids. "You find anything yet?"

The details came to Nolin as he ushered Nick into his reading room, stacked on three walls with the usual, floor-to-ceiling shelves of law books. "Your estranged wife, correct? The one you're thinking of divorcing?"

Nick spread himself unceremoniously into the easy chair. "You were gonna find out if she's spending my money. Is she?"

Nolin snapped his fingers and moved to the oak filing cabinet on the fourth wall. He pulled out a file and leafed through it for a moment before sitting on the couch. "You understand, Mr. Van Horne, that I have no power of sub-poena, not until there is an actual petition filed and we are in the discovery process. And as you know, bank records are not public. We were only able to make some discreet inquiries. We don't know, for example, where exactly she's spending her money."

Nick crossed and uncrossed his legs, spun his fingers in circles. "Yeah, yeah, yeah. Whatever. So what do you got?"

"Barbara Baxter Van Horne. Age thirty-four. Married. Owns a single-family residential dwelling on State Road A1A, assessed value $177,000. Claims a homestead exemption. Current on her taxes. One car registered in her name, a 1989 Volkswagen, fully paid. Seems to be using a single account at Barnett Bank for all her expenses."

"That's it? The Barnett account?"

"So it seems."

"She's not getting anything out of First Volusia?"

"Apparently not. Isn't the account at First Volusia in your name?"

"Yeah. But we're still married, so doesn't she get access or anything?"

"No, sir. It has to be a joint account for her to have access. And you closed the only joint account you had, correct?"

Nick hung his head, dejected. "So where's she getting all the money?"

Nolin flipped a page in the thin folder. "As far as I can tell, Mr. Van Horne, there doesn't seem to *be* that much money. Besides, she does have the boutique on Seabreeze."

"No way." Nick shook his head. "No way that stupid place pays for everything."

Nolin closed the folder and dropped it on the coffee table. "I don't know what else to tell you."

Nick stood, stuck his hands in his pockets to jingle his coins. "You don't have to tell me nothing. All you lawyers; you're all the same. Well, I gotta get going. I'm already late for the Jet Skis. I don't need any more information, all right? So I don't want you spending any more of my money on this."

Nolin lifted an eyebrow. "You're telling me, then, that you don't need representation in a matrimonial?"

Nick scowled. "Matri . . ."

"A divorce."

"Oh." Nick considered the question a moment. "Uh, not at the moment, no. But I'm not ruling it out in the future, you understand." He thought that over, liked the sound of it. "In fact, yeah. I *do* want a divorce, just not right now. Okay?"

Nolin shrugged. "Whatever you say."

"In the meantime, I hope you realize how sensitive a situation this is."

Nolin didn't have the foggiest. "Absolutely."

"With my family's standing in town and all, you know how damaging any publicity would be."

Now Nolin understood, and suppressed a smile. "I can appreciate your concern, Mr. Van Horne. As you know, an attorney-client relationship is strictly confidential. Our dealings are absolutely private."

Nick's eyes opened a fraction. "Yeah." He nodded. "And don't you forget it. Unless you want the bar association to yank your license. And don't think I can't have it done. I have some, shall we say, *influential* friends in Tallahassee."

Nick opened the door for himself and got into his brand-new green Monte Carlo. Nolin waited for it to turn the corner before he started laughing.

Jamie Hotchkiss stuck his grimy feet into a pair of Nike sandals, strung the credentials around his neck and grabbed the camera off the passenger seat. The beach was already getting crowded, and he needed to hurry. He walked toward the water's edge, crossed two lanes of traffic at the high-water mark and weaved through a menagerie of tourists in bright shorts, businessmen in loafers and housewives with toddlers to find the racers, their machines and, most important, their fans.

Yessir, the babes were flocking, just like he figured. Despite the chilly breeze off the greenish-brown water, the Jet Ski groupies bravely sported their thong bikinis. By the dozens, firm young buttocks faced shoreward, tanned and goose bumped.

Jamie adjusted his press badges. He'd spent hours

smudging the date so no one would realize he'd dug them from the trash following the last race three months earlier. Then he adjusted the zoom lens of the Nikon he'd found on some tourist's blanket two days earlier. Carefully, he half-pressed the shutter until, with a sudden whir, a trio of bare bottoms came into stark focus. He snapped off a couple of frames, put on his best salesman's smile and walked up behind the girls.

"Beautiful day, ain't it?" he asked after a while.

At just under six feet, with dirty blond hair and a dimple, he would have drawn their attention anyway. With the credentials and camera, they were as good as his.

"Nice enough," said the shortest of the three, a long-haired brunette. "You a photographer?"

Jamie affected a blush. It was a trick he'd lived off of for years. "Well, I shoot freelance for *Personal Watercraft* magazine." They looked at him blankly. "You know. Jet Skis. Wave Runners."

"Oh yeah." The tallest girl nodded. "I get that once in a while. You know, just to see what's new."

"Sure," Jamie agreed. "You've probably seen some of my work. Remember the issue with the South Beach race? I shot most of that." He smiled broadly and extended his hand. "Jamie Hotchkiss."

One by one, the girls shook his hand and introduced themselves: Tiffany, Monica and Kristin. It was Monica, the tall one, who asked him what he'd been waiting to hear.

"So, Jamie, you ever take pictures of other things? Or just Jet Skis?"

Jamie smiled again and went to work.

No matter how he adjusted them, the blasted headphones chafed his ears. He had no idea how teenagers spent blissful hours in them, whole days in them. Within minutes of donning them, he wanted to tear them off, fling them into the surf.

Outwardly he maintained a Zen-like calm, sitting cross-legged on his towel, invisible in the dark shades, headphones and Walkman clipped to his shorts. Casually he checked his watch for the fiftieth time and, for the fiftieth time, cursed inwardly. Those damn Van Hornes! Where the hell were they? They didn't even have the courtesy to be on time for their own stupid party!

He looked again out at the racecourse: three orange buoys set in a large triangle, with two of the markers forming a line parallel to the beach. If he'd done his homework properly, the tank was just about halfway between the southern mark and the eastern one. But if they didn't start soon, it would all be for naught.

The race had been scheduled for low tide, to maximize spectator room on the beach, and that's what he'd set his float for. It was already an hour past low and rising quickly.

True, there were always at least a few people in the water even before the race. He *could* set it off now. . . . But then the only targets would be the acolytes tuning their masters' machines and a few of the bikini set who were wading in and out of water to their knees.

He had no particular love for the bikini bimbos, and the racers' helpers were certainly Jet Ski operators themselves and therefore fair game. But the statement he wanted was best made with some actual wet-suited racers. Live on ESPN, for the entire world to witness via satellite. No, he would wait. It would be worth it.

He scanned the crowd again. The miserable matriarch, Joanna Van Horne, had finally arrived on the VIP platform in a bright yellow miniskirt, white blouse and a white jacket. She was only about twenty years too old for that look, but that had never stopped her before, he remembered. Even she was looking anxiously toward the street. Obviously it was the moron son holding things up now.

He turned quickly as a high-pitched whine cut through the buzz of the crowd and the rumble of the surf. One of the racers sped straight out to sea, turned around and sped back. Who knew why? Perhaps to impress the girls, who were starting to look bored as they stood in groups and gossiped. Three of them lounged unnaturally on a Jet Ski for a photographer, who darted like a puppy from side to side, taking pictures of as much upturned and thrust-out flesh as he could manage.

From behind him a cheer went up, and he turned to see the pudgy form of J. Robert Van Horne climb the platform steps and lamely hug his stepmother. A high-pitched squeal from the loudspeakers preceded her voice, welcoming everyone to the World's Most Famous Beach for the First Annual Daytona Offshore 100.

He smiled to himself and adjusted his Walkman. It was going to work out after all.

Nick grimaced, wished yet again he'd remembered to bring what he never went to the raceway without: earplugs. Because yet again the pack rounded the far marker and shrieked back toward the beach.

What the hell was he doing here, anyway? The turtle trial was supposed to start the following week. He had only seven days to work with. He should be out interviewing killers, not standing around watching a bunch of dumb Jet Skis.

Murder-for-hire was among Daytona's favorite pastimes, with at least one arrest every other month. Still, he had no idea where to begin. He tried to remember the newspaper headlines, the TV reports from the county jail or the scene of the crime. In almost every one, it seemed, the hit man was someone known to both customer and victim. Who did he know who could pull off something like that? Certainly not the twins. They'd be lucky not to kill each other by accident. Besides, having somebody you knew do it seemed almost as bad as doing it yourself. That's the first place the cops would start asking questions. There was probably a limit to how much friends in high places could do if it was obvious even to the greenest rookie that your pool guy had knocked off your wife.

No, there had to be a better way. . . . He'd taken the last gulp from his glass when the old light bulb came shining through again. He smiled as he confirmed to himself once more that he'd always go far because he was always one step ahead, always one notch smarter than the crowd.

The fact that every murder-for-hire he'd seen on the news had been committed by a friend of the family proved absolutely that that was the wrong way to go. Hah! Every single one of those cases was a *failure*, with the murderer going to prison or worse.

No, thank you. He would find an outsider. Somebody with no ties to either him or Barbie. Preferably someone with no ties even to Daytona. Someone who visited town but rarely, didn't know anybody here and was prone to violence and easy money. Someone, he smiled again, like a biker. And he knew just where to look. And as soon as this blasted race was over, that's just what he'd do.

Once again, the horde of banshees rounded the mark and headed away from the beach. Once again, he pushed the play button on his Walkman. And once again, nothing happened.

God damn it, he swore to himself. *God damn it all.* He'd waited too long. The water was too high now. The aerial was completely submerged, and it wasn't going to happen. All that time and money and planning. Wasted. All because of that lard-ass Van Horne showing up an hour late. Damn him to hell.

He bit back his anger and thought. There was still a chance. He'd have to time it with a trough of a wave, when a bit of wire was most likely to stick out above the surface. It was a long shot, but at this point, it was better than nothing. All he could do was try.

Nick winced again. It wasn't that they were particularly loud. They weren't, at least not compared to stock cars. They were just *annoying*, with a ridiculous high-pitched whine that lessened only for a blissful moment as the riders slowed to round a buoy. A swarm of mosquitoes. That's what they were. Just as persistent, just as irritating.

He swigged the rest of his vodka martini and turned to the table to make another, glancing sideways to see if his stepmother would notice. As usual, she was feigning total absorption in the race: standing upright in white pumps and miniskirt, eyes straight ahead, hands cupped around her wineglass. He had to admit, grudgingly, that she still cut a decent figure, for a woman of forty-six. Back when his dad had taken up with her, she'd been downright spectacular. He'd had trouble sleeping at night, thinking about her swimming in the pool or sitting in the kitchen in her purple kimono.

Much of that unnerving attraction was gone, thankfully, now that he'd learned to parlay his name and bank account into an active social life. The Daytona Debs hung on his every word, breaking dates and rearranging vacations to accompany him somewhere. Alas, they weren't much fun. Plus they were *so* expensive. With money of their own at home, it took real gold and real diamonds to impress. And, eventually, they wanted the whole thing: a ring, a big wedding, the name.

Not like his little Cherry, whose heart he'd won with a $24.99 ankle bracelet. She wore it all the time, he'd noticed, and usually not much else. That was the nice thing about Boardwalk babes: they never expected much. A decent $15 meal and a couple of six-packs of beer would get you everything you wanted. He recalled again the previous week, when she'd invited one of her girlfriends along. The three of them had split a magnum of champagne when the girlfriend and Cherry started getting friendly. It had rattled him, and he'd remembered an important appointment and escaped. He'd been able to think of little else since.

Next time, he swore, he wasn't going to freak out. Next time, he'd do them both, and have plenty left to spare. In fact, he wondered if she wasn't there now, on the beach. He picked up the binoculars and started scanning Bimbo Row along the water's edge. Quickly he settled on two possible sets of butt cheeks. Both were darkly tanned, firm and perky Both were bisected by a bright red strip of fabric. Now as soon as they turned a little bit . . .

But they didn't turn, and instead kept their eyes locked on the racers. *Damn them!* What the hell was so interesting about a bunch of cretins riding Jet Skis that they couldn't look away even for a minute? Hell, he'd met some of the racers. They weren't even rich! He couldn't understand the fascination with drivers, either, but at least some of them took home hundreds of thousands of dollars every race.

He darted the binoculars between the red-thonged girls for a while longer. Neither turned around, and out of sheer boredom he lifted the glasses toward the Jet Skis. Rounding the southern mark, they were, bouncing through the small chop out toward the seaward mark. A guy in a yellow wetsuit and blue helmet was in the lead, followed closely by a guy in a green wetsuit and red helmet. Or maybe Green Wetsuit was about to lap Yellow Wetsuit. Who knew? Who cared?

He followed Yellow Wetsuit up to the far mark. . . . Well, that was odd. The water around the orange buoy seemed darker than everywhere else, almost purple instead of green. Yellow Wetsuit slowed to take the turn, leaning toward the beach and sticking his left leg out to pivot around. . . . And he was gone.

Nick blinked, dropped the binoculars to see the whole picture. Sure enough, Yellow Wetsuit's Jet Ski sat in the water next to the buoy, but Yellow Wetsuit himself had disappeared. Within moments, Green Wetsuit was right on top of the idle Jet Ski, turning around it, trailing his leg when the water exploded in front of him, fell over him, swallowed him. And he was gone, too.

But he wasn't, completely. The crowd saw it the same moment Nick did, and as a group stepped back from the water's edge. A woman screamed, then another, as the phalanx of mechanics and gofers stood motionless by their trailers and corporate tents. Because still attached to the throttle of the little fuchsia water scooter, still driving it in ever widening manic circles, was Green Wetsuit's forearm, the thin spiral kill-switch cord still strapped to the wrist.

Nick watched with dropped jaw as the single-handed Jet Ski bounced off one boat, then another, knocking their riders into the now frenzied water before ramming a third racer head on. Both boats stopped dead for a moment before erupting in an orange ball of flame.

The remaining racers slowed to an idle, then saw why the water around the buoy was so turbulent: dark fins, more than a dozen, surrounding the riderless Jet Skis, slicing through the purple murk. Without warning, another wave exploded over Green Wetsuit's Jet Ski, shook the big plastic machine, then, amazingly, dragged it underwater.

The crowd screamed as one when, a few moments later, the boat popped back through the surface and settled low in the water. Green Wetsuit's forearm was gone.

Nick watched in stunned rapture. Five abandoned Jet Skis sat near the far buoy in various states of disrepair. The remaining dozen were back on the beach, their riders gesturing wildly at the water. The crowd of spectators murmured uncertainly, not knowing exactly what to expect next or even exactly what had happened. And everywhere, Jet Ski bimbos clung to boyfriends, strangers, one another.

Slowly it dawned on Nick what a wonderful, beautiful thing had just occurred. There would be no yellow caution flag, no prolonged delay as crews cleared wreckage and soaked up spilled oil from the track. That was it. The race was finished. He could go home.

TWO

...

"You know what those bastards down at Beach Patrol told me?"

Joanna sucked down a cigarette in anger. She only smoked now in anger, or in the presence of Winston officials, to demonstrate her loyalty to her biggest sponsor.

"They told me they couldn't kill them. That they didn't have the boats or the equipment. And even if they did, they wouldn't know which ones were responsible and that some kinds are protected or endangered or some such nonsense."

She took another powerful drag. Nick watched in awe as the glowing orange tip moved visibly down the paper.

"It's a crazy world," he mumbled.

"I should have them all fired. I should pick up the phone and get every last one of those cocksuckers fired."

Nick cringed. The C word was second only to the M word in implied carnage among Joanna's pantheon of traditionally male epithets. It wouldn't pay to be a smartass right now. Instead he stared down at the elaborate card-board-and-foam model of RaceWorld, the $120 million theme park Joanna had dreamed up two years earlier. It would feature exhibits, restaurants, Jet Ski rentals, a water slide and, most important, a strip of beach where visitors could race actual replica, turn-of-the-century cars on the sand.

She had planned to unveil it that afternoon, after the Jet Ski race, but decided to postpone in light of the day's events. She wanted her announcement to lead the newscast, not play second to "Sharks Eat Jet Skiers." They had quietly loaded the model and charts and artists' renderings back into the van and taken them home.

"Well, never mind. We'll have a quick memorial service for them tomorrow and be done with it. We still have the Offshore Challenge on Wednesday. We'll announce RaceWorld there." She stubbed out her cigarette, pulled another from the pack and lit it. "How are you coming with your project?"

Nick prepared to whine that she'd only given it to him that morning, then saw how fast her new cigarette was disappearing. "I'm, uh, meeting a prospect tonight," he gulped.

"Good. Don't screw this up. If that motherfucker judge rules in her favor, we may as well kiss RaceWorld good-bye. And you know what that means?"

Nick gulped again. The M word. He nodded weakly.

"Right. No inheritance." She kicked off her pumps and started pulling the blouse over her head. "Now get out of my sight."

Amee leaned over the table, lined up her cuestick and heard the sharp crack of a ball bouncing on linoleum. She lifted her eyes to see her new assistant chase it down, bend over awkwardly to grab it and scamper back to her table, mouthing the word "sorry" to Amee on her way.

Amee dropped her head in disgust for a moment, took a breath and nailed the eight ball into the far corner. Game.

She collected her money from her Joe and glanced around the room. Only two other customers were waiting. Both had eyes glued to the new girl, Lori. Amee had hired her to help out at night during the busy season, and paid her a flat rate of $3 a game. Lori was an abysmal pool player, but she was a big girl with long blonde hair, and none of the customers was complaining. In fact, Amee was making more money than she ever had on her own.

"I'm taking a break, Peaches," she shouted, snapping her cuestick into the rack on the wall. "I'll be back in a few."

She unzipped her fanny pack, found her box of Marlboro Lights, pulled one out with her lips and kicked the door to her "office" shut behind her. It had been a long day, but a good one. More than $150 so far, not counting her share of Lori's take, and the night was still young. She threw her legs and bare feet up on the metal desk and blew smoke toward the yellowed poster stuck to the ceiling.

It was of a thin girl with a model's face and long dark hair, taken in black and white. She was nude, but sat sideways to the camera with her knees drawn toward her chest. The only thing you could see was her left breast, a slight swelling capped with a long, dark nipple. She'd only noticed the poster several months after she'd taken over the pool hall, and could only imagine what the previous tenant had done while staring up at it. The door echoed with three quick knocks and she took another long drag. Never a moment's rest. There was a brief pause and then three more knocks.

"What now?" she shouted.

The door swung inward followed by a round head. "Are you Cherry?"

He had medium-length blond hair, bright blues and a permanent dimple. He'd stood by the wall for the last hour nursing a beer, staring down Lori's bikini top, but hadn't bought a single game. She blew a stream of smoke at his face. "Who wants to know?"

"Well, I guess I do," he replied politely. "Jamie Hotchkiss. A couple of friends suggested you and I could do some business."

Ah, so the middle-class looks were only a front. He was just another Boardwalk hustler. That, she could deal with. She nodded him in, and he stepped through the door and shut it behind him. He wore a soiled T-shirt, surfer shorts and a pair of yuppie sandals a size or two too small.

"Couldn't find any tourists with your shoe size?" she asked.

His eyes widened as he glanced down at his dirty feet. "No," he said quickly. "I, ah, bought these. They were on special. Real cheap. So I got 'em even though they're kinda small."

He had the trace of a hillbilly accent. Kentucky. Or Tennessee, maybe. "So what business are you in, exactly?"

"Well, ma'am, I'm actually a driver. You know. A race car driver?" He nodded solemnly. "I've done the dirt tracks where I grew up and I thought I'd come down here to break into the big time."

He stood so earnestly, waiting for her approval. She laughed out loud. "What, you want me to sponsor you? Drive a Top Shots Billiards car?"

The blue eyes moistened into a puppy-dog softness. "Oh, no, ma'am. I guess I've realized that getting into NASCAR might take a little longer than I thought. It might be weeks, maybe even months before I get my own car. In the meantime, I'm just trying to make a living, you know? A buck here, a buck there."

She finished one cigarette and lit another. "Well, there ain't much for you to do around here. I mean, you're cute, but not so cute that some guy from Buffalo's gonna pay five bucks a pop to see you in a thong, if you see what I'm saying."

"Oh, no." He dug an envelope out of his pocket. "See, I have pictures. I, uh, heard you know some people who can use these."

She held out her hand and he passed her the envelope. Who the hell had told him she bought pictures? She hadn't done that in almost a year, not since she left the House of Babes. Amee opened the drugstore envelope and pulled out a stack of color prints. Jet Ski bimbos. Three of them, sitting on top of, next to and around a bright orange Wave Runner. She flipped through them one by one. The girls were licking their lips, flaring their nostrils, sticking their butts at the lens, everything, in fact, except the one thing she was looking for: taking off their bikinis.

She threw the photos on the desk. "You ain't got dick. You only got one or two in there where you can even see anything. Who do you think's gonna buy that?"

He quickly straightened the pile into a neat stack, bent to retrieve two that had slid off the desk. "But what about all these?" he protested. "You can see their asses in every single one!"

She took a final drag from the bit of tobacco left above the filter and stubbed it out. "Okay, Einstein, I'm gonna explain a business principle to you: Nobody pays for something they can get for free. Nobody. Not you. Not me. Not girlie magazines. In Daytona, bare asses ain't even a dime a dozen. Now get out of here. I gotta get back to work."

"But what about this one?" He flipped through till he

found the shot in which the tall girl's top had, in her exertions, migrated south. "See?"

She stood, realized she only came up to his chin. He wasn't half bad-looking. Not long on brains, though. "Where, Jamie, do you think I can sell a picture of some chick sitting on a Jet Ski with one boob hanging out?"

He looked puzzled. "*Playboy?*"

She nodded. "*Playboy.*" She pointed up to the ceiling. "You see that? That's the kind of girl, that's the kind of picture that's *almost* good enough to get into *Playboy.*"

Jamie stared upward, slack-mouthed. "Whoa. Who is *she?*"

Amee glanced up at the dog-eared poster again, annoyed. "The fuck should I know who she is? My point is, *you're* never gonna shoot anything like it."

He hadn't taken his eyes off the ceiling. "She's hot. I mean totally hot."

Amee grabbed the photos and shoved them back into his envelope. "Okay. Time to go. Here." She unzipped her fanny pack, pulled out a $5 bill, stuck money and envelope in his hand. "Here's five bucks. Go to the store and buy a copy of *Hustler.* You get your girlfriends to do some of the things the chicks in *there* do, and we'll talk. Until then, get the fuck out."

She grabbed his waist and spun him around. Reluctantly, he pulled his eyes away from the ceiling and reached for the doorknob. "It was nice meeting you."

Amee shut the door after him and looked into the mirror to adjust her bikini. She tilted her head upward to look at the poster. What the hell did that girl have that she didn't? She pulled one bright-red triangle down, looked in the mirror to see the effect, looked back up at the poster. She snorted, pulled her top back on and went out into the pool hall.

·   ·   ·

He looked back down at his notebook, checked his math and then, with gloved hands, put another small lump of the heavy putty on the scales. Getting hold of it was easier now than it ever had been, what with all the unemployed arms dealers in Czechoslovakia and Russia. Thank God for the end of the Cold War.

He removed the final lump from the scales, piled it onto the others and gently kneaded the mass into a half globe. The exact shape wasn't crucial. It wouldn't be cutting through metal or propelling a spray of shrapnel. No, the correct amount was much more important than the configuration, and he double- and triple-checked his calculations.

Carefully he inserted the thin detonators, ran the wires to a junction box. He'd already laid a sheet of plastic underneath, and he folded it over, forming a doubled seam to act as the first barrier against the water. Four hours for the epoxy to set, another four for the silicone sealant around the wire leads. Two hours for final assembly and then six to swim it out to the site.

And the race wasn't for another two days. Plenty of time.

Amee slid deeper into the tub, lifted her toes up onto Nick's chest. He tried to ignore the dirt ground into her soles from running around barefoot on the filthy Boardwalk all day, just as he tried to ignore the forests of mildew on the tiled walls. When he got home, he'd need a shower to wash away this bath. No matter. Now wasn't a time to nitpick. Now was a time to celebrate. He sipped at his champagne.

"Nicky baby? I had this idea for the business. You tell me what you think. Right now I'm making five bucks a game, about six games an hour during the busy time. What if I raised my rates to twenty bucks a game? Then I could make four times as much."

Nick closed his eyes and, momentarily forgetting the mildew, leaned his head back against the tile. She was in the throes of one of her brainstorms again.

"Or I could make twice as much, and only work half as many hours."

He snorted. "Maybe you could set your rate at two hundred a game. Then you'd only have to shoot one game a day."

She pinched a fold of flesh on his chest with her toes, making him yelp and spill some of his champagne. "I'm *serious*! Don't make fun of my ideas or I'll kick your fat ass out of my tub!"

Nick poured himself some more champagne, set the bottle back on the toilet-seat lid. For a moment he considered reminding her whose money was paying for the tub, but then thought better of it. He was in too good a mood. "Sorry, baby. Please tell me more about your idea."

Amee smiled. "That's better. Okay. Right now, guys pay five bucks to shoot a game of pool with me in my bikini. Don't you think they'd pay twenty a game if I was topless?"

He blinked, realized she was serious. "Cherry, you can't go topless."

"Why not?" She sat up straight, lifting her breasts clear of the bubbles, and arched her back. "Don't you think they're good enough?"

Nick felt himself tingle. He imagined her dancing around the pool hall, rubbing up against the various sleazeballs and bozos, her boobs hanging free, and he felt himself awaken. "Sure, baby, they're great. That ain't the problem. Your outfit's already barely legal. You drop the top, then the pool hall becomes a strip joint. No way is the city gonna permit you for that on the Boardwalk."

Amee was speechless with anger. "Why the hell not? They got a shampoo parlor in the back of the pizza place. Hookers sell blowjobs in the photo booths at the arcade. All the gay pimps are out on Ocean Drive, but I can't take my top off to play a game of pool, for Chrissake?"

He wondered if she'd let him videotape her shooting pool topless. She probably would. "I know," he agreed. "It's not a fair world."

She slipped back in the tub, chugged the rest of her champagne and pouted. He was always a sucker for that. Besides, he was dying for an excuse to tell her.

"Anyway, you won't have to worry about shooting pool much longer," he said, reaching for the bottle to refill her glass.

"Why not?"

"Let's just say my financial worries are about to become history. And *you* won't have to worry about working another day of your life."

Amee smiled, scooted forward to sit on his lap. "Why? What's happening?"

He shouldn't tell her. He shouldn't tell anyone. That's how these things fell apart. Oh, what the hell. "My estranged wife is about to become my former wife."

She clapped her hands. "You're getting a divorce!"

He grinned, took another sip. "I'm gonna be a widower," he whispered.

Amee's eyes grew wide with amazement and, he saw with satisfaction, genuine awe. "Nicky, I'm so proud of you!" She clapped her hands together, squeezing gobs of Mr. Bubble into the air and onto the tiled floor. "When, Nicky? When you gonna do it?"

Nick glanced at his wrist, remembered he'd taken off the Rolex in the first moments of pawing and grabbing at the front door to their love nest. "Within a couple of hours, I should be a free man."

"Oh, Nick!" She slid farther forward, bent down for a long, wet kiss. "I can't tell you how much you turn me on," she whispered. "This is the end of all our problems, isn't it? You'll get all the money now, right?"

One hand reached up to grab from below, the other stretched around to grab from behind. Fondle as much as you can, whenever you can, was his rule. You never knew when it would be gone. "Not exactly," he explained. "It's not like she's got the money. That's Joanna. But this puts me in a better position."

She slapped at his hand. "Don't pinch. How many fuckin' times do I gotta tell you? I don't like to be pinched."

He cautiously moved his hand back onto her chest. "Sorry."

"Now explain 'not exactly,' " she demanded. "What does killing her do, if it doesn't get us more money?"

Women, he thought angrily. They were the same. All of them, all of the time. Still, he couldn't piss her off. She'd promised that Lori would come over later. "Barbie's damn turtle lawsuit is wrecking Joanna's plans for the company. In other words, she's screwing with my inheritance."

Amee sat still for a moment. "I thought you told me once that Joanna was actually younger than you."

For a Boardwalk bimbo, she was sharp, he thought. "She is. By a year."

"So she's probably gonna live as long as you. Probably longer."

Nick paused. He hadn't thought of it that way. "Yeah. I guess."

"You guess." She laughed, pushed off his lap and slid back to her end of the tub. She reached over to the toilet lid for her cigarettes, lit one and blew smoke at him. "Great. Basically, Joanna's got you doin' her dirty work.

You make her richer, she gives you diddly squat. Good thinking, Einstein."

He hated when she called him that. Where did she get off making fun of him? At least he'd seen the inside of a college, which was a hell of a lot better than dropping out of some bum-fuck high school near Cleveland. God damn it, though, she was right. Joanna *was* using him, and what would he get out of it? Nothing more than he was getting now. A stupid little eight grand a month. Anything more, he had to beg Joanna for.

Joanna. He sounded it out again. *Joanna.* God, he hated that name. What was his old man thinking? He didn't have to marry her. He could have kept her in a condo somewhere, gone over whenever he needed some, and nobody would have been the wiser. Joanna. Now *there* was his real problem. If he had any balls, he'd have her dealt with, too. Hell, he had plenty of money. All he'd have to do was . . .

He blinked twice, allowed himself a confident smile, refilled his champagne glass and took a sip. "What makes you think Barbie's the only one I'm taking care of?" He waited till she looked up, took a slow, casual sip.

The look of wonder returned. "You're gonna . . . ?"

He shrugged carelessly. "As soon as he's done with Barbie, he does Joanna."

Amee was speechless.

"The order's important, you know. 'Cause the old man had a soft spot for Barbie. If she outlives Joanna, she gets a chunk. This way, see, everything comes my way."

She shook her head and smiled. "Nicky, I'm sorry I got mad. I shoulda trusted your business sense."

She leaned forward, took a deep breath and plunged her face into the bubbles over his lap. He started in alarm, jerking his head back against the tiled wall with a sharp *crack.* Waves of pain drowned out all else, and he groaned in agony.

Amee finally came up for air, licked her way up his chest to his mouth. "I planned a special treat tonight," she whispered, biting his lip. "But I better let you get home."

Nick winced back tears. "Why?" he managed finally.

"For your alibi, silly. The cops are gonna come to you right off the bat. You gotta prove you weren't there."

Gingerly he pushed on the back of his skull. Pain stabbed through him again. "Oh, yeah. That."

She studied him in silence. "Nicky, maybe you better let me help you. I think maybe I got a little more experience with this sort of thing."

"With what? Having people knocked off?"

"With doing business with, you know, this type of people."

"This type?" He wondered whether he was bleeding.

"Bums. Like you shouldn't meet this guy again, in case the cops are watching."

He decided he wasn't bleeding. A skull fracture, maybe. A concussion, definitely. But not bleeding. "What guy?"

"The shooter, for Chrissake! Who you think we been talkin' about all this time? The Pope?"

He had no idea who she was talking about. She didn't even realize how much pain he was in, or that she'd caused it. The selfish bitch. "Why would I want to meet him again?"

She pushed herself off his chest, sat up straight. "To pay him the rest of the money. You know: half before, half after?" Her shoulders suddenly sagged. "Tell me you didn't give him everything up front."

A jolt of fear hit his stomach, twisted it. He'd never even stopped to worry about this. "Why wouldn't I pay up front?" he asked defensively. "This way, I don't *have* to meet him afterward."

She shook her head sadly. "You know, it's a good thing you were born rich, 'cause otherwise you'd be in the gutter drinkin' paint thinner by now." She took a deep breath. "Okay. Let's go get it back. How much?"

He gulped. "Ten."

Amee thought she would cry. "You gave him ten grand. And he told you he'd kill your wife. And that was good enough for you."

"He seemed honest."

She shook her head again. "So who is he?"

"His name's Lance. I don't know his last name. And I didn't tell him *my* real name," Nick said proudly. "I wore a disguise."

"Brilliant. So who is he?"

"A biker. Found him in a bar."

She scrunched up her nose. "A biker named *Lance*? What bar?"

"That place on Main Street. Across from the cemetery. You know: the Iron Spike."

Amee held her breath for a long moment, then screamed, slapped his ear. "Nick! You're *so* fuckin' stupid! Do you have any idea *how* fuckin' stupid you are?" She stood, stepped out of the tub. "The Iron Spike is a *fag* bar. *Fag* bikers go there. You want your house redecorated, you go to the Iron Spike. You want your wife *killed*, you go to Mike's Tap!"

He held his ear with one hand, the back of his head with the other, shut his eyes against the pain. "Jesus Christ . . . The fuck was *I* supposed to know? They were all wearing leather and chains and shit!" He opened his eyes, saw her standing over him, soap suds sliding off her body. God, she was beautiful. "It's all right! Tomorrow I'll go back there and get my money back."

She grabbed a towel and started drying off. "Forget it. You're never going to find Lance again. He's down in South Beach by now, bragging to his boyfriends how some complete *moron* gave him ten grand!"

She finished with the towel and threw it at him. "Now get the fuck out of my bathtub."

Mathematics was never her strongest suit, so she added all the numbers in both halves of the ledger again. And, once again, she came up with the same depressing result. Her assets were tens of thousands less than her liabilities. What's more, she had nothing left to borrow against. What little equity she had in her house had been mortgaged first. Next came the credit cards, and she had wisely stopped after maxing out two.

She sipped a glass of wine and looked around the dining room, assessing value. An old, scratched table, a garage-sale sideboard she'd never gotten around to refinishing, rickety chairs. The lot would get her maybe $50. A *Southern Living* home and college-student furniture. Such was her life.

Barbie sighed deeply, refilled her glass and grabbed the towel off the countertop. She returned to the living room, pulled open the sliding glass door and padded softly onto the deck. It was her favorite part of the house: weathered, light-gray wood, bordered by sea oats and a matching gray privacy fence.

She bent beside the Jacuzzi and flicked a switch on the side. The pump began a gentle rumbling, and a few feet away, bubbles gurgled to the surface of the sunken hot tub. It was a beautiful night: cool but not cold, a fresh ocean breeze. Only a thin layer of clouds off the water marred perfection. She set her wineglass on the deck, pulled off her long-sleeve T-shirt and sweatpants and climbed down the steps, nestling the small of her back against a stream of bubbles.

With another sip from her glass, she started running through the possibilities again. Income from the store barely paid the rent and utilities, so there wasn't much she could do there. The old Volkswagen wasn't costing her much but also wasn't worth much. It was the house that was killing her, pure and simple. The mortgage payment was just over $1,900 a month, which was $1,900 a month she no longer had.

She needed a roommate. That was it. Someone to take one of the bedrooms and pay $950 rent. Yeah, sure. Who in Daytona Beach well off enough to pay $950 a month was going to *want* a roommate? Only students didn't mind roommates, and Daytona wasn't exactly a college town. She wouldn't mind sharing with a professional woman who lived normal hours and kept to herself. But students, with their angst and weird ideas and weirder schedules, they were something else entirely.

No, the answer was plain. She would have to bite the bullet and sell the place. It was the only way. She could probably get enough to pay off the credit cards and get square with the lawyer. Enough, at least, to make him start the trial. And if he started the trial, he would finish the trial. He was too afraid of the judge not to. That way, the turtles would at least get a fighting chance.

Yes, tomorrow she'd talk to a realtor. It was the only way.

After three hours of drywalling, the vinyl chaise lounge seemed as comfortable as the deepest, most luxurious divan. Nolin spread himself on it, with one hand popped open a longneck Bud, flipped the cap onto the concrete with the bent nails, chipped plaster and other accumulated trash.

The first swig was cold, ice cold, and he let it slide down his throat slowly. He let out a long, satisfying burp and turned to survey his work by the light from the lone, dim bulb hanging from the ceiling. His second "project" house, it was. Just like the one on the river in Holly Hill, only better. He'd finished the outside first, pulling off all the old siding, replacing it with stained wood, re-shingling the roof, replacing the crumbled concrete driveway with brick.

He'd started on the interior about a month earlier: ripping up shag carpet and dirty linoleum to get down to bare floor, tearing down flimsy paneling, adding a skylight, nailing up new Sheetrock. He studied his calloused hands, still slightly warm and swollen from the evening's exertions, and took another swig of beer.

Whatever had possessed him to waste years of nights and weekends becoming a lawyer, he wondered for the two- or three-millionth time, when what he truly loved was working with his hands, building things? Or perhaps now building things was fun, a hobby, while writing briefs and filing motions was work. Maybe if he built houses for a living and lawyered in his free time, maybe then he would trade his loves for his hates. He took another long swig from his bottle. Maybe not.

He turned back toward the sea, which lay dark and still beyond two-by-fours that framed what would become a sun room, with ceiling fans and huge hurricane-vulnerable glass windows. It would be the only room, save the bathrooms, with tile floors instead of hardwood, his grudging acknowledgment that it would, eventually, flood. Because it was a good two feet lower than the rest of the house, he hoped that maybe the natural disaster gods would spare him, and never let the storm surge rise above the threshold into his living room.

Outside, he heard a rustling in the dune. He put down his beer and clapped twice.

"Pedro! Come!"

The dune became still. After a moment, the rustling resumed.

"Pedro!" he shouted this time. "Don't *make* me come in there and kick your butt!"

The creeping ivy and sea oats parted, and a small tan-and-brown dog stepped out, stopped and stared at him sheepishly.

"Pedro? How many times have I told you not to go in the dune at night, huh? Now come here and sit!"

The dog stared at him silently, finally walked between two studs and sat before Nolin. He bent down and squeezed his head, scratching under his chin and behind his ears. "Good boy. That's a good boy."

He'd adopted Pedro that New Year's Eve. He'd seen him almost every day he worked on the house, wandering up and down A1A. Then one day he realized he hadn't seen him in more than a week. On a hunch he went to the Humane Society and, sure enough, in Cage 14 was the familiar pointed snout, the dark eyes. The lady said he had labrador, shepherd, collie and about five other species in him, and had another two days before his stay of execution expired. He'd paid her the $50 on the spot. Even a month later it still made him nervous not to have him on his leash. Pedro had had a tendency to run into the street his first couple of weeks with him, and it had scared Nolin to death.

"There. That's a good boy." The watch on his wrist beeped twice, and Nolin stared out the framing to the north. It was almost time. "Sit, Pedro. Stay."

He stood, walked up the two stairs, grabbed another

beer from the cooler, pulled the chain on the bulb and returned to the sun room. From a nail in a stud he removed a pair of rubberized binoculars and draped the strap around his neck, lifted them to his eyes, adjusted the focus. The optics were excellent, and the huge lenses picked up what little light was available and magnified it, so that every detail on the wooden dune crossover stood out clearly despite the gloom.

Rarely did he have to wait more than five minutes. On that night, he waited less than two. A wooden gate swung open and a tall woman strode onto the crossover, down the ramp and skipped down the steps to the beach. Long, graceful legs and arms, a slim waist, long dark hair; *God*, she was beautiful. She ran down the sand and waded into the water, waited for a wave, dove under it, swam five, ten, twenty strokes through the dark water and stood to walk back out.

He tweaked the focus knob a touch and held his breath. It had become a nightly ritual: knock off by nine and wait in the shadows for his uninhibited neighbor. He loved it. Someday, eventually, maybe, he'd work up the nerve to meet her. After he'd moved in. After he had the place put together. Maybe then. Bump into her one day as she went to check her mail. Someday.

Suddenly she bent over, dropped to her knees. He lowered the glasses a hair and saw her smiling broadly, petting a pointy-snouted dog as it tried to lick her face. And then his breath caught in his throat. It was Pedro, licking her hands, wagging his tail like he'd never been petted before.

Nolin dropped the binoculars and stared out into the dark in horror. The son of a bitch must have snuck off! *Now* what was he going to do? He put the glasses to his eyes again, saw her checking his collar for a name tag.

Damn it all! He hadn't bought one yet. She was liable to take him for a stray, call Animal Control . . .

"Pedro!" He slipped through the wooden studs, started running down the short crossover to the sand. "Pedro! Come!"

Yeah. Right. Like *that* had ever worked. He slowed, began wondering what in God's name he would say once he got there: Hi, I'm Nolin. That's my dog and you've got a great ass? He should go back. Right now. He could still slip back to his porch; Pedro would come home on his own.

He froze in his steps. She had glanced up, smiled. He gulped, started walking again.

She looked up again. "Cute dog. Is he yours?"

"Pedro," he stammered. "Pedro."

She stood, nipples erect in the cool breeze. She stuck a hand out. "It's nice to meet you. I'm Barbie."

He dropped her hand. Her nipples were *so* long. Longer than he'd ever seen. Almost an inch, it seemed. Why did nipples need to be so long?

"Are you an astronomer?"

A moment of sheer panic: She'd been talking to him . . . And he'd been staring at her chest. Shamefully he jerked his eyes upward, wondered what she'd said, tried to think of something clever, something urbane.

"Huh?" he managed finally.

She pointed at the binoculars around his chest. "Were you looking at the stars?"

"Yeah. I was looking at the stars." He'd finished before he even knew what he was saying.

Together they lifted their heads to the sky, to the clouds that had been rolling in off the ocean all evening. "But I couldn't find any," he added weakly.

Barbie searched the sky in vain. "Yeah. Too bad. I love looking at the stars, and the planets." She smiled. "I'm kind of into astrology, you know? How the heavenly bodies affect our lives?"

He smiled back, kept his eyes locked on hers.

She crossed her arms, rubbing them with open palms. "Well, I'd love to chat, but I'm getting kind of cold." She bent to pet the dog, then waved a hand at him. "It was nice meeting you, Pedro."

She turned and scampered up the steps, along the walkway and through the open wooden gate to her patio. Nolin waited on the beach, silent, his eyes fixed on the closed gate. Ten minutes later she still hadn't come back out. He grabbed Pedro's collar and dragged him back to the house.

THREE

...

Tylenol 3, Nick decided, was a hoax. A placebo for those too stupid to figure out they'd been had. That's what the Raceway doctor had given him for his concussion. Codeine, he'd said. Take two every four hours, he'd said. Nick had taken six, and it hadn't done a bit of good.

The interminable memorial service for the "Fallen Jet Skiers," as the city had taken to calling them, hadn't helped either. What a total fraud. The mayor, the City Commission, the County Council and every weasel politician in between had made a speech, going on about the morons like they were war heroes. All they'd done was ride around in circles on water bikes, for Christ's sake, and been unlucky enough to fall off near some hungry sharks.

They'd filled First Baptist, the biggest church in town. Probably the only time they'd seen the inside of a church, what was left of them, anyway. Served the bastards right. He snorted, recalling all the little groupies in their black spandex minidresses, bawling into their hankies as they walked past the five coffins, empty except for a forearm in one, a bit of leg in another. That was all the Marine Patrol had been able to salvage.

The mayor, meanwhile, had yammered about having called in the best shark experts in the world, who'd all assured him that it had been a freak incident, an isolated event, and that there was no reason to close the beaches. Nick wondered if the tourists would be dumb enough to buy it. Couldn't they remember what happened in *Jaws*?

The car behind him honked impatiently. Nick scowled, noticed the green light and stepped on the gas. He flipped a middle finger at the rearview mirror for good measure and squeezed his throbbing head. The doctor had said the pain would last at least a couple of days. Then he'd dug some mildewy grout out of his scalp, asked if he'd fallen down in a public shower.

That bitch Amee. She'd get hers. He'd take care of Barbie, then Joanna, then he'd get Amee, too. There were plenty of women in Daytona who'd die for the chance to put out for J. Robert Van Horne, plenty of *fine* women. James Bond would never have taken any lip from some Boardwalk tramp. Neither would he, and she'd best not forget it.

Who did she think she was? Kicking him out of the apartment *he* was paying for? And all that crap about him being stupid: It wasn't *his* goddamned fault the Iron Spike was a gay bar. How the hell was he supposed to know? Sure, it was easy to look back and criticize. But where the hell had she been when he was putting out feelers, asking the hard questions, interviewing his candidate?

Gay bar. Gay *biker* bar, for Christ's sake. Who ever heard of such a thing? And of course *no* one there that morning had heard of any Lance. Couldn't remember seeing him there last night. No, come to think of it, they couldn't remember *Nick* having been there, either. And then they'd snicker and turn away.

Damn homos. They all stuck together. Well, he'd get the last laugh. Once he had his money, he'd find somebody to take care of old Lance. And maybe he'd talk to a couple of the city code inspectors about checking into the Iron Spike. Make sure they had their sneeze guards properly installed around the salad bar. Or maybe he'd just have the place torched.

On a last, desperate hope that maybe he had indeed found the one, honest, man-of-his-word gay biker, he'd cruised down Seabreeze Boulevard, peered in through the window as he passed the Harmonic Age. Sure enough, there she was. No bullet holes, garrote scars or knife wounds.

Well, he'd fix that. This time he'd get a real biker, not some candy-ass mama's boy.

He was the essence of grace: long, tapered body, streamlined snout, smooth, scythelike tail. A million years of evolution hadn't brought even the tiniest change. He hadn't needed any. Lightning fast, agile, awesomely powerful. Not a bump or an appendage wasted. Perfection.

He sliced through the murky waters, homing in on the signal he'd known since birth. A slow pinging that triggered electrical impulses along the long, thin vibration sensors buried on either side of his great head.

Quickly he found the source, and slowed to bump the familiar figure: a dark, four-limbed creature standing on the sandy bottom. Slowly he nuzzled up against it, with one dark eye saw the stream of bubbles escaping from near the creature's top. He relaxed, enjoyed the stimulation of the limbs rubbing either side of his snout, flipped over to have his belly stroked.

And then, on cue, a limb reached into a side pocket and pulled out the little food, slid it carefully into his jaws. There were two more little foods, which he swallowed whole, even though he wasn't particularly hungry. He had eaten well the day before. He had eaten big food. Three of them, and pieces of two more, pieces he had stolen away from smaller, weaker competitors.

Eating, though, wasn't a question of hunger. It was what he did, especially when he heard the signal. He had to eat. The slow sound meant little food, and a visit with the limbed creature. The fast sound meant big food. Today was little food. And strokes.

He nuzzled his enormous head upward for more.

Joanna paged through the album as she waited. The photos had faded somewhat through the years, but not badly. She was glad she'd opted for the acid-free paper, even though it had cost five dollars more at a time in her life when five dollars meant something.

"He's still in there, Mrs. Van Horne," the perky young voice on the phone told her. "I can have him call you as soon as he's free."

"I'll hold," Joanna insisted.

The Muzak came back on and Joanna cradled the handset between ear and shoulder. It was always best to hold for the Honorable Marvin Julius Weathers, for he was a busy man, what with his twin roles of Speaker of the Florida House and chairman of the Coalition for Decency. Even busier now, on the brink of the new Legislative session: meetings all day; deals to cut; arms to twist; fresh, young college interns to screw.

Joanna smiled to herself. She couldn't complain. He'd always done right by her, even before that afternoon a decade earlier when he'd seen the pictures and come to understand that it wasn't just her husband he needed to respect. She turned the page in the album and gasped. No matter how many times she saw that one, it still amazed her. First that it had happened at all, and second that she had allowed it to be photographed.

Like the other photos, it was a Polaroid, and showed the backside, from the waist down, of a strapping young black man, the starting tailback of the Florida State Seminoles. Kneeling before him was a naked, nineteen-year-old Joanna Montgomery. She wore no makeup, but her face was unlined, fresh and smiling. And behind her, grabbing her generous bosom with both hands, was a drunken but clearly recognizable M. J. Weathers, then the 'Noles' second-string wide receiver.

Joanna shook her head at the photo, wondering again how they'd all managed to get in the picture. The camera must have had an auto-timer, no doubt. Her memories of the event were sketchy and faded, obscured by the fog of alcohol and pot that had precipitated their little party. She had been the jock fraternity's "little sister," terrified to tell her parents that she had flunked out. The frat brothers had graciously put her up in their house, passing her from room to room as their outside social lives demanded.

She had been assigned to Weathers' room for about a week, and had actually grown to like him, when his buddy Troy had stopped by one evening with a bottle of Wild Turkey and a dime bag. One thing led to another, and before she knew it, they were all three naked, in and out of the twin bed, pawing each other like the porn movie they'd just got done watching. Somewhere a Polaroid camera appeared, and they shot the whole cartridge.

Joanna decided later it must have been Troy's camera, because that's who blackmailed her with the photos just a few months before she was to marry racing magnate Bobby Horn in Daytona's Wedding of the Century. By then, Troy had long since suffered his career-ending knee injury, blown what money he'd earned in his brief NFL stint and had been in and out of jail on cocaine charges. In retrospect, he had done her a favor. The photos, after all, were a much more powerful tool in her hands, and worth a whole lot more than the $2,500 Troy had bargained for. And with his overdose a year later, there was no telling where they might have wound up if she hadn't bought them.

At one time she had considered incinerating all the photos save for the one useful shot. But as the years passed, she was glad she hadn't. She had come to enjoy reminiscing about how she once looked naturally, before the series of tucks and lifts and suctions. And, truth be told, looking at herself in the various porn-star poses still made her hot, made her wonder if she could still manage . . .

The Muzak clicked off in Joanna's ear.

"Speaker Weathers."

Joanna smiled. Not M. J., or just Weathers, but Speaker Weathers.

"Good afternoon, M.J. It's your favorite multimillionaire."

The line clicked again, as M.J. switched off the speakerphone. "Hullo, Joanna," he drawled. "What can I do you for today?"

"How are things?" she teased. "How are your buddies in the God Squad?"

A brief pause. M.J. had heard this bit before. "What is it you need, Joanna?"

She wasn't through teasing yet. "Don't you want to know what I'm looking at?"

She heard the line become muffled, heard M.J. call his secretary "sweetheart," ask her to close the door on her way out. "You know, Joanna," his voice returned clearly, "I'm sure you could find plenty of guys in Daytona to re-create that night for you. You seem awful hung up on it. What's it been, twenty-seven, twenty-eight years?"

Joanna laughed pleasantly. "Now M.J., you *know* that's not my favorite." She flipped the page on the album. "You know which one I'm looking at right now, don't you?"

M.J. knew. She had shown it to him once. Not the original, of course, but a snapshot of the photo. It had been fuzzy, but clear enough to show M. J. Weathers and Troy Jefferson, their arms around each other's shoulders, huge grins on their stoned faces as they proudly displayed the evidence of Joanna's handiwork. Of course, Joanna had snapped the picture herself, so that one photo, taken out of context, implied something else entirely. Something a God-fearing, race-baiting, gay-bashing, Bible-thumping public servant would be hard pressed to explain.

"I don't even remember it," he said calmly. "Neither do you, I bet. Besides, I was a kid. It was three decades ago."

"Save it. You were already president of the student senate, Campus Crusade and College Republicans. And if I remember right, your election campaign called for firing all homosexuals from the state colleges." She snapped the album shut, shifted into business mode. "Anyway. That's not why I called. I want to know what's happening with my RaceWorld bill."

"I shouldda known. Now Joanna, why can't you just come to the point? How many times do I have to tell you that you don't need to blackmail me? Have I *ever* turned down one of your bribes?" M.J. sighed. "Okay. RaceWorld. Like I told you last week, it ain't a bill. Bills gotta be filed, and then pesky freshman members ask dumb questions about them. I'm doin' it as two amendments on two separate bills. The first one grants a waiver to the coastal construction set-back line along the Daytona Beach–Ponce Inlet Corridor. The second allocates eighty million dollars for redevelopment projects east of the set-back line between Sebastian Inlet and the Georgia border. The restrictions are written so that only RaceWorld qualifies."

Joanna doodled on her desk pad, drew a giant, three-dimensional dollar sign, wrote out an eight followed by seven zeros. "So when are you planning on introducing them?"

"I already told you. They'll be inserted as technical amendments by the staff. It's no big deal. But I've got something for *you*: What the hell's going on with that lawsuit? I thought you were gettin' that dismissed?"

She squirmed in her chair. "We've hit kind of a snag with that."

"I read about your snag. Your idiot son plants piles of chicken eggs on the beach. And now the judge can't wait to rule against the county. Nice going. You realize, don't you, that if the judge finds in her favor, it could take years of appeals to get it overturned? And all that time, not a shovel gets turned on RaceWorld? Not to mention the possibility it might not *get* overturned?"

"He's not my son," Joanna corrected. "He's my stepson. In fact, he's older than me."

"Whatever. Point is: You don't get things in order down there, it don't make a lick of difference what I do up here. I could set aside eight hundred million, and it would just sit in the Treasury collecting dust."

Joanna wondered about his sudden enthusiasm. He'd never sounded so interested before. Perhaps she'd been overly generous with her carrot: ten percent of RaceWorld's net for as long as he lived. She did, after all, still have a pretty persuasive stick. Perhaps she'd modify the agreement—after he'd slipped the language into law.

"Don't worry yourself about it," she said. "RaceWorld will make you a millionaire."

"I'm already a millionaire."

"You can never be too rich, or too thin. I'll talk to you soon."

Joanna paged backward through the album. It was amazing how far M.J. had moved in the world since that night. He'd never actually started a game until his senior year, and even then he hadn't been very good. Now, having taken over the right wing of the state Republican Party, M.J. had a great shot at Congress. Or even governor.

She smiled, wishing M. J. Weathers a long and prosperous career. She shut the album, walked to the wall safe behind the giant aerial photo of the racetrack and tucked it away.

Amee stood on tiptoe to wave bye to Dave from Charlotte, the night's first customer, as he walked off down the Boardwalk, $40 poorer than when he'd walked in.

She smiled, satisfied. She'd played him well, letting him win the first two games, and then beating him, barely, with what looked like a lucky shot. Then she beat him consistently and handily, figuring his ego would keep buying games until he'd won again.

Eight games from one Joe wasn't bad for the early evening lull when customers were scarce. She turned and headed for the bar, where Rick already had two rumrunners poured and waiting. She pulled a Marlboro Light from her fanny pack *en route* and had already sucked down two lungsful by the time she sat down.

A few gulps of bubble-gum pink drink later, though, the exhilaration of earning $40 in less than an hour wore off, and she fell back into the dumps she'd awakened in. She'd fucked up last night. Big time. She'd pushed that schmuck too far, and had the uneasy feeling she wouldn't be able to reel him back.

The fool needed her help, not her insults. She berated

herself for not biting her tongue; it was something she'd never been good at, and this time it had cost her. This guy was rich: not owned-a-hardware-store-or-gas-station rich, but *real* rich. Millionaire rich. A chick didn't get many shots at guys like that, especially guys that rich who were also that dumb.

If she played Nick right, she'd have more money than she'd ever dreamed of, a hell of a lot more than she'd ever make scamming pool games. She had to be smarter, and treat him like any other Joe whom she needed to play for a while. She had to stroke him, make him feel important, smart, powerful, until she had him where she could finish him. With Nick, that could take months. She had to ease into a position where he'd trust her, tell her things, like where he kept the cash in his house, how much money he had in his checking account, what the code was for his ATM card. And, if he was serious about doing his wife and stepmom, he would be in line for some serious dough. Like enough even to try to marry the fool, get in his will . . .

She had a daydream she hadn't had since she was nine —herself in a white, flowing gown, a veil over her face, walking down the aisle—when she noticed the heavy smell behind her, a thick combination of sweat, mildew and sex.

"Don't you ever wear any other clothes?"

She turned to find Jamie, the wanna-be race-car-driving pornographer. He had another day's growth of erratic facial hair and wore the same grungy T-shirt and shorts he had the day before. "Don't *you*?"

He smiled, showing off the deep dimple in his left cheek. "I had a busy night *and* a busy morning." He pulled another packet of photos from his shorts and set them on the bar. "Didn't have time for a shower."

Amee blew a stream of smoke into the air, set down her

cigarette in an ashtray. "More chicks in bathing suits?" she asked, opening the packet from the one-hour lab and pulling out the inner envelope.

"I did what you told me. I bought a copy of *Hustler* to study, and I saw right away what you were talking about. Can I have your other drink?"

Amee pushed the second glass toward him and stared at the first photo. It was one of the girls from the day before, except she was in bed on all fours, looking down through her spread legs at the camera. She wore only a gold ankle bracelet and a hungry sneer.

"That's Monica," Jamie added helpfully. "She was the best. I got a real good one of her further down, holding a rolling pin."

She slipped through the stack, each new picture more explicit than the last. One had Tiffany lying back, legs open, back arched, face screwed up in feigned ecstasy.

"That's a good one, huh?" He smiled proudly. "You can see right up inside."

By the middle of the roll, Jamie had gotten the girls to start playing with assorted props: a hairbrush, kitchen implements, various pieces of fruit, stuffed animals. A few shots further, he'd gotten them to start playing with each other.

"And you met these chicks for the first time yesterday?" The pictures were amateurishly shot, with bad lighting and worse composition. But the girls were all pretty and all young. Not a dimple of cellulite among them. She could get $200 or $300 for the stack without even trying. "Who are they?"

Jamie knocked back half his drink. "They're roommates, here in town. Two of 'em wait tables at the Quarterdeck. The third one, Monica, sells timeshares." He picked up the pile Amee had finished with. "You know, they're just the sweetest gals I ever met. They really want to help me out. I don't have a place to stay, so they took me in. They made me dinner last night." He nodded sincerely. "They're like sisters to me."

Amee got to the last picture, a family portrait of the three surrounding their new brother. Jamie sat on a tattered couch, drunk and naked, each arm around a bare girl, each hand cupping a bare breast. All three girls lent a hand to cover his privates.

"These are your sisters? Where are *you* from, Kentucky?"

He grabbed the photo and shoved it into his pocket. "West Virginia. This one ain't for publication. It's just a souvenir."

Amee shook her head, drew a long puff from her cigarette, crushed the butt in the ashtray. "What did you promise them?"

"I didn't *promise* nothing. I told them I'd try to get them shoots with *Playboy* and *Penthouse*, and that could get 'em into modeling and acting. But before the big boys would even look at 'em, they had to be in smaller magazines first, like *Hustler*. So what do you think, can you sell 'em?"

"Maybe." She lit another cigarette. "I might be able to get a hundred or a hundred fifty. For the set."

His eyebrows narrowed. "And how much is your take?"

"For this?" She shrugged. "I'd do it for fifteen percent."

Jamie took a deep breath. "Okay. So if you sold 'em for a hundred, that means you'd keep . . ." He added figures, mouthed out calculations, closed his eyes. "No, wait . . ."

"Fifteen dollars." She sighed. "Which means you'd get eighty-five."

"Right. And if it was one fifty, then . . ."

"Twenty-two fifty for me, a hundred twenty-two fifty for you."

She eyed him carefully. He was a total cretin, but had a certain charm. What he'd done with those girls was impressive, if he was telling the truth: met them in the afternoon, had them modeling porn for him that night.

"You're pretty good with girls, huh?"

He smiled modestly. "I'm okay, I guess. My friends tell me I do all right with the women."

She nodded. "You can pretty much talk them into anything, huh?"

"Well, not *anything*. But women listen to what I have to say. I'd say I have that ability. You want I should go back and get some more pictures?"

"No, no. These are fine. But how would you like to start doing some driving sooner instead of later?"

He tilted his head skeptically. "What kind of driving?"

"NASCAR driving."

His face melted in awe. "You serious?" he whispered.

"You'll never guess who my boyfriend is." She popped down off her stool. "Follow me to my office."

Nolin laid the two-by-four across the sawhorses, rummaged for his tape measure and pulled it the length of the stud. *Pedro*. Just friggin' brilliant. And then to make sure she noticed his blazing intellect, he'd repeated it: *Pedro*. He turned to the corner where he'd banished the mutt. "See where your shenanigans got us? Bad dog!"

Pedro perked up his ears, then laid them flat when he realized he was still being scolded. Nolin marked the wood, rewound the tape and drew it back out on the other side. Measure twice, cut once. *God*, she was beautiful. Long, lean, perfect skin. Just like she'd looked through the binoculars. And now, thanks to his traitor dog, his beautiful, long, lean neighbor knew that he was a friggin' pervert. Spied on naked women from the safety of his porch. One hand for the binoculars, one hand for himself, no doubt.

He bent for the circular saw, pushed the guide against the wood and pulled the trigger. The machine screamed to life and he slid it forward, slicing through the pine like butter. He grabbed the trimmed piece and held it to the nearly complete frame for what would be one of five picture windows along the seaward wall.

I was looking at the stars. Yeah. *I was looking at your breasts. Could I call you sometime?*

Any hope of trying to see her socially was pretty much shot to hell. He hadn't been able to stop thinking about her all day, through the routine motions in divorce court, through the lunch meeting with the cuckolded husband and new client, through the afternoon of staring out the window while pretending to read briefs. He bet she even knew how to sail. Probably owned her own boat. Of course. Why not? Probably an Ivy League grad from a moneyed family, now that he'd totally blown his chance with her.

He'd already spent hours dreaming up scenarios to salvage a second chance: Follow her to see where she did her grocery shopping, and then happen to run into her in the produce section. Or wait until she checked her mail one evening, then go out to pull his own rusting relic of a mailbox from the ground. Sure, he'd tie the wrought-iron pole to the tow hitch on his truck and yank it clean out. That would impress her.

And then, when he'd caught her eye, he'd walk over, introduce himself and pretend like the other night had never happened. In the off chance she remembered him and asked if she hadn't seen him on the beach that other night, he'd play dumb. No. That wouldn't work because of that damned Pedro. Eventually she'd see him. Unless he could hide him away somewhere . . . No, he'd just start barking. And anyway, what were the odds that she wouldn't remember his face? He certainly had gotten a good, long look at hers.

He sighed, reached for the drill. She would have been perfect: the woman he'd been waiting for since his dad died. Someone to fill that enormous void, and he'd finally found her. The only sailboat-owning, independently wealthy, well-educated woman in greater Daytona Beach. And he'd blown it. Or rather, Pedro had blown it for him.

"Bad dog," he called over to the corner again before plunging the whirring bit into the stud. It was only when the drill stopped its whine that he heard the knock. Pedro leapt to his feet, tail wagging furiously, and Nolin turned around. She was smiling shyly, wearing a blue sundress and holding a six-pack of Bud longnecks.

"Hi. I didn't mean to barge in, but you didn't answer the doorbell. And the door *was* open . . ."

Nolin gulped, tried to remember the script he'd worked out for this meeting. "Not hooked up. The doorbell."

Her dress clung to her thin figure, slid gracefully down long legs. A thin, white coral strand decorated her left ankle above white sandals. She was absolutely stunning. He stared, speechless.

She grinned nervously. "Well, I'm sorry if I disturbed you. But I thought that since we're neighbors and all." She lifted the six-pack of beer. "This *is* what you were drinking last night?"

Oh, God. Not only had she remembered he had a beer in his hand, she remembered *which* beer. He nodded weakly.

"Well, I saw you come in a couple of hours ago and decided to drop by and get your opinion on something. If you're busy, I can come back some other time—"

"No!" Nolin startled himself. "I mean, now is great. I was just . . ." He dropped the drill and wiped the sawdust on his hands onto his jeans. "Finishing up. Please, have a seat."

"Tell me." She lifted her left foot onto a stack of wood like a hunter above a kill and put her hands on her hips. "Do I look like a slut?"

Nick huddled uncomfortably in his leather jacket. The joint either didn't have air conditioning or didn't have it turned on, and between the heavy jacket and the full beard pasted onto his face, he was hot, sweaty and itchy.

Over his beer mug he again surveyed the establishment, which was either a bar doing a side business in tattoos or a tattoo parlor serving alcohol. Either way, he wondered how it had gotten a license. Probably by threatening to beat the living crap out of the health inspector, he decided.

He turned from the bar, shuffling peanut shells underfoot, and out of the corner of his eye checked out the clientele. Big, bearded, smelly. Wearing denim, leather, both or, among those in the tattoo chairs, pretty much nothing at all. Yelling and laughing, guzzling huge mugs of beer. He understood now what Amee had meant about the Iron Spike. That place had potted plants hanging in the windows and over the bar, while any foliage brought into Mike's Tap would almost certainly expire within minutes. If the thick gray air didn't get it, one of the patrons would probably piss in it. A particularly foul-smelling man had already urinated out the front window, banging himself dry against the frame.

Which one was it? he wondered again. Which of the guys looked most like a Crawdad? The newspaper article didn't have a picture. It just described the man acquitted of aggravated assault and attempted murder after the witness disappeared. He didn't dare ask. It would probably be the window pisser, who looked to be the meanest son of a bitch in there.

On the other hand, a mean son of a bitch was just the sort of man he was looking for. He'd already seen what a polite, well-mannered biker would do with his money. He finished his beer, turned back to the bar and waited for the long-haired barkeep to wander over.

"I'll have another. And I'm looking for Crawdad." He slipped a twenty onto the bar.

The barkeep set the foaming mug onto the cigarette-burned wood and nodded his head at the near corner, where a half dozen bikers and their molls sat in various states of undress while grungy tattoo artists poked their flesh with needles and ink-filled guns.

One man lay on a couch completely naked except for his boots, while a gap-toothed woman applied the finishing touches to a green-and-purple snake that began on his shoulder, slithered over rolls of chest and belly fat, through a patch of dark hair and onto his shaft. He winced and growled as the woman poked the outlines of a pair of black snake eyes. She had already finished the fangs and nostrils.

Nick gulped, hoped desperately that wasn't his man. He averted his eyes quickly and lit upon a voluptuous young blonde in a black bikini getting something done on her back. He looked again at the bikini top. It seemed painted on, the way it hugged every contour. He blinked and realized it *was* painted on. No, worse: It was *tattooed* on.

"Nice tits, huh?"

Nick looked up, saw that a heavyset man in dirty jeans and a faded black leather jacket had walked up beside him. He carried a beer mug and grinned maliciously, reached out to pinch a matte-black nipple. She smiled at him, then at Nick.

"See, last year, they busted my old lady 'cause I had her ridin' nekkid, so she wouldn't have to keep pulling off her clothes," the biker explained to Nick, who nodded quickly.

It was a Daytona Bike Week tradition. Guys lined Main Street, chanting "Show us your tits" at the women and cheering as the women on the bikes would lift their shirts obligingly.

"This time next week, she won't even have to wear her bottoms and no one'll know the difference." He reached down to pinch her left cheek through the leather bikini. "So long as she shaves."

The girl smiled at Nick again, and he looked away quickly, noticed the faded red lobster on the back of a giant hand, over the letters L-O-N. Lon. As in Lon Stanko. As in Crawdad.

"Did you do that yourself?" Nick pointed at his hand.

"My first tattoo," he said proudly. "I did it with a needle and some paints. That's all you get in a maximum security facility like Union Correctional. Whatever you can steal with your own two hands."

"It's very nice," Nick said sincerely.

"Damn right." Crawdad stretched an arm around Nick's shoulders, positioned it gently so the crook of his elbow squeezed Nick's neck. "Mister, you didn't come here to look at my skin art, and you didn't come here to look at my old lady's titties, either."

Nick glanced back at the bar, saw the bartender drawing two drafts.

"That's right. Johnnie told me you was lookin' for me. He's my friend, see? Like everybody in here is my friend. Nobody's gonna say a word if you never leave here." He spun Nick around to look into his face and belched violently. "Now. You here for business? Or pleasure?"

It had been too long since he'd done a night dive. Even a short one, on a bare sand bottom like he was doing, was better than a lot of daytime dives on coral. All the critters came out at night, and even though he only saw the ones that swam within the beam of his headlamp, it was still a whole lot more interesting than in the day, when most of the baitfish, rays, crabs, sharks and eels hid from predators.

He kicked gently, holding the metal box out in front, stopping every now and again when a blacktip or a sand shark cruised by, passing close to examine the strange creature in their domain. It wouldn't do to antagonize them. No telling how they'd react, not at night: feeding time.

Quickly he came to the marker he'd placed that afternoon. He dove a few feet to the bottom, buried a small anchor in the sand, and let the box rise upward until it was about six feet from the surface and its attached wire just broke through, then clamped the nylon cable tie into place. It wasn't as elaborate as last time but would, if it worked right, be even more spectacular.

Finished, he turned and started back toward the dinghy, switching off his light and flipping over to swim on his back. Every once in a while a graceful black shadow passed in silhouette against the starlit dark blue.

God, he loved night dives.

Nolin realized after an awkward half minute that her question wasn't rhetorical. She would stand there until he answered. Which explained everything. She had appeared, unbeckoned, like a Venus on the halfshell, but only to chew him out for gawking at her like the hopeless reprobate that he was.

"Well," he began uncertainly. "I don't think there's anything to be ashamed of about the human body. I go skinny-dipping myself, every now and then. . . ."

She frowned, set the six-pack on the ground and climbed onto a plank lying across the sawhorses. She bent her left knee, twisting first left, then right, like a fashion model.

He blinked, puzzled for a moment before realizing he was off the hook. She wasn't talking about last night after all! She wanted to know what he thought about her dress. Hmmm . . . Should he compliment her on how it clung to every goose bump? How it was obvious to the planet that she wasn't wearing a bra?

"It's very nice," he said politely. "And you really can't tell whether you're wearing underwear or not." *Aarrrrgh!* He shook his head quickly. "What I mean is, and it's certainly not a reflection on your sensibilities whether you do or you don't—"

"I'm *talking* about this." She pointed at the coral anklet. "Do you think the ankle bracelet makes me look like a slut?"

He looked down at her ankle, bewildered. "Do *you* think it makes you look like a slut?" he asked cautiously.

She jumped down off the plank, grabbed two beers and handed him one. "As a matter of fact, I do. See, I think it would help my business if I wore one, but I don't want to look cheap. It's such a small step, you know, between looking cheap and being cheap."

Nolin watched as she sat down across from him on an overturned milk crate, crossed her long legs. He studied the string of coral beads draped across her foot. "I guess I never thought of it that way. But you know? Now that I think of it, it seems like half the women in Daytona are wearing them nowadays."

"So you *do* think it makes me look like a slut." She took a sip of her beer. "Not that it matters. Even if it brings in more business, I don't think it would happen fast enough. I'm in a lawsuit, you see, and I'm way behind on my bills. My attorney told me he'd drop me if I can't pay by next week. And then the judge will rule against me."

"Not necessarily," Nolin said, sensing an opportunity to redeem himself. "Just tell the judge you have to switch lawyers and he'll postpone everything for a while."

"Not this judge."

"Sounds like Antoon." He took a swig of beer. "You're right. He never grants continuances. I've tried. You pretty much have to die to get one. Which case?"

She smiled shyly. "So you're an attorney, too. But you don't recognize me? You've never seen me on TV?"

"Never watch it."

"Well, I think the official name is Save Our Turtles, Inc., versus Volusia—"

"The Turtle Lady! Sure, I know who you are. You're the one trying to get cars off the beach because they run over baby sea turtles."

She nodded. "The way this town's reacting, you'd think I was trying to make them give up sex."

Nolin grinned. "No, in this town, you'd have an easier time banning sex than banning cars from the beach. A lot of them think it's *better* than sex."

She laughed out loud. He studied her face, the sculpted features, the smoky eyes. He remembered it from some-place, but couldn't recall where.

"This *is* a strange place," she agreed. "Bikers, race car rednecks, drunk college students, bums, escaped cons. And everybody pretends like it's all perfectly normal." She took another sip. "Sometimes I wonder why I stay. I mean, if I lose the turtle suit, I guess there's nothing keeping me."

"You don't have family here?"

"Not anymore. My mom died a few years ago. My dad is"—she waved an arm out toward the ocean—"who knows. He ran away when I was an infant."

"No boyfriend, fiancé?" He smiled. "No one who's gonna come barging in here any minute to kick my butt?"

She smiled sadly. "No. No boyfriend, no fiancé. Although, technically, I guess I still have a husband. We've been separated almost two years. It's just a matter of signing the papers."

Nick's heart sank. "Oh. I see. Well, sometimes, you know, couples realize how much they miss each other after they've been apart for a while. They find they can't bring themselves to go through with a divorce and end up back together, more in love than ever."

Barbie looked at him quizzically and laughed aloud. "It's nothing like that. It has nothing to do with love. It never did. That was the problem." She thought a moment. "All the years I was growing up, Mom groomed me to marry well. That was all that mattered. To make up, I guess, for the fact that she didn't. Anyway, so when the most eligible bachelor in town gave me a ring, I pretty much figured I'd died and gone to heaven. My mom acted like I was getting away with grand larceny. That I was marrying way over my head, that I couldn't possibly deserve everything I was getting. I guess I bought into it. I didn't stop to ask myself whether I loved him, or he loved me. Anyway. The reason we haven't signed the papers is his family image. His father got divorced to marry a much younger woman, and he and his stepmom are afraid it'll look bad if he got a divorce, too."

He snorted. "That's crazy! And what are *you* supposed

to do, meanwhile? Never get married again just so this guy won't look bad at the country club?"

She shrugged. "I didn't mind. What did it matter? I've been using my maiden name, my own money, I have my own business. As far as getting married again, I haven't met anyone I've even been remotely interested in." She sipped her beer and grinned. "Until maybe now."

Jamie sat in the straight-backed chair, staring at Amee's navel. It was an outie, pierced with a tiny golden ring. Funny, but he hadn't noticed, and he'd always considered himself fairly observant about that sort of thing. Maybe it was only an outie some of the time, and an innie the rest.

"You're not paying attention," she scolded.

"I am so. I walk into her store, hang around till no one else is there, get her to go in the back, shoot her, make it—"

"Shoot her in the head," Amee corrected. "You gotta shoot her in the head."

"Shoot her in the head, make it look like a robbery and get out the back door."

"Good." Amee smiled. She sat on the edge of her desk, lifted her feet onto Jamie's chair and tucked her toes under his thighs. "I think you've got it."

"And where do I get the gun?"

"I'll get it for you."

"And what do I do with the gun?"

"Take it with you. We dump it in the ocean afterwards."

Jamie thought about it, shook his head. "I dunno. It don't *sound* that easy."

"What part?" she asked patiently. "What part doesn't sound easy?"

"Like how do I get her in the back?"

Amee smiled. "If you can charm the panties off three

babes you just met, get 'em to spread their legs for your camera, don't you think you can talk *one* into getting something from the back office for you? Tell her you're buying an outfit for your girlfriend, and you need the phone to call her to get the right size. I don't know. You tell me. What sort of shit does a chick like that fall for?"

"I dunno," he repeated, looking up shyly. "I never killed anybody before."

"Nothing to be ashamed of." She shook her head with conviction. "There's gotta be a first time for everything, right? Besides, I promise not to tell Nick that you don't got any experience. And when you get this done, he won't even care. He'll be so grateful you can't imagine."

"And you're sure I'll get to drive in the Crown Cola 400?"

"You have my word. Your own car, your own pit crew and whatever else you need to give those rednecks a run for their money. Besides"—she moved her feet out from under his thighs to rest them gently on his crotch—"a fringe benefit of partnering with Cherry is you get to hang out with Cherry socially, if you know what I mean."

His eyes scanned her from brown toes all the way up to dark brown eyes. "I've never needed to kill anybody to get girls."

"Really?" With one hand she swept her hair out of the way, with the other she untied the knot behind her neck. Her breasts swung free. "You wouldn't just be getting girls, you'd be getting Cherry. For example: How many orifices do your new girlfriends let you use?"

His eyes were now glued to her chest; she felt a tremor beneath her toes.

"I told you. They give me the run of the house."

Amee rolled her eyes. "How many different *holes* do your girlfriends let you into?"

He blushed. "Oh, that. Well, one of them only does sex, but the other two give me blowjobs, too."

"Oh yeah? Well, with Cherry, you get a three-orifice woman. And if you're really good, Peaches out there can join us, and that's another three. So between the two of us, we've already got your girlfriends beat, six to five."

"Oh." He thought for a moment, then blushed even deeper. "*Oh!* Well, I ain't never done *that.*"

"Like I said, there's gotta be a first time for everything." She squeezed him between her toes. "So what do you say? You with me?"

"I dunno, Cherry. Shootin' somebody like that. It don't seem right, somehow." He thought a moment longer, glanced up at her nipples again. "How about a shot in the Crown Cola *and* ten grand?"

With a sigh, she found the strands to her top, reached behind her neck to retie them. "A shot in the Crown Cola and five grand."

He smiled happily and stuck out his hand. "Deal."

Nick understood now why the guy had urinated out the window instead of in the men's room. The first thing he'd have to do when he left would be to stop at a decent establishment and wash his hands, which at the moment were spread against the tiled wall—a wall stained with grime, mildew, urine and God only knew what else.

The girl's hands moved firmly down his chest, his sides, his groin, his legs and finally his ankles. She was barefoot, and didn't mind kneeling on the sticky floor, just as she didn't mind traipsing around in only a leather bikini bottom in the nastiest biker bar in town.

"He's not carrying," she said in a sweet young voice.

Crawdad grunted. "See if he's wired."

She began patting him down again, this time more

probingly. He felt himself awaken. Perfect. That's all he needed was to get a hard-on for the psycho's girlfriend. Give him just the excuse to gut him like an animal. Like he needed an excuse.

"I can't tell through his clothes," she said.

"Then take his goddamned clothes off," Crawdad growled.

Nick turned his head in alarm, saw the biker flick a cigarette butt in the general direction of the urinal.

"Don't get excited. Just makin' sure you ain't a cop." He reached in his jacket for a pack of Camels and pulled one out with his teeth. "You *ain't* a cop, are you?"

Nick turned back to the wall. The girl had taken off his jacket and was unbuttoning his shirt. "No, sir."

"Good. 'Cause if you are, and you lie and say you ain't, then that's entrapment. You know that, dontcha?"

She pulled off his shirt, squeezed between him and the wall to undo his belt. "If you say so, sir," Nick said in a shaky voice, wondering for a moment what James Bond might have done in this situation before realizing the absurdity of the thought. Bond would already have killed the biker, bedded his woman and have been on his second martini. The notion of bedding Crawdad's woman aroused him even further, just as she unzipped his pants and yanked down both trousers and shorts, pulling the elastic outward to let him pop free. He didn't know what was worse: her seeing it, or her not even noticing. It didn't matter. If Crawdad saw, he was a dead man.

"No wires," she reported.

"Good. One more place to check."

Nick wondered what he meant when suddenly he felt her wiggling in, probing, searching. He winced back tears, but realized he was growing even harder. Just as suddenly she was gone.

"Nothing."

"Good," Crawdad said. "Now go wash your hands. You don't know where that asshole's been, if you know what I mean. And *you* can turn around."

Nick reached for his pants.

"I said *turn around*!"

Nick dropped his pants, closed his eyes and turned to face Crawdad.

"Well, ain't you somethin'," Crawdad said. "Fake beard, pants down at your knees and a raging hard-on for my old lady. Put that thing away."

Nick complied, zipping up his pants, stuffing his arms back into his shirt and buttoning and buckling as fast as he could. The girl walked back from the sink and returned to Crawdad's side.

"Now tell me, mister." Crawdad reached an arm behind her, slid his hand inside her bikini bottom. "So who is it you want killed?"

Nick gulped. "Who said I want anyone killed?"

"Well, I'm just guessin' you ain't here for financial advice." Crawdad removed his hand, held it beneath wide, grimy nostrils and inhaled deeply. "Who am I supposed to do? Business partner? Mother-in-law? Girlfriend's husband?"

"Wife," Nick said softly.

Crawdad nodded, like he should have known. "Obvious choice. Never fails. You can't live with 'em, you can't chop 'em into little pieces and stick 'em in a storage unit. What, she cheat on you?"

"No." Did he have to tell him why? "It's a long story."

"Just went bad, eh?" Crawdad said understandingly. "It happens. When?"

"Soon. It has to be before next Monday. But the sooner the better."

Crawdad twisted and untwisted strands of his beard. "Rush job. Don't like 'em. Too easy to screw something up." He grinned, baring a row of skewed teeth. "I think I can fit her in. If the price is right."

Nick lowered his eyes. "Well, I don't have a lot."

Crawdad shrugged. "You can't afford it, you can't afford it. I got plenty of work."

Nick gulped. "How much?"

"Normally it's twenty bills. For a rush job, thirty."

His mind sped. He did the math twice and tried to hide his surprise. "So that's, what, three grand?"

Crawdad snorted. "*Thirty* grand."

"I thought a bill was a hundred dollars," Nick whined. He was sure of it. Every mobster movie he'd ever seen: a bill was a $100 bill.

A sneer spread across the biker's lips. "You thought wrong. For three grand, I wouldn't even bust her legs. Now this ain't some flea market. The price is thirty grand."

Nick frowned in dismay. He'd already blown $10,000 on Lance the Gay Biker, now this guy wanted most of what he had left. So much for his own big bonus. And how the hell was he going to pay for Joanna?

"I just can't afford thirty thousand," he said quietly.

Crawdad turned for the door. "Fine. Kill her yourself."

"Wait." Nick sighed in defeat. "Okay. Thirty thousand."

Crawdad smiled. "Name, address, work address if she's got one and a picture."

Nick pulled out his wallet, removed a photo and scribbled on the back. "This is about three years old but she pretty much looks the same. Only her hair is longer."

Crawdad studied the snapshot. "Whoa. You sure you want to be gettin' rid of somethin' like this?" He bent closer to the photo. "Wait a minute. I seen this lady before."

"You and half the planet," Nick said impatiently.

Crawdad snapped his fingers. "Now I remember! She's the naked chick from that poster. I *got* that poster at home. The Nipple Girl." He showed the picture to his girlfriend. "See? Ain't that her?"

Nick sighed. "You're right. That's her. The Nipple Girl."

"Why you want to go killin' a lady like this for? You got any idea what you can get for her? Especially with titties like that?"

Nick blinked. "*Get* for her?"

"Fifty, sixty grand, easy. Tell you what, you let me take care of her. I'll do it for free. She'll be out of your hair." He thrust his girlfriend at Nick. "I'll even give you this one."

Nick looked at the girl, who smiled back shyly. He imagined taking her home to show Joanna, shook his head. "Look, let's just keep it simple, okay? Just kill her. No white slavery. No wife swapping. Just kill her."

Crawdad looked at the photo again. "Damn shame, wastin' a prime piece of ass like that. *C'est la vie.*"

Nick blinked uncomprehendingly. "You'll do it, then?"

"My friend, go start pickin' out a tombstone." He shoved the photo in his jacket pocket. "That'll be fifteen now, fifteen after. You can leave it for me at the bar. You seem like an honest guy, so I don't gotta tell you what I'll do to you if you don't pay up afterward."

Nick reached for his wallet, remembered again what his last hire had done. And here he was about to give this guy $5,000 more than he'd given Lance. "Mr. Stanko, I hate to ask you this, but you're not by any chance gay, are you?"

Barbie knelt down, lifted her hair out of the way and pressed her ear against the mound of sand. "Sometimes I think I can really hear them in there." She sat back up and smiled. "I know it's just my imagination."

Nolin ran his hand over the mound. "You know, I've lived in Daytona fifteen years, but this is the first time I've been this close to a turtle nest. How many eggs are inside?"

"A hundred. More or less." She turned toward the sea, sat up straight, cross-legged. "They've come here for thousands of years, you know. Long before any people were even here. The Indians used to catch them, eat their eggs. But they never ate enough to kill them off."

He brushed the sand off his hand. "I guess you do know your turtles."

She shrugged. "I've read up. They're found in every ocean. They thrive in warm water. They haven't changed in aeons. The females lay eggs every other year. Of those hundred hatchlings, maybe fifty will avoid the seagulls and other critters and make it across the beach and into the water. Of those, most get eaten by fishes and crabs. Maybe one or two will grow to adulthood."

He studied her in profile, the pale eyes, the line of her nose, and knew again he'd seen her somewhere. "How'd you get so interested in them?"

Barbie laughed, flicked a small shell at the white surf line. "You'll think I'm a ditz if I tell you."

"You don't know that."

"You will. I can tell from the way you talk. You're very linear. You go straight from point A to point B. There's never any question, never any mystery."

Nolin smiled. "I don't know whether to be insulted or flattered."

"I didn't mean it in a bad way. I'm just saying I'm not like that, and that's why you'll laugh."

"I promise not to laugh. At least not until later, when I'm by myself."

She sighed. "My fortune-teller told me I was a sea turtle in a past life."

"Ah." He nodded effusively. "Fortune-teller."

"You know. Psychic. Seer. Medium. Whatever you want to call it. Anyway, I have one in Cassadaga I go to a couple of times a week."

"Sure. Cassadaga." He'd never been there, but had read the newspaper's annual Halloween story about the strange little town populated by mystics and spiritual advisers. He thought it all a crock.

"You think it's all a crock, don't you?" She turned to him seriously. "Okay, so it probably is. I know most of 'em are just con artists, but I thought Madame Rosa was different. For a while I did, anyway. Lately I haven't been too sure. Anyhow, the one time she told me I lived in the sea in a past life, I just *knew*, right away, that she was right. Even now, when I close my eyes, I can still see coral reefs, and fish, and when I look up, the surface of the sea."

"Maybe you're just remembering a nice dive you've done."

"I've never been diving in my life. I'd *like* to, but I can never get past the first class. It's something to do with my ears. Anyway, I think she's right about the turtles. There's something sort of mystical about them. The way they coincide their trips to the beach with the phase of the moon. Did you know"—she put a hand on his knee—"that a female turtle swims hundreds, even thousands of miles but still returns to the exact same beach to lay her eggs? Now, when scientists can explain *that*, maybe I'll put more faith in them and less in Madame Rosa."

Nolin glanced nervously at her hand, still on his knee. He tried to keep from shaking, looked out at the starlit water. A soft breeze drove gentle waves onto the sand. "So how come they're still disappearing? The turtles I mean. I thought they're protected now."

"They are. From hunters. But not from condos that undercut the beach. Or from streetlights that confuse the babies and lure them onto the road. Here in Daytona, they're not even protected from cars running over their nests. Not to mention all the pollution."

Nolin nodded. "That's right. That's one of your main points in the lawsuit, isn't it? About the pollution destroying the habitat of an endangered species."

"Ever notice how much oil and antifreeze and God knows what else drips onto a supermarket parking lot?" She lifted a handful of sand, let it slip between her fingers. "Well, that's exactly what cars leave on the beach, too."

To his chagrin, she removed her hand from his knee to stroke the turtle nest again. "That's the whole reason I got a house way down here near the inlet. The sand's so soft that most drivers don't want to risk getting stuck." She brushed the damp grains off her hands. "Tomorrow will be different, though. Tomorrow every idiot between Jacksonville and Miami will be parked right here."

"Oh yeah." Nolin remembered hearing an ad on the radio. "Some speedboat race, right?"

"*The* offshore speedboat series of the year, if you believe the hype. Four hours of the biggest, noisiest, dirtiest boats in the world, tearing up the water, spewing unburned gas, leaking oil. The whole shebang."

"I can't wait. Why here?"

Barbie shrugged. "Probably something to do with the Van Hornes' RaceWorld scheme." She sat up straight. "Did you see that?"

He sat up also and stared out at the water. "Where?"

She pointed. "Out where they have those buoys set up."

He squinted, shook his head. "I don't see a thing."

"It's gone, now. I'm pretty sure I saw something, though. Something dark, just out beyond that marker. It looked like, I don't know, one of those little inflatable boats." She peered a bit longer. "Maybe it was nothing. Just a dolphin or something."

"Or a shark." He grinned. "Maybe the same one that ate the Jet Skiers is coming back for more."

"I was there that day." She shivered at the memory. "It was amazing. One moment everything was fine. The next, a feeding frenzy. It was like they were teaching us a lesson. We can poison the land all we want, but we better leave the sea alone. Or else."

"Maybe they just hate Jet Skiers." Nolin shrugged. "Can you blame them?"

"They *are* pretty annoying. And smelly, and noisy, and rude. No, I guess I can't."

He lay down on the cool sand, stared into the clear sky. This night, *all* the stars were out. "So what's RaceWorld? I've never heard of it."

She turned toward him. "Oh, it's this monstrosity the Van Hornes want to build. Sort of a racing theme park. There'll be Jet Ski rentals, boat racing, exhibits, three-dollar Cokes. But the biggest attraction's supposed to be a quarter-mile strip where tourists can race old-time cars up and down the beach. It was going to cost like a hundred million or something, but Joanna figured a way to scam the state into paying for most of it."

"Down here?" Nolin asked in alarm. "They want to build that *here*?"

"Uh-huh." She nodded. "Land's cheaper than in Daytona proper. They've already bought off whoever they need to buy off to get it done."

He shook his head in wonder. "I haven't seen a word about this in the paper."

"That's because they *own* half the paper, or just about. The paper will write about it when the Van Hornes are good and ready to have it written about."

A series of previously random thoughts coalesced in

his head. His breath caught in his throat as he tried to remember the address listed for Barbara Van Horne, née Baxter. "How come *you* know so much about it then?" he asked as nonchalantly as he could manage.

She laughed. "Because when you marry into the family, you learn a lot of stuff, even when they don't want you to."

Nolin sat silently for a minute. Shock slowly became anger. The one woman he'd met in years who seemed like she could be The One, and that asshole Van Horne had made her unavailable. His client's estranged wife, and here he was. On the beach, drinking beers. Working up his courage to reach out, casually touch her forearm. Perfect.

Well, to hell with it, he thought bitterly. He'd see her if he wanted to, and that was that.

And then J. R. Van Horne would file a complaint with the Bar, and they would process it, and a judge—with his luck Antoon—would hear it, and he would be disbarred. He shook his head in disbelief.

"Is something wrong?"

"I just can't believe"—he turned to face her, saw the earnest eyes, the full lips he suddenly needed so badly against his own. To hell with J. R. Van Horne. He'd tell him he wasn't going to represent him anymore—"that they're going to ruin the last piece of undeveloped beach in the county."

Barbie sat glumly. "Me neither. Or actually, I *can* believe it. I can believe it pretty easily. And they'll do it, too, unless by some miracle I win this lawsuit."

Nolin grinned. "That's right. If you get cars off the beach, I guess that goes for race car rides on the beach, as well. I bet they're worried sick about how Antoon's gonna rule, especially after that stunt with the chicken eggs."

"Yeah. That's got Nick all over it. He's such a loser. I must have been out of my mind to marry him. You know

he goes to all the hearings? Except he doesn't want anyone to know that the family has an interest in the outcome,
so he wears glasses and a fake beard."

"Aha." Nolin recalled the odd figure behind him at the
chicken-egg hearing. "Things become clearer."

Barbie stood, brushed sand off her dress. "Well, I don't
mean to be a party pooper, but I've got to wake up early.
The curse of running your own business, I guess."

Nolin picked up her sandals, handed them to her. "Can
I walk you the rest of the way home?"

She smiled. "I would be honored."

They began walking, occasionally touching at the
shoulders and elbows. Nolin's nerves crackled at every
contact. "I'm glad you came by."

"I'm glad I did, too."

"Thanks for the beer."

"You're welcome. Next time you can bring it."

Yes! There would be a next time! "Maybe later this
week? Or this weekend?"

"I would love that." They reached her dune crossover.
She reached for the weathered two-by-six that served as a
handrail. "Well, this is where I get off."

Nolin stood awkwardly, toeing the sand. He couldn't
remember the last time he'd been in this situation. Was he
supposed to put his arm around her? Or would that be too
forward? Before he could react, she had pressed against
him, reached up onto tiptoes and kissed him lightly.

"Good night, Pedro."

His dog's name rattled around his head as, once again,
he watched her climb the stairs and slip through her gate
before he turned away to walk home.

FOUR

...

The sun was out again, and for the fourth straight day it was unseasonably warm. Amee ached to take off the T-shirt and shorts and take advantage of the sunshine to maintain her tan. She turned an olive green when she didn't get enough sun, and olive green just didn't bring in the Joes like nut brown did. Still, the little red thong would turn too many heads out on the street, and this was one morning she didn't want attention.

She glanced again at the clock on the lamppost. It was almost quarter after. He was already a half hour late. Served her right for picking a moron. She glanced back up at the clock and reached for the handlebars on her bike when a dirty orange Datsun pulled up alongside the curb.

Jamie gave her a big grin. "Hey, Cherry! Sorry I'm running a little late." He leaned over to push the passenger door open for her. "My roommates didn't wake me up early enough, and when they did, they were all getting ready for work. So I jumped in the shower with one of them, you know, to save a little time? But I think it actually slowed things down instead." He smiled again. "You know how *that* goes."

Amee swung herself into the seat and slammed the door. "I've been standing here for a half hour, asshole. If you ain't up to this, just tell me, okay? I could get a hundred other guys"—she snapped her fingers—"like that."

Jamie lifted his hands defensively. "Okay. All right. I'm sorry. Keep your shirt on. I'm here now, ain't I?"

Amee shook her head, reached to open her knapsack, pulled out a towel. "Here."

"What do I need that for?"

"Inside, numbnuts," she hissed. "I got it for you last night. It's only a .22, so remember what I said about shooting her—"

"In the head, I know. I'm not a *complete* moron." He took the towel, reached inside and removed the pistol. It was a tiny automatic, barely the size of his hand. "This? I'm supposed to kill somebody with this? I had a bigger gun back home to shoot squirrels with."

"Fine. You think of a way to sneak a rifle into her store, go for it. Until then, shut the fuck up."

Jamie examined the gun unhappily. "I don't like it. But you're the boss, I guess." He squinted through his window at the store across the street. "Is that it? The Harmonic Age? What's that, like a music store?"

"She sells crystals and shit. You know, New Age stuff."

He watched three women standing around a dress rack. "Which one's her?"

"See? That's why you were supposed to get here a half hour ago. To see who opened up. Lucky for you, I was here to save your ass." She pointed through the window. "The skinny one in the yellow dress. Now let's go through this once more."

Jamie rolled his eyes. "We've been through it enough

already. I browse until I'm the only customer left. I ask to borrow her phone, I follow her back into the office, I shoot her in the head—"

"How many times?"

"I empty the gun. Then I pull out the drawers, make a mess and get out the back door. I meet you at the boat race, and we ditch the gun tonight."

She nodded. "Good. And don't touch anything metal or glass or they'll have your fingerprints. Got it?"

"Yeah, yeah, yeah. When do I get my five grand?"

"Don't worry about it. You'll get your money."

"And a crack at your orifices."

"And my orifices."

"And a shot in the Crown Cola."

"And a shot in the damn race. Now get going. She'll close for lunch if you don't hurry."

Jamie opened his door, shut it again. "Hang on a minute . . . That word, orifices." He dug underneath his seat, pulled out a crumpled paper napkin and a pen. "I want to write it down before I forget. I like to use a new word at least three times every day. See? And I've already used it once."

She stared at him as he scratched the pen on his thigh until the ink began to flow. "You gotta be fuckin' kidding."

His eyes opened wide. "Oh no. It really helps. I want to build up my vocabulary. You know that people get their first impression of you based on the kind of words you use? You might want to think about building your own vocabulary, too."

"I don't fuckin' believe this."

"Orifices. How do you spell that?"

She shook her head and spelled it for him.

"Great. And that means: holes." He wrote carefully, folded the napkin and stuffed it into his T-shirt pocket. "Oh yeah, I know what I wanted to ask you. How come you're called Cherry? Is that your favorite fruit or something? I mean, you ain't a virgin, are you?"

She looked at him a moment. "Do I look like a virgin?"

"I didn't think so. So how come Cherry?"

She sighed. "It's French. French for dear."

"Oh." Jamie nodded. "Okay. Cherry means dear." He dug out his napkin. "Let me write that down, too."

Amee groaned, reached for the door handle. "I'm outta here. Meet me at the boat races."

Pedro. She thought his name was Pedro.

He mulled it over and over. How was he going to correct her without embarrassing her? And if he did embarrass her, would it shame her into avoiding him? Perhaps correcting her could wait a few days. Or weeks. Or months. After all, what was a name? A collection of vowels and consonants chosen by his parents. Douglas. Pedro. What did it matter?

Nolin was lost in the abstraction and therefore didn't notice the Monte Carlo pull up in the circular driveway, didn't see his visitor until he was standing behind him clearing his throat. He turned and smiled. J. R. Van Horne. Just the man he needed to see. "Good morning, Mr. Van Horne."

Nick held up his hand, walked in with legs spread, knees bent, and stood in front of the desk. "I have some legal-type questions for you."

"What happened to your legs?" Nolin asked.

Nick scowled, winced. "Don't ask."

Nolin shrugged, motioned him toward the chair. "Sit down, please."

Nick winced again. "I'd rather stand."

Nolin shrugged again. "Well, Mr. Van Horne, I didn't

expect to see you today, but I'm glad you stopped by. There's something I need to discuss—"

"First off," Nick began. "Say hypothetically I hire somebody to do some work, and pay him up front, and then he doesn't do the work. What can I do about it?"

Nolin watched him shift his weight from one leg to the other. "I'd start by complaining to the trade association that represents him. Like if he's an electrician, file a complaint with the electricians guild. There's no legal remedy there, but sometimes they can help resolve things."

Nick thought for a second. "What if there's no trade association?"

"Then you have to sue him. How much did he stiff you for?"

Nick thought again. "Ten grand," he said carefully.

"Then that's circuit court. That's a hundred-and-five-dollar filing fee, and you have to pay to serve the guy with the papers. Then there are attorneys' fees. You can get attorneys' fees and court costs back if you win."

"But in court, would I have to explain what the guy was supposed to do? Or could it be enough that he stiffed me?"

Nolin blinked. "You mean you want to go in there, tell the judge that there's this guy who owes you money, but you don't want to explain why?" He chuckled. "He'd toss the both of us out on our ear."

"I was afraid of that." Nick meditated a moment. "So I guess it's the same if, hypothetically, I hire somebody for a job, and he does something that's got *nothing* to do with our deal. Say, hypothetically"—Nick mumbled now—"he fucks me instead. I guess the judge would want details on that, too, huh?"

Nolin recalled the stiff-legged walk. "Hypothetically fucks you . . . financially? Or physically?"

"Would it make a difference? To the judge?"

"No."

"Then forget it. I'll deal with it some other way," Nick muttered. "I got some other questions, about my wife. If something happened to her, what happens with her legal affairs?"

Nolin raised an eyebrow. "What do you mean *happened* to her?"

"You know. Hit by a bus. Drowned. Anything. I mean, I'm still technically married to her. Do I get stuck with her bills?"

"Ah," Nolin said. "No, I don't believe so. Not bills that she incurred after you were separated. Any debts she had before that, though, are legally yours."

Nick nodded. "Okay. And what about legal problems."

"Problems?"

"Yeah. Like if somebody was suing her . . . Or she was suing somebody. Hypothetically. What happens to those?"

Nolin watched him carefully. The questions had strayed well beyond those of the typical husband seeking a divorce. "Well, if she's a defendant in a suit involving a dispute that predates your separation, then yes, you're a party. As to suits in which she's the plaintiff . . ." Nolin hesitated, saw Nick's eyes narrow. "There, the judge would immediately dismiss the lawsuit."

"A lawyer couldn't keep pressing it," Nick asked casually. "Like in her memory or something?"

"It doesn't work that way." Nolin saw suspicion melt into relief. "Why do you ask? Is your wife prone to falling in front of buses?"

Nick winced, adjusted his trousers. "Don't be a smart-ass. Just covering all my bases, that's all. So what was it you wanted to talk about?"

"Hmmm?"

"When I came in. You said you wanted to talk about something."

Nolin affected an innocent look, inwardly scrambled.

"Oh yeah. No big deal. Just doing some bookkeeping and found that you still have sixteen thousand dollars of your retainer unspent. You want me to transfer it back to your mother's account?"

Nick thought for a moment. "Any way you can just return it to me?"

"Sorry. She was pretty clear when she opened the account. Any refund goes to her."

Nick nodded. "Right. Sure. Well, you hang onto it. I might be needing your services soon." He attempted a grin and turned for the door, walked out in the same bowlegged manner he had walked in.

Through the window, Nolin watched him open the door to his Monte Carlo, heard him curse as he lowered himself into the driver's seat. He waited till the car was gone before he turned to the cabinet to pull out the Van Horne file.

Jamie stood in front of the blouse rack, flipped through them while the lady in the yellow dress helped a pair of high school girls in cutoffs and halters pick out crystal necklaces and earrings. He waded through a bin of scarves as she sold a book on massage oils and three sample bottles to a clean-cut, effeminate young man in a perfectly pressed gray suit.

Jamie eyed him suspiciously, guarding against the likelihood that he'd make a pass at him. He left, though, without any overt moves, and Jamie moved to the large jewelry display while she took care of the only other customer in the store, an older lady with long, brown legs protruding from a black minidress. She, too, finally left with a shopping bag tucked under an arm.

He engrossed himself in the jewelry, picking through gold chains, as he heard his target approach.

"Sorry it's been so busy. Can I help you find anything?"

Jamie turned with a smile, which suddenly froze on his lips. It was his first good look at her face, and he realized at once she was the girl on Cherry's ceiling. His eyes moved to her chest, but the strangely enticing breast in the poster was invisible beneath the flowing fabric.

"Yeah," he began, feeling himself press uncomfortably against the gun jammed in his waistband. "I was looking for one of these, but I need to call my girlfriend to make sure it'll fit."

Barbie glanced at the thin gold ankle bracelet between his fingers. "They're one size fits all." She pointed to a tiny catch on a series of removable links. "They're adjustable."

"I just want to be sure," he said lamely.

She studied his nervous eyes. There was something peculiar about this one. "Why don't you describe your girlfriend for me."

Jamie tried to picture one of his new roommates, but all he could see was that damned poster. The gun's metal felt cold as he pressed against it even harder. He closed one eye and thought of Cherry. "She's got dark hair, about five-foot-two, and she's got really nice tits . . . uh, excuse me, boobs. Although her butt's kinda big."

Barbie suppressed a smile. "I meant, describe her bone structure. Does she have thin limbs, like me? Or thicker?"

"Oh." He blushed. "Thin ones. Like you."

"In that case, any of these should fit without a problem. They all fit me."

Jamie looked down, saw she was wearing a string of pink coral beads around her left ankle. The pink matched her toenails and her cloth sandals. He thought of the thin gold anklet that Cherry wore.

"What's the difference between beads and the gold chains?" he asked.

"Well, it's a matter of personal preference. I tend to feel that coral suggests fun, carefree, casual. Gold is dressier. You see a lot of professional women wearing gold ones nowadays, both with bare legs and over panty hose." And they all happen to be sluts, she thought. "Is your girlfriend a professional woman?"

Jamie grinned. "No. Not exactly." He felt the gun shift slightly when he laughed and remembered his mission. "Well, I guess I need to call her to see what kind she prefers."

Barbie shrugged, motioned to the phone on the counter next to the register. "Help yourself. As long as she doesn't live in Paris or someplace."

He looked at the phone in dismay. It was right out in the main display area, within clear sight of the plate glass windows. "I, uh, need to borrow your phone book." He noticed her brow furrow in suspicion. "To get her work number. I don't know it off the top of my head."

Barbie strode past him toward the rear office. Jamie fell in behind her, studied the back of her head, where the long, straight hair fell over her bare neck. Such a beautiful neck, and those wonderful nipples he was never going to see. A damned waste. Suddenly it struck him: He was going to kill her. He was going to put his gun up against her head and pull the trigger, and her blood and brains would spill out.

"Where does she work?" Barbie asked as she opened the door to her office. "Your girlfriend."

"Oh, uh, Top Shots. Top Shots pool hall." He watched as she rounded her desk and pulled out a phone book. He thought of the various animals he had killed: squirrels, rabbits, deer. How they shivered, less and less alive, until the spirit drained from them and their eyes went dull.

"Let me see . . ." She bent over the desk across from him, head down.

Instinctively he tilted his head to look down her sundress when he remembered the gun. He looked back through the door at the empty store and focused on the top of her head. Her hair swirled clockwise, away from a tiny bare spot. A perfect target. She flipped pages. He drew the gun. It was just like the woods. The small and weak died so the big and strong could survive. He pointed at the center of the swirl. He closed his eyes. He pulled the trigger.

Nothing happened.

He opened his eyes, pulled harder, saw her move her finger down the page. He stuffed the gun back into his shorts, tried to loop the barrel through the drawstring like he had before, fumbled, missed . . .

She was staring at him, mouth wide open, finger pressed against the middle of the phone book, eyes fixated on his hands, which were plunged into his shorts, over a huge bulge that pushed through the fabric.

He smiled, looked down, didn't dare let go of the gun. "You, uh, find the number?"

"I have it right here." She lifted her eyes to meet his. "Shall I write it down for you?"

Jamie swallowed, realized he wasn't going to get his hands out of his pants until he left the store. "You know what? I just realized I forgot my wallet." He turned for the door. "Let me go get it, and I'll be right back."

Barbie watched as he walked briskly past the racks of dresses, pushed the front door open with his shoulder and ran up the street.

God, he realized, was behind him one hundred percent, and hated speedboats every bit as much as he did. The wind had grown even warmer, swung around to the south-southwest and, a consequence of Volusia County's northeast-facing shoreline, completely flattened the waves.

Barely a six-inch ripple remained, breaking in long running streaks against the sand.

Conditions couldn't have been more perfect for the flat-bottomed, overpowered, fume-belching behemoths to charge at wide-open throttle down the racecourse, crushing any and all hapless sea life in their path. Conditions also couldn't have been better for the tiny, bobbing aerial to pick up the weak radio signal that would bring the afternoon to a premature but powerful conclusion.

Behind him a covered stage had been erected on the sand, on which the various luminaries had already gathered. One table supported big bowls of ice cubes and various bottles of refreshments to quench the luminaries' thirst. Another table was covered with a large green piece of felt that concealed something that, presumably, the luminaries planned to unveil at some point in the festivities.

He turned his attention back to the water, where the boats were already rumbling. Soon. Very soon. Though the earplugs leading to the Walkman remained silent, he began shaking his head to the tune that ran through his mind.

At the edge of the crowd, Amee Mosher gyrated to the beat from her Walkman, waving her arms, shaking her buns. She didn't know the song, she didn't even like the radio station. She didn't care. She was going to be rich, and it wouldn't be long now.

She spun, stepped to the side, dropped to the sand, stood straight. She opened her eyes and noticed a scrawny surfer standing before her, mouth agape, staring at her chest. She smiled at him, licked her lips and pulled the errant red triangle back into place, then laughed aloud as he scurried away.

Tonight she would reward that moron, and tomorrow night, she would tell Nicky, and he would reward her. And then they would live happily ever after. Or however long it took for her to devise a way to separate him from his money.

She felt a hand on her waist and turned her head to the beat. It was the moron. She ground her rear against his crotch, pulled out her earphones, settled back into his arms.

"Well? Have you earned a night with Cherry?" she whispered.

"She thinks I'm a friggin' pervert. She thinks I play with myself."

Amee stiffened, turned to face him. "Who thinks you're a pervert? Nick's wife? Why is she still alive?"

"It didn't work. The gun you gave me." He reached into a paper bag. "Here."

"Not here!" she hissed. "Are you nuts?"

Around them, beach bimbos in their bikinis and bubbas in their stained T-shirts stood waiting for the start of the races.

"No one's paying any attention to us," he said defensively.

She grabbed the paper bag from him, stuffed it into her knapsack, then reached into the knapsack with one hand.

"It jammed," he complained. "I squeezed and squeezed, but it wouldn't fire."

She took her hand out of the knapsack, fastened the snaps and thrust it at Jamie's chest. "You moron. You didn't release the safety."

"Safety?"

"Safety. You know. The little thingie on the side? You push it forward before you can fire it?"

"I know what a safety is," he said indignantly. "But *you*

didn't tell me *this* gun had one. Not all guns do, you know. How was I supposed to know?"

"Oh, Mr. Great Big Hunter Man can't figure out how to use a fucking little .22. Perfect. Well, a deal's a deal. You go back there and finish it," she ordered. "This time flick the safety off."

"I can't go back there!" he whined. "She'll call the cops if I set foot anywhere near there!"

Amee crossed her arms. "I send you to kill her, and instead you wank off in front of her?"

"I didn't wank off," he whispered, looking around to make sure no one was listening. "It's these shorts. They don't have no pockets. And the gun was gonna fall out. I had to grab it."

She rolled her eyes. "Okay. Here's what you're gonna do. Park across the street from her store. Then, when she leaves to go home tonight, follow her. When she gets to that part of A1A where it narrows to two lanes, you run her off the road and shoot her."

"You want me to shoot her on the street? Out in public?"

"Make sure no one's around." She heard the roar behind her, saw that the boats had started their engines, raised her voice. "You must have seen how empty the road is down here. Just make sure there's no cars coming. Got it?"

"Got it. Run her off the road and shoot her in the head," he shouted, then realized the boats had stopped racing their engines and everyone could hear him. A blond-haired guy with a Confederate-flag T-shirt and ponytail was staring at him. He glared back until Bubba looked away. "Then what?" he whispered.

Amee shook her head sadly. "Come by the pool hall."

● ● ● ●

Nick turned the knobs until the glasses focused on the row of bimbos lining the water's edge near the finish line. With the warmer weather, they had broken out their skimpiest bikinis, and all he could see was buns. Big, small, flabby, firm. Buns everywhere.

He groaned and set the binoculars on the table, grabbed the edge until the wave of nausea passed. There was a time, not too long ago, when he could have spent all day staring at young girls' asses. No more. Rear ends were no longer a mystery.

"Where the hell have you been?" Joanna hissed. "I had to lunch with the Budweiser people myself."

She was, as usual, dressed way too young: transparent white blouse, red miniskirt, bright red pumps and the ubiquitous gold anklet. He would introduce her to Crawdad, he decided. Tell him that *she* thought he was gay, too.

"I'm running a little slow today, so back off," he said through gritted teeth. "Mom."

She glared at him for a few moments. "Well, come on over here. The races are about to start." She moved to the front of the platform. "And after the awards ceremony, we'll announce RaceWorld. Why are you walking like that?"

Nick grimaced as he pulled up beside her. "It's nothing, all right? Just pulled something getting out of the car."

The emcee announced their presence over the PA system, and Joanna smiled and waved at the applauding crowd. "Did you take care of . . . everything?" she asked through her smile.

"It's done, okay? So get off my case."

The first two boats in the series rumbled south to the start line. One bright red, representing Budweiser, the other yellow, sponsored by Chiquita bananas, each carried 1,500-horsepower engines built into its stern, enough to drive them at more than 120 miles per hour across flat water. Three helmeted men in matching coveralls stood behind each boat's console, although only one held the steering wheel.

"You know those things cost ten million each? They could buy five race cars with that," Joanna said.

"Budweiser already *has* five race cars." Nick winced. He had to stop raising his voice. Somehow the muscles in his diaphragm linked up with the muscles . . . farther down.

"I wonder what those other guys do while the driver is driving," Joanna mused.

"Something worthwhile, I'm sure," Nick said. On the sand below him, a beer-bellied bubba had his hand down his girlfriend's shorts. "Something worth the respect of all these classy spectators."

Joanna shot him a glare, then turned back to the start of the race. The course was one mile long and the boats began from an idle. The yellow lights blinked on and off down the pole erected on a flatbed truck, until finally the green one lighted to the accompaniment of a piercing shriek. Suddenly the boats were spewing exhaust, their bows thrust high into the air, rooster tails growing behind them. A few seconds later the roar of their engines arrived, blasting across the beach.

Nick watched the Budweiser boat take a half boat-length lead, then stretch it to a full length. Closer they came, a quarter mile away now. Then only three hundred yards. Then two hundred. And then the bow of the red boat lifted out of the water even farther, dragging her clear out of the water, until she stood upright on her stern, propellers screaming, and then the bow continued its arc, coming over to complete the back flip, coming down, down . . . right on top of the Chiquita boat.

The crowd groaned collectively as space-age carbon

composites crunched and smashed, taking loads in directions never imagined by the engineers, until the still-racing propellers on Budweiser finally sheared off, sending fragments of red-hot titanium slicing through her outer hull and into the integral fuel tank.

The explosion drowned out the crowd, which by then was screaming, and the fireball quickly consumed the plastic and metal carcass, sending waves of heat across the water toward the beach. In the ensuing pandemonium, it took some time before anyone noticed the dark fin that sliced this way and that, snatching bits of matching coveralled racers into the depths.

Jamie struggled down the page, one boring paragraph at a time, finally flipped to the next one. He couldn't believe he was reading. He hated reading. It was so slow, so dull. He'd never understood why, after TV was invented, people bothered with it.

But, he had to fit in, and the only place to hang out across from the Harmonic Age was a bookstore that had little tables on the sidewalk where you could sit, drink coffee and read a book. Jamie couldn't see how come they couldn't set out some radios and TVs for people who didn't like reading, but realized that was probably an argument he wasn't going to win.

The owner was probably a snob, some English major in college, probably didn't even own a TV. Besides, everyone else was reading, so he forced himself to grab a book from the best-seller rack and take a table next to the building, facing across the street. He closed the book again, stared at the cover. It showed a dark haunted house, and a bald, evil-looking vampire. He was pretty sure he'd seen the movie, and he even remembered liking it, but how they'd made a decent flick out of such an awful book he'd never understand.

He turned back to his page, picked up where he'd left off. If only he had his Walkman. If he was listening to music, it wouldn't seem like he'd been reading so long. He eyed the waitress at the next table, where a couple wearing matching tie-dyed shirts sat with open magazines.

He smiled at her as she walked by, trying to get another look at her chest. She was wearing a tight, ribbed T-shirt with nothing underneath except a nipple ring. God, he wanted to see her naked. Maybe tomorrow he'd come back with his camera and press passes. Maybe he could get her to come to his new roommates' house. Four girls at once. Now *there* was an idea.

He was busy thinking of pickup lines when, out of the corner of his eye, he noticed Barbie Van Horne shake her front door to make sure it was locked and turn toward her white Volkswagen. It was time. Nonchalantly he set his book on the table, dropped five sticky quarters on the table for the coffee and stood to walk over to his car. He felt his waistband, panicked for a moment, then remembered he'd left the gun under the passenger seat. He allowed himself a smile. This time things would go perfectly, and he'd be $5,000 richer, with a good chance at the $250,000 prize money for winning the Crown Cola 400 come July. He couldn't begin to imagine what he would do with such staggering wealth. But one thing for sure, he'd get himself a new car. Maybe one of those new Trans Ams they just came out with. Now *that* would be cool. With a car like that, he'd be able to get any chick he wanted.

He watched his quarry lower her convertible top, settle into her seat and start her engine. He reached for his door handle, pulled and nearly broke his fingernails off. It was stuck. He turned, saw her look over her shoulder and pull into traffic, and gave another sharp yank on the door, this time accompanied with a kick. Still it wouldn't budge. Panicked, he shook the handle violently, then looked inside the window and realized it wasn't stuck. It was locked, with his keys dangling quietly from the ignition. Why? He *never* locked his doors! There was nothing inside worth stealing.

Then he remembered. This time there *was* something worth stealing. The gun. He had rolled his windows and locked his doors to keep the gun from getting ripped off. Brilliant. He turned to look down Seabreeze but could no longer distinguish Barbie Van Horne's taillights from the rest in the stream. He gave his Datsun a final kick for good measure and turned to go find himself a wire hanger.

FIVE

...

The floodlights provided an eerie cast to the race-way's infield, giving the grass almost the same blue-green hue the ocean had had that afternoon. Nick stood at the plate-glass window atop the Winston Tower, staring down at the two-and-a-half-mile "tri-oval" of concrete below. Tomorrow was the first day of qualifying. The pits and workshops would be filled with tobacco-chewing rednecks who, somehow, had become the heroes of America's fastest growing spectator sport. The clean, well-kept infield would become home for their beer-swilling kin, who would sit atop their rented U-Haul trucks with binoculars, watching their local-boys-done-good make left turn after left turn, hour after hour, breaking only to get more beer out of the cooler or get into fights with rival clans. By the end of Speed Week, the infield would be trashed, the concrete marred with a few hundred more rubber streaks, and the Van Horne family would be about $20 million richer.

Behind him, Joanna hit the rewind button once again, bringing the tape back to the few hundred feet before the accident. She leaned forward intently and pressed play. Nick sighed, finished his gin and tonic. She had been watching the tape for nearly an hour. On the table beside her sat the still-not-unveiled model for RaceWorld, with its little exhibit hall, its little Van Horne Needle thrusting skyward, its little plastic figurines of parents and children walking the beach and enjoying the many, all-included-in-the-same-low-price attractions.

"There, you see that?" Joanna hit the rewind button, brought it back a few seconds, let it roll forward again. In one frame, the Budweiser boat was charging along in full control. The next, her bow had begun its fatal rise out of the water. "You see that? Sharks."

Nick shuffled painfully forward to just behind the couch. "Where? All I saw was the boat flipping out of control."

"No!" Joanna slapped the remote control onto the coffee table. "One accident, okay. But two? I tell you, it's those same sharks from before. Once they taste human flesh, they never go back to fish."

Nick poured himself another drink, stiffer even than the last, which in turn had been more so than the one previous. "Maybe we just weren't meant for this water thing. Maybe we should stick to racing on land."

She stared at him icily. "How many times do I have to tell you? More than ninety percent of our revenues come from the five big races each year. So the three raceways bring in fifty million, give or take. We have to exploit the other forty-seven weeks out of the year, otherwise we're never going to make any real money. You think Michael Eisner would keep Disney World open just five weeks each year? Or Bill Gates would sell computers for just one month out of the year? Of course not."

Nick took a big gulp, swallowed it down. His headache wasn't getting any better. Neither was his butt-ache. And he wouldn't have either one if not for Joanna's damned beach theme park. "You know, even making money just five weeks out of the year, you're still the queen of Daytona Beach. Isn't that what you always wanted?"

Joanna pressed the eject button, walked over to the VCR to grab the tape. "Now you listen to me. If you think I'm about to abandon RaceWorld because of some stupid fish, you've got another think coming. Now here." She thrust the tape at him. "Take care of it."

"Take care of it?" He looked at the cassette cartridge. "What the hell am *I* supposed to do?"

"Eliminate them. You're having that bitch wife of yours eliminated, right? Find someone to do the fish."

Nick laughed, immediately regretted it as his hemorrhoids throbbed. "Joanna, they're not just *fish*. They're sharks. They're huge! One of 'em swallowed a Jet Skier whole!"

"Kill them."

"Chrissake, Joanna, didn't you ever watch *Jaws*? You can't just kill them. They keep coming back. Year after year after year." Nick caught her glare, held it, finally looked away with a dry swallow. "Who the hell in this town knows anything about sharks, anyway?"

Joanna moved to the couch to step into her heels. "That, Nick, is no longer my problem. Now it is your problem. You have until the end of Speed Week. If we don't announce RaceWorld by then, we'll end up paying a fortune in advertising. No, I take that back. *You'll* end up paying a fortune in advertising."

She strode out of the suite, and he heard her clicking down the hall to the elevator. Nick moved back to the picture window, studied the tape in his hand with disdain, and downed the rest of his drink.

· · ·

See, Barbie, there's a couple of things I need to explain. First off, my name's not Pedro. Second, I represent your husband in your divorce. And third, I think he might be trying to kill you.

No. Too direct. Nolin shook his head, turned around her mailbox, up her driveway. Perhaps a more casual approach would be better. He'd wait for the conversation to take the appropriate turn, then nonchalantly bring up the salient information. Yeah, right. And how, exactly, would the conversation wind up on the topic of dim-witted, murdering husbands?

He pulled up to the front door, put his finger on the doorbell, then pulled away. He peered in through the glass panel beside the door, saw a long, tiled foyer leading straight back to a sliding glass door overlooking the darkening beach. He turned to face the scraggly lawn fronting the road, looked at the orange sky turning purple.

Another day, that's what he needed. He'd sleep on it, and tomorrow at work he'd think of a smooth way to explain everything. Besides, what was there to explain? The name thing: well, that was just an honest mistake. And the stuff about her husband: again a simple mistake. He didn't realize when he met her that her husband was a client. No big deal. He certainly wasn't trying to trick her. And as for the murder thing. Well, granted he had no definitive proof. And this *was* Daytona Beach, so nothing was too farfetched, and she certainly deserved to know that her husband had been asking about the financial implications of her death.

He turned again toward the door, saw now that it was open and Barbie was leaning in it, arms stretched across the opening.

"I was wondering whether you were going to stand there all night."

She wore a white knee-length pullover and white coral jewelry around her neck and wrists. "I didn't know whether you were going to come over tonight or not." She nodded at the bottle of wine he held in his hand. "No beer tonight?"

He swallowed, handed her the bottle of Chardonnay. "I thought you might like this instead." He followed her into the house, noticed the sparse furnishings. The living room had but an old, beat-up blue couch, a green ottoman and a driftwood-and-glass coffee table. Opposite the kitchen's long counter, the dining room was bare save for a picnic table and some folding chairs. In rooms with redwood-beamed cathedral ceilings and enormous picture windows, the effect was comical, as if squatters had taken over an abandoned mansion and brought in the belongings they'd used on the streets.

"You have a beautiful place," Nolin said.

"Thank you." She fished a corkscrew from a drawer. "Excuse the furniture. Or lack thereof. As you can probably guess, I'm one of those millions of foolish Americans who's cash poor and house rich. I was at an RTC auction and couldn't resist the price, even though it cleaned me out."

Barbie popped out the cork and poured two glasses. She handed him one and clinked her glass against his. "Cheers."

He took a sip, swallowed. Not bad, considering he'd never really cared for the stuff. He watched her pull a tray of cheese out of the fridge, grab a box of crackers from the cupboard and bend over to check the oven. Okay: It had to be now. There would be no better time.

Nolin cleared his throat. "I'm, uh, sorry I'm running a little late, but something came up at the office. Something quite interesting, actually—"

"I've got a chicken in the oven. It'll be another half

hour or so. You want to wait in here, or go out on the deck?"

Nolin shrugged, flustered. He almost had it out. "The deck sounds good."

She pulled open the sliding glass door and climbed down three steps onto the weathered gray planking. He followed, slid the screen door shut behind him and watched her set the cheese and crackers beside the sunken Jacuzzi. She lifted off the vinyl cover, folded it and laid it aside.

"I turned the heater on this up about an hour ago." She dipped her toes in, swished them around for a few seconds. "I hope it's hot enough for you."

It took a moment for this to register before Nolin's mouth went dry. She wanted to go hot-tubbing with him! "I didn't bring my suit," he said lamely as he watched her pull the terry cover-up over her head. She was, of course, naked underneath.

She tossed the dress onto the deck chair. "Well, I'm afraid I'm clean out of men's swim trunks. I could lend you a pair of my running shorts. They might fit."

Nolin shook his head. The only thing worse than being naked and staring at her body would be wearing clothes and staring at her body. Like he was doing now. He dropped his eyes and started undoing his belt. "No, that's okay. I guess I don't really need to wear one after all."

Amee put her eye to the peephole, confirmed it was, indeed, Nick waddling up the walkway. She turned nervously to the mirror in the hall. He had that "No Boardwalk tramp can talk to J. R. Van Horne like that" scowl on his face. She'd have to talk fast tonight, reassure him that, yes, Cherry Mosher understood that his station in life was well above hers, and that, yes, she understood completely that he could easily find a dozen others to take her place.

She fluffed up her $29 haircut, mashed her lips together to smooth the bright red gloss and tugged at the uneven seams of her neck-to-toe, red lace body stocking. As an afterthought, she pinched each nipple until it poked through the fabric. As soon as the knock sounded, she pulled open the door, lounged sinuously against the door-jamb, put on her best smile. "I've been waiting for you."

She arched her back to thrust out her chest and, as hoped, saw the scowl disappear, the mouth fall open and his eyes wander hungrily up and down her body. "What's all this about?" he asked finally.

She took his hand and drew him in, immediately started undoing the buttons on his shirt. "I just wanted to make up for the other night. I was mean to you, and I had no right to be."

His eyes narrowed and the scowl returned. She saw he was still determined to teach her a lesson. Quickly she fell to her knees.

"Damn right, you didn't," he said with as surly a voice as he could manage while watching her take his trousers' zipper tab in her teeth and pull it downward. "And don't you forget it," he mumbled.

"Oh, I won't." She pushed the door shut behind him, pulled him onto a couch to finish undressing him. "So tonight, I'm your sex slave." She struck a pose, one hand in the air, the other on her hip, and twirled around. "What do you think?"

He ran his eyes up and down again; she could see that the body stocking had his head spinning. "You look all right," he said guardedly, then seemed to remember something. "Is Lori coming?"

Amee smiled. The greedy bastard. He wasn't going to forget her offer. "Oh, she'll be here soon enough. I've got her at Top Shots by herself. She'll close up at eleven. In time for round two? But first lie down, I've got a treat for you."

Nick smiled broadly, lay as directed, belly down on the couch. It was clear he'd shown her who was boss. And she was bending over backward to make up for it. He watched as she poured from a small flask into her cupped hand.

"Massage oil. To loosen you up." She placed her greased hands on his shoulders and started kneading. He closed his eyes and moaned softly. "I also got another surprise for you. Wanna hear it?"

"A third girl?" he asked hopefully.

"No." She moved down his back. "It's about that thing we were talking about the other night. About your wife, remember?"

"Oh. Yeah. What about it?"

"Well, I think all your worries are over. I found someone to take care of it."

He opened his eyes, turned his head to face her. "Who?" he asked suspiciously.

"This guy. You won't know him. He's sort of a beach bum. Mooches off chicks. Not bad good-looking. Anyway, I told him you'd pay him five thousand bucks."

She watched as he considered this, his fat lips twisting and poking. What the hell was his problem? Five grand for a killer was a *great* price, even for Daytona Beach. "You know, Nicky, that five grand is a steal. Getting somebody killed usually costs a lot more, especially if you get someone with experience."

He snorted. "Tell me about it. How'd you get him for just five?"

She reloaded her hands with oil. "Well, I sort of also told him you'd let him drive in the Crown Cola 400."

"Drive *what* in the Crown Cola?" he demanded.

She kneaded deeper, moved down into the small of his back. "You know. A race car."

"Hah!" he laughed. "Whadya think, I just pick whoever I want to drive in these stupid things? No sir, they got sanctioning bodies to protect the *integrity* of the *sport*, to prevent just this kind of thing. No way. Tell him forget it."

She bit her lip. By now the deed was done, provided the moron hadn't screwed up again. What was she supposed to do when he came for his money? "But Nicky, you can get just one of your own drivers in the race, can't you? Just this once?"

"Look," he growled. "There's no way I could get something like that past Joanna. Besides, I already found somebody for the job. And yes, thank you very much, I'm paying a whole hell of a lot more than five grand."

She moved her hands down onto his great, pale buttocks. "Maybe you could call your guy off, tell him you changed your mind?"

Nick thought for a moment, grunted. "Forget it. Giving this guy a deposit was painful enough. I don't even want to think about what he'd do if I tried to get it back."

She massaged silently for a while. Okay, she would have to take care of the moron. That should be easy enough: She'd take him out into the woods and pop him, something she would have to do eventually, anyway. So long as *she* was able to take credit for the murder. She was going to be really pissed if *her* guy did the job and *his* guy took the credit.

Oh well. Same as always. She had to work twice as hard to get half as much respect. But never mind. She had bigger fish to fry. Tonight she had to secure her spot as the next Mrs. Van Horne. She leaned forward to kiss him on the neck, poured more oil into her palms, greased her fingers.

"Nicky, you're doing a wonderful job with your wife."

She bit his ear. "But have you thought about what to do with Joanna? Maybe I can help, baby."

He grunted. "Do more of what you were doing there."

She smiled. "Oh, you like that, eh?" She slid her oiled hand over loose flab. "I bet your wife never did this for you. Don't you want me to do this to you every night? Don't you want me to live in your house, do this to you anytime you want?"

Amee poked a greased finger down between his buttocks.

Nick screamed.

Nolin took a sip of his wine, munched another cracker. He had a while ago stopped worrying about how to tell her those terribly important things he needed to tell her. Now he was too busy falling for her.

"So how'd you and, what's-his-name, meet?" he asked, sinking deep into the water until the bubble jet was positioned on the small of his back.

"Oh, it's a trite enough story. I guess you have to understand the Daytona social scene for it to make any sense. Everything revolves around the Van Hornes. They're the town's royalty, and everyone aspires to go to the same parties, serve on the same boards, donate to the same charities, and so forth." She smiled over a sip of wine. "It's stupid, I know. But that's the stuff you're made of when you grow up here. And so when Nick actually *talked* to me at a Christmas party, and then *called* me up the next day to ask me on a date, well, that was it. I was Cinderella, about to be rescued. My mom thought it was great. It was in the gossip column of the paper, all her friends were talking about it. We were married within six months."

Nolin stared into her eyes, big and oval, separated by that perfect nose. A model's nose, small and straight. That was it. She must have been a model. That was where he recognized her from. "You know, there's something I don't understand about the Van Hornes. It seems an awful Old World name for such a white trash family."

Barbie giggled. "See what you miss out on not growing up here? That name is a fraud. Joanna invented it after she married into the family. The name was originally Horn. Like what a bull has. Or a car. But Joanna always had this inferiority complex. She bought into that old-money thing, where it wasn't enough to be rich, you had to have inherited it from, I don't know, ten generations back. So twenty years ago, she legally changed the family's name to *Van Horne*. She changed all the signs at the track, had the city rename Horn Boulevard *Van* Horne Boulevard. She even went to the paper and sat down with the publisher to explain that they could mention the change in one article, and after that they couldn't refer to the plain old *Horns* ever again."

Nolin chuckled. "And the paper went for it?"

"The publisher decided he wanted to keep his job, so yeah, he went for it. Even Nick had to have his name changed, to John Robert. Joanna thought J. Robert sounded more old-money than Nick. Thought that if they all had hoity-toity names, then the Palm Beach and Martha's Vineyard set would start accepting her invitations to watch the Daytona 500 from her skybox."

Nolin laughed again. "Interesting family. I can see how you might have felt out of place."

"Like a loggerhead turtle out of water."

She stood suddenly, twisted around to grab the bottle of wine. Again he glimpsed those fantastic nipples. They weren't erect like when she'd pulled off her dress, but still proved fascinating, still almost an inch long. Where had he seen them before? A magazine, maybe? Or a movie?

He quickly averted his eyes as she spun back around to refill her glass, then his.

"So," she began as she replaced the bottle behind her. "How come a nice guy like you doesn't already have a wife and kids at home?"

He shrugged, then sank into the water to his neck. "I guess I never really tried hard enough to find someone. Plus, *you* know how hard it is to meet anybody nice in this town, especially if you don't like car racing, or Bike Week or Spring Break or driving your car on the beach. Shoot, you're practically a heretic."

She laughed. "Tell me about it. At least you're not suing to take away one of their God-given rights, like I am."

She sank into the water, lifted her feet out. Instinctively he grabbed her ankles, studied the soles. Long and thin, they were, with toes to match. Just like his.

"I know, I have freak feet." She had lifted herself off the built-in bench so she lay parallel to the surface and a few inches beneath it. "They look okay from a distance, but I could never model sandals, that's for sure."

"No. There's nothing wrong with your feet. I like long toes." He looked up her legs, across her submerged belly and chest to her face. Aha! Modeling. So that *was* where he'd seen her. "I knew I recognized your face from somewhere! You're a model!"

"Not exactly. I did some modeling years ago. You know, to pay bills for college. Ads for local boutiques, stuff like that." She pulled her feet from him. "But that's not where you recognize me from."

"It's not?"

She stood up to reveal her breasts. "I'm the Nipple Girl. From the poster."

He stared slack-jawed. That's right! The girl from the poster! They'd been all over town five years earlier. An artsy, black-and-white profile of a thin, angular model sitting knees bent and head laying on her arms. And one long, dark nipple protruding from her chest.

"That was you?" he asked incredulously.

"You seen tits like these anywhere else?" She sat back down. "That poster gave me the first clue that marrying into the Van Hornes was a serious mistake."

"They were mad you did it?"

She sighed. "See, I never gave permission for that poster. That shot was done in college, when I was modeling for a friend of mine, an *ex*-friend of mine, for his portfolio. I agreed to pose nude so long as he promised not to take pictures that showed anything. Well, he never told me about *that* shot. And it wasn't until years later that he printed the poster."

"Let me guess. Until after you'd married Nick."

"You got it. Two days after I married Nick, to be exact. We went to Bermuda on our honeymoon. When we got back, that poster was in every cheesy T-shirt shop in town. Joanna threw a fit. She screamed, called me a slut, accused me of hiding my past, scandalizing the family." She shook her head. "She considered having the marriage annulled, but decided against it because that would have attracted even more attention to it: 'The Nipple that Broke Up the Royal Marriage.'"

Nolin chuckled. "And what did Nick have to say?"

"Nick had to say exactly what his stepmother wanted to hear. He felt as betrayed as she did, that he had no idea, et cetera, et cetera. And foolish me, I actually felt like I'd done something wrong. Like I *had* betrayed their trust by not remembering those pictures and telling them about 'em. See what growing up being taught that rich people are better than you are just because they're rich does?" She sipped her wine. "I wasted three years of my life in that marriage."

"How come you haven't divorced him?"

She shrugged. "Joanna begged me not to. She thinks divorces in the family hurt them, socially. She attributes her not getting into the Palm Beach set to the fact that she's a second wife, and that Bobby divorced his first wife to marry a girl thirty years his junior. So she didn't want a divorce, especially one so soon after the nipple poster. And I honestly didn't care one way or the other. I had no intention of finding someone else. So I just let it go. Now, with the turtle lawsuit, I can barely afford *that*, let alone the bills for a divorce."

Nolin gazed at her, wondering where she'd been all these years. He thought again of the terribly important things he'd come to tell her. How would she react now if he told her he was her husband's attorney? Even more important, he had to tell her about Nick's peculiar questions about her death.

"So." She smiled. "Do you think I'm a long-toed, long-nippled slut freak, and wish you'd never met me? Or do you think I'm a long-toed, long-nippled slut freak, and wish you'd met me sooner?"

He shook his head earnestly. "I don't think you're a long-toed, long-nippled slut freak. Well, I mean, your toes *are* kinda long. And I suppose your nipples are, too. But that doesn't mean anything. I mean"—he lifted one foot out of the water—"I've got long, thin extremities, too."

She smiled coyly. "So I noticed."

He blushed violently.

"Oh come on. Don't get all shy on me now." She stood, walked across the tub and took his hand. "I mean, it's okay for you to ogle me through your binoculars? But it's not okay for me to notice your . . . extremities?"

He put his other hand on her waist. This was happening too fast. He had to tell her. "Barbie, there's something I need to tell you."

She sat on his lap, put her arms around his head. "What?"

He swallowed. "I heard the oven buzzer go off about twenty minutes ago."

Jamie hit his head against the window, awakened and sat upright with a start. He must have nodded off, that's all. No harm done. The sky behind the house was the same dark gray it had been the last time he looked. More important, the white VW was still parked in the driveway.

He twisted the radio knob to turn up the volume. It seemed to have grown softer as the night had worn on. Or maybe it was just that the miserable choice of music the night DJ had picked had dulled his hearing. The Doors, Van Morrison, Janis Joplin, the Beatles. His favorite station, and more significant, the only station his radio would pick up since the tuning control had broken, had become some sort of oldies-but-goodies station at two A.M. Who listened to that crap? How about some Ace of Base, or Smashing Pumpkins? He ought to call the station manager and tell him that the overnight DJ sucked. Hell, *he* could do a better job.

And there, even before the sun had broken the horizon in the east, came his first brainstorm of the day. He would become a radio DJ. How hard could that be? You played some music, you read some news and took some phone calls when you had a contest going.

He nodded to himself. That's what he'd do. He'd call the station manager, tell him the night DJ sucked and that he had a much better format for those hours and would be happy to help him out. He wondered how much a job like that paid. A lot, he guessed. After all, if you were on the radio, you'd be pretty famous. They'd have to give you pretty good money. Plus there were the fringe benefits, like concert tickets and T-shirts and stuff. It occurred to him that he'd also be able to tip off his friends about contest questions, so they could call in and win.

Jamie stretched his legs to pull his little notebook from his rear pocket, then rummaged around beneath the seat for a pen. He flipped through to an empty page, then wrote in careful, capital letters: NEW JOB—NIGHT RADIO DJ. Beneath the header he wrote out all benefits to such a job: GOOD MONEY, FREE STUFF, FAMOUS—BETTER CHICKS. He drew a solid line, put his pen between his lips to ponder what negatives might go with it. Finally he wrote: LOUSY HOURS.

He flipped back through the pages, glancing at the various headers—video-store manager, bartender, race car driver, airline pilot, used car salesman. He shook his head sadly: so many things to do, so little time. At least he'd definitely have a shot at race car driver, once he finished with this Van Horne chick. He returned his little book of ideas to his pocket, looked up in time to see the front door open and a tall skinny guy step through, turn to kiss Mrs. Van Horne and then walk down the path toward the street.

Jamie slid further in his seat as the guy turned down the street, walked two houses, climbed into the pickup truck in the driveway and then drove back past where Jamie's orange Datsun sat parked, nose pointing out, among some shrubs in a vacant lot.

Jamie peered over the steering wheel to see the taillights disappear in the distance, then wiped the sweat from his brow. That had been close—too close. A perfect witness, the chick's boyfriend, picking him out of a lineup as the suspicious guy in the car across from her house the morning she was killed. Fortunately, the guy hadn't even turned his head toward him as he passed. He did have a big smile on his face, though. Like he'd just gotten laid.

Jamie smiled, turned up the radio again, and sat daydreaming about Mrs. Van Horne. She was the chick in the poster on Cherry's ceiling, all right. He was sure of it. Kind of bony, yeah, but still pretty hot. That was probably why Mr. Van Horne wanted her killed. Caught her sleeping with this other bozo.

The opening riffs of Van Halen's "Pretty Woman" came through the tinny car-door speakers, and Jamie cranked the volume knob as high as it would go. He started strumming his air guitar, realizing that the first thing he would buy with his $5,000 would be a really nice radio for his car, when he noticed Mrs. Van Horne in gym shorts, tennis shoes and a sports bra, a canvas bag slung over her shoulder, unlocking the driver's side door of her VW.

Jamie reached his hand beneath the passenger seat, pulled out the towel-wrapped pistol, carefully unwrapped it, checked to make sure the safety was off and set it on the seat. He waited for her taillights to come on, then her white reverse lights, and then turned his ignition key.

The radio went dead as a soft click came from under the hood.

Sweat beaded his lip as he frantically released the key and tried again. Again the click, and then nothing. Across the highway, the VW backed into the street, stopped, then lurched forward.

Jamie pounded the wheel with his left hand, ran through the familiar procedure step-by-step: left foot pushing in clutch, right foot ready on the gas, gear shift in neutral, ignition key to "on."

Still nothing.

He pounded the wheel with both hands, swore that his stupid, piece-of-crap car had screwed him for the last time, when he noticed that now no sound whatsoever was coming from the radio. Slowly at first, then with increasing speed, he slammed his forehead on the steering wheel.

SIX

...

Nolin drove slowly, studying the small houses on either side of the road. A casual visitor might not notice anything out of the ordinary, he decided. The streets were tree-lined and tidy, the homes well tended and neat. But here and there were hints that Cassadaga wasn't just a run-of-the-mill town in the Florida Bible Belt.

In the backyard of a concrete-block house, he caught a glimpse of half a dozen men, all bald, all wearing bright orange robes, sitting in a circle on the grass. Two houses down, a three-story Colonial had a giant wooden cutout of the Hindi symbol for "Om" mounted above the portico. And up the street a bit, a front yard was decorated with a small white-flowering shrub arranged in an enormous pentagram.

Nolin grabbed the "Guide to Spiritualists" he'd picked up at the visitors' center, unfolded it and scanned it as he drove, making sure of the address.

He slowed his truck, came around a gentle curve and

saw the white mailbox with the red lettering: MADAME ROSA CASTILLA MURDO, SEER AND MEDIUM. He turned into the driveway, set the parking brake and stepped out.

He chuckled to himself as he saw the number on one of the posts supporting the porch—777—and wondered how much of a fight there'd been for *that* address when street numbers had been assigned.

"I have been waiting for you, Meester Nolin," a Hispanic voice sang out from inside. "Please, won't you come in?"

He hesitated a moment, then pulled the screen door open and stepped through. Inside was dark, intentionally dark, with cloth hangings over the windows. As his eyes adjusted to the gloom, he saw a Spanish motif: a bullfighter's cape and sword, a pair of castanets, a small photo of the Alhambra. She smiled when she saw him, and waved him to the seat across the table from her. He moved to it, pulled out his chair and sat.

"How are you today?" she asked pleasantly.

"I'm very well, thanks." He studied the bright blue eyes, the makeup, the long, manicured fingernails on short, stubby fingers. "You know who I am?"

She laughed. "Madame Rosa knows many things, Meester Nolin. How may I help you today?"

He smiled. "Don't you know already?"

"Ah, a skeptic. It's so nice to have one every once in a while!" She laid her hands on the table, on either side of the grapefruit-sized crystal ball. "How was your drive here? From your home in Holly Hill, in your 1989 Ford pickup truck?"

And suddenly he knew. Suddenly he understood why the receptionist at the visitors' center had a computer and modem on her otherwise quaintly decorated nineteenth-century desk, why a pair of binoculars lay on the little table by the window.

"It was fine." He grinned. "Except, of course, I traded in the truck two nights ago for a BMW, although I suppose the new registration hasn't made it into the state Motor Vehicles database yet."

Madame Rosa's smile remained frozen on her lips as her eyes narrowed slightly, then widened again. "Ah, yes. Now I see the new car, although you still have the truck's aura about you. You like the new car, yes? It is very beautiful."

"I was only kidding about the new car. Don't you think your spy in the visitors' center would be able to tell the difference between a Ford pickup and a BMW?"

She lifted her arms from the table and crossed them across her ample bosom. "Is there something I can help you with? Or did you just come here to insult me?"

A bit of the Spanish accent had fallen away; Nolin noticed a touch of Texas or Oklahoma underneath. He reached into his jacket pocket and pulled out a money clip, laid it on the table. Madame Rosa's eyes fixated for a moment on the folded stack of fifty-dollar bills.

"I'm sorry if you feel insulted. I didn't come here to do that." He pulled off the silver clip, counted out two bills. "How much is your normal fee?"

"Fifty dollars for a half hour, eighty for an hour."

"More than a mechanic, less than a chiropractor." He nodded his head, counted out five $50 bills on the table. "Well. I'm prepared to give you three hours' worth of money right now for your help. Help which, by the way, will not take any more of your time than normal."

She nodded for him to continue.

"You see, a very good friend of mine is one of your clients. She believes what you tell her. Don't ask me why, but she does. Anyway, I have some information that I want to tell her but, because of my own personal circumstances, I can't."

"What kind of information, Mr. Nolin?"

"It's about her husband. He's up to no good with her, and I've got this uneasy feeling he may try to hurt her. Now, I can try to protect her, but I think she'd be a lot safer if she was on her guard, too."

She eyed the money, then looked up at him. "You're asking me to base my evaluation on your information? How do I know it's true?"

He snorted. "You don't have a problem using Department of Highway Safety and Motor Vehicle information in your *evaluations*, and you know how inaccurate a lot of *that* stuff is. Plus the reason I'm here is I really care about this woman. But I think she'd be very angry with me if she knew how I came to learn this stuff about her husband."

She sighed. "It's unethical to influence a psychic forecast for the sake of two hundred and fifty dollars."

"Really?" He counted out another bill. "How about for the sake of three hundred?"

She shook her head. "If people learned that Madame Rosa changed her predictions because of bribes, they would never again trust—"

"Three-fifty?" He counted out another bill.

"—what I or any of my colleagues here—"

"Four hundred."

"—tell them, for fear that—"

He peeled off two more bills. "Five hundred dollars."

Madame Rosa looked at him, looked at the pile of fifty-dollar bills, leaned across the table to gather them up and stick them in her blouse. "Who is she, and what do you want me to tell her?"

Crawdad sat crammed in one of the tiny painted iron chairs the Book Nook had on its stretch of sidewalk, his massive legs stretched out under a glass-topped patio table. With fingerless leather gloves he poured back his third beer, motioned at the passing waitress that he wanted another.

"Just a little while longer, Jasmine." He stroked his old lady's bare arm.

It was a gray day, and although not quite cold, was on the chilly side. That morning had promised sunshine and he'd had her wear her usual warm-weather costume of high-heeled ankle boots and ruffled socks.

"It's okay," Jasmine said demurely, crossing her arms to keep herself warm.

"That chair's not too cold for you now?" he asked, recalling the yelp as she'd put her newly-tattooed-but-otherwise-bare bottom in it.

"No. I'm fine."

Crawdad resumed his study of the Harmonic Age storefront. It looked like a terrible place for either a hit or a snatch, with big windows facing one of downtown's busier streets. Inside, his target was showing a skimpy dress to a great, big, fat woman.

The more he watched her, the more he knew he should snatch her, despite what that dipshit Van Horne said. She looked five-foot-nine, five-foot-ten, easy, with most of that in her legs. He wished the hair was blonde. Light hair typically fetched a better price than dark, although that depended on the total package and the tastes of the individual customer. A lot would depend on eye color. Blue had fallen out of style, but gray or green would up the price considerably.

The fat woman left the store, and Barbie bent to pick up something off the floor. Crawdad nodded in admiration as her dress hiked higher up her thigh. Yes sir, she'd bring a nice price indeed. And he'd just tell Mr. Bigshot Executive, Mr. J. Robert Van Homo, that he'd shot her and buried her in the forest, and where the hell was his remaining fifteen grand? Shoot, he might even ask for a little tip on top, and royalties every few months probably wouldn't be out of line, either. He smiled, thinking of the pudgy, nervous little weasel. It would be just like collecting lunch money back in junior high.

"Baby, why don't you go check out that store? I need to know what color eyes this chick's got."

Jasmine nodded, took another sip of coffee from her mug and got up to walk across the street.

Nick shut off the motor and stared through the windshield at the dilapidated old house. Stucco flaked off the walls, which themselves leaned pitifully, as if weary of a long, dreary existence and just waiting for the big storm that would sweep them into the sea. The building had no number on it, yet there could be no mistaking it: the only house on the east side of A1A just inside the Flagler County line. Just like the *Daytona News-Herald* article had said.

As proof, parked right in front of him, was the car: a faded orange Karmann Ghia with the personalized tag BLCKTIP, Romer's long-ago surfer nickname, according to the article. Nick opened the door and stepped out, slowly standing upright. The soreness was gradually diminishing. With the help of Preparation H, so was the burning.

He walked to the door, rang once, twice, a third time, then, despite the NO TRESPASSING sign, started through the dune grasses and sea oats around the house to the sound of a power tool. A side window looked into a room piled high with surfboards and lumber, but Nick saw no sign of Romer and continued around to the rear of the house. There, a sliding glass door opened onto a vast workshop filled with surfboards in various stages of assembly.

The power tool noise had gone away; Nick looked

around nervously, stepped inside. Tiny bits of fiberglass, foam and wood littered the bare concrete floor. He took a step forward, saw a hallway leading back into a darkened room with a blue glow, took another step and saw the source of the light. It was one of those glass wave tanks with the blue fluid that rolled back and forth, except it was bigger than any Nick had ever seen.

He moved to it, transfixed by the waves as they slowly rolled one way, broke against the side, then back the other way.

He never saw the forearm that dropped him to the thin carpet until it was already across his throat, holding him down against the cold floor. He looked up in terror at blazing eyes set amid a face constructed entirely of acute angles.

"What are you doing in my house?"

Nick managed a choked gasp in response, tried futilely to push the arm off his throat.

"You're trespassing. I'm within my rights to shoot you. You were a burglar. I was asleep. I feared an imminent threat to my person and my property. So I shot. I can guarantee you the police would buy that lock, stock and barrel. So explain why I shouldn't kill you right now."

Tears came to Nick's eyes as he kicked his legs, tried again to free his throat. "Can't breathe," he finally squeezed through.

The arm relaxed a millimeter, and Nick sucked in air. "I rang the doorbell. Three times," he explained.

"And I didn't answer it. What did that tell you?"

The tone and the eyes demanded a response, Nick realized. "That you didn't want to be bothered?"

A wicked smile curled the lip, exposing two rows of sharp teeth. "Very good. So why, then, did you choose instead to invade my privacy and break into my house?"

"I need to talk to you. It's very important."

"So talk."

The man still lay across Nick's chest, his arm still securely pressed against Nick's throat. Nick thought about asking if he could sit up, decided against it. "You're Randall Romer, right? The guy who used to be the state attorney? I mean, I only assumed because this is the house—"

"I'm Romer," the man said flatly.

"I came here because—" Nick blinked. "Don't you know who I am? Don't you recognize me?" Nick tried to turn his head to the angle in the flattering publicity shots the paper always used.

"No," Romer said.

Nick tried to hide his disappointment. "Oh. It's just that I'm on the TV every once in a while. And I'm in the paper all the—"

"I don't watch television, and I *never* read the newspaper." Romer squinted. "You're not that stockbroker I sent away for ten years, are you? The one who ripped off all those old people?" He smiled his wolfish smile. "Oh, I bet your dance card was filled every night, huh? Bet you were the belle of the ball. Tell me: Was it better with soap? Or without?"

It took a moment for Nick to realize what he was talking about, and when he did, sweat broke out on his brow as he recalled Crawdad's savage grin afterward. *No, not again!* "No!" he shouted. "I mean, I'm not him at all. I've never sold any stocks. I'm, that is, my family . . . You know who the Van Hornes are, right?"

Romer cleared his throat like he was about to spit. "You're not one of those scum, are you? That's my biggest disappointment: Eight years in office, and I was never able to put a single one of those bastards away."

Nick's mind spun gears. "Uh, no. I'm not *one* of them. I just work for 'em."

"That would have been my crowning coup: the Van Hornes, Daytona's white-trash-turned-royalty. A bunch of thieving scum, the whole lot. Another couple of months and I could have had the old man, his tramp wife and the kid. All three on bribery and mail fraud. I think I could've gotten state time for the kid."

Nick gulped. "Well, I don't really know them that well. The old man died a few years ago, though. The tramp wife is running things now. That's who I work for."

Romer scowled. "So what does she want?"

"Sharks. I guess you're some kind of expert?"

Romer's eyes narrowed. "What do you mean? Who says I am?"

"Lots of people, I guess. I asked a friend of mine for a shark expert, he sent me down to a surf shop in Ponce Inlet. The guy there said Randall Romer was the closest thing to an expert Daytona had ever seen." Actually the guy had said: that crazy son-of-a-bitch state attorney. "He even dug up an old article from the newspaper. They quoted you about surfing at the Inlet, and how come so many sharks bite surfers—"

"Screw the newspaper. Endorsed my opponent, the bastards. Over the porno tapes. Editors didn't want anybody interfering with their God-given right to rent *Debbie Does Dallas* and whack off. To hell with Florida law. Just enforce the laws we *want* you to enforce."

Nick lay very still, watching Romer stare vacantly at him, through him. The details of the controversy came back to him now, how God-fearing Randall Romer had taken a literal view of the obscenity statutes and gone beyond shutting down the peep shows and sex clubs on U.S. 1 like he'd promised in his campaigns. Instead he'd gone after video-store owners for carrying porno cassettes, even subpoenaing them for their lists of customers. Romer had put his flawless record on the line for his crusade: In twenty years as a prosecutor, first as an assistant U.S. attorney, then as the elected state attorney for Volusia County, trying everything from racketeering and counterfeiting to extortion and murder, he'd never lost a case. Ever. Not until the blue-haired grandmother and jury forewoman had stood up after a full ten-minute deliberation and told the judge that while *she* personally wouldn't watch such filth, she didn't think it violated obscenity laws for others to do so.

Romer's fall afterward had been swift and complete. He failed to return to his office, or even call in, for two weeks after the verdict, and when he did return, it was as a surly, withdrawn tyrant. His wife left him, took the house, took everything. And when it came time for re-election, the voters disavowed him as well. Though he'd taken nearly seventy-five percent of the vote in his first two elections, he won only thirty percent in the election that threw him out of office.

"I personally think it's a lousy newspaper, myself," Nick offered.

Romer's eyes regained their focus. "So what about sharks?" he asked suspiciously.

"Well, sir, you seem to be as much an expert as there is about them, at least here in Daytona Beach, and I was hoping—"

"Most misunderstood fish on the planet, the shark." Romer's eyes lifted up to the wave tank. "Absolute apex predator of the sea. Perfect in every way, and everybody hates it."

Romer lifted his stringy body off Nick, brushed bits of Styrofoam and wood from his shirt and moved to the wave tank. On the wall above was a varnished teak plaque displaying five triangular teeth. One by one he pulled them from custom-carved indentations and turned back toward Nick.

"This is from *Carcharhinus limbatus*, the blacktip." He handed Nick a hard triangle, an inch on each side. "This accounts for ninety percent of shark attacks in Florida. Almost all of them are on surfers."

Nick felt the serrated edges of the tooth, nodded admiringly.

"They don't mean to bite us. We're not their normal prey. But the water's so murky near river mouths, the visibility is terrible, all they can feel is the vibration as the surfer paddles out. These they can sense from miles away, along the lateral line that runs right back to the tail. They can also sense the surfer's actual electrical field through tiny little holes, the ampullae of Lorenzini. Biologists still haven't figured out exactly how they work. Just like they haven't figured out why sharks never get cancer."

Nick felt more than saw Romer's evangelical gaze as he turned the tooth over in his hands. "Really?" he answered pleasantly. "That's interesting."

"Oh, it's more than just *interesting*," Romer mocked. "Here we are, helpless before this dread disease that, sooner or later, will get every one of us if something else doesn't get us first, and this primordial fish, something that's barely evolved in millions of years, is completely immune. Of course, when you're that perfect, why would you *need* to evolve?"

Nick nodded, passed him back the blacktip tooth. "It seems that you might be just—"

"This one is from a tiger shark." Romer handed him a slightly larger triangle. "Another species classified as dangerous. Because, I guess, it has the audacity to defend its territory. This is from a bull shark. This is from the favorite of the big and small screen: *Carcharodon carcharias*, the great white, the best known and the most feared. Which is not completely deserved. Because this one"—he held up a narrower tooth, slightly smaller than the great white's—

"comes from the most unpredictable, most ferocious thing out there: *Isurus oxyrinchus*, the mako."

Nick took the tooth, studied it with genuine curiosity. "Really? Worse than the great white?"

"*Worse* is pejorative, but in that context: yes, worse than a great white. A great white will hit when he's hungry. When he's not hungry, he'll just bump or even go away. Not a mako. He hits for the sake of hitting. Voracious feeder. Easily excited, faster than hell. Bite first, ask questions later. Nothing's safe in the water when a mako's around."

"Huh." Nick looked up from the teeth. "Sounds like the one that showed up at the boat races."

Romer fell silent, studied Nick closely for a minute. "Actually, no." He grabbed the teeth out of Nick's hands and replaced them in their plaque. "A mako is a pelagic fish. He doesn't hang around shallows. Whatever it was, it wasn't a mako."

He smiled broadly at Nick, then stepped back into the workshop, put his face down close to an eight-foot-long board with a gentle hollow ground out of its centerline. Nick looked around the room, counted four other boards in various stages of completion. He peered through an open door and noticed stacks of finished ones, brightly colored and shiny, nearly filling the side room. Other boards were mounted on the walls. Every one was more than seven feet long.

"Nice boards," he offered.

Romer turned from his examination, looked Nick up and down. "Are you a surfer, Mr. . . . ?"

Nick glanced around the room quickly, noticed a large stainless steel box under the kitchen counter. "Mr. Box," he said. "Nick Box. That's Box: B-A-C-H-S. Am I a surfer? I guess anybody growing up in Daytona has done his share of surfing. Not much anymore, though."

Romer shot him a look of disdain, picked up a sanding block and turned back to the board. "It's actually a highly complicated means of locomotion. Much more complicated than these nose-pierced cretins nowadays understand. The management of kinetic energy along a wave front, constantly remaining at the point in the curve where the forward vector just balances the down vector. It's a beauty these kids will never appreciate. All they want to do is chop, chop, chop. Up the face, down the face, tear it up. Like those moron snowboarders they have out West. Everything's me, me, me. Look what I can do. Look how I can deface God's creation."

Lightly, he sanded a high spot on his board. "Barely a step above Jet Skiers, they are. This board, for instance, I'm experimenting with a displacement-saving hollow that runs from the midpoint aft to the fins. Since we lose laminar flow at about a third of the way back, it doesn't do much good to continue a foil shape past that point. Try and explain that to any of the geniuses down at the pier and they look at you like you're from Mars."

Nick listened politely, wondering what the hell laminar flow was, and why Romer thought he was in the least bit interested in it. Still, he was the shark expert. Finally Romer seemed to have shut up.

"About those sharks, then," Nick said pleasantly.

Romer didn't look up from his sanding. "What about sharks?"

"I was hoping you could help me with a problem." Nick waited for a response, got none. "Like I said, I work for the Van Hornes, and as you might know, they sponsored those races where sharks showed up and ate the racers."

Romer reached for a torpedo level, laid it against the board and sighted down it with one eye closed. "They were in the sharks' domain, and the sharks ate them.

Besides, they were Jet Skiers and speedboat racers." He put the level back down. "I'm a busy man. I don't have time to serve on any panel of inquiry or committee or whatever else the city might be doing to cover its ass. I frankly—"

"Oh, no," Nick interrupted. "We don't want you to study the sharks. We want you to kill them."

Romer stared at him silently. "You want *me* to kill *sharks*?"

Nick nodded. "Oh, yes. Joanna was quite clear. Kill the sharks. All of them. She'll pay you quite well. In fact, I'm authorized—"

"Get out."

"But you're the only guy in Daytona—"

"Get out before I kill *you*." Romer picked a cordless scroll saw off the floor, revved it. "Yeah. They'll think *you* were attacked by a shark by the time I get through with you. Now, get out!"

He stood, advanced on Nick with eyes blazing and power tool screaming.

Nick stumbled back over a foam slab, caught himself and waddled quickly out the back door.

Jamie stared straight ahead through the windshield, unable to blink for fear he would miss her. His Datsun sat parked on the street, four spaces behind her VW. The meter had a good two hours' worth of quarters in it, even though her store was scheduled to close in another few minutes.

The pistol lay on the passenger seat beneath the sports section of the newspaper. The safety—he had checked it four times—was off, as was the car radio. The engine, however, was on, and idling roughly. He wasn't about to risk another screwup over a balky engine. And, for the first time since he'd traded a nice video camera for the car a month ago, gas wasn't an issue. He could idle all night, if he needed to. The needle stood at full, courtesy of the $15 that Monica, the most generous of his new roommates, had lent him after borrowing a set of jumper cables and rescuing him.

Yup, that Monica sure was a classy chick. Not only was she the best looking of the three, with the tightest ass and the firmest tits, but she was the nicest, too. He would have to reward her somehow, he nodded to himself. Maybe as soon as his photography gig started taking off, he'd do a special spread with just her. Help her get into *Playboy* or *Penthouse* or one of the other top-shelf magazines. Maybe put in a good word for her, too, if someone wanted to use her in a movie or on TV.

Unlike others he'd heard about, ol' Jamie Hotchkiss wasn't about to forget those who helped him on his way up. No sir. Once he made it, he would reach down with a helping hand. That's how he'd been taught. One good turn deserves another. He'd help out Kristin and Tiffany, too. Probably not get them into the movies, like Monica, but maybe something else in show biz. Shoot, he could be their agent, set up gigs, arrange publicity, for a cut of their contract.

He wondered how much an agent got. Thirty percent? Forty? He would need more clients, then. More chicks. He gazed out across the street at the Book Nook, where the waitress with the nipple ring worked. She was probably working there tonight. She was pretty hot, too. He would be sure to sign her up. Maybe after he finished tonight he would come back and have a cup of coffee out on the street, maybe get to know her a little—

A giant Harley-Davidson roared by his door, startling him. He watched it rumble down Seabreeze, the enormous rider straddling it, a tiny German war helmet sitting comically atop the mop of red hair that flowed to his shoulders. Maybe that's what he'd get with the $5,000 instead of a car: a Hog. Man, that would be cool, tearing up the road on a big machine like that. And chicks dug Hogs, especially in Daytona. He'd have to look into it.

He turned back to the Harmonic Age and his heart nearly stopped. The lights had been turned off. Quickly he craned to see the parking spot four spaces ahead of his. Sure enough, the VW was gone. He swore to himself as he pulled into traffic, cutting off a Cadillac that honked in anger. He ignored the other driver's hand waving and gunned ahead, tailgating the car in front of him as he searched desperately for the convertible. How the hell had she driven off without his noticing?

God damn it, James, you have to pay attention! What the hell had he been thinking of? Helping out Monica, that's what it was. Well, that's what he got for being too smart for his own good. Always thinking, never an idle moment: that was his hyperactive brain. He couldn't imagine what it would be like *not* to have ideas all the time, to be brain-dead like some of the kids he'd grown up with, but Christ Almighty, he wished he could keep it in check sometimes, stay focused on the task at hand . . .

There! Three blocks ahead, just now turning onto A1A. He pressed the accelerator to race through a yellow light, then another and he, too, was turning south onto A1A.

Methodically he weaved through traffic until only the Harley separated him from the VW. Okay, easy does it, he told himself. He had plenty of time before the road narrowed to two lanes and grew deserted. He just had to make sure he was directly behind her by then. No problem. The Harley was sure to turn off on Dunlawton, just like most of the other cars.

He rehearsed in his head the steps he would take: first, wait until no other cars were around on that empty stretch of Wilbur-by-the-Sea. Then, pull around her like he was trying to pass, cut her off and drive her off the road. He'd stop like he was checking to make sure she was okay and then, after checking for cars again, he'd pop her in the head four or five times and get the hell out.

Simple and sweet. He'd meet up with Cherry, get his money and find out about when he could start practicing for the Crown Cola. He'd never raced on a big track before, never even raced on a paved track, for that matter, and he'd need a little bit of work. He fully intended to finish in the money, whatever it took, so he wanted to start early.

Ahead of him the Harley was still between him and the VW, and Jamie started to get a little nervous. The traffic lights of Dunlawton Avenue were in sight now, and still the Harley hadn't moved into the right lane. With his luck, this would be the one biker who lived in the ritzy South Peninsula. Most of the other traffic slid to the right to turn and cross the high-rise bridge to the mainland, but the Harley kept going straight, through the light, barely a car length behind the VW.

Great. He *had* found the one biker who lived on the South Peninsula. He ran a hand through his hair to calm himself and consider his options. He could pass the biker and get between him and the VW. But that wouldn't help, not if he kept following them. No, he would just have to stick it out, hope that the biker got impatient enough with Barbie's just-over-the-speed-limit driving to race past her. And if he didn't, well, he'd have to think of something, and fast.

The VW sped up a touch, and Crawdad twisted the throttle a hair to keep up. She lived down here, he knew, but wasn't sure exactly where. Not that it mattered.

He'd watch her go into her house, wait a few minutes, park nearby, break in from the beach side, grab her, tie her up, throw her in the back of her car and be in Miami by midnight. She'd be out of the country within forty-eight hours, and in the harem of some sultan or prince or tribal chief by the end of the week, the lucky bastard. With $30,000 from Van Horne and, say, $50,000 for delivering a nice, tall, green-eyed white woman to his old Union Correctional acquaintance Gatortail, he'd be flush for a while, a couple of months at least.

It would be enough to have the bike detailed, maybe get that airbrush painting of Pamela Anderson he'd always wanted on his gas tank. Hell, he could probably spare a couple of grand to send home to Ma. He could get something nice for Jasmine, too. Maybe a leather vest or a new pair of boots. Although the waitress at that bookstore had looked pretty fine, as well. He'd noticed her checking out Jasmine's tattooed bikini. Maybe he'd get her to move in with them for a while.

He smiled at the thought, then glanced at the rearview on his handlebar. The dickhead in the little Jap car was still there, and still riding his ass. He had half a mind to pull the big Colt revolver from his jacket and fire through his windshield a couple of times. That would make him back off.

He thought again of Barbie Van Horne's long, long legs, and what a waste it was just to sell her off like that without getting a piece for himself. But, no, she was certain to put up a fight, and every scratch, every bruise was hundreds or even thousands off the price. It was bad business to damage the goods like that. Maybe he'd take it out on her husband again. He smiled at *that* thought, nostalgically remembered his prison days.

Ahead, the VW sped up again, and Crawdad turned the throttle again to keep pace.

• • •

Barbie looked into her rearview mirror in annoyance, saw that awful Harley still there. It was the loudest motorcycle she'd ever heard, even after suffering through two dozen Bike Weeks in her lifetime. The thing was behind her, yet loud enough to drown out her radio.

She turned up the volume button and, finally, the strains of Van Morrison's "Moondance" overcame the bike's exhaust pipes. She nodded to the music, flipped the lever on the rearview so the single headlamp wouldn't blind her and let her foot rest a bit more heavily on the accelerator.

Her new friend Pedro was supposed to come over again tonight, and she was going to attempt to cook him dinner, having charred the previous night's chicken to a crusty, inedible black lump. But, boy, had it ever been worth it. They'd eaten cold-cut sandwiches in bed, instead, and talked and made love through the night. She should be exhausted, she knew, but felt instead a boundless exhilaration. She'd been anticipating this evening all day.

It had been years since she'd felt anything like this, not since . . . Well, come to think of it, she'd *never* felt like this. Not with the guys she dated before she married Nick, *certainly* not with Nick, and not even remotely with the one or two losers with whom she'd had dinner-and-nothing-else-thank-you-for-a-lovely-evening since her separation. Finally, she'd met someone whose idea of conversation wasn't bragging about how he'd picked up two coeds at once last Spring Break by telling them he was Don Wheat, the founder of Tahitian Tropic sunscreen. Or explaining to her in excruciating detail how that no-account bum Dale Earnhardt had cheated Ernie Ervin out of the Winston Cup points lead with that dirty piece of driving last Sunday. Had she seen that? No? Well, they were replaying it on ESPN 2, and they could go over to his place and watch.

Quickly she went through in her head what she needed to pull together for dinner, what she would wear, what to drink. There would be no burned chicken tonight, no sir. It wasn't until she'd pulled into her driveway that she noticed idly that the annoying biker had disappeared.

SEVEN

•••

Nick paged through the file again, this time actually reading the clippings and reports in the half-inch-thick folder. He'd had the publisher of the paper drop the packet by his office the day before, but he'd only skimmed it to find an address. Now he read more closely to learn more about the man who had dared to threaten him. The man who'd knocked him to the ground, humiliated him. Who the hell did he think he was? Well, he'd find out all about him and then decide how to make him pay.

He struggled to keep his place in the long article about his record as state attorney after his first term: higher conviction rates for murderers, rapists, child molesters. Even tax cheats and embezzlers. *Blah, blah, blah, blah*, the article went on and on. Best front-line prosecutor in the state, maybe the nation, according to some bar association survey.

Yeah? If he was so fucking smart, how come he was

living in a dirty little shack? He paged backward through the clips, came to a profile from before he was elected. There was a photo of him holding a crossbow and the head of a boar he'd shot on the two hundred acres he had lived on at the time in backwoods Flagler County. He looked even more intense and angular than he did now, Nick thought with a shudder. He began skimming the article, and a chill went up his spine: youth surfing champion three years running in high school, valedictorian of his senior class, appointment to Annapolis Naval Academy, two tours in Vietnam with the Navy SEALs, a stint at the postgraduate school in Monterey, then Stanford Law School, then back home to northeast Florida and a job with the U.S. Attorney.

A SEAL. A fucking SEAL. Nick didn't know a lot about the Navy's elite corps, but knew enough to be afraid. A trained killer, he was. He trembled again, reconsidered his vow to punish Romer. Perhaps, since there'd been no witness to his insults, there would be no need to make him pay. Perhaps it would be better just to let it go.

He paged back some more, blinked at a *Washington Post* story about a secret Navy project in Key West, an off-shoot of the one where they'd trained dolphins to plant explosives on the hulls of ships. This one, though, had instead tried to work with sharks, trying to train them to respond to certain sounds, to perform certain tasks. The article was slanted toward the idea that the whole thing was a complete boondoggle, even though a couple of experts said they thought it might work, if the sharks were trained early enough after they were born.

The Navy's official comment was no comment, as was the comment of a northeast Florida prosecutor who, according to documents obtained by *The Washington Post*, had spent two years in Key West on the project, part of it ostensibly during a second tour in Vietnam. Romer had flatly denied knowing anything about it, and the local paper didn't seem to have followed up.

Nick nodded his head. No *wonder* the guy had reacted so violently to Nick's proposal to kill the sharks. They were like his pets. He trembled again, flipped through more pages, came to an article about Romer's wife of twenty-one years divorcing him over the porn-tape crusade. Nick blinked as he read the next part: He had not fought for anything: not the house, the cars, the boat, anything. He clucked to himself, shaking his head, wondering what kind of mental illness must have possessed a man to do something like that. He'd never heard of such a thing. A man capable of that was capable of anything, he realized apprehensively. Well, he'd figure it out later.

Right now, he needed a drink. He stretched his arms, eased his buttocks forward to the edge of the couch and only then noticed the face that filled the muted big-screen television across the room.

It was Crawdad, taken off his driver's license. Nick scrambled for the remote control, patted all the cushions, finally found where it had slid down between them, pointed it at the set and hit the mute button.

. . . Stanko is among the first of this year's motorcycle enthusiasts to visit Daytona Beach. He remains comatose at Halifax Medical Center, where doctors treated him for two broken arms and a shattered kneecap. Police are looking for the hit-and-run driver who left the scene before a resident noticed Stanko lying in the street underneath his motorcycle. . . .

The news anchor and his willowy blonde co-anchor shook their heads sadly, reminded viewers of the importance of Motorcycle Week to the local economy and admonished everyone to pay extra careful attention in the coming days to watch out for our two-wheeled friends on the road. In other news, there was another huge turnout for the Daytona 500 practice session, Marty would have details . . .

Nick hit the mute button again, shook his head slowly. Amazing. Just fucking amazing. Of all the bikers in this ridiculous town, of all the fat, grungy thugs terrorizing the streets on their noisy toys, some road hog had to choose *his* to run over. He pieced through the implications and, slowly, his amazement and anger turned to loathing and fear: He would have to return to that biker bar and find somebody else.

His sphincter puckered at the thought. Then he remembered the $15,000 he'd already given to Crawdad and it puckered some more. He would have to get that back! Or else tell Joanna what had happened.

He heard footsteps on the stairs, turned to see Joanna in her nightgown, coming to watch the Raceway clips. She sat in the chair beside him and reached over to grab the remote control from his hand. As always, a wave of Oedipal guilt washed over him. She always wore a sheer nightie in the evening hours. And she never wore a robe. And he always found himself sneaking a peek.

"How's your little project coming?" she demanded in an icy tone.

The guilt receded immediately, replaced again with fear. He gulped, nodded at the television, where a police spokesman was offering a reward for information in the hit-and-run on the innocent motorcyclist in Wilbur-by-the-Sea earlier that evening.

"Not too good," he admitted.

The steam from the hot tub rose into the cold air, condensing into a thin mist that stuck to Nolin's face and hair. He leaned back against the jets and sighed contentedly.

"Thanks for a wonderful dinner. It's the best meal I've had in . . . ever. It's the best meal I've had ever."

Barbie laughed, slipped back into the tub across from him. "Now I *know* you want something."

"I'm serious. You should open a restaurant."

"No way. I took my business courses. Most restaurants fail. Especially in this town. The favorite food of the natives is fried shrimp, and the favorite food of tourists is Pizza Hut."

"So what's holding you here? Your umpteenth annual Speed Week–Bike Week–Spring Break?"

She groaned, lifted her feet onto his lap. "You know, I had the loudest biker—"

"Motorcycle enthusiast." Nolin wagged a finger. " 'Biker' is pejorative. The Chamber doesn't like it."

"Sorry: the loudest *motorcycle enthusiast* on the planet behind me most of the way home. I couldn't hear myself think."

Nolin nodded. "Yeah. They could muffle their exhausts, but they don't. And then they ride around at full throttle outside your house at two in the morning all Bike Week. I've always wanted to figure out where they live, drive up there on my vacation, take the muffler off my truck and then drive in circles around *their* houses all night. See how *they* like it."

"They'd like it fine. They'd just come out and shoot you."

He shook his head sadly. "Another pejorative myth about motorcycle enthusiasts. As the Chamber and the City Commission tell us, our two-wheeled friends are *not* mother-rapers and father-stabbers. They are doctors and lawyers, dressed in costume to enjoy a week of camaraderie each year among ten thousand fellow motorcycle enthusiasts. And each spends an average of three hundred dollars a day during a week-long visit, so, after factoring in the multiplier effect, they have a positive impact on our local economy of about seven hundred trillion dollars."

She laughed. "You've got it down, haven't you? What do you do, work for the Chamber?"

"I had a client who tried to sue them one year to keep the biker, er, excuse me, the enthusiast parade from passing by his store. He was tired of the vandalism and the litter and the doctors and lawyers pissing on his door."

"And? What happened?"

Nolin ground his thumb into the palm of his other hand. "Squished like a bug."

"It's amazing. This whole town is so completely brainwashed by this stuff. And then they wonder how come we attract every deviant and escaped psycho on the East Coast. You know this afternoon I had a woman, good-looking, about twenty-seven, twenty-eight years old, walk into my shop. She was wearing a pair of biker boots."

"So? Lots of women in Daytona wear biker boots."

"That's *all* she was wearing. Except for a black thong bikini that was either painted on or tattooed on. I couldn't tell."

"Really," Nolin muttered, trying to picture it.

"And the day before, this surfer guy came in, asking about an ankle bracelet for his girlfriend. Next thing I know, he's got his hands down the front of his shorts, grabbing himself, and then he runs out. He dropped a little piece of paper. It said: Orifices, holes, cherry, dear. I think maybe it was supposed to be a poem."

"So when you say 'good-looking,' how do you mean? Like blonde? Big bazoongas?"

Underwater, she grabbed a bit of thigh between her toes and pinched. He let out a howl.

"Let that be a lesson to you. Not only are they freakishly long, they're astonishingly powerful, as well."

He grabbed her foot and lifted it out of the water. "It's

funny, mine are freakishly long, too. But they're not even a little bit powerful."

She lifted his foot out to study it. "It's all in the breeding. My great-grandmother was a trapeze artist in the circus, and my grandfather was the first man to free-climb the face of El Capitan in Yosemite."

"Wow," he said, impressed. "You're kidding."

She smiled. "Yeah. I am."

He dropped her foot disgustedly, shook his head. "Serves me right."

Barbie traced a finger down his big toe, around his ankle and up his calf. "I wonder what would happen if a man with freakishly long toes were to mate with a woman with freakishly long toes."

"You'd either get a baby with chimpanzee toes, or no toes at all."

Her mouth fell open. "You're kidding."

Nolin smiled. "Yeah. I am." He pulled her toward him. "You want to practice some more?"

She turned up her chin in a pout. "I thought you wanted a blonde. A blonde with big bazoongas. I thought—" But his mouth was already on hers.

"We've got a slight problem," Joanna said quietly. This time the album remained in the safe behind the aerial photo. This time, he had called her.

"I can tell from here in Tallahassee that you got a problem," Weathers said, his Panhandle drawl firing on all cylinders. "I keep looking in the Daytona paper for a certain obituary, maybe an article about a prominent local lady in a tragic accident. But I ain't seen nothing. And then I hear from a buddy of mine who happens to be a golfing pal of the good Judge Anthony Antoon that he can't wait for Monday to stick it to that quote pompous lardass county attorney unquote. I put two and two together, and the outlook don't look promisin', does it?"

Joanna breathed silently into the phone. He had no right to talk to her like this.

"Now maybe you can explain what you plan to do about it."

She held her temper. She could destroy him. End his career overnight. It would take one phone call and a messenger to run the photo over to the paper's city desk. "I told you, we just had some bad luck."

"Well, let me tell you: There ain't no such thing. I didn't get to my position by relying on luck. You're responsible for making your own luck, and you obviously haven't been taking that responsibility seriously. So don't go tellin' me about bikers and car wrecks. Serves you right for relyin' on that idiot son—"

"Stepson. And only technically. He's older than me."

"So you say."

She waited through an awkward silence. "Look, I told you I'd handle the lawsuit problem down here, and all you have to do is—"

"Don't tell me what I have to do. I already done it. There's eighty million hidden in the appropriations bill for RaceWorld, and we ain't gonna see a dime of it 'cause of some fuckin' turtles and *your* daughter-in-law."

"Estranged daughter-in-law."

"Look, just shut up, okay? Let me think a moment. You obviously have no idea of the political risks I'm taking monkeying with the budget like that. Just shut up for once in your life."

Joanna shut up, her hands shaking with anger. One phone call. That's all it would take. But no, not yet. She still needed him. Until the $80 million was safely in her account, she needed him.

"All right. I'll take care of it," Weathers said finally.

"But I thought—"

"Shut up, already. I'll take care of it. If there's one thing my daddy taught me, it's that you want somethin' done right, you'd best do it yourself."

"Do you want me to meet you somewhere, give you—"

"No. I don't want your help. It's likely to get me killed. You just keep that idiot son out of my way, that's all."

Joanna listened to the silence after the click for a few seconds, then hung up.

Nick pressed the fake mustache firmly against his upper lip, held his breath to stifle another sneeze. He glanced down at the $26.95-plus-tax Pick-Me-Up Bouquet in his hands with disdain; he'd be glad to get rid of those. Still, to get into a hospital without a lot of questions, there was nothing like them. The elevator pinged three times, the doors opened and he strode out, following the signs for patient rooms to the right. Quickly he came to 316, turned the knob and stepped in.

Immediately his sinuses were under assault. Through watery eyes, he scanned the room, counted fifteen, twenty, twenty-five, thirty, *thirty-seven* floral arrangements. They covered every inch of bureau, desk, chair space and much of the floor as well in the private room. Nick made his way through the foliage toward the sounds of a tinny television, stepped between two giant rubber tree plants to where Lon Stanko was propped up in the adjustable bed watching a *Baywatch* rerun.

"That you, Jasmine?" Crawdad growled, then turned to see Nick emerge through the greenery. "The fuck do you want?"

His bulk was covered in a cotton gown from pasty white feet to a sunburned neck. Each arm was in a cast from bicep to wrist, as was his left leg from mid-thigh down. They had apparently bathed him, for the grime from around his malignant eyes and squashed-in nose was gone. Even the red curls of his beard glistened softly. In belated response, Nick sneezed violently. With the third explosion, his mustache flew across the bed in a cloud of mist.

"Chrissake," Crawdad roared. "You come to a hospital with a raging cold? What are you, some kind of psycho?"

Nick sneezed again. "Allergies. From all this." He waved a hand around the room.

"Oh. Tokens of sympathy from the community. Those tulips over there are from the mayor, the mums from the Chamber, the roses from the Hotel/Motel Association. Plus they're giving me a complimentary week at the Marriott. That big mixed assortment is from the police and one of those rubber plants is from the sheriff. The rest of the stuff came in while I was asleep this morning."

Nick stared in disbelief. Only in Daytona would a hired thug on his way to a murder be given the red carpet. "What happened?"

Crawdad shrugged. "I was followin' her home. This punk tried to get past me and cut me off. I wouldn't let him in. He tried again, only this time he was wavin' a gun. I reached in my jacket to grab mine when the cocksucker ran into me. I went over the top, landed on my arms. So here I am."

Nick studied him silently, up and down. Casts meant broken limbs. Meant he was out of commission for at least several weeks.

"I can tell you this much," Crawdad continued. "I hope he's settlin' his affairs, saying goodbye to his momma and his sweetheart. Because he's a dead man. No doubt about that, no sir."

Nick cursed his luck under his breath, wiped his nose on his sleeve. "So when do you get out?"

He stared at the television, where big-bosomed life-guards dragged a wiry surfer out of the waves and gave him mouth-to-mouth resuscitation. "The doctors want me for about a week. They tell me I was in a coma through the night. Fuck if I know. Don't remember no coma."

Nick chose his words carefully. "So in other words, you can't do the job."

Crawdad turned to him slowly. "What are you, deaf? I told you: I was on my way to do it last night when this happened. It's because of *you* that I'm here, all busted up."

Nick studied the cast on the leg, decided there was no way he would be able to stand, let alone walk. He swallowed, growing braver. "Look, I appreciate the effort. But I'm not paying for effort. I'm paying for results. You obviously are in no position to do what I need done, by the date I need it. Because if it's not done by Monday morning, it's of no value to me. Therefore I need to find someone else immediately." He held Crawdad's stare, swallowed again. "Therefore, I have to ask you for my deposit back."

Crawdad's eyes narrowed slightly, his mouth turned up on one side. "What did you say?"

"I said," Nick began, more confident now, "that I want my fifteen grand back, and I want it back now."

In a flash, Crawdad's hand shot out toward Nick, and tears of allergy became tears of pain. "What did you say?" Crawdad asked again, his voice barely a whisper.

Nick's mouth opened, closed. His hands squirmed, moved toward Crawdad's cast-encased arm, moved away again. No, he reasoned through the agony, if he tried to pull the arm away, Crawdad would make it hurt even worse. "Nothing," Nick managed finally.

Crawdad eased his grip slightly. "That's nice. Because the first time, I thought you said you was backin' out of a deal. And I don't like people who go back on their word. Do you?"

Nick shook his head, his breaths coming fast and shallow, his hands squirming. Crawdad shook his massive head, too. "Good, 'cause I don't like 'em, either. Fact is, I hate 'em. Now. I'll do what I told you I'd do. And I expect to see the rest of my money, plus, say, ten grand to compensate for my injuries and my lost time. Sound fair?"

Crawdad tightened his hold. Nick winced, nodded furiously.

"Well, I knew we could come to a reasonable agreement." Finally he opened his hand, drew his pulleyed and counterweighted arm back inboard of his bed, and returned his attention to *Baywatch*. "You know, just once before I die I'd like to have Pamela Anderson."

Nick, still hunched over, hands covering crotch, turned and shuffled through the foliage toward the door.

"Thanks for stopping by," Crawdad called. "Just leave the flowers on the nightstand."

Lori bent at the waist, lined up the cue ball with the solid yellow that lay inches from the corner pocket and missed it completely. Not just missed it completely, but managed to scratch, yet again. With a pout, she stamped her foot on the floor as a middle-aged tourist retrieved the cue ball and set it on the felt.

Amee sighed and turned back to her rumrunner. It was hopeless: Lori was never going to get any better. She had been playing pool now twelve hours a day, every day, for over two weeks, but she still hadn't picked up the slightest bit of game. Not, judging by the size of her Joe's eyes as he stared at her over the table, that it seemed to matter.

And there, Amee decided, was the secret to getting rich. It didn't matter how well Lori played or didn't play. Just so long as customers came in primarily to see her falling out of her bikini top, and so long as she brought in more than Cherry was paying her, she could remain the world's worst pool player and still make Amee a lot of money. And if one dumb blonde in a thong could nearly double Amee's income, then how much would a second dumb blonde, or a third, or a tenth bring in?

That's what she would do, Amee decided. After she'd gotten her hands on some of Nicky's dough, she would add three or four more tables and hire another couple of chicks. And all she'd have to do would be to count the money. Or maybe she'd hire somebody to do that, too. Isn't that what rich people did? Hire other people for things they couldn't be bothered with anymore? Even fun things like keeping track of all their money?

Speaking of which, she wondered, where the hell was the moron? He hadn't shown up the previous night, like he was supposed to, but that wasn't really surprising. No doubt he'd freaked out afterward. Probably hadn't expected so much blood and stuff. Probably hiding out somewhere, gathering his courage to come collect his money.

She'd give him his money, all right. No problem, Jamie boy, let's go out for a ride in your car. Out to the woods by the river, where I buried it to keep it safe. Too bad he wasn't more reliable. She would have liked to have kept him around awhile, at least until she'd gotten rid of Joanna, maybe even Nicky, too.

She glanced at the clock over the bar, saw it was already past noon. She sighed, realized he wasn't going to come to her, that she would have to go find him. A billiard ball clattered onto the floor, rolled toward her with Lori in hot pursuit. Amee bent to pick it up, handed it back to Lori. "It's supposed to stay *on* the table," she said dryly.

She followed Lori back toward the table, patted her bare bottom encouragingly, smiled at the customer and watched his eyes light up. That's right, we're lesbians.

And if you hang around long enough, we might let you watch. She winked at him, knowing he'd be good for another hour now, at least, and walked back into her office.

Jamie Hotchkiss. She picked up the phone book, replaced it immediately at the notion of Jamie paying a monthly bill. Where did he say he lived? She thought back through their meetings, recalling the first, when he'd stood at the side of the pool hall holding a beer. He hadn't told her, she realized, had only bragged about the three girls he'd shacked up with. She snapped her fingers and reached for her desk drawer, grabbing the envelope with the nudie pictures. Sure enough, there was the address on the front. She tore off the receipt and stuffed it into her bikini bottom, closed the door to her office as she left and gave Lori another fondle as she passed.

"Be back in a bit, Peaches," she sang as she opened the front door. "Hold down the fort."

The airplane rose and rose, pointed its nose toward the ceiling and immediately tumbled out of the air, well short of the wastepaper basket, joining two dozen other failures on the hardwood floor.

Nolin squinted at the wedge of paper. Obviously a design flaw. The craft was not balanced. The center of effort was too far forward, giving the nose the tendency to pitch upward at the slightest disturbance. He grabbed another sheet from the respondent's brief and began folding it. First in half, then each half over on itself. Not everyone could make paper airplanes like this. It would be something he would teach his son. Or his daughter. Or both.

He smiled to himself again. She had mentioned children, and he hadn't freaked, hadn't made excuses that he needed to go, that he had an early day tomorrow, that he had a load of laundry that needed to go in the dryer. Before he was hopeful, but now he was certain: He had found her.

He creased his final fold, bent the nose downward for improved performance at supersonic velocities and let it fly. The long, narrow craft flew fast but low and nose-dived into the edge of the Oriental rug. Back to the drawing board.

He thought again of his visit to Cassadaga and Madame Rosa, and the $500 he'd thrown down the toilet because of his paranoia. *Of course* Van Horne was hoping Barbie would have a terrible accident. He knew that he would have to pay through the nose for alimony, and couldn't bear the thought of giving her a cent, let alone tens of thousands of dollars every month. How could that dumb, fat slob know that his ex was already getting serious with somebody else, that he probably would have barely a month or two of payments before she remarried?

He smiled to himself again. Finally, in his life, everything was working out. He would finish the beach house, and, depending on which one they liked better, they would live together in one and sell the other. That money would be more than enough to pay off her legal bills. She could keep the store, maybe even hire a part-time clerk to help run it, in case she got pregnant or something, and they would live happily ever after. Now all he had to do was dump Van Horne. And, at some point, explain to Barbie that his name wasn't Pedro. But that could wait. And, if it came to it, he could rename the dog, and keep Pedro for himself. It was, after all, just a name.

He glanced again at the letter he'd typed that morning:

Dear Mr. Van Horne: Due to a recently discovered pre-existing relationship that could constitute a conflict of interest, I must at this time end my representation of you re: your matrimonial. Blah, blah, blah, blah, blah. Douglas Nolin.

Short, sweet, to the point. Leave me alone. Find some other shyster. That would be that. He could forget that he'd ever had any dealings with Van Horne, and he'd never have to explain anything to Barbie. He'd already pulled another sheet of paper from the long, tedious brief he should have been reading and started yet another airplane design when he saw the big green Monte Carlo pull into his driveway and jerk to a stop. The door opened, and J. Robert Van Horne lurched out of the car and, bent at the waist, staggered up the stoop. Nolin turned to his desk, grabbed the one-page letter and stuffed it into an envelope as Van Horne wobbled through his door.

"Ah, Mr. Van Horne, what a surprise. In fact, quite a coincidence—"

"Here." Nick threw a brown paper bag onto Nolin's desk. "I need you to hang onto that."

Nolin carefully tugged at the bag's opening, peeked inside at two videocassettes and a plain white envelope. His stomach sank. He didn't even want to know. "What're those?" he asked warily.

"Never mind. You just stick 'em in your safe. I'll be back for 'em in a week."

Nolin studied Van Horne. He didn't look at all good, with dark circles hollowed out beneath bleary and blood-shot eyes. "*Why* do you want them in my safe?" Nolin asked finally.

"You're my damned lawyer, aren't you? I want you to hang onto 'em. That's all. If for some reason I *don't* come back for them next week, then you open the letter."

Nolin nodded sagely. "And then what am I supposed to do?"

"It's all in the letter, okay?" Nick straightened, grimaced, bent back over.

Nolin twisted to look into the bag again. He didn't like any of it. Still, he had to know what was on the tapes. . . . "Why don't you just keep them in your own safe?" he asked.

Nick scowled like he'd never heard anything so stupid. "Then who's supposed to open the letter if I don't come back?"

What the hell could be on the tapes? Barbie had posed naked for a poster. Could she have done a video, too? No . . . She *wouldn't* have . . . No. That was ridiculous. Van Horne wouldn't be asking him to hold onto dirty videos of his ex-wife. That didn't make any sense. No, it was part of some paranoid fantasy, that's all. A part he had no interest in, and wanted only to wash his hands of once and for all. The longer he saw Barbie while continuing to represent her husband, the worse the Florida Bar would come down on his head.

"I don't know, Mr. Van Horne. I'm awful busy. In fact"—he reached for the envelope containing the letter he'd written—"that's what I was getting ready to tell you when you walked in. I've got some big trials coming up and I really need to lighten my caseload—"

"What?" Nick demanded. "What don't you know? All I'm asking is that you put this bag in your safe for one week. How much could that possibly add to your *caseload*?" Nick began to laugh, then stopped short, grabbing himself in the crotch. "I mean, I'm paying you *money* to leave something in your safe and not do anything. What could be easier?"

He really didn't look good, Nolin decided. In fact, he seemed to acquire a new ailment each time he saw him. *What the hell was on those tapes?* He knew now that he just had to find out. If it was something about Barbie, he wasn't going to be able to sleep until he knew.

Slowly he nodded. "Okay. I'll do it."

Nick nodded back. "Good. Now was that so hard?" He turned and started hobbling through the office door. "I'll see you in a week."

Nolin watched him ease himself slowly into the enormous sedan and drive off before he went back inside and sat at his desk. He pulled the cassettes out of the bag, laid them atop the clutter, stared at them. They were black, with not even any labels on the side. He pulled the white envelope from the bag, studied it, front and back. It was high-quality, 25 percent cotton rag, letterhead stock. Rich man's stationery. Except for the Van Horne logo, it was completely blank, and sealed.

He set it down and turned back to the tapes. He drummed his fingers on them, imagining their contents. *They were blackmail tapes of Barbie screwing another man, two or three other men, to make her agree to a fast, free divorce.* His eyes widened. What if they were of Barbie screwing one *particular* other man in her hot tub?

He stood up quickly and walked the tapes into his living room, plugged the first into his VCR, flipped on the television and stepped back a few feet.

On the screen, a dozen Jet Skis roared through a turn, their riders' left legs stuck out into the water as they rounded the floating mark. The camera followed the racers for a while, then panned the crowd at the beach, focused on a trio of bikini-clad girls who stood facing the water, moved to a mother holding her little boy's hand, then to a profile of a middle-aged man sitting cross-legged in the sand, listening to a Walkman.

Nolin hit the pause button, rewound it slightly and let it play. He knew the man on the screen from somewhere. Even in profile, he recognized the face. He just couldn't recall where ... The middle-aged man adjusted his Walkman, and the camera moved back to the racers. Suddenly, the lead racer went down around the far mark.

He hit the fast-forward button. The rest of this he'd seen, repeated a million times, on the news. He grinned. Despite the savage shark attack, the city had done absolutely nothing. No extra lifeguards, no beach closures. This close to the prime tourist season, they had hoped the whole thing would just go away. The recording ended, turned to snow. Nolin pressed the eject button and pushed in the other tape, fast-forwarded through the leader.

This one was the speedboat race. Again the camera panned the crowd, lingering longest on women who were both young and unclothed. The race began, and the camera followed the two boats as they tore through the water along the beach until they neared the finish line. Then the red boat leapt into the air. Again Nolin hit the fast-forward button, watched as the camera pulled back for a wide-angle shot of the spectators all lining the beach, pointing out toward the flaming wrecks of the boats.

Except for one. Nolin slowed the tape down to normal speed and saw the Walkman guy again, walking back to the line of parked cars on the beach, getting into a Karmann Ghia and driving off.

Nolin ejected the tape, rapped the remote control onto his palm as he racked his brain about the tall, angular man with the Walkman. Finally he walked to the kitchen to set a kettle on the stove to steam open Van Horne's envelope.

EIGHT

•••

The numbers on the wooden post holding up the sagging carport were faded, but legible. Amee rode her bike up the sidewalk and let it fall on the grass, cursing loudly as the pedal caught her calf and drew a thin red scratch across brown skin. She was already in a foul mood and could feel it getting worse.

She had ridden up Seabreeze to get to the house, fully expecting to see police tape and a CLOSED sign on the door of Harmonic Age. Instead, she'd seen Nicky's wife, wearing a cute little top and miniskirt, showing scarves to some blue-haired tourists from up north.

Amee rang the doorbell and waited impatiently until a tall brunette wearing a long T-shirt answered the door. Inside, two other girls still in nighties peeked across the dim living room.

"I'm here to see Jamie," Amee announced. "You must be Monica."

Monica eyed her up and down, lifting her nose slightly

at Amee's bikini. "He's not feeling good today. Can I give him a message?"

Amee snorted. "He's gonna feel a fuck of a lot worse by the time I get through with him."

She squeezed past Monica and marched over the faded orange shag rug in the living room, began poking her head through doorways. She'd checked two bra-and-panties-strewn bedrooms and one bathroom on one side of the house and crossed the main hall leading to the other when the short brunette and the chesty blonde took up station in front of a closed door. Each wore panties and a T-shirt and stood with crossed arms and a defiant look. Monica joined them and crossed her arms, too.

"Excuse me. But I need to talk to your boyfriend," Amee said.

"He's sick," Monica said. She seemed to be their spokeswoman. "What about?"

Amee smiled broadly, put her hands on her bare hips. "Private business."

This was too much for the blonde. "Screw you! Who the hell do you think you are, busting in our house like this?"

She smiled again. "I'm Jamie's photography agent. You know, the one who sells all his pictures?"

The girls traded worried looks, unfolded their arms. The blonde pushed a strand of hair behind her ear, thrust out her chest a bit. "Oh. Have you, uh, seen any of the stuff he took of us?"

Amee nodded sadly, sighed. "Tiffany, right?" She ran a hand down her side from breasts to buttocks. "You got great tits, but you need to work on your ass. Cottage cheese don't sell pictures." She turned to the short brunette. "And you, you got a nice firm butt. But really. Don't you think you ought to invest in a boob job?"

Both girls stared at Amee in horror. Tears came to their

eyes and they ran down the hall into their rooms, slamming doors behind them. Monica stood quietly. "You got
any complaints about me?"

Amee reached past her for the doorknob. "With you I
got no problems. Well, nothing a pair of scissors won't fix.
Guys don't want to see the Black Forest down there, know
what I mean? They get scared they might get lost."

Monica blushed and stepped back. Amee stepped forward, turned back. "You don't, by any chance, play pool,
do you?"

Nick drove north along A1A at below the speed limit for
the first time in his life. Inside, his stomach was a tight
ball, spewing out acids that burned his throat.

He couldn't believe what he was about to do. But what
choice did he have? Besides, it would be better to get
killed by this lunatic than sodomized by another foul-
smelling biker. He'd heard those SEALs could crush a
man's windpipe with their fingers, or jab a pencil into the
brain through the nose. He nodded to himself soberly.
He'd have to keep Romer away from his windpipe. Or any
pencils.

More quickly than he wanted, the high-rise hotels of
Daytona gave way to the expensive mansions of Ormond
and the subdivisions and condos of Ormond-by-the-Sea.
Before he knew it, he had crossed the empty dunes of the
state park and had pulled onto the gravel fronting Romer's
ramshackle beach house.

Cautiously, every nerve ending on high alert, he
stepped from his car, crossed to the front door, peered
through a narrow jalousie window. Nothing but gloom.
The whole house was nothing but mildew and gloom,
except for the workshop in back.

Remembering Romer's lecture about his privacy, he

rang the bell once, twice, three times. No answer. Back in the driveway sat the Karmann Ghia with the ubiquitous long board sticking out the back, as if Romer had to be ready to hit the road at a moment's notice to track down the big wave.

He rang the doorbell twice more, got no reply and slowly started around back. Step by step, stopping twice to pick sandspurs off his socks, he moved through the brush until he was on the back porch. He knocked on the sliding glass door, called out Romer's name, turned in frustration and gasped. Quickly he crouched behind a rusty barbecue grill.

Out in the water, maybe a hundred feet from shore, stood a man in a wetsuit. And beside him was a dark gray dorsal fin, at least two feet tall. Nick's jaw fell as the man stroked the fin, eliciting a fast thrashing of the giant tail that broke the surface. Nick breathed heavily, felt himself losing his balance and grabbed the grill for support.

Rusted legs gave way and the grill toppled off the concrete patio with a loud crash. In the same instant, Nick half stood and Romer snapped his head around. For a moment their eyes locked, Nick's bulging and wide, Romer's dark and narrow, before Nick stood, turned and ambled into the fastest run of his middle age. Through the sea oats and dune scrub, ignoring the sandspurs that dug into his flesh, across the gravel drive, into the driver's seat.

He felt for the ignition key, remembered it was still in his pocket, shifted his bulk uncomfortably to jam his hand into his hip pocket, down, down, down further. There! He pulled his hand, but it wouldn't budge. It was stuck! He leaned back and forth, tugging at his hand, looking out his window at the corner of the house where Romer would emerge at any moment, an official, hardened-steel Navy SEAL knife in his hand. He began to whimper, struggling with the damned keys—*why in God's name did they make the pockets so small?*—when he felt the cold metal under his chin.

He stopped struggling, wondered how Romer had snuck up without him hearing, turned his eyes to the left, saw him standing outside the car holding a spear gun through the open window. He still felt the point under his chin.

"Hello again, Mr. Bachs," Romer said coolly. "Mr. Bachs who works for the Van Hornes but isn't part of the sleazebag family. Particularly not that fat, lazy lardass J. Robert Van Horne."

"Please don't shoot me with that thing."

Romer nodded to the spear gun. "This? You won't feel a thing. You see, I've always thought it crude to kill fish with those pivoting tips that don't come back out the way they come in. So I make my own tips: razor sharp. So that I need to hit a vital organ and kill the animal instantly. Of course, if I miss even a little, the spear goes clean through and the fish gets away. Of course, I never miss."

Nick gulped. "I came to talk to you."

"You came to spy on me."

"Nuh-uh, I came to talk. I just, uh, got a little panicked. But I came to talk."

Romer nodded once. "So talk."

Nick swallowed again, his mouth dry from the prick of the point under his chin. "Can you please move that thing away from my throat?"

Romer smiled. "The spear? I already have." He showed Nick the whole spear gun, now completely outside the car. "What you feel is the cut the tip left behind."

Nick looked down in horror, saw the blood staining the front of his shirt, moved his hand to his warm, wet neck and fainted.

●　　●　　●

"Please, please, pleeeeeeeease, let go!" Jamie wailed.

Even in the darkness under the bed, Amee saw the tears in his eyes. She kept a constant pressure between thumb and forefinger. "I'll let go when you get your ass out from under there."

"Okay," he relented. "I'm coming. Don't pull!"

He wiggled slowly toward the edge. As he moved, Amee moved back, keeping her grip, slowly getting up on her knees. When he emerged, she squatted to stand, yanking him upward.

"Don't pull!" he shouted, scrambling to keep pace. "Now what?"

"Lie down," she demanded.

When he complied, she finally let go. Immediately he covered himself with his hands, shielding himself from her awful fingers. "You don't have any idea how much that hurts," he protested. "How'd you like it if I did that to your tit?"

She got in bed with him, shrugged. "I might like it."

"Not if I did it that hard," he pouted.

"You deserved it." She began stroking his chest and belly. "So what happened after you ran the biker off the road?"

"I didn't *mean* to run him off the road. He was being a dick. I was trying to get in behind her and he wouldn't let me. So I showed him my gun. You know, to scare him."

"Great. So now he knows you have a gun. My gun. Perfect. I bet he told the cops."

"I doubt it. 'Cause otherwise he'd have to tell 'em about the gun he was pulling out of his jacket. That's how we wrecked. I saw his gun and turned to get away. I musta skidded. Anyway, next thing I knew, I was turned around in the ditch and the car was stalled. The biker was lying on the road near his Harley."

"You didn't check on him?"

"Jesus Christ, Cherry, the cops were gonna be there any minute. Plus the guy was gonna shoot me, and you think I shoulda stuck around to make sure he was okay?"

Amee stroked lower on his belly, started sliding under his hands that still formed a protective shield over his privates. "Not check on him to make sure he was okay," she said calmly. "Check on him to make sure he was dead."

Jamie blinked. "What, kill *him*, too?"

Amee shrugged. "Why not? You just said he was ready to shoot you."

He shook his head. "I don't know, Cherry. Killing Mrs. Van Horne, now I got a good reason for doin' that. But that biker, I got nothing against him. He wasn't doin' nothing."

She sat up. "I think there's something you don't understand about life. If there's something you want, you have to go out and get it. You don't let anyone stand in your way, especially not biker trash. If you want to make some money, if you want to drive at Daytona, you're gonna have to get the job done. Mr. Van Horne's getting impatient. Now. What did you do with the car?"

Jamie timidly opened his hands to give her better access, ever mindful of the terrible pain she could inflict. "I ditched it in the woods up near High Bridge. Covered it with some branches."

"And the gun?"

"Buried it. About a mile south of the car."

"You'll need to go dig it up this afternoon. And tonight you'll go take care of Mrs. Van Horne. It didn't work at her store, it didn't work on the drive home. Fine. Do her at her house."

"At her *house*? How?"

"You're a smart boy. You think of a way." She reached around back and undid the knot, pulled her bikini top over her head. "And to help you think, I'll give you a kiss to make it better."

Jamie's eyes widened in terror at the thought of the permanent disfigurement she could do, then relaxed a bit, then closed as a wide smile spread across his face. A light knock sounded on the door.

Amee lifted her head slightly. "Come in."

Monica stepped in, closed the door behind her. She had lost her panties and was holding the bottom of her T-shirt up above her navel. It was clear she had spent the past twenty minutes with scissors and razor. "You think the magazines would be interested in me now?"

The boat was bobbing, going nowhere. Just bobbing. Fishing, probably. Nick hated fishing. He hated water, period. Just the thought of it nauseated him. In fact, he felt like throwing up right now. Why would he dream about boating? He hated boating. He wished he would wake up.

A splash of cold water hit him in the face. "Wake up," a voice commanded.

Nick woke up, saw Romer's dark face surrounded by blue sky. He realized he was freezing, turned his head to look around and wished he'd remained asleep. He was buck naked, tied to a surfboard, bobbing up and down in the slight swell. Romer stood next to him. The deserted beach was about 150 feet away.

"So, you ready to tell the truth?"

Nick tried to move his hands, realized he couldn't budge them. Of course he couldn't. A Navy SEAL would certainly know his knots. He felt nauseated again. "You're not going to let me drift out to sea, are you?"

Romer laughed. "It amazes me how a guy can live by the water all his pathetic life and still not know a damn thing about the tides." He grabbed the surfboard and spun it around so Nick's head pointed offshore. "See, the prevailing wind this time of year is southeast. The easterly

seabreeze is even stronger. So unless there's an unusual
westerly to take you well offshore, all the tide does is take
you away from shore, then bring you back to shore, away
from shore, back to shore, until at some point a spring tide
washes you up on the beach. That's why drowning victims
almost always come back."

Nick felt the vomit rising, struggled to keep it down,
knowing Romer would probably let him choke on it.

"That's the good news, as far as drifting out to sea goes.
Now the bad news: This is the time of year we *do* get lots
of westerlies with all the cold fronts coming through.
Right now for instance. Feel how warm the air is?"

Nick shivered, his pale, doughy flesh covered with
goose bumps.

"Well, you probably don't, being naked and all. But
believe me. It's warm. Unseasonably warm. That's
because the wind is out of the south, pulling up all that
warm, moist air out of the Gulf of Mexico and the
Caribbean. And you know what that means, right?
Exactly. It'll go west as the cold front approaches. And this
time of year, it might sit in the west for, oh, a day or two.
Perfect surfing wind, a westerly. Especially with a big
northeast swell, that west wind makes those big boys stand
right up. Nice, clean, long break. California conditions."

Romer shook his head wistfully. "Anyway. That westerly will also push things out beyond the reach of the daily
tides. In fact, if it can get you fifty or sixty miles offshore,
it'll put you in the Gulf Stream, and then God only knows
where you'll wind up. Maybe Cape Hatteras. More likely,
Ireland, or even Norway. Of course, there's a chance
you'll catch the Canary current off Cape Finisterre and be
pushed southwest right into the trade winds and the northern equatorial current." Romer laughed. "And that could
put you right back on this beach: in about two or three
years. What's left of you, anyway."

Nick retched violently, sending a spume straight upward. Romer dodged it easily, then turned the board on its side to let Nick puke into the water.

"But to answer your question: No. I'm not going to let you drift out to sea."

Nick finished vomiting, took a series of deep breaths. "You're not?"

"Nope." Romer shook his head, let the board down into the water again. "I'm going to flip you upside down and let my trained shark devour you."

Nick felt his mouth go dry, saw a wicked smile on Romer's lips.

"See, that's why I took your clothes. The cops, they aren't too good with bone fragments. But clothing, that's where they'll make an ID every time." He laughed softly. "I know what you're thinking. You're thinking: He wouldn't feed me to the shark like this; it would ruin his board. But that's the best part. Remember I said *trained* shark. Lots of people, even ichthyologists who should know better, think sharks are mindless brutes, nothing but strength and hunger. They have no idea how intelligent these animals are because they've never bothered to study them. Well, I have. And I've found that not only are they trainable, some also *want* human contact. Take Bruce, for example. I've trained Bruce since he was born. He comes when I call him, and he'll be as playful as a kitten or as hungry as, well, I guess as hungry as a shark, depending on the signal I use. But he won't even damage my board. No, he'll just pass by right next to you, and his rough skin will slice right through those ropes. Then he'll tear you to pieces. Or he'll swallow you whole. I never know."

Nick's jaws moved, but nothing was coming out. Quickly, he had to tell him about the tapes he'd left with his lawyer, the letter. Why wasn't his voice working?

"Well, I'm sure after listening to me blather, being

eaten by sharks will seem a welcome relief. I'm sorry I go on so; I guess I'm used to rambling. You know once in a conspiracy case I did a five-hour closing argument? Convicted all seven, too." He reached for his waist and unclipped the bright yellow Walkman, started adjusting the knobs. "Anyway, I'm sorry it has to end like this, but I suppose there are worse ways to go."

"Like the electric chair," Nick finally blurted.

Romer blinked. "Excuse me?"

"That's what they do to murderers, you know," Nick spouted self-righteously. "They fry 'em in the electric chair. And that's what'll happen to you, too. I've got a lawyer."

"I *am* a lawyer, and a fat lot of good it did me. Anyway. They'll never prove anything. Especially if Bruce eats you whole. They'll think you ran away to Tahiti with your bimbo—"

"I gave him some videos. And a letter. To be opened if I don't return by the close of business."

"Videos." Romer watched Nick carefully. "Videos of what?"

"You know of what. Dead Jet Skiers. Dead boat racers. You. Your shark." Nick swallowed, gambled on a hunch. "Your Walkman."

Romer's eyes flashed, and Nick pressed his advantage.

"Yeah, I read all about you. You hate TV. You hate music. You don't even have a radio in your car. But you go out and buy a two-hundred-dollar underwater Walkman? And you, who hate Jet Skis and powerboats, you go out of your way to watch them race? And take your Walkman with you? So you can listen to music, which you also hate, while you're there?"

Romer stood still, stared at Nick with cold, unblinking eyes. "You're lying. You're making this up as you go."

"I'm not!" Nick croaked. "Believe me, I'm not that smart."

Romer stared another minute. "No. You're not, are you? But you *are* smart enough to watch tapes of the races and figure out what happened. You probably watched them a million times to see why your races kept blowing up. Of course, there's nothing provable. Hell, there isn't even probable cause to come search my house, let alone bring me in," Romer mused aloud. "But with the police chief in your pocket, you wouldn't need probable cause. And they'd bring all the evidence they need with them. So you could have already gone to the cops with what you got. But you didn't. You came here instead. Why?"

Nick swallowed again. "Because—"

"To blackmail me," Romer continued. "Of course. The tapes are at the lawyer in case something went wrong. Well, with all your resources, you must know I don't *have* anything. All the money's gone. I gave it away. And my surfboard business hasn't exactly taken off. So the question recurs: Why are you here?"

"I'm not here to blackmail you," Nick said, now more confident that he wasn't going to die in the jaws of Romer's pet. "I'm perfectly willing to pay a reasonable fee for one night of your . . . expertise."

Romer stood silently for a moment. "How much?"

Nick calculated quickly. "Five thousand?"

Romer scoffed, started fingering his Walkman.

"Okay, twenty!" Nick blurted.

The angular head tilted for a moment, considered the offer. "What do you want?"

Nick licked his lips. "I need to borrow your shark."

Weathers stroked the long barrel one final time and tucked it into the specially cut slot in the foam. He patted the night scope, its power pack and the ten shiny cartridges all in a row. He shut the case, flicked the snaps, hit the light on his way out and climbed into the forest-green Ford Expedition. The $30,000 sport utility vehicle still had that new-car smell Weathers loved so much, despite his frequent jaunts to the hunting lodge. He got to the end of the dirt road, looked left and turned right, flicking the truck out of four-wheel drive for a smoother ride down to Daytona.

God, he hated leaving the lodge like that. It belonged to the cable television lobbyist, who'd given it to Weathers for the week in anticipated appreciation of his personal interest in a bill that would, in the now highly unlikely event that it passed, levy the telecommunications surcharge on the cable industry.

Perhaps he'd mention to the lobbyist that he'd had a harder time than expected lining up the necessary votes in the Finance and Taxation Committee, and another week or so in the lodge should ensure the bill's defeat. That and maybe an evening with one of his firm's younger associates, he was thinking in particular of the blonde with the long legs.

He had seriously considered preserving his long weekend by hiring out the task at hand. In fact, he was reasonably sure one of his colleagues from Miami a few years earlier had had a similar thing done with a loud-mouthed community activist who was threatening to run against him. But he knew if he asked for a referral it would come back to haunt him. Soon enough, either the colleague or the contractor would no doubt need a favor, or two, or ten. Joanna with her damn pictures was bad enough. One blackmailer was plenty in the life of any politician.

Garth Brooks skipped a note on the CD player and Weathers grimaced. Why bother if it wasn't going to work right? Now he'd have to take it back to Capital Ford and complain to the owner, the one who wanted an exemption to the state's Growth Management Law so he could build a Hyundai dealership on land that had been set aside for a state park, back when the bunny-huggers had held sway in the House. Maybe he'd try the next Expedition in a different color, maroon perhaps. If he didn't like it, he could always go back and get green again.

He flicked on the cruise control and stretched out his legs. Another five hours to Daytona to clean up Joanna's mess. Damn her and those wretched Polaroids. He should have taken care of them, and her, a long time ago.

On the other hand, had he done that, she never could have given him 10 percent of RaceWorld. An easy million and a half a year. *That* he could live with: a safe, reliable income he could depend on as he struck out for higher office. After all, it would take a while before an investment in a congressional seat started paying dividends. He'd need a few years to acquire the power and seniority necessary to attract the favor of Washington lobbyists, particularly those with the really well-heeled clients. And a man had to eat in the meantime.

Those Polaroids, though. He really would have to do something about them. It wouldn't do at all if, one day as chairman of the House Armed Services Committee, he were to get a breathless call reminding him of the gory details and asking for yet another favor for Van Horne Enterprises.

Yes, he would make those pictures a top priority. A nice, clean burglary would do it. Grab all the jewelry, all the silver, everything in the safe, including, most likely, a well-worn photo album. How much might such a thing cost? Perhaps he would check into it tomorrow or the next day, whenever he finished.

He sighed, wiggled his hips and stretched his legs some more. Another four hours and fifty minutes to Daytona.

• • •

Madame Rosa held up both palms, eyes shut tightly. She began swaying to and fro.

Nick checked his watch impatiently. "Cut the crap, all right?"

Rosa opened her eyes, studied him suspiciously. He was in full disguise mode: beard, mustache and plain-glass, horn-rim spectacles.

"I know all about you. Your real name is Rosalind Jones. You're from Tulsa. You're about as psychic as I am." He waved a hand around the room at the faux-Spanish decorations. "This is all bullshit."

Rosa pulled the shawl off her head, picked up a folding fan and began fanning herself. "Who are you?" she asked, the Spanish accent gone.

Nick pulled open his jacket and removed a money belt. Quickly he counted out ten $100 bills and laid them on the table. "You don't need to know that. You just need to know that I'm good friends with Mr. Franklin here." He held up one of the bills. "You have a regular Friday customer. Barbie Baxter."

She looked down at the stack of bills, back up to Nick's face. "I don't discuss my clients with others. Everything's strictly confidential. Sort of like a priest, or a lawyer."

Nick snickered, picked the money off the table. "Really? Then I guess we have nothing to talk about." He turned for the door.

"Wait a minute!" Rosa called out, an Okie twang infecting the words.

Nick turned slowly.

"I might as well hear you out. Now that you're here, I mean."

Nick laid the thousand dollars back on the table. "You're the one who got Barbie on this sea turtle kick, right? Don't try to deny it. I know it's true. Anyway, I just want you to give her one more piece of advice about the ocean, okay? How does that sound? A thousand bucks for one sentence. And another thousand if she follows through."

Rosa stifled a gasp, but couldn't keep her eyes from widening: Two thousand dollars for one sitting! Plus Barbie's regular $50 fee, plus the $500 her boyfriend already put up; more than five weeks' worth of income! She could take a vacation. Go to Atlantic City, or even Las Vegas!

"Tell me what you wish me to say and let me meditate. If it is in her aura, I will pass it along," Rosa said, the Spanish pronunciations and inflections creeping back into her voice. "Otherwise I cannot."

Nick groaned. "Whatever. She loves to go swimming at night. In the ocean. Tell her she has to go tonight. Tell her all the turtles and dolphins and fishes and whales and all the other animals will be having a harmonic conference. That this is the one night when all the kindred spirits of the sea meet in the ocean of life."

"Señor, I will not speak of harmonic convergence." Rosa turned up her nose. "I am a traditional seer."

"Tell her whatever the fuck you want. Just make sure she goes swimming tonight."

Rosa set her hands on either side of her ball and closed her eyes. "I must see."

Nick shifted his weight from one foot to the other, checked his watch, bent to peek out the window. "Come on, Madame Jones. I ain't got all day. She's gonna be here any minute."

Rosa opened one eye suspiciously. "Why do you wish for her to go swimming tonight?"

"It's her birthday." Nick turned away from the window. "And, uh, we're having a party for her on the beach. A surprise party."

Rosa shut her eyes again. It didn't make any sense, a surprise party on the beach. Where would everyone hide? Well, that was *their* problem. Two grand was two grand. "I see it is in her being, in her spirit to do this."

"Well, hallelujah. You'll tell her, then?"

"When will you bring by the second thousand?"

Nick grinned. The almighty dollar had won again. "Tomorrow." He turned for the door. "If Barbie shows up at her party tonight, I'll come by first thing in the morning."

He hurried down the dim hall, pushed aside the screen door and waddled to the car. Things were still sore, but the salt water had actually made him feel better. Or maybe it was the prospect of finally getting rid of Barbie, and actually having a hand in it. Maybe that's what all the fuss of do-it-yourselfers was about.

He slammed the door, pulled a U-turn in the narrow street and headed back out toward the interstate. He hadn't gone two blocks when he saw approaching the familiar outline of the VW Cabriolet. Quickly he slouched as low as he could, put a hand over the left side of his face and held his breath.

Barbie drove down the street, parked in her usual spot and got out, just slightly off balance. Something had happened. She'd seen something, but couldn't figure out what. She looked back down the street, shrugged and turned down the path to Rosa's parlor.

NINE

...

Weathers set the parking brake, stepped out of the truck and stretched out his once-lanky, now filled-in frame. He grabbed his hunting case and an overnight bag and walked up the rest of the drive to the stately river mansion, the property of Jimmy Poole, the lobbyist for Daytona Raceway. He entered the empty house, walked past the art-gallery trinkets, through the back door and down a wooden walkway toward the *Checkered Flag,* the Van Hornes' fifty-four-foot luxury trawler, tied to the end of the dock. A fifteen-foot, rigid-bottomed, inflatable runabout hung on hoists off her aft deck.

Weathers ignored both vessels and instead grabbed a four-foot-long, three-foot-thick bundle of plastic and unrolled it onto the gray planks. Aluminum slats clicked into place as he put a bellows pump to one of the valves and began pumping. In twenty minutes, he had prepared himself a ten-foot dinghy, complete with a 9.9-horse-power Evinrude outboard, and had it tied to the dock at the bottom of a wooden ladder. Weathers looked at the quickly darkening sky and checked his watch. Sure, he had time. At least for one beer.

He headed back up toward the house, hoping that good ol' Jimmy kept a supply of cold ones in his fridge.

Outside, the sky over the ocean was dark, dark blue, with the few clouds reflecting back the orange from the sunset across the river. Amee ignored it, instead scanned the Boardwalk up and down for Jamie's familiar blond head. The moron was late again, and she had important instructions.

She turned and watched Monica, her new thong-clad billiards hostess, line up a shot and knock it in. What she lacked in breast size, she made up for with long, long legs and a decent pool game. She was already out-earning big, blonde Lori at the next table.

Monica sunk her final ball and walked over to her Joe, an acne-faced kid in Bermuda shorts, T-shirt and baseball cap, a Canadian Spring Breaker. She gave him a big hug, kicking her foot up in the air like in the old movies, and a demure kiss on the cheek. She didn't object when the kid's hands slid down and grazed her bare buns. Nor when he pulled out a twenty to pay for his game and told her to keep it.

Amee smiled. Now *that* was customer service. She wondered again what it would cost to pay off a couple of city commissioners and the Boardwalk cops to let her girls play topless. She could easily double, maybe triple her income. Make it that much sooner that she could pick up a third and fourth table. And then a third and fourth girl. Between that and the money she'd make off Nicky, she was finally going to be rich.

The bell at the top of the door jingled as three Joes, their pockets and fanny packs emptied, went out and Jamie and his goofy smile came in. Amee marched to the door, grabbed his arm, dragged him past the tables, past Monica's waving, through the back door and into her office.

"The fuck have you been?" she snapped when the door was shut behind them. "You were supposed to be here two hours ago."

He put his hands on her shoulders, let them slide down her arms. "Whoa, take it easy. I'm here now, ain't I?"

She pulled his hands off her and sat on the desk. "Did you get the gun?"

Jamie lifted his shirt to show her the handle sticking from his waistband. "That's what kept me. I couldn't remember if it was fifty paces east and sixty paces north or sixty east and fifty north."

Amee lowered her head into one hand and squeezed. "Why didn't you just do it fifty and fifty? Then you woulda had to remember just one number."

He blinked, nodded slowly. "Oh yeah. Good idea." He patted his pockets for a pen. "I oughta write that down. Anyway, I ended up borrowing a metal detector from this guy on the beach. Told him I'd lost my keys hiking in the woods. What a nice old guy."

She rolled her eyes and sighed. "Okay, now that you got your gun back, there's been a change in plans. You're not going to Mrs. Van Horne's house tonight. You're going to the hospital."

"The *hospital*? Why, what happened? Is she okay?"

Amee sneered. "Your concern is touching. No, it's not her. It's some business partner of Nicky's. He screwed him somehow. I didn't get all the details. Anyway, he's in room three-sixteen at Halifax. You go in, put a pillow over the gun and shoot him in the head until it's empty."

"Wait a minute," he said, raising his hands. "I ain't killing *two* people for five grand. I ain't *that* cheap."

"No one's telling you to. You get five grand for this one, plus another five for the wife, all right?"

"And a chance to drive in the Crown Cola?"

"And driving in the Crown Cola. Now go get some clean clothes. Buy some flowers like you're visiting somebody."

Jamie stroked his chin. "Are you sure this is a good idea? Shooting somebody in the hospital? Won't somebody hear?"

"It's just a .22. If you use a pillow, nobody will hear a thing. Here, gimme the gun." She grabbed a cushion off the mildewy old couch in the corner and pushed the muzzle into it. A "pop" sounded in the office and a cloud of cotton filling blew into the air. "See? You can hardly hear it."

Jamie stared at the ceiling. A small round hole had appeared in the paper poster, barely an inch above Barbie's head. "Did you know that's her?"

"That's who?" Amee asked.

"The chick in the poster. That's Mrs. Van Horne. Amazing, huh?"

Amee stared at the photo. "*That's* his wife? Nicky's married to the Nipple Girl?"

"Ummm. And I gotta say, she's just as pretty in person."

Amee scoffed. "Gimme a break. Except for them freaky nipples, she's as flat as a board. You couldn't get her pictures into *Screw* or *Jugs* or *Hustler* if you paid *them*."

Jamie shrugged. "I'm just tellin' you like I see it. Speaking of which, that was pretty good, this afternoon, huh?"

"Yeah. I suppose it wasn't bad." She remembered Jamie lying there like a log, waiting for her and Monica to work on him. Now, Monica was a different story altogether. She wouldn't mind getting together with *her* again. "Where's Monica from, anyway?"

Jamie nodded with pride. "I guess I'm pretty good in the sack. I suppose I must be, huh? To satisfy two good-lookin' chicks at once? You know, a couple of years back I had four at once. Did all four of 'em, too, one after the other: boom, boom, boom, boom."

Amee pushed herself off the desk. "Right, Jamie. You're the best. Now, why don't you get going. Nick said the nurses have a shift change at ten. That'll be the best time."

"You really think I'm pretty good? 'Cause I been thinkin' a good way to make a little extra money might be to be like a male hooker, you know? I figure, I get laid a lot anyway, I might as well get paid for it, you know?"

She pushed him toward the door. "Sure, Jamie, anything you say. You can be a NASCAR driver, and an airline pilot, and a tree surgeon, and a submarine captain, and a gigolo, and whatever the fuck else you want, all right? But tonight, right now, you got to be a killer, okay?"

He turned toward the door, then turned back for a final point. "I mean, it's not like I'm making this up. Just the other day, a guy on the Boardwalk asked if I did tricks. So you figure there's gotta be a pretty good market."

She stared for a moment in renewed amazement. "He was *gay*, you moron! He wanted to know if you'd let guys stick their dicks up your ass. Now *go*!"

Jamie considered this new piece of information, shrugged. "How much you suppose they'd pay for that?"

Amee shook her head, pulled open the door and shoved him out.

Nick scanned the beach in one direction, then the other. Nothing. Completely deserted. He set down the binocu-

lars, grabbed the black metal box with the attached coil
of wire and ran down the dune, fell in the soft sand at its
base, got up and continued waddling toward the water.

He stood for a moment at the border of wet sand and
dry. He'd always hated this moment. The water was
always cold. And usually it had slimy things floating in it
that brushed up against him and scared the daylights out
of him. Why would anyone want to swim in the ocean,
anyway? That's what pools were for, for God's sake.

He looked nervously up and down the beach, then cautiously waded in, sneakers, jeans and all. A small wave
approached and suddenly wet his legs to his knees. He
suppressed a shout. Somehow it was colder, a *lot* colder,
than that afternoon. With gritted teeth he waded out until
he was thigh deep. There. That would be perfect, he
decided. With a clumsy thumb he pressed the single button on the metal box. A tiny green LED bulb began blink-
ing. Just like when Romer had demonstrated it.

He undid a garbage-bag tie from around the coil of wire
and flung the black Styrofoam ball at the end away from
him. Quickly now, with chattering teeth, he reared back
and threw the softball-size metal box as far as he could. It
flew about ten feet and plopped into the water. He shook
his head; he'd always hated softball.

As Romer had instructed, he made sure the Styrofoam
ball was floating and still attached to the box by the wire.
He watched it sway in and out with passing waves and
decided he'd checked it out just about enough. He turned,
waddled, then splashed through the surf, out onto the
beach, and started running back up toward the gutted
house he'd picked as his base. The wind stung through his
soaked blue jeans and his teeth chattered all the more as
he climbed the dune and retreated into the shelter of a ply-
wood wall.

He huddled for warmth and swore aloud, first at Joanna

for making him go through all he'd endured, and then at Barbie for tricking him into marrying her in the first place. He'd get even, though. Tonight was it. Tonight he'd take charge, once and for all.

"You know, I haven't got a lick of work done on my house since I started seeing you."

Barbie flipped herself around in the tub, nestled against him. "Yeah, but you've been getting laid a lot more."

His hands began caressing her neck, moved down to her shoulders, her chest. Her back arched in anticipation. He wondered whether to broach the subject of Nick Van Horne's strange videotapes and even stranger letter, the one that spoke cryptically about a business arrangement and advised police to search Randall Romer's house. What the hell was all that about? Drugs? Counterfeiting? And what exactly were the videos supposed to show? Sure, they proved Romer was in town the days of the Jet Ski and speedboat races, but surely there were easier ways of proving *that.* As long as none of it had to do with Barbie, he really didn't care what the tapes and the letter were about. Still, his uneasiness about Van Horne had returned.

He stroked down her smooth, soft sides, down past her hips. "Maybe, but getting laid doesn't pay the bills."

"No, but it's a hell of a lot more fun, isn't it?" Barbie collapsed in a soggy heap against his body, sighed. "Tell you what. Starting tomorrow, I'll help you with the house every day. I can handle a hammer and a nail as good as the next six-dollar-an-hour, pot-smoking bum."

Nick's eyes widened. "Seriously? You'd help me?"

"We could get up early every morning and do it before work. That way we'd have some daylight, too."

He had never hired casual help because he'd been trying to save the money. But a second pair of hands would get him through the grunt work in half the time. "God, that would really speed things up. We could finish the exterior in the next week, and then all the drywalling the week after that." He stroked her damp hair. "We could be finished this spring."

"Good. Then you can stop obsessing about it while we're making love."

"I *never* think about the house while we're making love. Trust me." His hands wandered down her thighs. "And you know what else? In return for helping me with the house, I'll take over your lawsuit for you."

She turned around to face him. "You don't have to do that."

He shrugged. "Why not? I want to."

She bit her lip. "The lawyer I got now said he's losing half his clients because he's representing me. The same thing would happen to you. There's a lot of pressure to make sure I lose."

"I doubt it. My clients aren't as politically well con-nected as his. Anyway, I thought Antoon was so pissed about the chicken\eggs thing that he was going to rule against the county."

"My lawyer says even if that happens, the county would appeal, and appeal again, and keep appealing right up to the U.S. Supreme Court. He said it would cost a fortune."

Nolin tilted his head, lifted his chin. "I could get into that. Arguing before the United States Supreme Court. I guess I'd have to call myself J. Douglas Nolin."

She blinked. "Douglas?"

He froze for a moment. "My middle name," he answered weakly. "Anyhow, appellate procedure was my favorite thing in law school. I'd really enjoy going before appeals judges. They're a sharp bunch, you know."

She leaned forward to kiss him. "You're so sweet to me."

"Sweet nothing. I just can't see you pissing away all that money on some shyster. What's he charge, like a hundred an hour?"

"One-seventy in court, a hundred out of court."

Nolin shook his head. "What did Shakespeare say? Kill all the lawyers?"

Barbie laughed out loud. "*You're* a lawyer!"

"True, but I never tell anybody. Have you ever noticed, that's why lawyers call themselves attorneys? It's because *lawyer* sounds so sleazy. You know, there's a technical difference. You're not an attorney until you're representing somebody. Like if I take on your case, I'm your attorney. But I'm still a lawyer."

She kissed him again. "Well, I think you're a very sweet lawyer. I hope Shakespeare doesn't kill you." She smiled broadly. "You remember you were making fun of me for going to a fortune-teller? Well, she predicted I'd meet you. She said I'd get another lawyer, and the turtles would win their beach back, and all my problems would be over."

He raised an eyebrow. "Really? She said that? What else did she say?"

"Well, I saw her again today, and she saw more about my past lives. Turns out I had several in the sea. Most of my psychic history, in fact, has been in the ocean."

Nolin nodded. "Interesting. Anything else?"

"I was a dolphin. Before I was a turtle, I mean."

"Hmmm. Nothing else? Nothing about any dangers on the horizon? About sharks lurking in the waters?"

Barbie shrugged, shook her head. "Why? Should I be looking out for one in particular? One with long, thin fingers, and long, thin toes, and a long, thin—"

"*Okay*, no need to get into that." He kissed her neck. "Seriously, though, she didn't say anything about any dangers?"

"No. Why are you so interested? I thought you didn't believe in psychics and seers and all that stuff."

"I don't." Especially when they took your money and didn't keep their end of the bargain, he thought crossly. "Just curious, that's all."

"Well, she didn't say anything about dangers." Barbie sat up straight with a grin. "But she *did* say I had to go swimming tonight. In the ocean. You know, I haven't done *that* since we started seeing each other, either."

He recalled instantly the many nights he'd watched her through his binoculars running naked in and out of the water. "No, I suppose you haven't. What's so special about tonight?"

"It's something about all the spirits of the water creatures coming together in Pisces. It won't happen again for fifty years or something. I'm not too clear on it. All I know is it's tonight and I want to do it. And I want you to come with me."

He thought of how cold the water would be this time of year, and of how the sharks had torn the Jet Skiers into so many bits of flesh and neoprene. "Gee, Barbie, I don't know. I'm not into this cold-water stuff. Why—"

"Come on!" She tickled under his arms until he squeezed them against his sides. "Don't be such a baby. Besides, you said you liked to go skinny-dipping every now and then, remember?"

"Yeah, but in the middle of winter? Can't we wait for the water to warm up a little?"

"Oh, I guess the water's warm enough for *me* to go in while you ogle through your binoculars, but it's too cold for *you* to go in?"

His face, already flush from the hot water, darkened even further. "I *wasn't* ogling, I was looking at the sky; I . . ." He saw her smirk, gave up. "All right, you win. But at least let me get good and hot in here first, okay?"

• • •

Through the night glasses, the single house with the tall, pointed roof stood out in bright detail among its squat neighbors. The tall privacy fence hid the deck area, and a long dune crossover extended to the beach.

Weathers put down his binoculars, tossed the small dinghy anchor overboard and pressed the kill switch on the small outboard. A damp mist hung in the air, and he zipped his hunting parka against it. At least it was a calm night. It could be hours, he knew, or perhaps not at all tonight. That was okay. He was used to waiting and not even getting a shot at something. Those were the dues you had to pay whenever you hunted anything: ducks, moose, deer. Troublesome wives.

Quietly and efficiently, he attached barrel to stock, night scope to barrel and battery pack to scope. With practiced ease he slipped five cartridges into the breech and worked the bolt to move one into the firing chamber. He lay down across the inflatable to face the shore and peered through the glasses at the empty beach. Over the privacy fence, steam rose in intermittent clouds: a Jacuzzi. A good sign, he knew. She was home. And what would feel more refreshing, more bracing after a soak in the tub than a nice, cold dip in the ocean?

With his free hand he searched the floor for his open can of Miller Genuine Draft, drained the last few ounces, crushed the can and flipped it into the water before opening another. With any luck she'd come out soon; he only had four cans of beer left.

Jamie tiptoed along the deserted corridor, searching the doors for room numbers. Just as Cherry had promised, the floor was empty of nurses; he'd seen only one since getting off the elevator. If challenged, he would tell them he was visiting his cousin in room 216. Oh, he was on the *third* floor? His mistake, sorry. He held the basket of pink carnations surrounding a stuffed Winnie-the-Pooh he'd lifted from the nurses' station counter like a talisman, proof that he belonged there. Sweat, meanwhile, accumulated under his arms and on his forehead.

This was crazy. Why had he agreed to it? Oh yeah: another $5,000, he remembered. That was it. Enough for a motorcycle, although not a nice one like that Harley. He could probably get a pretty decent Hog for $10,000, if he could wait until after doing Mrs. Van Horne for a new set of wheels.

He had a bad feeling about her. It was like she had some sort of guardian angel, and no matter what he did, he wouldn't be able to hurt her. He shook his head to clear away negative thoughts. *Come on, James*: Be all that you can be, he told himself. Finally he came to a door with 316 on the smoked acrylic sign next to it. He turned the knob and pushed silently inward, stepped into a forest of green growth.

Bewildered, he closed the door behind him and turned to step among the potted plants and trees. Ahead he heard faint noises, like animals. A television, he guessed. Jamie wiped the sweat onto his sleeve, pulled the gun from his pocket and set it inside his basket of flowers for quicker access. Quietly he began stepping among the flowers, over a cactus and through a jumble of rubber trees and ferns.

Ahead and to the left came the soft noises. He edged in that direction and soon came to the wall. Carefully, one soft step after another, he eased through the greenery, his heart hammering in his ears, almost overcoming the soft grunts that seemed just ahead . . .

Gently he pushed aside a heavy fern, and his breath caught in his throat. Not two feet away was a darkly tanned blonde, naked except for a black, seemingly painted-on bikini and sitting astride the chest of a very hairy man, presumably the room's patient. And behind her was the waitress from the Book Nook: *his* waitress! She was also naked except for her nipple ring, which she teased between the fingers of one hand while the other hand groped the painted-bikini woman. Both girls smiled at him demurely.

The man on the bed noticed something amiss, lifted his head and grunted, *"You!"*

Even upside down, Jamie recognized the pushed-in nose, the blazing eyes of the biker he'd run off the road.

"You!" he screamed again and began waving his cast-bound arms on either side of his women. "I'll kill you, you son of a bitch!"

Jamie screamed, dropped the Pooh basket and tripped twice on various potted plants on his way to the door.

It would be pneumonia, Nick knew. Crouched on the concrete slab, naked from the waist down, with the wind swirling through the framed-in porch, he would catch his death. He shivered again, rubbed his arms to keep warm and again cursed Romer for not telling him to bring a set of clothes to change into after he'd planted the transmitter.

No, instead that maniac had suggested a wetsuit. Like he would even own one. He was catching a nasty cold, and it was all Romer's fault. Romer's and Barbie's. Romer's and Barbie's and Joanna's. Romer for not warning him he wouldn't dry out after he'd been in the water, regardless how warm a night it was. Barbie for tricking him into marrying her, then leaving him, then filing that pain-in-the-ass lawsuit and finally for not dying two nights earlier and causing him all this extra trouble. And Joanna for, well, being Joanna. For torturing him through the years with that plump, ripe body she would tease him with, then make him feel guilty for wanting, and finally for putting him through this ordeal just for a stupid theme park.

Sure, it was easy for *her* to sit and criticize. She hadn't been swindled, sodomized, threatened at spearpoint and prepared as a shark hors d'oeuvre. She'd get hers, though. And soon. Maybe he would rent the shark gear from Romer again. Problem was, though, that Joanna never went in the ocean, either. He'd have to find a way to get the shark into the swimming pool. But then afterward he'd have to get the shark out. And clean up all the blood before the cops got there.

He shuddered at the thought. No, he'd need some other method for Joanna. Certainly Romer would think of something. He seemed pretty resourceful, although expensive. It had cost him $20,000 just to rent his equipment. That, plus the $10,000 he'd wasted on Lance the Gay Biker, $15,000 on Crawdad the sodomizing biker and another $5,000 to have Crawdad taken care of so he wouldn't come after him for the remaining $15,000. . . .

That was his $50,000 right there, not counting the $1,000 he paid that fortune-teller out of his own pocket. He wouldn't be able to skim any of it for himself, and wouldn't have any left to pay for Joanna's demise. Maybe Romer would work on credit? After all, Nick would be a wealthy man after Barbie and Joanna were gone, with full control over his own money. No more running for Joanna's signature every time he wanted to cash in a CD or savings bond. No more of those insufferable parties Joanna kept dragging him to. And no more races, either. He might agree to award the Winston Cup trophy at the end of every season, but that would be it.

Nick felt a sneeze coming, braced for it, and still smashed his head on the two-by-four he was leaning against. He rubbed his forehead gingerly, thankful, he supposed, that there hadn't been a nail protruding from the stud. He picked up the binoculars and stared at her house. Still the same lights on, still the steam rising from the back porch. Still no sign of her.

He shifted slightly to rearrange what portion of his bare buttocks contacted cold cement; he had sat in soaked pants and underwear for a while before finally deciding they weren't going to dry anytime soon. He reached to check his jeans, draped over a sawhorse. He sighed: still no drier. Eventually he was going to have to pull those wet clothes back on to go home.

What if that phony gypsy hadn't told her to go swimming tonight? What if Barbie had missed her regular appointment? What if she already had plans for the night, and couldn't go swimming, regardless of Madame Rosa's suggestion? Nick scowled, realizing his elaborate scheme was pretty much a house of cards, ready to fall apart at any instant, leaving Barbie rich and him dying in intensive care with fluid in his lungs.

He sneezed again, less violently this time. As he twisted to wipe clear, sticky snot onto his sleeve, he noticed a blur on the dune crossover two houses down. Quickly he pushed the binoculars to his eyes, saw his estranged wife, tall, thin and naked, tugging at something behind the gate. Finally she pulled it out, and Nick saw it was a man. Equally tall, equally thin and equally naked. Together they scampered across the walkway and down the stairs and ran across the sand, steam rising from their bodies.

Nick fumbled for the yellow Walkman, found it on the floor behind him, held it out in front of him between two studs, and pressed the play button. A small red LED began to blink slowly. Still pointing the Walkman, Nick lifted the binoculars to his eyes and held his breath.

• • •

Weathers laid his binoculars on the dinghy floor and picked up the rifle, flicking the safety with his thumb and activating the battery for the night scope. In a few moments, the image through the scope was bathed in soft green hues.

At the center of the cross hairs was the outline of a woman with long flowing hair, then a man, then the woman again. He swore at the motion of the dinghy, which, magnified through the 20-power scope, seemed to lurch beneath him. He shifted his weight so he lay completely athwart the little boat, the rifle resting on the inflated gunwale, his duck-booted feet dipping into the water.

There, much better. The images of the woman and man came together, then apart, then together again. The cross hairs lined up on the two heads as they turned as one. Well, if the boyfriend had to die, too, that's the way it was going to be.

He took a deep breath, had begun slowly exhaling through his nose and gently squeezing the trigger when the rest of the wind was knocked from his chest and sky became water and water became sky.

"Jesus Christ!" Nolin yelled. "This water's fucking freezing! Did your fortune-teller say anything about the spirits of the sea dying of hypothermia? Or maybe heart failure?"

She ducked under, arose and splashed him. "You know, I shouldn't tell you this, because it will only encourage you, but I don't feel any particular kinship with ocean creatures tonight." She thought a moment. "Which reminds me. Rosa also wished me a happy birthday. And my birthday isn't for another three months. Isn't that weird? The first time I went to her, she knew my birthday, and my middle name, and where I lived and everything."

Nolin rubbed his arms. "I recommend a new psychic, before this one gets me killed."

Barbie sidled next to him, put her hands on his hips and pulled him closer. "Come on. It's not that bad when you get used to it. Actually, it feels kind of warm now, doesn't it?"

Nolin snorted, sputtered, nodded at her chest, which alternately surfaced and sank in each passing wavelet. "If it's so goddamn warm, then how come you got your high beams on?"

She reached out a hand underwater. "Funny, it seems to have had the opposite effect on you."

She stretched upward to kiss him, spun him around. He pulled her close, felt the chill fall away and suddenly froze. He had seen it out of the corner of his eye: a glint of green, then an enormous black shadow bursting through the surface, the silhouette of a man, then a splash, then nothing. He pulled his lips away and stood very still, put a hand over her mouth when she tried to question him. Whatever it was, it was gone.

"We need to get out," he said quietly. "Right now. Without a lot of noise."

"What? What did you see?"

"Later," he hissed, and turned her toward the beach. Slowly they walked toward the shore, then faster as they got into thigh-deep water, then ran as they were in the surf.

Safely on the sand, he turned to her, panting. "You're never going to believe this."

TEN

...

Nick stood up, stumbled backward, barked his shins on a stack of two-by-fours, finally sat down again. He put his hand over his heart, willed it to slow down. The shark had come, all right. The same one he'd seen that afternoon at Romer's underwater petting zoo. But who the hell had it eaten? His binoculars had been trained on Barbie and her boyfriend when he'd noticed a green wink, searched for it, fearing it was the box he'd thrown out into the surf, somehow risen to the surface.

It wasn't though. He'd seen it clearly enough, for that split second before the view was instead filled with the head of the shark, rising straight upward from beneath. He shook his head. He had to get out, before Barbie and boyfriend called the cops. He crawled to the sawhorse, and that's when he noticed the dog.

It stood silently, staring, a curious expression on its face. Nick froze, stared back. He hated dogs, and dogs generally hated him. He tried a stilted smile. "Nice boy," he said, voice quavering.

The dog tilted its head slightly, stood its ground. Nick reached slowly for his pants and underwear, grabbed them with one hand and started drawing them back. The dog lunged, snapped the pair of jeans and BVDs from his hand and raced out between the studs framing the rear of the porch. With brisk strides, he was down the dune and out on the beach.

Nick scrambled to his feet, stepped through the frame for a sliding glass door. "Come back here right now!" he hissed. He watched the dog run in a quick circle, drop the clothes and start barking loudly. Nick glanced nervously up and down the beach, saw a light come on in the house to the south, and ducked back inside. On the sand, the dog grabbed the clothes, ran in another two circles, dropped them, and barked some more.

"Owwww!" Jamie yelled, shaking his head. "Be careful, will ya?"

Amee straightened, pulled the levers on the vise grips apart, grabbed the cactus spine between thumb and forefinger and laid it on her desk, adding it to the existing row of eight.

"Just shut up, okay? Stop being such a baby." She leaned over his face, positioned the vise grips over a short spine sticking from his forehead and locked the tool down.

"Aaaaaaahhhhh!" he screamed, pulling his head violently away, leaving the blood-tipped spine between the vise grips' jaws. "Don't you have a pair of tweezers or something?"

"Sure. At home. I'll go there in another three hours. You want to walk around like that till then? This is the only thing Rick had that would work. So shut the fuck up." She laid the spine with the others and prepared to pull another. "So how do you know it was the same guy? I thought you didn't get a good look at him the other night."

"No! *He* recognized *me*! I told you, he had these two chicks on him, and then he looked up and said he was gonna kill me!" Jamie became still as she approached with the vise grips again, stared up at the bullet-scarred poster on the ceiling. "This whole thing has been a disaster, right from the get-go."

"No, *you've* been a disaster right from the get-go." She pulled another spine. "Let's see: You've screwed up with Nick's wife, what, four times? Now this one tonight makes oh-for-five."

"Well, I ain't going after that biker guy again. You can just forget about it. No way. That psycho's liable to tear my head off with his bare hands. In fact, I'm thinking maybe I ought to get out of town for a while. You know? Let things settle down for a bit?"

She reached for his face and yanked another spine. "Don't be a pussy. Besides, I thought you said both his arms were broken."

"He's still dangerous." Jamie shook his head warily. "You know, they say a crazy guy has the strength of ten normal guys. Forget it, Cherry. I ain't goin' anywhere near him."

Amee realized he'd dug in his heels. "Okay. Forget about him. Besides, he isn't going anywhere for a while. We need to concentrate on Mrs. Van Horne. That's the important one." She stroked his face, pockmarked and red. "How'd you manage to fall on a *cactus*, of all things?"

"The guy's a celebrity or something. He's got like a million baskets of flowers, potted plants, boxes of candy." Jamie gazed at Amee's chest bursting from her bikini top, remembered the painted one worn by one of the biker's chicks. "I wonder why your boyfriend wanted him killed?"

Amee recalled her argument with Nick about using Jamie. He already had Barbie taken care of, Nick had said. Right. By the biker who Jamie ended up putting in the hospital. Whatever happened, she had to make sure Nick never found out about that. The guy was probably putting the screws to Nick, now that he was laid up.

She shrugged. "Who knows? Nick hires guys from time to time. You know, to help out at the Raceway. I guess this guy didn't work out."

Jamie shook his head. "So he's havin' him killed. Great. I hope *I* never piss him off."

She paused over the last spine, stuck in the corner of his lip, and yanked it out. "You won't. So long as we take care of his wife. Tomorrow night. We'll do it together." She reached a hand down his pants. "Tonight we'll do something else, at your place, okay? Me, you and Monica."

Jamie instantly forgot the biker. His eyes lit up greedily. "Can we bring in Tiffany and Kristin? It's been a couple of years since I've had four at once. And I'd kinda like to keep in practice."

Nick tiptoed up the stairs, got to the landing and took a deep breath. So far, so good. He'd made it home without incident, wearing only his windbreaker, his still-soaked shoes and his golf shirt wrapped around his waist. The last thing he needed was to explain any of it to Joanna. He snuck down the hall, to where the light shone from her open bedroom door. He steeled himself and quickly strode forward.

"John Robert!" she called.

Nick stopped, swallowed, turned into the room and

opened his eyes. Joanna was sitting at her vanity, brushing her hair. She was wearing one of her see-through peignoirs, unlaced in the front, so that her bosom seemed on the verge of tumbling out. She looked at him in the mirror.

"Why are you wearing your shirt like that? What happened to your pants?"

Nick shrugged carelessly, like he couldn't be bothered to keep track of such minutiae.

She frowned. "Well, you'd better get your black suit ready. We'll have to make an announcement to the press, probably before the race. But the race will go on as if nothing had happened, and we'll carry on through our grief."

Nick gulped. "What, uh, will have happened?"

Joanna turned to face him. "After finally realizing you are incapable of performing even the simplest task, I decided to take care of the Barbie problem myself."

Her left breast had escaped from the peignoir, bobbed slightly up and down as she breathed. Nick felt a twinge in his loins, tried to suppress it. She was his *stepmother*, for Chrissake. "You mean, she's, uh, already taken care of?"

"As we speak. An old friend of mine is handling it personally." Joanna flipped some loose strands of hair back with a shake of her head. "If not tonight, then tomorrow morning. Certainly by the race."

Old friend. Old friend. The phrase referred to someone specific, he knew, but couldn't remember exactly who. Someone important. Nick felt a cold sweat break out on his lip and brow, remembering the long, thin shape in the shadowy figure's hands before he was snatched by the legs and dragged under. "How? How's he doing it?"

"Oh, he mentioned something about the versatility of

a deer rifle. But don't you worry about it. Let's just say your beautiful wife will be permanently cured of her habit of running around naked on the beach. And the police will have yet another one of those unsolved mysteries."

Old friend. Suddenly Nick remembered. It was that politician, Withers, Walters, Webber. Whoever. The guy Joanna had the pictures on. The guy making sure RaceWorld got all that state money. A wave of panic overcame him, and he struggled to keep his composure. No matter what happened, he had to make sure Joanna never even suspected his involvement. She would kill him, without a doubt. With her bare hands. Worse, she'd hold it over him the rest of his life, take it out of his trust fund. No more cars. No more girls. He'd be better off dead.

Nausea built in his stomach, spread slowly upward. His stepmother turned on the stool, exposing a smooth, just-waxed leg up to her hip, but he'd lost all interest. Fear had overcome lust.

Joanna stroked lotion up and down her legs, only then seemed to notice the loose breast. She tucked it back in coyly. "You know, Nick, there's no reason to be embarrassed about having . . . desires for me. We're not *actually* related, you know. And as you point out so often, I *am* younger than you." She teased her hair between her fingers. "So, now with Barbie gone, there's really no reason for us . . . not to get to know each other a little better, don't you think?"

The nausea climbed up his throat. He grabbed his mouth and turned for the bathroom, big white buns flapping in his wake as the golf shirt fell off his waist.

Joanna clucked disgustedly. "Remember we have our party tomorrow night, after the race, and then the

Thompsons' on Sunday," she called after him, then turned back to her vanity and resumed brushing her hair.

"It was a guy with a rifle, and a night scope, and he was aiming right at us." Nolin waved the flashlight as they walked down the sand. "Right out there."

She clung to his arm, still damp beneath her sweats. "Out in the water? Standing or swimming?"

"I'll give you standing or swimming." He pinched her bottom through the thick cotton fabric, drew a howl of protest. "I told you. He was in a raft, or maybe a little boat."

"And you saw all this, how? On such a dark night?"

"There's enough light. The stars. The lights onshore."

"Sure. And then a giant shark came up and grabbed him." She nodded agreeably. "And this guy had a rifle, with a . . . what again?"

"A night scope. You can get 'em in military surplus stores, gun catalogs." He noticed her eyes narrow suspiciously. "I know because I defended a gun nut once. Boy am I glad I lost that one. He was a real kook. Militia commander, survivalist, the whole bit. Anyway. There are two kinds of night-vision sights: one that shows you stuff in infrared, and one that makes everything look green. That one gives off a green glow when you look straight through it. Which is what I saw, and which is why I know it was aimed right at us."

Barbie nodded again. "Right. Of course. And this person wants to kill me . . . why again?"

Nolin sighed. "Look. All I'm saying is that there's a whole town here that wishes you and your lawsuit would go away." He again debated telling her about Nick Van Horne's strange behavior, again decided against it. The more he thought about it, the more outlandish the whole thing seemed. Maybe she was right. Maybe he *had* had a bit too much wine. "I don't know. After all that shark stuff with the Jet Skis and the boat races—"

"The sharks didn't have anything to do with the boat accidents," she said quickly. "They only showed up afterward. I mean, what do you *expect* them to do when you got a bunch of bleeding bodies in the water? You can't blame 'em for that!"

Nolin smiled. "No. Far be it from me to blame a sea creature for anything bad. I mean, hey, sharks are people, too. Oooowwww!" he howled, rubbing his butt where she'd pinched him. "I didn't pinch you that hard!"

"You deserved it. You were making fun of me."

"Still, you didn't have to rip my flesh off. I'm gonna have a bruise for—"

"Give me the light a second." She pointed it down the beach, broke into a jog, stopped over a dark piece of flotsam. "A raft like this, maybe?"

He studied the gray rubber, about two feet square, torn at its edges. He poked it with a stick, as if afraid it would spring back to life. He turned the swatch over, immediately saw the Zodiac logo.

"Where's the rest?" Barbie whispered. "It wouldn't have eaten it, would it?"

Nolin shrugged. "Beats me. All I know about sharks is from movies. I guess they'd eat anything." He looked out to the mist-shrouded water. "But I suppose that if the boat was torn up, the weight of the outboard would sink it transom first. Maybe the rest of it's at the bottom, out there."

A familiar bark sounded down the beach. They both waited, heard it again.

"That's Pedro," Nolin said. "Pedro! Come!"

Barbie scrunched up her nose. "Pedro? You named your dog after yourself?"

Nolin realized his slip. "It's a long story. Pedro! Here, boy!"

Pedro bounded out of the fog, a package of rags in his mouth. He deposited them at Nolin's feet and then turned to Barbie to get his head rubbed. Nolin sifted through the clothes, separated a pair of forty-two-inch white cotton briefs from a tattered pair of blue jeans. He felt the pockets, removed a brown leather wallet. He opened it quickly and, though it wasn't a total shock, his breath still caught in his throat when he saw the driver's license. Wordlessly he passed it to Barbie, who took it in both hands and studied it for a long minute before looking up, mouth agape.

He reached out for her shoulder. "I guess I've got some explaining to do."

Nick absolutely dreaded returning to Romer's place in Flagler. His first visit, Romer had nearly choked him. On the second, he'd come at him with a spear, then tied him naked to a surfboard and threatened to feed him to his shark. This time he'd probably want to dissolve him in acid or something. Quietly Nick crept through the sea oats, past the window of the room filled with surfboards, turned the corner onto the patio and nearly ran right into Romer.

Romer held up his belt sander threateningly, pulled the mask off his nose and mouth. "Where is it?"

Nick resigned himself to his fear. "Where is what?"

"The radio transmitter. The Walkman. You didn't bring it back."

Nick's eyes widened as he tried to recall what he'd done with it. He remembered pushing the button, waiting, seeing the fish hit the rubber dinghy and eat Joanna's friend. What had he done next? Stumbled backward, reached for his clothes, lost them to the dog . . . He must have dropped it on the floor!

"I forgot it," he mumbled. "It's at home. I'll bring it by. Don't worry."

Romer tinkered with the belt sander, ran his fingers along the curves of the surfboard. "So why are you here? If you forgot the Walkman, then why'd you come?"

Nick swallowed hard. "I need your . . . expertise again."

"Why? What went wrong?"

"It ate the wrong guy."

Romer set the sander down. "The wrong guy."

"Joanna had arranged with one of her friends to take care of it. He was out in a dinghy with a rifle, and I guess he was splashing his legs or something."

Romer shook his head. "Well, Bruce might not be so hungry if he ate last night. Depends if he's in a growth spurt. You might have to wait awhile before you try again."

"I don't think she's ever gonna want to swim in the ocean again. Not after last night. The shark jumped clear out of the water with that guy in his mouth." Nick shivered. "Anyway, I can't wait a few days. She's gotta die this weekend."

Romer held a wooden template against the board, marked a high spot with a piece of chalk. "I'm not a hired killer. I rented you some equipment because I needed the money. What you did with it is your concern. Now I want the equipment back."

"Don't worry about the equipment." Nick gulped again. "You'll get it back. I promise. But look around: I bet you could do with a little more than twenty grand, right?"

Romer put his tools down, crossed his arms.

Nick licked his lips, on a roll. "Like, here you are,

making all these surfboards, and what do you do with
'em? Stack 'em in a spare bedroom." He gently stroked
the board on Romer's workbench. "I bet babies like these
are worth, what, two hundred, three hundred each,
right?"

Romer scoffed. "More like seven or eight hundred. You
offer me three hundred, and I'll have to kick your ass."

"You're right, eight hundred. Maybe even a thousand
each. But you can't sell them out of a broken-down shack
up in Flagler No offense." Gears turned in his head as
Nick remembered friends who owed him favors. "In fact,
I know a store with a fantastic location that'll come
vacant, if something should happen to Barbie. She sells
crystals and incense and all that New Age shit, but I bet
you could do a hell of a business selling surfboards."

Romer studied his half-finished board, glanced at the
stack of finished boards overflowing from the spare bedroom. "What's it cost?"

"That's the best part. The banker who holds the note
is a personal friend of mine." Nick smiled, tallying the
race tickets he'd given him, all the pert, young Raceway
groupies he'd sent his way when his wife was out of
town. "He'd be more than happy to let you have it for
free for the first year, and something *real* reasonable
after that."

Romer tapped his fingers on the surfboard, thinking.
Nick saw that he was close, real close, realized he would
have to start promising money he didn't have.

"And to help set up the place, decorate, advertise, so
on, maybe I could kick in a hundred grand? Cash? And if
you do Joanna, too, say, another two hundred grand?"

"And when"—Romer shot Nick a sardonic smile—
"would I be *doing* her?"

Nick shrugged. "Soon. But after Barbie. Definitely

after Barbie, but I'd leave the specifics up to you. Surprise me."

Romer thought for another few moments, sighed and shook his head. "As tempting as the prospect of earning a living off my work is, I'm afraid I can't accept. I can't justify killing for money. I put too many of those scumbags in prison to become one. Thanks, but no thanks."

Nick's jaw dropped. "Are you serious? You killed, what, five Jet Skiers and another five offshore boat racers, but you can't kill two more? What are two more?"

"Yeah, but Jet Skiers and boat racers are subhuman. Jet Skiers especially. They hog the waves, they have no sense of grace, they stink up the air with their fumes, and that incessant whine from those engines . . ." He shook his head, picked up his belt sander. "It's grounds for legally justifiable homicide. Same with the boat racers, to a lesser degree. They deserved to die. And I'll bet you there are fewer Jet Skiers out on the water right now because of what happened. You could say I've performed a public service."

Nick's brain went into overdrive, began spitting out a whole new pack of lies. "Well, that's all *I'm* doing!" he blurted. "Who do you think sponsored those races? That's right: Joanna and Barbie! The two of them want to bring those assholes to Daytona six times a year. Race after race. They think Jet Skiing and boat racing are the fastest-growing spectator sports in the country! I'm just trying to stop them!"

Romer set his sander back down. "So now you're some kind of environmentalist? You want to kill your ex-wife and stepmother because they're bringing dirty, polluting boats to Daytona? And I'm supposed to believe you?"

Nick licked his lips for a moment until the right answer came to mind. "No, I won't bullshit you. I'm doing it because I'm tired of them pissing away my inheritance.

I'm the only *real* Van Horne among them, but they spend it like it's theirs! There'll be nothing left by the time they're done."

"So it's nothing more than basic, craven greed, then." Romer nodded. "All right. I can live with that. You're telling me that if they die, then this RaceWorld theme park and all its Jet Ski rentals and races and all that shit dies with them?"

"Mr. Romer, you're talking to one of the laziest men you'll ever meet. All I want to do is let Daytona Raceway take money from dumb rednecks and give it to me. I shake the winner's hand, give him a trophy and that's that. I couldn't give a rat's ass about RaceWorld, or Jet Skis or any of that crap." Nick raised his left hand, palm outward. "Scout's honor."

Romer eyed him suspiciously. "It's the right hand, and it's supposed to be three fingers. You were never even a Cub Scout, were you?"

Nick lowered his head, recalling the long-ago humiliation of being thrown out by his den mother. She had caught him playing with himself while spying on her as she changed into her bathing suit. "So you'll do it?"

"Tonight." Romer lifted the mask back over his mouth, pulled it back down to speak. "I'll expect that hundred grand tonight, too. The deed to the store can wait until Monday, but the money I want to see tonight. Here. Ten o'clock."

"You got it. I'll be here." Nick turned to leave, suddenly had an afterthought. "She seems to have this new boyfriend she's hanging around with a lot. If you happen to, uh, eliminate him, too, I wouldn't have any problems with that."

"Really? I'll keep that in mind. Oh yes, and just so you understand completely: If those ocean races continue after Barbie and Joanna are gone, or if you so much as turn one shovel of dirt for RaceWorld, then, Mr. Van Horne, you and I will have some business to discuss. Fact of it is, I'll hunt you down like a dog. Just so you know."

Romer scowled, fired up the belt sander and turned his attention back to the surfboard, grinding with a practiced touch at the chalk marks. Nick shuddered and walked back to his car.

Nolin knelt on the floor, ran his fingers along the irregular line marking the stain on the concrete slab. "Someone was definitely here last night. Someone wet." He pointed to the fallen sawhorse. "The piece of white cotton on that nail matches the hole in the underwear. I think it was Nick. He must have waited here, then gone down to the inflatable after dark."

Barbie surveyed the half-finished Florida room with arms crossed over her T-shirt, hands rubbing her forearms. "So he's really dead."

Nolin stood and put his arm around her shoulders. "I think so, yes," he said softly, massaging her neck. "Are you all right?"

Barbie shrugged. "I guess, considering that my husband, who was trying to shoot me, was instead swallowed by a shark. And that my boyfriend was technically working for him, and technically has a different name than what I've been calling him all this time. Apart from all that, I guess I'm just peachy."

He pulled her into his arms and squeezed tightly. "I'm sorry. That's all I can say."

Barbie nodded. "I know. I just wish you'd told me from the beginning, instead of waiting until everything went to hell."

"I'm sorry," he repeated. "It's just, I didn't have any idea, none, that you were his wife, until we'd already started seeing each other. And the only reason I didn't dump him as a client was because I got suspicious about what he might be up to. You know I even went out to that psychic of yours and gave her five hundred bucks so she would warn you about him? I guess looking back it sounds pretty stupid, but at the time, I couldn't think of any other way of doing it without your finding out that I represented him."

She stared over his shoulder at the water, flat now with a strong southwesterly knocking down the ground swell. "Well, you ought to go get your money back from her. She never mentioned a word about it." Barbie pulled herself free and walked to the framed doorway, stared up at the thickening cirrus clouds. "So what do we do now?"

"I don't know what we *can* do." Nolin came over to stand behind her. "I mean, I don't think we can prove a word. The rifle's somewhere on the bottom out there. Like the rest of that dinghy. But all we got is his wallet and some clothes. Maybe we should just let Joanna deal with it."

"I suppose." Barbie shrugged. "I guess this takes care of all my financial worries, though. Nick's father wrote his will so I'd be taken care of if Nick were to die before me. He knew Joanna didn't much like me. I guess it's sort of funny how things turn out, huh?"

Nolin nodded, hugged her from behind.

"Can we go now? I'm not feeling too well." She turned to grab his hands. "I think I'd like to lie down for a while."

He nodded again, started to follow her through the framing, stopped, broke away to step back inside. He returned a moment later with a bright yellow Walkman.

"I didn't know you had one of those," she said.

"I don't." He turned it over, shook it. "I guess Nick must have brought it. To help him pass the time while he waited."

"I guess. Although he never had one while we were married." She started leading him down the path to the sand. "Then again, he never had a rifle when we were married, either."

Pedro fell in step behind them, pausing once to stare at something in the breakers. He barked twice and bounded to catch up.

"So when I ring the doorbell, you sneak up behind her with the wrench. Hit her as she's opening the door, then I'll help you carry her to the back. Then we'll figure out how to get her down to the ocean. All right?"

Amee waited for a response, heard only the chatter of a sports announcer and the whine of race cars. Finally she stuck her head out of the bathroom and saw Jamie, still naked from their afternoon romp, sitting at the foot of the bed, eyes transfixed by the television, mouth open. She emerged from the bathroom, a towel around her body and hairbrush in hand and stood between him and the thirteen-inch RCA. He craned his neck to look around her. Without warning, she raised the hairbrush and brought it down hard between his legs, earning a tremendous howl.

Jamie curled into a ball, grabbing himself. She turned and looked at the television, where a green car and a red car bumped each other as they chased a yellow car. The announcer chattered, the engines whined. Amee turned back to the bed where Jamie lay grimacing, his eyes watering but still locked on the television set.

"Whatcha do that for?" he protested.

"You haven't been listening to a word I said, have you? Just watching that stupid race."

"*Stupid?* It's only the biggest Winston Cup race of the year! Wallace and Martin, neck and neck, with Earnhardt just two car lengths back until he had to pit early last lap. Now—"

"Shut up. I'm gonna go over the plan one more time, and you better pay attention."

Reluctantly Jamie pulled his eyes from the TV. "Yeah, yeah, yeah. I'm listening."

"You get there just as it's getting dark, break in from the beach side and go hide. She comes home after closing the store. Remember, she closes a little early on Saturdays. I show up and ring the doorbell—"

"And I come up behind her and whack her in the head as she's opening the door. I know. See? I was listening the first ten times. You didn't have to hit me."

"And what do you do if she's late?"

"Hang tight."

"And if I'm late?"

"Hang tight."

"Good." Amee smiled. She should have taken a more active role a long time ago. Jamie was basically good, just needed a lot of guidance. "And now, I have a surprise for you. Remember what Monica did the other day?"

She dropped her towel and ran a hand over the razor-burned pink skin between her legs. "Doesn't this turn you on?"

But Jamie's eyes had migrated back to the television, where a black car was trying to pass a yellow car. His penis lay unprotected, a dark purple welt running across it diagonally from her blow. Amee wound her arm back and let fly with the hairbrush once again.

Madame Rosa leaned back in her chair, lifted her feet onto the table and took another long drag from her Virginia Slims cigarette, grimacing as the orange-and-yellow Tide detergent car tried and failed to squeak past the Miller beer car. The Tide driver was from her hometown, in fact, had been a boyfriend once, if having done it with him in the girls' locker room, up against the door in the towel closet, counted as having had him as a boyfriend.

She'd toyed with the idea of walking up to him after a race and seeing if he remembered her, if he wanted to have another go at her in the locker room. But he'd never finished in the Top Ten in points, though, had never even won a major race. She couldn't see throwing herself at a driver who wasn't consistently in the Top Five, or who hadn't won Darlington or Talladega at least once. It wasn't like she was some cheap NASCAR tramp.

She flicked the cigarette over the base for the crystal ball she was using as an ashtray; the ball itself lay on a crumpled Cheetos bag on the floor. The front door had a CLOSED sign on it, and Rosa lounged in spandex leggings that stretched over an ample bottom and a loose tank top that barely contained a sagging bosom. It felt nice, she thought, not to have to be in costume all day. It was a luxury she gave herself only on race days, when much of her clientele was either screaming their heads off in the Raceway's littered infield or hunkered down over a television set with a twelve-pack of cheap beer.

The TV went to a commercial, one of the annoying car dealers with the shouting salesman, and Rosa reached for the mute button on the remote. She set down her cigarette and reached for the travel brochures she'd picked up the previous evening: Las Vegas, New Orleans, Atlantic City, as well as a splashy booklet describing the Carnival Cruises from Fort Lauderdale to the Bahamas. She'd never really considered a cruise before she'd picked up the brochure, but the more she thought about it, the more it appealed to her. There was gambling, the chance to pick up men, but also sunbathing and shopping. Best of all, it promised five gourmet meals a day. All you could eat. It wasn't that much more expensive than a nice hotel, either. All she needed was to collect the $1,000 from that guy.

She sighed and popped a can of Busch. It figured the weasel wouldn't pay up. She should make him. She ought to go to his house and collect it. Just show up and make a scene until he paid. In fact, tonight would be the perfect night. He and his shrew stepmother would host their annual post-race bash at their house on the river. Watered-down drinks, black-tie, moldy-oldies wedding band, the works. Yes, that's exactly what she'd do. She'd go down there in full Madame Rosa regalia and demand payment for services rendered, or else threaten to put a hex on the house and everyone in it. That ought to make him cough up the money in a hurry. Even if it didn't, it would certainly get the attention of the gossip columnist for the local rag and win some free publicity. She would need to remember to take some business cards with her.

The television was showing the race again, and Rosa turned the sound back up. Yes, that's exactly what she'd do, as soon as the race was over. In fact, she'd run by Barbie's house first, to make sure she'd met her friends for the surprise party on the beach. That way she'd have proof that she'd held up her end of the bargain.

Rosa took a long swig of beer and settled lower in her chair. It was funny, though. She didn't think Barbie and her ex were on speaking terms, and suddenly here he was planning a surprise birthday party for her. She thought about it another moment, then shrugged. She'd long ago given up trying to understand the Daytona marriage.

She gave a long belch and leaned forward as the Tide car made another run at the leaders.

Crawdad jabbed his finger as far as it would go between the cast and his arm, scratching furiously. Then he switched arms and repeated the procedure, gritting his teeth until pain drowned out the itch.

If only he had a hanger; he cursed again his stupidity for sending both Jasmine and Lola out at the same time. But he supposed it was a worthy sacrifice. Lola was starting on a bikini tattoo, in bright red, and Jasmine was getting a nipple pierced. He supposed he should also consider himself lucky. It wasn't every biker who could find two old ladies who got on so well together. Still, he wasn't happy. And, as usual, it was money problems weighing heavily on his shoulders.

Jasmine told him the bike-shop guy had come out to the hospital to check out his Hog, and it wasn't pretty. He was looking at $15,000 to make everything right, including a new paint job. And that was just to put it all back the way it was, never mind getting Pamela Anderson airbrushed on the gas tank.

He needed money, and he needed it fast. More than anything, he needed to get the hell out of the hospital. He couldn't do deals lying on his ass all day. He was losing his edge, doing nothing but watching talk shows and getting blowjobs. It had been days since he'd kicked the shit out of anybody. He would get out; that was that. That very night, as soon as Jasmine got back to help him on his Harley, he'd go over to that chick's house and finish what he'd started when that dipshit kid had run him off the road. He shook his head, recalling the scared face above him the previous night. What the hell had he been doing? Who had sent him?

Someone was trying to take him out, that was sure. But why send some kid, especially some kid who couldn't tell his ass from a hole in the ground? His first guesses would have been Walnut or Squid. Neither had ever liked him, and both would love to get their grubby little hands on his tittie bar take. On the other hand, both had the balls to do the job themselves, not send some pimple-faced punk.

Well, that would be his next job, after he sold the chick in Miami. He might have to wait for the casts to come off before he took out whoever was after him, but that didn't mean he couldn't start asking questions.

He lifted his eyes back to the television and smiled: The black Mr. Goodwrench car had just knocked two others into the wall and taken the lead. Now *that* was good car racing. One day he'd have to meet that Dale Earnhardt, maybe buy him a beer, or a chick. Hell, he might even lend him one of his.

Slowly at first, then unbearably, the itch started under his right cast again. Crawdad cursed aloud and contorted his arms to cram a finger underneath and scratch like crazy.

His nose pressed against the glass in the owners' box, Nick watched idly as the two cars knocked from the race by the black car limped off the track and into the pits. Two skinny, helmeted guys in coveralls that matched their dented wrecks crawled out the windows and stormed around, kicking the crumpled fenders and waving their fists at the far turn, where the black car was opening an ever-wider lead.

Good, Nick thought. No caution flags. The damaged cars had come off the track under their own power without anyone else running into them and stopping the race. The faster that son of a bitch won, the faster he could get the hell out of there.

He racked his brain, trying to remember the combination to the safe in Joanna's room. He'd come upon it once, snooping around in her lingerie drawer, but hadn't thought to write it down. He could have kicked himself. Oh well, it just meant he had to root around in there first, get the number, and then get Joanna's little pocketbook out of her safe. The one with the emergency "grease" money, in case a city commissioner or county council member became suddenly recalcitrant just before a key vote.

He'd overheard her talking about it to the chair of the Planning and Zoning Commission once, and thought she said she kept $250,000 there in large bills. He couldn't decide whether to take just $100,000 or the whole quarter million.

If he took only what he needed, the rest might get locked up in probate upon her tragic death. On the other hand, if he took it all and she noticed it missing before she died, she'd kill him. First she'd cut his nuts off, and then she'd kill him. Of course, she was likely to do that even if he took just the hundred grand. Of course, he didn't even know how much was really there. Maybe she'd just bribed somebody last week, and hadn't had time to replenish it. In which case *Romer* would cut his nuts off and feed them to his shark.

Nick shuddered at the thought and looked back down on the Raceway. More than 150,000 people *paying* real money to watch cars drive in circles for four hours. Morons, all. But morons who kept him rich, so he supposed he shouldn't be so harsh. He checked his watch again impatiently, and looked for the black car leading the remaining pack. One hundred and seventy laps done, thirty to go. It took close to a minute for each lap, so he had another half hour of this, barring any yellow flags.

He groaned and glared at the black car. Come on: *win*, already.

Once again the pinging sound came from shallow water, and he dutifully turned around to home in on the signal. It had never sounded without food having been nearby, so he picked up his speed, swishing through the water with his massive tail. Yet just as it seemed he was close, the pinging stopped.

He lunged through the surface, just in case, but there was nothing. Bewildered, he turned back toward deep water. He'd eaten a full meal just the day before, but rational considerations weren't his forte. If there was food, it should be eaten, and four times now, food had been signaled, then not delivered.

He began a slow patrol of his territory when the signal sounded once again. And once again he turned his giant snout toward the shallows and raced in.

Nolin popped the cassette back in, snapped the lid shut and pushed the play button. A small red LED came on, but neither spool on the tape moved. He shook the machine and stared at it. Still no movement. He hit the stop button and the light went off. He pushed play and the light came on, pushed stop and it went off.

"Baby, do you have earphones for one of these?"

Barbie kept flipping through the channels of her old, rabbit-ears, nine-inch black-and-white set. "No. I don't believe in tuning out the outside world like that."

"Yeah. I kind of figured." He opened the battery panel, pulled out four AA cells and pushed them back in place. "Well, I can't figure this out. It seems to come on, but nothing happens. How are you supposed to listen to a tape if the tape drive won't engage?"

"Maybe it's broken." She flipped through the dial, stopped at the channel that had been showing the race. "Can you believe they haven't said a word about it? They just ran the race like nothing happened."

Nolin set the Walkman on the table and walked over

behind Barbie. "Well, honey, given what you've told me about Joanna, did you think she would postpone her single biggest cash cow of the year just because her stepson died?" He began massaging her shoulders. "Plus, she might not even notice his absence yet. Maybe she thinks he just stayed out late, didn't get home by the time she left for the track."

Barbie shook her head. "Not Joanna. Not on the day of the Daytona 500. She'd have a stroke if he was a minute late, let alone miss it entirely. No, she must know he's missing. You're right, though. Whatever reason he's missing can't possibly be important enough to stop the race."

The tendons in her shoulders tensed even more, and Nolin pushed down hard with his thumbs. "It's okay, baby. Remember what he was trying to do when he died, all right? There's no reason for you to feel guilty."

"Oh, I know." She let her head loll back, her shoulders droop. "I guess I can't help but blame myself. If I hadn't filed that turtle lawsuit, none of this would have happened."

Nolin moved his thumbs to her back, rubbed until she groaned. "Come on, baby. That's crazy talk. Just because you sued—and I might point out, sued the *county*, not him—just because you sued doesn't somehow justify his trying to kill you. Nick died because he got unlucky while he was trying to shoot you in the head. In my opinion, he got what he deserved. And now it's done.".

Suddenly she was tense again, leaning toward the television. "No, it's not," she whispered. "Look."

The television scene had shifted to the winner's circle, where perennial anti-hero Dale Earnhardt was spraying a bottle of champagne over a crowd of cheering groupies. Behind him stood Joanna and J. R. Van Horne, applauding sedately, waiting to present a giant trophy to Earnhardt and his team.

"So he's alive after all," Barbie said softly. "I guess it wasn't him last night."

Nolin knelt to study the black-and-white picture more closely. "Apparently not. But that *was* his wallet we found. Whatever it was I saw last night, Nick had something to do with it."

He stood up again, went to the table to retrieve the dysfunctional Walkman. Quickly he pressed play, then stop to watch the LED light come on and go off.

"Baby, remember I told you about those videotapes? Well, I think it's time we see what Randall Romer had to do with this."

ELEVEN

...

Jamie crouched low among the dunes, carefully scanned the houses fronting the beach. There were no lights on, no movement visible through the windows.

Suddenly he was sprinting up the dune, reaching for the top of the wooden privacy fence, swinging his legs over. And then he was falling, falling, falling. His right ankle crumpled under him as he hit a bed of white pebbles. He looked back up with a grimace and realized that the ground inside the fence was a couple of feet lower than outside.

Jamie struggled to his feet and limped past the hot tub, past a chaise lounge to the sliding glass door and knew he was in luck: The door was centered between two tall, thin, multipaneled windows. Quickly he pulled off his T-shirt and balled it around his left hand. He steeled himself, punched a pane of glass. The pane shattered, but left a curious stinging in his hand. He pulled his fist back and felt himself growing woozy: Sticking into the T-shirt was a triangular slab of glass the size of his palm. The white cloth turned dark red in an expanding circle.

He bit his tongue and gingerly pulled out the glass, tossing it aside. He unwrapped the T-shirt, saw the shard had sliced cleanly between middle and index fingers; as he moved his fingers, he could see the tendons shifting inside. Lightheaded again, he reached out for support, resting against the glass door, which slowly began sliding open.

When he realized what was happening he wanted to kick himself. It was unlocked. Unsteadily he limped inside, closed the door behind him and picked broken glass from the floor. A potted plant stood nearby; he dropped the pieces into the pot and slid the plant to hide the empty pane.

He noticed a clock on the kitchen wall, saw it was already past six and began to panic. She'd be home any minute. Quickly he knotted the bloody T-shirt around his hand and scurried through the darkening rooms looking for a place to hide. He settled on the kitchen and wedged himself beneath the sink, his head tucked between the side of the cabinet and the disposal, his wounded hand between his knees. He shifted around so the small pipe wrench in his pocket didn't dig so much into his hip.

His hand began to throb, and he felt his ankle swelling inside his tennis shoe. That, he decided, was the last straw: He'd had enough of the killer's life. He'd been in a car wreck, his face still hadn't healed from falling on the cactus, and now he'd sprained an ankle and cut himself open. The money sounded good, but it was going to get him killed.

His hand throbbed harder, and he remembered the white tendons moving around inside his hand, the blood squirting out through the gaping hole. The lightheadedness came back, accompanied by a claustrophobic attack.

Jamie hyperventilated, then passed out.

It was a strange feeling, Crawdad decided, to have cars honking at him, flashing their lights, weaving, before finally swerving out and passing him, usually with an angry gesture. Crawdad didn't care. It was his goddamned road, too, and he had as much right to it as they did, a sentiment he dutifully expressed to each passing motorist with a scowl and a flipped middle finger. Otherwise he just leaned against the backrest of his Hog, crutches lashed to the rear fender and a cast-encased arm on each handlebar as he rode along at fifteen miles per hour: the fastest he could go in first gear.

That was the only thing he couldn't manage because of his injuries. He could work the clutch and the front brakes despite his broken arms, and the rear brakes with his good leg. But working the gear shift with the broken leg was out of the question, something he'd learned in the hospital parking lot while acquiring some bruised, maybe broken, ribs.

He swore aloud as a pothole sent ripples of pain through his limbs, and swore to himself that the next time he saw the punk who did this, he would first break every bone in his scrawny little body, then run over him several times with the Harley.

As he neared the stretch of A1A where the chick lived, though, he again wondered how he was going to drive her down to Miami by himself, and hoped to hell that her car had automatic transmission and cruise control. If it didn't, he'd have to have one of his old ladies drive him down. Either that or steal a car with automatic and cruise. Come to think of it, he would steal a *nice* car *and* have one of his old ladies drive him down. Sure, he'd take Lola. Sort of introduce her to the business a little.

He passed a deserted stretch and slowed the bike until he was barely moving, eased it into the overgrown vacant lot across from the house. There he leaned on his good leg, pushed the heavy machine onto its kickstand, untied his crutches and hobbled unsteadily across the road.

The convertible VW was in the driveway, and he paused by the driver-side window. Stick shift. Fucking figured. He continued up the pathway, up the two stairs to the door and tried the knob. With a quick glance up and down the deserted road, he pulled the gun the punk had dropped in the hospital room from his waistband and shoved it into a jacket pocket, then pulled out a canvas satchel.

Balancing on his good leg, he pulled out two stiff pieces of wire on wooden handles, felt around the keyhole and quickly heard the soft "click" from the knob. With a sneer, he turned the knob and hobbled in.

Romer pushed his little inflatable through the tiny swell, waded until he was thigh deep and hopped aboard. The wind was already blowing nearly twenty-five knots from the west, and he let it push him offshore.

His life in the morning would be very different from his life these past years, he thought ruefully. He'd be rich again, and reintegrated into society, such as it was in Daytona Beach. He'd have a business to run, bills to pay and appearances to maintain. Chamber of Commerce dues, Kiwanis breakfasts, those insufferable Halifax Club luncheons. The mere thought sickened him.

Still, it was a way to win the recognition he deserved for his work, his lifelong pride: the best hand-carved surf-boards on the East Coast. Those money-grubbing weasels at Big Kahuna and Ron Jon who'd turned down his lines, they'd be knocking down his door. And he could tell them to screw themselves. With his own store, he wouldn't need them. And maybe after he'd built up a name for himself, he could ignore all the crap that went with running a business and just stick to shaping boards.

He glanced down in the black water and wondered where Bruce was. He'd miss him. With the shop all day and making boards at night, he wouldn't have much time to play in the water. Perhaps it was just as well. Ultimately Bruce was a wild creature, and deserved the opportunity to roam the oceans like his cohorts, not remain tied to some freak human. Tomorrow, maybe, he would say bye to him, and then avoid the water for a while. In a few days, or weeks, a month at most, Bruce would understand that he was on his own.

There was already a slight northerly component to the wind, and the dinghy was drifting south as well as east, away from the empty beach. Along the shore, the western sky had acquired an unhealthy, pale orange cast. The front would be a doozy, he could see already. He would need to wrap things up quickly before it hit; there'd be no fighting a strong norther in a ten-foot inflatable.

Romer leaned to pump the bulb on the gas tank and flip the choke switch on the big Evinrude. At twenty-five horsepower, he was seriously overpowered, and could skim over the waves at nearly twenty knots. He lowered a crude wood-and-foam muffler over the engine cowling and yanked on a cord.

The motor instantly roared to life. He adjusted the choke, fitted a blue-painted length of PVC pipe over the handle, slid to the front of the dinghy and twisted the pipe to open the throttle.

· · ·

Nick stood in his underwear and socks, his ear at his bed-room wall. It had to be soon; all of Daytona's leeches and suck-ups would be in his home soon, and he wouldn't get an opportunity later.

Come on, bitch, he thought impatiently. Finally he heard the noise he was waiting for: the gurgling of water pipes. He kept his ear to the wall a half second longer to make sure he wasn't mistaken, then ran out his door, down the hall and into Joanna's room, shutting the door softly behind him. She was in the adjoining shower and, as usual, she'd left the door to the bathroom open. He saw the occa-sional white flash as her butt bumped the shower stall's glass door.

Quickly he crept to her dresser and opened the third drawer down, began sifting through the various night-gowns, teddies and other lingerie Joanna liked to parade around in. He came upon a black fishnet body stocking and held it for a second; it still had the store tags on, and he wondered for a moment what she would look like in it.

He heard splashing from the bathroom, and tossed the fishnet aside. There, in the corner, was the slip of paper he'd remembered. He grabbed it and ran to the safe across from the desk, hurriedly dialed the numbers. He pulled it open and rooted through envelopes and a photo album before seeing the purse in the back.

In a moment he had it back in his room, next to a leather overnight bag he'd pulled from his closet. His heart pounding, he yanked the zipper open and pulled out stacks of green bills. They had an unfamiliar face on the front, and his breath caught when he saw they were thousand-dollar bills. They seemed to be bundled in stacks of fifty bills each, and there were ten stacks.

Droplets erupted on his forehead as he did the math, and his eyes darted around the room while he weighed his options. He only needed two stacks to pay Romer his deposit, but four more would be enough to pay for Joanna, too. He threw six stacks of bills into his overnight bag, hesitated, then grabbed the remaining four stacks, as well.

He shoved the bag under his bed and ran back to Joanna's room with the empty purse, tucked it back in the safe, shut it, spun the dial and pushed the aerial photo of the Raceway back in place. He was ready to breathe a sigh of relief when he noticed the slip of paper with the combination still clutched between his fingers.

Beads of sweat came to his lip as he ran across the plush carpeting to the dresser, nearly stumbling over a wastebasket, and pulled open the drawer again. He plunged his hand to the bottom of the satin and silk underthings, dropped the slip of paper in the corner. A long breath escaped his lips; he'd made it. He started closing the drawer when he noticed the body stocking again; he'd always had a thing for fishnet. He tugged at its collar and pulled it out. Where had she gotten it, and why hadn't he seen it before? It had the whiff of her perfume; he put it to his nose and breathed in.

Only then did he notice the silence. The shower had stopped. He turned in alarm, and she stood there quietly in all her naked glory, save for a towel wrapped like a turban around her hair.

"You want me to model it for you?" Joanna asked softly. "Or do you just want to inhale it?"

He found himself staring, jaw slack. Her nipples stared back like big, brown eyes; it was the first time he'd seen her fully nude, and he found himself getting aroused. Out of the corner of his eye he noticed the photo over the wall safe, and his heart stopped: he must have slammed it too hard, and it had bounced slightly open. He had to get to it before she saw it, or it was all over.

Joanna took a step toward him and knelt on the shag orange carpeting. "I'm going to let him out before he suffocates."

Nick gulped, shifted his weight to the other foot and decided to let her.

They'd rung the doorbell, knocked on the doors, peered in through the windows, and still hadn't seen anything. Barbie tugged at Nolin's hand, tried again to pull him away.

"We really shouldn't be doing this," she whispered loudly as Nolin pried at the side window with a screwdriver.

"Nothing's going to happen," he whispered back.

"Either we're going to get arrested or he's going to shoot us. That's what's going to happen."

Before she could say another word, he'd jimmied the window open and was pulling his gangly frame through. She heard a muffled crash, then a curse, then saw his face reappear. "Damn surfboards weren't stacked very securely."

She handed him the flashlight. "Yeah. Doesn't he realize burglars might get hurt breaking in?"

"Funny. Go around front and I'll let you in."

She scampered through the grasses and waited for the front door to crack open, then, with a quick glance up and down the road, silently slipped in.

"I can't believe I'm doing this," she said, following him down a dimly lit corridor. "Why are we doing this again?"

They came to the source of the light: a fluorescent tube shining on a long, thin aquarium that rocked back and forth, sending a viscous wave to and fro.

"These things are so cool. I can stare at 'em for hours," he said.

"If we leave right now, I'll *buy* you one for Christmas, and you can stare to your heart's content," she said hoarsely.

Nolin played the flashlight around, saw the unmade mattress on the floor. "Christmas isn't for ten months."

"For your birthday, then. *Please*, Pedro, I mean Doug, let's get out of here, okay?"

"Aha!" He stepped across the mattress to a small bookshelf, pulled out a photo album, squatted on the floor to examine it.

With an exasperated sigh, she stepped between mattress and piles of rumpled work clothes to squat beside him. "What?"

Nolin flipped to the start of the album, where the first few pages featured snapshots of Romer accepting a plaque from the governor, sitting on a rock by a lake with a beautiful woman, standing in ski gear before a panorama of snow-covered mountains, toasting his staff at an office Christmas party. "Pretty normal stuff, right?" He flipped pages. "Until about here."

Barbie's heart hammered inside her chest. The photos of vacations and work, wife and colleagues ended, and were instead replaced with underwater shots of a giant gray shark with sharp white teeth, a huge black eye and a peculiar jagged notch on its dorsal fin. Nolan flipped through the pages, came to a horrific one of the shark snapping into a bloody piece of meat.

He turned the page and they both gasped: It was a newspaper clipping of a blurry photo transferred from a videotape of the Jet Ski race, and clearly showed a wet-suited body being dragged underwater by a shark with a notch on its dorsal fin.

"Who *is* this guy?" Barbie whispered.

• • •

Amee fidgeted in the vacant lot, still astride her bike, impatiently scanning the highway in front of the house. Still no sign of Mrs. Van Horne, although, somehow, her car was already in her driveway. That was curious: How had she gotten to the store?

She must have gotten a ride, or used another car, they had decided. Amee had dropped Jamie off nearly two hours earlier, and the VW had already been there. Jamie had snooped around, finally ringing the front doorbell to make sure she hadn't taken a day off work or something. It would have screwed up their plan if she were home, but no one had answered the door, and they'd gone ahead.

She looked over her shoulder again where the Harley was stashed in some bushes and nervously watched awhile. She didn't have time to get mauled by some dope-crazed biker right now, but she didn't have any way of stopping one, either. *Damn* the moron for dropping the gun in the hospital room. It would have taken care of any biker, and would have made short work of Barbie Van Horne, too.

Instead, they had only the pipe wrench, meaning there would be a lot of screaming and blood. She shook her head sadly and wondered again what to do with the moron after it was over. The smart thing would be to kill him, and use somebody else to kill Nick after they were married. After all, that could take months, and she didn't know if she could manage Jamie on the side for that long. On the other hand, he *was* kind of cute, and him and that roommate of his, Monica, were something else in the sack. She wondered if Monica would sleep with her once Jamie was gone.

She stopped daydreaming and scanned the road again. She had to pay attention. The moron was likely to foul up somehow, and she had to be ready to pull things out of the fire. Plus she had to wrap everything up by midnight, when Nick was supposed to come over to her place, expecting a threesome with her and Lori. The thought made her cringe. She'd lost interest in Lori since Monica came along, and Lori and Nick together would make her stomach turn.

Maybe Monica wouldn't mind a fat slob like Nick, just once, for business. She'd have to run it by her and see. Maybe after the Barbie thing was finished she'd run by the pool hall on her way home and ask her.

Amee rubbed her bare arms and wished she'd brought a windbreaker to wear over her T-shirt. She *really* wished she'd brought a pair of shorts to wear over her thong bottom. It had been such a nice day earlier, but now her buns were freezing. She saw headlights approaching from the north, and she peered out at them.

Her heart sped as the car slowed, left blinker flashing, and finally turned into the driveway. Amee stepped off her bike, dropped it into the grass and crouched low. Across the street, the driver's door on the old Pontiac opened and a woman stepped out, walked hurriedly to the front door, reached for the knob and quickly disappeared inside.

Amee stood slowly, moved to the edge of the clearing and began counting backward from one hundred.

He couldn't get out. He had stayed too long, and now he was too big, and he would never get out. He couldn't even move anymore. His knees were up against his face and he couldn't move a muscle. He thought to scream for help, but no one would hear him. He was all by himself. He had overslept, and now he would never be born. He began to sob to himself as outside, the doctors chastised him: "Who are you? Who the fuck are you, then?" He sobbed even harder. What kind of doctors were they, talking like that to a helpless baby?

He awoke with a start, bashing his forehead against the disposal in front of him, then the back of his head against the cabinet behind him. Tears came to his eyes as he tried to wince the pain away, momentarily forgetting his throbbing hand.

Outside the shouts changed to thuds. It was Cherry, he realized suddenly. She had come, right on schedule, and now was tussling with Mrs. Van Horne! She needed his help; he had to get out. With a lurch he pushed open the cabinet with an elbow and fell onto the linoleum. He uncricked his back and neck and stood, immediately fell. His ankle had swollen to the size of a small grapefruit during his time under the sink. He cursed, reached for the countertop to pull himself up, favoring his good ankle, took a deep breath and began limping toward the sounds of the struggle.

She'd kicked him. The bitch had kicked him right in his busted knee. He'd dropped the gun, but it was around somewhere, not far. He squinted in the gloom and there it was, just a foot from his face. He turned his head to where she sat against the wall, glaring at him, her hands and feet finally, and at great personal sacrifice, tied.

Crawdad examined the casts on his arms. Each had a visible crack down its length. "You have no idea how pissed off I am right now," he told her softly. "Now I'm gonna have to get both of these reset. You got any idea how much that costs?"

Madame Rosa glared at him hatefully. He'd yanked her in as she turned the doorknob, thrown her to the ground and tied her hands behind her before she even realized what was happening. Her long black hair lay in a ball on the floor, revealing the short blonde mop beneath.

"Mrs. Van Horne's expecting me," she lied. "She'll be here any minute."

"Good," Crawdad grunted. "I was figurin' I'd get forty, fifty grand for her. I might be able to get five for you. Only 'cause you're blonde. You'd be worth a lot more if you weren't so goddamn fat."

Madame Rosa skipped over the implications of his estimate to defend her weight. "It's not something you can help, you know. It's in the genes. If it's your destiny to be full-figured, then you're full-figured. Besides"— she nodded at his generous beer belly—"you're one to talk."

"Yeah. You're a great talker. A big fat talker. I guess you're gonna need a gag." He pulled a soiled blue neckerchief out of a back pocket and wiggled across the floor, his arm casts stretched out before him. "I don't think I could take a five-hour drive listening—"

Without warning, Madame Rosa kicked her feet out in unison, the leather heels on her sandals smashing into Crawdad's knees with a loud crack. Crawdad howled in agony and the entryway light flicked on in the same instant.

Jamie stared at the scene before him in bewilderment, his bloody hand tucked against his belly, his good hand wielding the pipe wrench above his head.

"Grab the gun!" Madame Rosa screamed.

Jamie saw the pistol lying on the floor against the wall. He began limping toward it when he noticed how familiar it looked. The hairy man on the floor slowly lifted a screwed-up face at Jamie, and Jamie stopped dead in his tracks and yelped.

"You again!" Crawdad growled. "I'm gonna rip your scrawny little head off, you son of a—"

"Please don't kill me, sir," Jamie begged, falling to his knees. "I can explain the accident. I really didn't mean—"

"Get the gun, you fucking moron!" Madame Rosa screamed again.

Crawdad crawled on one leg across the hall and retrieved the gun, pushing the safety to the off position. "Shut up, the both of you!" he shouted, and pointed the gun at the door, which suddenly pushed open.

Amee surveyed the scene, fixated on the gun pointed at her head and the large hairy head behind it. "Oops, wrong house," she said.

"Cherry?" Jamie asked. "Who are these people?"

"That's a real good question." Four pairs of bewildered eyes turned to Romer, who had appeared from nowhere and stood in bare feet and a black wetsuit behind Crawdad, the point of his spear gun just grazing the biker's neck. "Sir, why don't you drop the gun, and then we can sort all this out."

Nick mingled through the crowd of sycophants and clingers a mile above his black Italian loafers. Tonight, he *was* Double-Oh-Seven, and everyone there knew it. The Raceway groupies in their too-short party dresses, the society wives with their expensive faces, even the bartender, who didn't bat an eye when Nick asked for a martini "shaken, not stirred," all of them knew there was something different about him, something to be reckoned with.

Because tonight, he would have it all. Tonight he would become sole ruler of the NASCAR empire, and all the petty serfs and peasants knew this from his bearing, his stride, the cut of his tux, the way he idly played with a cuff link while he listened patiently to their pathetic little stories, that it was *his* ring they would have to kiss from now on, not Joanna's. Sure, the drivers held some celebrity cachet among the circle of fawning admirers who listened to them explain how their cars done run real good, how the "tahrs" had been runnin' hot, but how the drivers through their expertise were able to keep 'em from blowin'. But the movers and shakers noticed when Nick moved among the tinkling of glass and the soft plunking of the baby grand.

Yes, because Nick had finally become his hero. For who other than James Bond would be able to sleep with the beautiful villainess, indeed, get a *blowjob* from the beautiful villainess, just before killing her? He would pay Romer his money, and he would carelessly offer an extra hundred grand to take care of his nemesis before morning. True, he wouldn't be able to dispatch Joanna with a laser in his belt buckle or a garrote in the winding stem of his watch, but allowances had to be made.

He nodded sympathetically at the story told by a young blonde with tanned, round, mineral-enhanced boobs bursting from her dress. But he didn't stare. James Bond never stared. Not until later, when they were in private. He noticed the time, gently touched the young lady's elbow, asked if she would excuse him a moment and would she mind if he called her next week? She tittered and wrote down a phone number on a chewing gum wrapper, which he slid into his pocket as he wandered to the bar to freshen his martini.

It would be important to create the impression that he'd never left the party, in case something were to go amiss. He'd fill his drink glass, and then fill it again right when he returned. He stepped as if toward the bathroom, and once he was in the corridor he kept going, turned, through a door and outside by the side entrance. From the bushes he retrieved the overnight bag he had dropped from his bedroom window and walked briskly to his car. He threw the bag in the backseat, opened the driver's door and started at the touch on his shoulder.

"Going somewhere?" It was Joanna, in her long, white, spaghetti-strap evening gown that clung to her curves and told everyone who saw her that, as hostess of the biggest winter party in Daytona Beach, she was bold enough to wear nothing underneath. "I was following you to the bathroom, in case you wanted a quickie."

She lifted her dress to her waist, showing him there was nothing physically in the way of such an event, not on her part anyway. She stepped closer, moved her lips to his ear. "I want you so bad," she whispered. "You make me so hot."

The shock and alarm faded, and Nick resumed thinking through his adopted persona: What would *Bond* do in this situation? Probably pat her on the rear, tell her he had man's work to do and leave. Or maybe, he thought with building excitement, he'd ad lib and take advantage of the situation. He'd have her again in the backseat, then put her in the trunk and blow up the car. Or push it off a high cliff. Nick scowled: He had handy neither bomb nor cliff. But he *did* have a sociopathic former prosecutor with a pet shark . . .

"I'm meeting someone who's doing some business for me. For us, really."

Joanna's eyes began to glow. "You mean about Barbie?" she breathed.

He casually checked his watch. "By now, she's no longer a problem."

"Dear, that's fantastic. Since *my* friend who was supposed to take care of it seems to have disappeared off the face of the Earth."

Nick swallowed uneasily, recalling the dark shape that flew out of the water, the silhouette of a man in its jaws. He cleared his throat. "Well, I don't want to be late."

She smiled wickedly. "You mind if I come along?"

He saw her tied to the surfboard, her white dress soaked and transparent, the giant jaws coming to avenge years of domineering and abuse. He flashed her a grin. "Not at all."

Romer slogged through the ankle-deep water and heaved Crawdad from a fireman's carry into the dinghy atop Jamie and Madame Rosa. The biker's knees smashed into the center wooden seat, and Crawdad howled, then let loose a string of graphic threats against Romer, his family and, particularly, his mother.

Jamie wriggled out against one of the inflatable tubes. "I know how it feels," he told Crawdad. "I busted a knee once, too. Never played football again. Could of had a scholarship, too. Listen, about the other night. I'm real sorry. I wasn't trying to cut you off or anything. It was just an accident."

Crawdad turned his attention to Jamie, his eyes narrowing to malignant slits. "If you don't shut up, I swear I'm gonna rip your little nuts off and shove 'em down your throat."

"That's if I don't rip them off first, you stupid moron," Madame Rosa added. "If you'd grabbed that gun when I said, we wouldn't be here right now."

Jamie went pale at the thought of choking on his privates as Romer bent over them. All three were bound at the wrists and ankles, and Romer tied their ankles to each other and also to the dinghy's center seat.

"Why don't the three of you shut up for a while?" Romer suggested. He stood, felt the wind whistle through his hair. "Second thought: Go ahead and shout your heads off. No one's going to hear you. Don't go anywhere. I'll be right back."

He sprinted across the beach, up the wooden dune crossover and in through the glass door. Amee lay similarly bound on the floor. Romer gathered her onto his shoulder, grabbed his spear gun and stepped back through the door, sliding it closed behind him. His hand slid over her bare bottom as he stepped nimbly down the stairs to the beach.

"Sorry," he muttered.

"Oh no," Amee said graciously. "I don't mind. I mean, you don't have to tie me up. A guy as good-looking as you, I'd do anything with."

He said nothing, continued toward the dinghy.

"Listen," Amee offered, "I don't know what you've got going with those three, but let me tell you that I can keep a secret. Let me go, and you can do whatever you want to them. I won't tell."

Romer slowed a bit, looked back over his shoulder at her face. "Lady, *you're* the reason I'm here."

Amee let out a snort. "*Me?* Why?"

He considered the question for a moment. "I guess you have a right to know. Your husband set this up."

"My *husband*?" Amee let out a breath of relief. "Mister, there's been a huge mistake. I'm not even married."

"Well, technically you still are, even though you've been separated for two years."

"I've *never* been married," Amee protested. "You're thinking of that other chick."

Romer slogged through the surf to where he had anchored the dinghy. "I don't think so. Your husband specifically described you as 'beautiful' and 'slut.' With all due respect and no offense intended, compare that other woman's appearance and dress to your own, and I think you'll agree I got the right woman." He dumped her uncermoniously into the dinghy atop the others. "Not that it makes a difference."

He pulled up the anchor and stowed it while his captives tussled with each other. With the dinghy so overloaded, he knew he was close to capsizing. He would have to play it safe, go directly downwind until it got deep enough. With a quick pull, the outboard began purring and Romer pointed the boat offshore. "Will everyone please settle down. This won't take long. Thank you."

Amee tried to work it so she could stretch her legs, while Crawdad glared silently at Jamie and Madame Rosa. Jamie, having secured a seat against the tube, stuck his bound arms overboard to let his throbbing hand soak in the cold water. He sighed with relief as the pain edged away.

Senses on full alert, he slowly cruised the shallows where the food signal had come from. He still wasn't very hungry, but he was pretty angry. Time after time, he'd come in on the signal, only to find nothing. Time after time after time. He was ready to hit something, anything, and hit it hard.

He turned quickly and headed back in his wake. Every nerve ending on his massive head and back tingled in anticipation. As soon as he sensed it again, he'd have it in his sights in an instant. No more cat-and-mouse.

It was around here somewhere . . .

There! It wasn't the food signal, but something even better: blood. And close by. Finally! The signal had kept its promise!

He whipped his head around, arched his back and swept his mighty tail through the water.

● ● ●

Crawdad stopped stroking his shattered knee long enough to stretch his neck and see the shore lights growing dimmer amid the rising waves.

"Who sent you?" he demanded. "Squid? Walnut?"

Romer stared silently out to sea. The others waited breathlessly to see how he'd react to the biker's tone.

"How much they pay you? Five grand? Ten? I'll give you fifteen not to. You don't even have to do them. I'll take care of them myself. That's just to *not* do me."

Romer kept a firm handle on the throttle and his eyes on the horizon.

Emboldened, Madame Rosa piped up. "May I just ask, sir, where you're taking us? And why?"

Crawdad snorted. "Where does it look like? He's taking us out here to kill us."

Madame Rosa, Jamie and Amee perked up, looked at Romer to hear his soothing voice reassure them and contradict the ill-mannered biker. Instead, Romer kept his eyes focused where the waves leapt angrily at the sky.

Crawdad laughed aloud. "What the fuck y'all think he was gonna do? Take us on a dinner cruise? He's gonna get into deep water, then put spears through our heads and toss us overboard!"

The others looked pleadingly at Romer. Finally he sighed and pushed the kill switch on the outboard. He pulled out the pistol he'd taken from Crawdad and dropped it overboard. "I want to apologize to all of you for what's about to happen. I mean that sincerely. I don't think of myself as this kind of man, but actions speak louder than words, so I guess I am."

Jamie blinked. "What?"

Madame Rosa elbowed him in the ribs. "He's gonna kill us, moron."

"Just think of today as an unlucky day," Romer continued. "It could happen to any of us. We wake up, everything's fine, and we get hit by a truck. Boom. It's all gone. Think of this as getting hit by a truck, being at the wrong place at the wrong time. An accident. Nothing personal. Although from what I saw in the house, none of you is exactly an innocent babe in the woods. You were all up to no good. What exactly, I can't say, and I guess it's none of my business."

"Come on!" Crawdad urged. "We can take him! The four of us, we can take him!"

Madame Rosa glared at him. "You want *me* to help *you*? You were gonna sell me into slavery, you asshole!"

Jamie lay stunned by the turn of events, his arms still soaking in the water, while Amee thrust her chest out as seductively as she could with her arms and legs tied. "You really aren't going to kill *me*, are you? I mean, I can think of a lot better things to do with me than kill me, can't you?"

Romer pulled a diver's knife from a sheath on his calf. "I have to tell you that I plan to cut your clothes away. Please don't struggle, and I won't cut you. I don't mean to inflict any unnecessary pain. And please don't worry about being naked in front of me. I'm not a sexual predator, and I'm not going to molest you."

Amee pushed herself toward him again. "You don't have to cut *my* clothes away! I'll *take* them off!"

He ignored her and leaned forward to start cutting through Crawdad's leather jacket. So he never saw the mammoth head pop up beside the dinghy, grab Jamie by the arms and pull him overboard.

Madame Rosa and Crawdad shrieked in unison as the cord tying their ankles to Jamie's ankles tightened. Romer felt the dinghy lurch, then go up on its side as the line from his captives' ankles to the center seat also became taut. Amee, Madame Rosa and Crawdad fell in with a splash as Romer used his weight to push the dinghy back on its bottom and his knife to saw through the cord tied to the center seat. If the dinghy flipped, the outboard would be doused and wouldn't start. He'd be as good as dead, with the wind and waves still pushing him out to sea.

Madame Rosa screamed and Romer cursed as he rubbed the knife's blade against the rope, slipping constantly as the nearly sideways boat was buffeted by waves and gusts of wind. With a sudden "pop" that nearly took his head off, the center seat ripped free of its mounts and flew into the darkness

Immediately the dinghy slapped back into the water. Romer picked himself off the floor and turned just in time to see Bruce circle back from the remnants of Jamie and take a giant chomp out of Madame Rosa, Crawdad and the dinghy seat, all in the same bite, putting an instant end to the screaming.

Amee clung to the dinghy's handhold with tied wrists. Somehow her ankles had come undone, and she threw one foot up over the inflated gunwale. Romer hesitated for a moment, then grabbed her ankle and pulled upward, slowly dragging her inboard. He didn't see Bruce return until his snout jumped back up, swallowing Amee's head, torso, bare buttocks and legs.

He fell back onto the floor of the dinghy in shock, then slowly lifted his eyes above the gunwale, which was now hissing loudly. He ran his hand along the outside and picked out a triangular tooth that had torn through the fabric and into the wooden floorboard. In the water, Bruce was in a classic mako frenzy, darting back and forth between remnants of various limbs, snapping at them and shaking his head vigorously.

Romer stared in awe, finally noticed he had something in his hands. It was a bloody foot, still encircled with a thin gold ankle bracelet. Slowly he pulled the anklet free, shoved it inside the cuff of his wetsuit, then reared his arm back and heaved the foot as far as he could.

It landed with a plop. Bruce immediately fixed on it and rushed it, swallowing it whole before returning to the patch of debris he was still tormenting.

Romer waited for the shark to finish cleaning up and settle down a bit before he pulled the start rope on the outboard. It caught on the second pull, and Romer pointed the bow back toward shore, dodging the bigger waves, jumping the small ones and trying as best he could to keep the punctured, port-side tube out of the water.

TWELVE

...

Barbie held the front door open as Nolin played the flashlight beam up and down the shelves one final time. His other arm was already loaded up with three photo albums.

"Come *on*!" She hissed.

"I'm coming," he answered calmly. "Let me get just one last look around. If only there was some actual proof that Romer brought the shark to those races."

"I thought you had videotapes of him at the beach? Isn't that enough?"

"Half the town was at the beach." He pulled open a dresser drawer for the fifth time. "We need something showing that the shark came to the races because Romer was at the races. Like if he was somehow calling it. . . . Wait a minute. You know what I haven't been able to find anywhere in the house?"

Barbie groaned. "Can we *please* leave?"

"Tapes. Cassette tapes. Not anywhere. But in both

videos, Romer is wearing a Walkman. In fact, it's just like the Walkman we found at my house.... No *wonder* it doesn't play tapes!" Nolin exclaimed. "I bet Romer modified it into some kind of radio transmitter, to call his shark."

He stepped back over the bed and walked toward Barbie. "I left it in the truck back at the park. Let's go."

Barbie started at the sound of tires on gravel, slammed the door just before headlights swung onto the house. "Great! He's home!" she whispered. "Now what?"

"Hide." He pointed the flashlight back along the main corridor. "In the surfboard room."

For just a moment, the new bravado vanished as Nick wondered how he was going to give Romer $300,000 in front of Joanna, when she had only given him $50,000. The worry nagged him until she grabbed his arm and pressed her bosom up against it.

"Are you sure this is the right place?" she whispered as he led her around the side to the back porch.

The nagging fear vanished, and James Bond was back. *Let* her see all her "grease" money, and let her know what was going to happen with it, and he would watch her face as surprise, then anger, and finally fear spread across it. "Be careful of the sandspurs," he warned as they stepped through the grass, and she pressed her breast even tighter.

They got to the patio and Nick stuck his face to the glass door to look inside, while Joanna hugged herself to keep warm in the whistling wind. "I can't believe she's finally gone." She walked up behind Nick and put a pudgy, well-manicured hand on his hip. "You know," she whispered, "with her gone, there's nothing to keep us from living like man and wife. Wouldn't that be nice?"

He glanced down at the outline of her curves in the

gloom. The thought both excited and repulsed him, and he remembered his date with Amee and her new girlfriend later that night. A tall dark-haired girl, and not a curly hair between them, Amee had promised.

"Yeah, sure," he said gruffly. "I'm kind of busy tonight, though."

"Oh." She pulled her hand back and crossed her arms. "Is it another woman?"

He said nothing and instead moved over to the kitchen window. She idly picked sandspurs off the satin gown.

"You know, it's not fair for you to keep seeing other girls and then come home to me. I thought I meant something to you."

He half wished the mean, domineering Joanna was back. He bit his tongue; she wouldn't be nagging him too much longer. "Okay, Joanna. I'll stop seeing other women," he lied. "I wonder where the hell Romer is?"

"Right here."

Nick turned to find Joanna's neck in the crook of Romer's arm, his spear gun against her back. "Who the hell is this?" Romer demanded.

"That's Joanna," Nick said. "You know. My stepmother."

"Your stepmother?" Romer stared at Nick quizzically. "You *brought* her here?"

Nick's heart raced. Surely he wouldn't kill her right *now*, right before his very eyes. Would he? "Sure," Nick shrugged, and let his breath out when Romer lowered the gun and unwrapped his arm from her throat.

Romer strode to the back door, unlocked it with a key on a chain around his neck and ushered them inside, flicking on a light in the corner of his workshop. "You know, it was a lot more work than we bargained for. There were four of them, and I ruined my inflatable. I expect reasonable compensation."

"*Four* of them?" Nick asked.

"There was her, her boyfriend, a big fat biker with two broken arms and a broken leg, and some gypsy woman. Her name was Rosa. At least that's what her charm bracelet said."

Nick stared at him openmouthed. Crawdad? Madame Rosa? What the hell was going on? They were conspiring with her, that's what was going on. Crawdad must have found out that Nick tried to have him killed, and was plotting something with Barbie. And Madame Rosa . . . Well, it didn't matter. "You killed them all?"

"They were there." Romer shrugged, turned his beady eyes back on Joanna, who had clung to Nick for protection. "A lesson I learned in Laos thirty years ago. There's no complaints about atrocities if there's no one left to complain."

Nick rocked back on his heels, forward again, trying to dispel the chill that had grabbed hold of his spine.

"You brought the money?" Romer asked.

Nick squeezed the handles on the overnight bag. "You're sure about Barbie, right?"

Romer reached inside his wetsuit cuff, pulled out the thin gold chain with the tiny heart-shaped pendant and threw it to Nick. "I figured you'd want proof."

Nick caught the chain. "I wonder when she started wearing an ankle bracelet." Then he recognized it and reeled backward, overcome by a vision of Amee, astride him in full naked splendor except for the trinket he'd just given her. "Oh no."

"What?" Joanna asked, digging her spiked heels into the floor to support his sagging weight.

"Oh no," Nick repeated, turning the chain over in his hand. Finally he raised a stricken look to Romer. "This girl was about five-three, a hundred and twenty pounds, nice ass, big tits? Wearing a red thong?"

Romer nodded. "So?"

"It was a birthday present." Nick fingered the tiny heart. "Are you sure she's dead? Maybe we can still save her?"

"Who *is* she?" Joanna demanded icily.

Romer thought about the job Bruce had done on the girl. "No, I'd definitely say she's beyond saving. What you've got in your hands is the only thing that wasn't returned to the food chain."

Nick rocked again, collapsed on the floor holding the anklet, the James Bond persona now completely vanished. He had *fed* her to his pet shark! Now he'd never get his threesome! Worse, Joanna would likely kill him.

Suddenly she stepped out from behind the heap he made on the floor and glared at Romer, arms crossed. "So, I take it that whoever this little tramp was, she wasn't Barbie. Am I correct?"

Romer's eyes narrowed as the scene in Barbie's house played through his head. "Did you hire that biker to kill her? And that idiot kid? Plus the guy with the rifle who got it last night. How many people did you hire for this?"

Joanna whirled on Nick. "The guy with the rifle? You mean M. J. Weathers? What happened to M.J.?"

Nick sat on the floor helplessly, clutching the overnight bag and the ankle chain. The thought occurred to him that he definitely couldn't let Joanna see how much money was in the bag; she'd know instantly where he'd gotten it.

Joanna turned back to Romer. "Obviously, I'm going to have to take care of this myself."

A crash sounded in the next room; Romer hit the light switch and dove across the floor into a pile of fallen surf-boards, coming to his knees with Barbie's ankle in his hands.

"Go!" Barbie screamed. "Get help! Tell them what happened!"

Outside the window Nolin hesitated, one arm holding two thick photo albums, the other still grasping Barbie's hand.

Romer stood, transferred his hold to around her neck and stared at Nolin. "Sure, you'd probably be able to escape. But I doubt you'd be able to get back in time. If you stay, you just might be able to help her. On the other hand, you might not. I'm a trained killer, you know. I could puncture her larynx with this little finger." He waved his pinkie at him.

"Just go!" Barbie repeated. "Tell them what we heard!"

"It's a tough call, I know," Romer said. "You could get killed if you stay. But would you be able to live with yourself if you left and she died? I doubt it."

Nolin swallowed, passed the photo albums back through the window to Romer, then hoisted himself back through the window. Romer whirled Barbie around and studied her head to toe. "Barbie Van Horne, I presume?" He turned to Nick, who had finally managed to pick himself up off the floor. "Why didn't you tell me you were married to the Nipple Girl? I wouldn't have wasted my time killing those others."

Romer waited until they had cleared the stone jetties before he tweaked the twin throttles forward an inch. The *Checkered Flag* surged forward, her turbocharged diesels spewing heavy smoke with the increased load before adjusting to the higher rpm. Nick stood on one side of him on the bridge, his overnight bag gathered to his chest, and Joanna stood on the other, rapping her fingernails on the teak console.

"Can't you go any faster?" she said. "I'm hosting a party I've got to get back to."

Romer stepped back from the wheel. "Be my guest."

"No!" she shouted. "I already told you we don't know how. That's why we have a captain."

Romer slid his hands back onto the stainless steel wheel and steered a hair to the right. The wind had risen to nearly gale force, and the *Checkered Flag* surged ahead of the building waves in the channel. "The Green Number Two buoy out here's got a broken light," Romer muttered. "It would really screw up our night if we hit it."

Finally he saw the dark shape off the starboard bow and slid the throttles forward another two inches. *Checkered Flag* lifted her bow in the air and began planing through the dark night.

"There," he said, flipping a switch on the console to engage the autopilot. "We'll be far enough offshore in just a few minutes."

Joanna leaned forward against the console and grabbed the handrails on the deckhead. "Far enough for what, exactly?"

"Far enough so that, with this wind for the next day or so, anything we throw overboard will be blown into the Gulf Stream. From there, the next stop is Cape Hatteras." He turned to Nick, who looked pale and green even in the dim red lamps of the bridge. "So did you bring all my money, Mr. Bachs? I'll expect an extra harbor pilot's fee, you know."

Nick suppressed an uncomfortable burp and lifted the bag. "All here."

Romer nodded and studied Joanna. She had kicked off her high heels once she realized the floor would be moving, but she couldn't do much about the long evening gown that clung to her as far down as her thighs. She left her post and maneuvered her way next to Nick to get in his face.

"So who was that slut you were so broken up about?"

she demanded. "You were buying her jewelry? And what else?"

Nick burped again, struggled to get air. He was starting to sweat, despite the chill. "She was nothing," he muttered.

"Nothing? Well, I have half a mind to cut your allowance. That ought to cut down on gifts to tramp girlfriends." She lowered her voice to a loud whisper. "If you expect to share my bed, you'd best make sure you're not sharing anyone else's. Do I make myself clear?"

Romer watched in amusement, shook his head. "Aren't you his *mother*?"

"Stepmother," Joanna snapped. "And mind your own business."

Barbie leaned her head close to Nolin's ear and shouted: "I'm sorry I got you into this."

Nolin barely heard her over the roar of the diesels. "It's not your fault. It's *their* fault." He tried to jiggle his hands again, but even his fingers were tightly bound. He tried his feet, but there was no play there, either. Romer was clearly not an amateur. "Maybe we can still talk them out of it. I'll tell them about the videotapes in my safe. Maybe that'll change their minds."

"The tapes of the boat races? I thought they were on my living room table."

"I won't tell them *that* part." He lifted his eyes to the little runabout secured on davits above their heads. It had an enormous, seventy-five-horsepower Johnson clamped to its stern, and was held aloft by two cables that ran through the hoists and down to a box on deck. A rotary switch selected between "manual" and "winch," with a lever next to it marked "locked" and "hoist."

He tried wiggling his fingers again, but still couldn't

budge them. He could've used his toes, but his tennis shoes were still on and tied. He looked in exasperation around the deck, and settled on Barbie's feet. Bare feet, with long, ungainly, wonderful toes; she had lost her sandals at Romer's house.

"Barbie," he shouted over the engines. "Turn around. See that little dial on that box?"

Romer eased back on the twin throttles, and the diesels rumbled down to an idle. "This is about far enough."

He pushed the kill switch, and the engines gasped and died. *Checkered Flag* quickly lost her forward way, and soon turned broadside to the wind and began to wallow. Nick's eyes grew wide; he let go of the grabrail to cover his mouth and ran out the cabin door.

"Be sure and puke to leeward," Romer shouted as Nick stumbled over the sill, staggered to the windward side of the boat and vomited into the gusty wind, which promptly deposited much of the stream back on his already damp tuxedo shirt. Five ejections later he collapsed in a putrid heap on the teak deck, the brown leather bag still clutched to his belly.

In his haste, he hadn't noticed Barbie manipulating the hoist-control box with her feet. And in his red-eyed agony, he didn't notice her scramble back into position just as Joanna and Romer walked through the cabin door and out onto the rolling deck. Joanna had picked up Romer's spear gun from the pilot berth in the bridge and carried it, infantry style, across her chest.

Joanna walked over to Nick and prodded his butt with a pedicured, pearl-enameled toe. "Come on. Let's get this over with so we can get back." She sniffed the air and made a face. "You smell awful. You'll have to shower and change. I hope you have another shirt pressed."

She looked down at her own dress, frayed at the hem, stained from spear-gun grease and God only knew what else. "I'll have to change, too, which means people will talk, make snide remarks about us both having showered and changed," she muttered. "Well, let them. To hell with them."

Nolin studied the control box out of the corner of his eye. If he could just step on the lever, they had a chance. A minuscule chance, sure, but it was better than getting skewered and left for shark bait.

Romer nodded to him in greeting. "I just want you to know that it's nothing personal. Think of it as a real unlucky day. As if you were to get hit by a truck while crossing the street. Just bad luck."

"Yeah? Well, I suppose a little stint on Death Row is just a little bad luck, too," Nolin blustered. "Like when the cops get hold of those videotapes from my safe. The ones Van Horne had me hold onto so he could blackmail you into killing Barbie."

Romer smiled. "You mean, by chance, the tapes you left on your girlfriend's living room table? Thanks, I got them. Not that they have enough evidence on them to prosecute anyone. Not without the Walkman, which, by the way, I took the liberty of retrieving from your car, as well."

Joanna snorted in frustration and shoved the spear gun at Nick. "Here. Hurry up and do it."

He studied the unfamiliar weapon with bleary eyes. "Why do *I* have to do it? I thought that's why we brought *him*?"

Joanna turned to Romer. "Well? What do we do now?"

Romer glanced at Nolin and Barbie for a moment, swayed from one leg to the other to counteract the swaying of the deck. He shrugged. "Nothing. We're ten miles from shore. They're bound. They can't swim. When we throw them over, they'll drown." He turned to Nick. "In fact, someone who fell in way out here, even if they *weren't* tied up, they wouldn't make it."

Joanna blinked. "What's *that* supposed to mean?"

"Can I just ask one question?" Barbie blurted. "Why?"

"Oh, shut up," Joanna snapped. "You brought this on yourself. I offered you a lot of money not to marry J.R. in the first place, then I offered a lot more to mind your own business and leave us alone. Well, the time for begging is over."

"Not you." Barbie stared at Romer. "I mean you. Why? The money? I can't believe that."

He considered the question for a moment. "Never take a surfer's waves away from him. The perfect wave is as close to God as we'll ever get in this world. Your damn theme park would have infested everything from Daytona Shores clear down to Ponce Inlet with those asshole Jet Skiers."

"*My* theme park!" Barbie yelled. "That's *Joanna's* idea from start to finish! That's why they're trying to kill me, because I'm suing the county to protect the sea turtle habitat! You should be after her!"

Romer's face darkened, turned toward Nick. "Is this true?"

"I can't believe we're arguing about this!" Joanna shouted. "Throw the two of them overboard right this minute or we're not paying you a dime!"

"Is it true?" Romer insisted.

Nick swallowed, fumbled with the spear gun.

"Kill them now!" Joanna demanded.

"It *is* true, isn't it?" Romer stepped toward Nick. "In light of this information, consider yourself in breach of contract. I'm not going to kill those two. I won't have them on my conscience." He glanced at a wild-eyed Joanna.

"But I think I *will* take you up on that offer about Joanna. Did you bring the two hundred grand?"

Joanna turned to Nick. "Two hundred thousand? To kill *me*?" She grabbed the overnight bag from him, yanked open the zipper. Her eyes blazed. "You got this from my safe, didn't you? *That's* why you were in my room, wasn't it?"

Romer kept stepping toward Nick. "Our agreement still stands? I kill Joanna, you pay me two hundred grand. Right?"

Nick swallowed again, lifted the spear gun, looked at it up and down for a safety catch. "She has to die after Barbie. Otherwise Barbie gets some of the money."

Joanna gasped. "You vile piece of shit! And to think I put that disgusting, shriveled little thing in my mouth! You're going to regret this day as long as you live, John Robert Van Horne. You point that gun at that son of a bitch and pull the trigger right now, you understand?"

Romer stopped two paces from Nick. "What's it going to be, Nick? You're the man. You've got the gun. You're empowered. You choose. Point the gun and pull the trigger. Kill me and you live under her thumb the rest of your pathetic days. Kill her and you're a free man. What'll it be?"

Nick's hands quavered. He looked at Romer, then Joanna. Her eyes burned through him. He swallowed again, found the safety and released it.

"Shoot him!" Joanna ordered.

Without warning he felt a tidal wave developing in his stomach, surging upward. He dropped the gun and rose to his knees, his head over the rail, his mouth spewing what little was left in his belly. Romer shook his head as Joanna bent for the gun, aimed it at him. He feinted left, cut right and sprinted for the leeward railing, then dove headfirst at the crest of a wave and cleared the bulwark as the spear whistled by his head.

He parted the waves cleanly as Joanna ran to the rail to search for him in the dark water, hands fumbling with the gun to reload. Behind her Nolin kneeled next to the hoist control, with bound hands pushed down on the chrome lever with all his might. It wouldn't budge. He repositioned himself to get his weight above it, and Barbie crawled over to help, all under Nick's bloodshot gaze.

"Joanna," Nick called feebly.

"Shut up," she shouted. "And come help me find that son of a bitch. He's out there somewhere."

"Joanna . . ." Nick tried again.

And the lever moved with a click, letting the runabout fall the ten feet from its davits down to the water, hitting the surface with a loud splash. Joanna whirled around, the spear gun loaded but not cocked, as Nolin and Barbie struggled to their feet.

"What the—"

And Nolin kicked her legs out from under her, sending them both to the deck. "Go!" he shouted at Barbie, and rose to his knees, then his feet, hopping toward the railing against the pitch and roll of the boat. "Over! Hurry!"

Nolin pushed Barbie over the side, then tipped himself over as Joanna's second missile dug its way into the teak caprail, a howl of anger behind it.

The cold water was shocking, then bracing as he gasped lungfuls of air between waves that broke over his head, bounced off *Checkered Flag*'s hull, then crashed over his head a second time.

"Over here!"

He turned and saw Barbie had made it to the runabout's side and was hanging by a handhold, trying to swing her legs over the side. He dog-paddled over and grabbed the second plastic handhold as the runabout began swinging close to *Checkered Flag*'s transom.

"Look! They're over there!" Nick was at the rail, pointing at the runabout as Joanna tried to load the third arrow in the quiver into the gun.

"I can't swing up like this," Nolin shouted between breaking waves. "We got to get something untied or we're gonna drown!"

Barbie lifted her legs to the surface, putting her feet on his chest. "Put your legs up here!"

A flash of steel whistled past their heads and stuck into the rigid bottom of the runabout, accompanied by a loud "Shit!" He let his legs float to the surface, and she grabbed at the loose ends of the knots with her toes, losing them with the rise of each passing wave, then re-grabbing them in the trough. Her arms strained at the effort as water splashed over her head.

Finally Nolin felt the pressure around his ankles slacken, and began pulling them apart. "Hold still," Barbie ordered. "Almost there . . . Got it!"

Nolin's legs were free. He took a deep breath, pulled up with his arms and swung one leg over the runabout's gunwale, then the other. He stopped to exhale, then turned to hook his bound hands under Barbie's and leaned back until a helpful wave sent her sprawling atop him.

"I'm exhausted," she gasped as above them, Joanna pointed at them and cursed at Nick.

"No rest yet," Nolin said. "She's trying to reel us back in. Quick, get that front cable off."

As they moved to either end of the boat, an electric motor started to hum. The loose cables began to take in their slack.

"They got the winch started!" Nolin shouted. "Quick!"

The cables were attached to the runabout with pelican

hooks secured with pins. He fumbled with immobile fingers against the wet metal, scratching and cutting his hands as the slack quickly disappeared.

"Got it!" Barbie shouted triumphantly behind him.

He watched the runabout's bow swing away from *Checkered Flag* as the single cable on the stern continued drawing straight. He swallowed hard; once it was taut, there would be no way he could force the hook open.

He slapped at it with the heel of his hand, opening yet another cut, but he saw that the pin had come free. With bleeding fingers, he pushed the gate off the tip of the hook and bent it open. The cable tightened and pulled the hook out of the metal ring at the stern. The next wave pushed the runabout beneath the swinging cables and away from *Checkered Flag*. They watched for a moment as Joanna waved a fist at them, then cuffed Nick in the ear, pointing at the far railing.

"Now we need to get out of here." Nolin studied the cord binding his fingers. Romer had picked Dacron, so it wouldn't stretch when wet. "And for that we're going to need our hands."

Nick gulped back another burp, wrapped his hands around the shaft of the spear and leaned his considerable bulk backward. Still the shaft refused to budge. He released it, wiped the sweat from his hands onto his tuxedo trousers, fought back another wave of nausea and tried again.

"Hurry it up, you moron!" Joanna screamed.

He cursed her under his breath. If she hadn't missed all three times, she wouldn't be needing him to dig this one out of the railing. He wondered wistfully what he had eaten that had given him such cockiness earlier. Or maybe it was just the sex. Whatever it was, it was gone now, and he knew he wouldn't dare lift a finger against her again.

"I don't believe it!" Joanna stood at the aft railing, the wind whistling through the torn gown that fluttered off to one side. "He's playing with her toes!"

Nick let go of the spear and walked back to the aft rail, squinted out into the dark night. "No. He's getting her to untie his hands. She's got amazing toes." He nodded.

Joanna turned to him in amazement. "The *spear*, you idiot!"

He stumbled back to the rail, leaned over to puke again, then grasped the shaft and threw his weight backward. The fluted rim at the back cut into his palms, but he had felt it move. More confident, he grabbed it again, clamped down tightly and pushed off the bulwark with his feet.

Helped by a wave, he flew backward, falling flat on his back and sliding several feet along the teak deck, the freed spear in his bloody hands and a satisfied smile on his face. "I got it!" But over the whistle of the wind and the slosh of the water, he heard a new sound: the high-pitched whine of an outboard.

Joanna turned toward him, mouth agape. "She untied him with her feet, and now they're leaving."

Nolin stood with knees bent, trying to absorb most of the shock as the little runabout leapt high off a crest and landed with a crash in the trough. He kept one hand on the wheel, the other on the throttle, easing off when the prop was ventilating to keep the engine from burning up, pushing it forward as they fell back in the water.

Barbie stood beside him, hanging onto the console with white knuckles. She let out a cry as they remained airborne for what seemed like a full minute before crashing onto the backside of the wave. "How many of those can we take?" she screamed.

He shook his head. "I have no idea. I've never driven

a rigid inflatable before. I'm trying to go around the really big ones, but some of these I can't help. I'm not even going that fast. You're sure Nick doesn't know how to drive that thing, right?"

"Positive. He's afraid to be out on a flat day, let alone in weather like this."

Her ears picked up a new sound, though, a deeper rumble over their own whine, and she turned around to see the red-and-green lights of *Checkered Flag* directly behind them, illuminating the spray kicking off the bow beneath as the trawler charged through and above the waves.

She tugged at Nolin's shirt and leaned toward his ear. "I take that back. Go *faster*!"

Romer squinted his eyes against the stinging spray, trying to catch a breath in each trough before the bow hit the next crest. His bare feet gripped *Checkered Flag*'s rubrail, and his fingers clawed the bronze lip of a porthole.

He had been creeping forward along the hull when the big diesels roared to life and the mighty trawler pointed her nose into the wind and waves. Somehow the girl and her boyfriend had managed to get the runabout in the water, climb in, untie each other and head back for home. He shook his head in amazement. Well, good luck to them. If they made it back, they certainly deserved it.

He held his grip while trying to relax his other muscles. He would need them for what he still had to do. He couldn't make any progress in these seas, but the waves would diminish as they closed land. Then he'd be able to work his way forward and climb the rest of the hull using the anchor hawse pipe by the bowsprit. Then he would take care of the Van Hornes once and for all.

Without warning the trawler hit an exceptionally large wave, washing his feet off the rubrail and leaving him hanging by his fingertips. Calmly he found the rail with his toes and reestablished his grip. Just a few more minutes . . .

Nick balanced against the slight roll by shifting his weight from leg to leg, focusing on the tiny boat still a hundred yards ahead. His nausea had disappeared, now that *Checkered Flag* was planing again, and he decided he rather liked driving her. In the future he would avail himself of the opportunity frequently. The society girls would love to go out on a big luxury yacht like this. In fact, he bet a lot of those stuck-up little prissies who were too high and mighty to wear a bikini on the public beach would probably go topless, or even better, if they were alone with Captain Nick.

"You know what? I kinda like this. I'm gonna do this more often."

He glanced at his stepmother, now falling out of her ragged dress. She stood with both hands on the console, her toes curled against the varnished teak sole. A larger-than-average wave made the cockpit lurch, and a spaghetti strap slipped off her shoulder to reveal a pale white breast that jiggled with the engine's vibration. She covered herself hastily.

"You know, you have really nice tits for a woman your age," Nick said expansively.

She glared at him with burning eyes. "Shut up and drive, idiot. You couldn't even figure out how to start the engines, remember? And don't think I've forgotten about your little deal with Randy Romer. You just wait till we get home. You think you have a tiny allowance *now*? Wait till I get done with it."

Nick's chest deflated and his shoulders sank. She was going to make his life a living hell. If only he'd turned the spear gun on her when he had the chance. Now it was too late.

"Speed up, or we're never going to catch them!" She slapped his cheek with a quick backhand. "You want 'em to get to the beach and go running to the cops?"

Meekly he lifted a hand to the throttles and slid them forward another inch. *Checkered Flag*'s bow lifted completely out of the water. He snuck a sideways glance before turning his eyes quickly back to the runabout's wake in front of him.

Well, maybe after they'd run down Barbie and her boyfriend, she'd calm down a little.

It wasn't the food signal, but it was familiar . . . Two separate high-pitched noises, moving quickly from left to right.

Yes, now he remembered. It was just a few days ago. The high-pitched noises, then a loud crack, and the noises stopped, and then: food! Lots of it! Just floating on the surface, waiting to be plucked down. He wasn't particularly hungry, but food was food. He would need to investigate.

Somewhere in the folds of his brain, an intercept course was plotted and, with a swish of his tail, he was off.

Barbie looked back over her shoulder, snapped her head forward. "They're gaining!"

Nick snuck a peek, saw the red-and-green running lights were now flying high above the water and closing fast. He ground his teeth, turned back to the mangled seascape ahead. Over the largest waves he could see the occasional blink of light from the beach. They weren't far now . . .

He would have to risk it. Slowly, waiting for a trough,

he pushed the throttle right to the forward stop and grabbed the wheel in both hands as the runabout flew off wavetops, bounced off the backs and instantly took off again.

His palms bled from where his nails wrapped around the wheel and dug in; only a couple more miles . . .

Romer felt more than saw the lessening of the seas. He turned his head into the spray and opened an eye. Sure enough, Ponce Inlet Lighthouse was maybe a mile and a half off and closing fast.

He took a deep breath and started inching along the skinny rubrail, reaching from porthole to porthole for fingerholds. Slowly he made his way forward until he was at the anchor hawse hole. There he waited a few moments, and the waves shrank noticeably.

With another deep breath, he leapt the few inches to the hawse pipe and swung his legs up to the bowsprit.

Nick steered sullenly, occasionally glancing at Joanna. It wasn't fair. None of it. Why couldn't *he* have a good life, too? He deserved it. After all, it was *his* granddad who started the track, not Joanna's and certainly not Barbie's. He could see her now, clinging to the console of the little boat, shoulder to shoulder with that lawyer. *His* lawyer, no less, the traitor. Probably was seeing him even before she moved out, the slut.

If only she'd been a better wife, none of this would have happened. Even if she'd just stayed out of his business, none of this would have happened, and Joanna wouldn't be cutting off his allowance. And Cherry would still be alive, dancing around in her bright red thong. Yup, it was all Barbie's doing. All of it. Come to think of it, Joanna had a point. He *would* be better off with her gone.

So when Joanna shouted, "Faster, idiot!" again, he was only too happy to jam the throttle knobs all the way forward. The bow lifted before him, blotting out the runabout, the wake, even the horizon.

Barbie watched, heart in her throat, as the big white bow loomed up behind. There were barely two boat lengths between them.

"They're almost on top of us!" she shouted, turned back forward and screamed aloud. "Pedro!"

He nodded, leaning to move their weight as far forward as possible and help the propeller take a deeper bite. "I see it. I'm just hoping they don't."

Not two hundred yards ahead was the silhouette of the unlit buoy, looming ever taller, a growing shadow on the horizon. Nolin tightened his grip on the wheel, preparing to jerk it starboard. He wondered idly if the hull would keep its hold on the surface or if they would flip over. Well, they would soon find out.

"Hold on tight, and get ready to lean left!" he shouted into the stinging spray. "Just another few seconds . . ."

Nick clenched his jaw; any moment now he would hear the satisfying crunch that would tell him he'd caught Barbie and her shyster boyfriend. He cocked his ears, listening carefully, waiting for any telltale noise. Any noise at all.

So that when Romer swung up and over the bowsprit not ten feet in front of him, the shock for a moment froze him, then drew a terrible scream from his lungs as Romer stood on the bowsprit, then like magic, like he had wings, suddenly took off and flew forward into the night.

And then the crash split his eardrums and his stomach in a sickening, soggy crumple of fiberglass on steel. *Checkered Flag* went airborne for a second, landed with a surprisingly soft plop as Nick bounced off the instrument console, then tumbled against the bridge's aft wall. His legs tangled with Joanna's, his hands caught in her hair, in the spaghetti straps of her torn dress. And suddenly they were up to their waists in water, the cabin sole sinking beneath them.

He stood, slogged through the open door toward the bulwarks, stared in bewilderment at the shattered bowsprit, at the buckled teak deck, then a hundred feet behind him at the solid, green, unblinking metal buoy. So *that* was the culprit . . .

"The bag, you idiot!"

It was Joanna, treading water just beyond the fast-disappearing bulwarks, pointing at the leather overnight bag bobbing in the water a few feet away. He began treading water himself as *Checkered Flag*'s deck sank beneath the reach of his feet.

"Go get it!" Joanna demanded. "It's *my* goddamned money."

He began stroking water toward the bag, watching the buoy the whole time. How the hell had *that* gotten there? How come he hadn't seen it? And finally he noticed the big gray fin, just a few feet away. He stopped moving, tried not to breathe as it circled him, edged toward the bag. His heart pounded. Surely it would hear him . . .

"What's the matter with you? Get the *bag*!" Joanna shouted, all the louder now without the rumble of the giant turbo diesels. "Oh, the hell with it. I'll get it."

She took three powerful strokes toward the bag. Nick gently pushed himself away as the fin circled the bag, bumped the bag; Joanna splashed ahead, heedless, reached for the bag, grabbed the bag. And the mighty tail swished once, the back arched, and enormous jaws spread and crashed down on the bag and an attached arm.

She screamed, grabbed at the bag with her other arm. "You son of a bitch, give that *back*!"

And the jaws snapped and the head shook, and the frenzy began. Wads of chewed thousand-dollar bills flew past Nick, along with bits and pieces of Joanna's arms, torso, and legs, still clad in skin-tight gown. Nick turned and began slapping toward shore, kicking his tuxedo-trousered legs as best he could. He felt the bump against his knees and kicked even harder, except he wasn't moving anymore. And then he saw the shark turn a few yards away, his tuxedo-trousered legs in its jaws.

And his vision darkened suddenly as he passed out.

Nolin leaned over the runabout's gunwale and picked out the scrap of pearl-colored gown. Tears and three ragged puncture marks marred the once lustrous fabric. He scanned the black surface for any more remains, but there were none. The shark had been thorough. Again he examined the piece of satin. Two seams joined at a point to give the fabric some fullness, and the remnant of a spaghetti strap was sewn to the edge. Part of the bust, he decided.

He sighed, wrapped his arms around Barbie and pulled her close. "I guess this resolves the moral dilemma of whether to pick them up."

Barbie turned her head from his chest to study the wind-rippled surface near the buoy. "It ate them *both*?"

"Every last bit. Except for this." He held up the scrap of Joanna's dress. By the time they had caught their breath and returned to the buoy, the shark was finishing his frenzy, snapping at empty water before finally submerging. "I guess he was hungry."

Barbie shook her head sadly. "Now what?"

Nolin shrugged. "Well, for starters, it looks like you win your lawsuit. The county attorney will drop his objections when I tell him what happened tonight. With the Van Hornes and their goons gone, it looks like the beaches will be safe for turtles after all. You did it, baby. You beat them."

Barbie sighed again, snuggled next to him to get out of the wind. "I can't believe Madame Rosa was in on it."

He nodded. "I guess you need a new spiritual adviser."

"Yeah. Serves me right for going with a crystal-ball psychic. They're all frauds." She looked up with the beginnings of a smile. "I'll go with tarot cards next time."

He laughed, pulled himself free to step back to the outboard. "I guess we better head in before the wind pushes us back out there." He pulled the starter rope and the big Johnson purred on the first try.

She looked over the runabout from stern to bow. "What should we do with this?"

He stepped to the console. "Whatever you want. It's yours, now. As well as the Van Horne house, all their bank accounts. Oh yeah: and three major stock car tracks in the Southeast."

"I guess I hadn't thought of that." Her eyes widened as an idea flashed through her head. "Can I do *anything* I want with them? Can I close them? Maybe turn them into marine biology research centers?"

Nolin nodded slowly. "You could, but as your attorney, I'd advise against that, unless you want three million pissed-off bubbas to come down here with their pickups and their shotguns. On the other hand, if you *sold* them, you'd probably net, oh, four hundred, five hundred million. You could open a dozen marine biology labs all over

Florida. All over the world, for that matter. Shoot, you could *buy* Woods Hole, if you wanted."

She thought it over in stunned silence. "Yeah. I guess I could."

He slid the throttle forward until it engaged into gear. "Where to?"

With a heavy sigh, she moved to his side and pulled his free arm around her. "Home."

Romer listened carefully as he lay face up, his ears submerged in the cold water. Nothing. Finally they were gone.

He turned onto his belly and began a slow, rhythmic stroke toward the beach, careful to avoid splashes or irregular movements. Bruce had gorged himself and calmed down, but it wouldn't take much to rile him back up. Romer stroked evenly, calmly. He could have stroked the twenty-five miles up to Flagler, if he wanted. But he could still walk faster than he could swim, and it had already been a long night.

As soon as he got home, he'd have to pack his things and leave, of course. The surfboards would have to stay behind. As would the wave tank. But he could make more surfboards, and buy another wave tank. He might even be able to hook up with Bruce again, someday.

He cleared his mind and concentrated on his stroke: left, right, left, breathe; left, right, left, breathe. Soon he could touch bottom, and then he was through the surf. He zipped up his wetsuit as high as he could, and began the long, cold walk home.

THIRTEEN

...

Circuit Court Judge Anthony Antoon stared down over his spectacles, his mouth slightly open, his pen lightly rapping his notebook.

"And that's how it stands, Your Honor," Nolin finished.

For a minute Antoon sat brooding, staring alternately at Nolin, then the county attorney. Nolin had asked for a sidebar conference at nine-thirty. It was now ten. Fifty prospective jurors sat on the opposite side of the railing, wearing big yellow "Juror" buttons and bored expressions.

"So I understand correctly," Antoon murmured, his voice low. "You suggest that if this case proceeds to trial, this entire story will come out, including the Van Hornes' employment of the former state attorney of this county and his . . . *trained* shark to murder your client in order to stop her lawsuit?"

"That's correct, Your Honor. We haven't gone to the police, because my client is satisfied the threat to her life is ended, and she has no desire for any publicity in this matter. However, if my client takes the stand, she will naturally testify to the measures that some in this community took to stop her." Nolin gathered his thoughts. This would be a tricky moment. "Testimony like that is sure to attract national press attention, including the tabloid television that I know everyone in this town is so tired of."

Nolin let that settle, hoping the threat had been subtle enough not to piss him off yet strong enough to convey the message.

Antoon turned toward the county attorney. "And the county's position, counselor?"

The county attorney cleared his throat, leaned closer to the judge. "Your Honor, I must again stress that my office had absolutely *no* knowledge of anything the Van Horne family may have done. None. But given the circumstances, we believe it's in the county's interest to avoid the type of publicity a public airing of these charges might bring."

Antoon rapped his pencil faster. "So you're saying . . . ?"

The county attorney grimaced painfully. "That we concede, Your Honor. From State Road 40 northward, and U.S. 92 southward, including all of the beach south of Ponce Inlet, vehicle traffic shall be excluded within thirty days. And traffic will be excluded from the remaining six miles as off-beach parking is added, no later than two years from the date of your order."

Antoon shook his head. "I guess, Mr. Nolin, that your client has managed the impossible. Write me an order, and I'll sign it this afternoon."

Nolin walked back toward his table, beaming at Barbie. She smiled back, gave his hand a quick squeeze but dropped it when she caught a stern look from Judge Antoon.

Antoon lifted his gaze to the prospective jurors. "Ladies and gentlemen, thank you for your attendance and your patience. However, the parties have agreed on a settlement, and your services will not be required. Please hand your juror buttons back to the clerk downstairs, and both I and the parties thank you for your time. You are dismissed. Court adjourned."

The judge ducked out the back way, the jurors filed out, the county attorney shut the snaps on his case and left.

Barbie and Nolin slowly gathered his papers and walked up the aisle, arm in arm.